THE FATE OF THE KING

THE FATE OF THE KING

The Bear King Book 2

CAL NEUBERT

I

Something in the Water

The mist-like rain mixed with the glow of the torches as the villagers of Sten were fast asleep. Only the guards remained awake as they patrolled the outskirts of the village like they always did. The harvest festival was in everyone's minds as dreams of glad tidings filled the air.

In the Great Hall, Jarl Toke was sleeping like the bear man he was as his son began to weep in the other room. Helga Styorrsdottir, Toke's wife and the queen of Sten, awoke to the noise and sat up in her bed.

"Would you like me to tend to him?" Toke asked, still more asleep than awake.

"No, no," Helga said, wiping her eyes of sleep. "I will fetch him."

She flipped her legs around the bed and stood up, stretching in the process. She grabbed a candle from the dresser and lit it as she left the bedchamber. A flash of lightning from outside caused thunder to roar as Helga began walking down the dimly lit hallway. As she entered the small room, the candle she held in her hand lit up the face of the small blonde boy that sat in his bed. The candlelight reflected off the boy's giant tears streaming down his face. He looked as though he had seen a ghost.

"What is the matter, Njal?" Helga asked, sitting down on the corner of his bed. She wiped a tear from his face.

The boy turned his head so that it was facing the outside world through the small entryway in the wall and said nothing to his mother. Helga turned to look outside the window but could only see the glow of the torches from the village and a quick lighting strike. A loud clap of thunder followed.

"Is it the storm?" she asked as she placed her hand upon his cheek.

"M...monster..." the boy replied, still looking outside in terror.

"My beautiful child," Helga began. "There is no monster outside. If there was, the guards would have seen it and informed your father and I. Loki is just playing tricks on your mind," she said, tapping his forehead. "You mustn't let him get to you."

"B...but I saw it, mother!" the boy exclaimed. "It took the form of a shadow and stared in my window! Then it disappeared in an instant!"

"I believe you, little cub," Helga started, her brown hair gracing her cheek. "I will go and have a look. You are safe, alright? If I do, in fact, see anything, I will fetch the guards and your father."

"Alright, mama..." the boy said before he hugged his mother. "Please be careful!"

"Are I not always?" she said, moving her body so her son could see the golden seax she had on her hip, even in her nighttime attire. "I love you, my son. Everything will be alright."

She gave the little Norseman one more hug before wiping his tears again with her thumb, then tucked him into bed with his fur blanket. She grabbed her small candle and gave him a little smile and a wink before leaving the boy's room.

As she shut the door behind her, a wild and horrifying scream echoed from outside that sent shivers up her spine. Njal wept from the other side of the door again.

"It is alright, Njal, I will have a look!" Helga said before stomping her feet rapidly to her bedchamber. Once she swung the door open, she noticed her husband Toke was already throwing his cloak on over his back and securing his sword to his waist. "What is happening, Toke?" Helga asked, grabbing her own cloak.

"I am not sure. Please stay with Njal and make sure he is safe," Toke replied.

"I will fetch the guards to do so. You are not going about this alone."

"This is not a debate; I will not put you in danger," Toke said, stepping close to his queen and putting his hands on her face.

"And I will not let you stare danger in the face by yourself," she replied. "I will fetch the guards to look after, Njal."

"Alright..." Toke said, realizing he wasn't going to

win the fight. He would smile at his wife's stubbornness under different circumstances, but now was not the time.

He stormed out of the doors to their bedchamber and continued to the front doors of the Great Hall. Once he and Helga exited, a wall of mist hit them in the face like a wave.

"Hjalmar, Ebbe," Helga said, looking at the two guards that awaited outside. "I need you to go inside and watch Njal..."

CRASH!

Everyone's heads turned towards the stables. Another blood-curdling scream followed.

"SVEND!" Toke shouted as he sprinted towards the stables.

His dearest friend opened the door to his house and stepped out. He was already in his battle attire, ready for anything.

"Where is the fight, my friend?" Svend asked, joining Toke in his all-out sprint.

"We are about to find out..." Toke replied. His boots making suction noises as he plowed through the mud.

Before Helga took off after her husband, she made sure the guards, Hjalmar and Ebbe, went inside to watch her son. As she did so, she noticed a shadow moving down by the docks. The torches that were usually lit there were not anymore. Suddenly, a flash of blue lighting showed that the shadow was wearing a hooded cloak. She squinted her green eyes and put her own hood of her green and black cloak up over her head. She began walking in that direction alone.

Toke and Svend continued their muddy trip to the stables.

"Could it be the Highlanders?" Svend asked, pumping his legs hard into the ground.

"I do not know," Toke replied.

After a few moments, the two men arrived at the stables and were shocked at the scene that lay before them. The gates were wide open and the cattle were spread out all around them. Toke called out for the stable keep, but there was no response. Another flash of lightning and a clap of thunder. The two warriors unsheathed their respected swords and examined the area. Mist was spraying their faces like they were standing under a waterfall. Toke called out for the stable keep again as he navigated through all the livestock, but just like the first time, no response.

"Toke!" Svend suddenly called out. "Come and see this..."

The Jarl of the Bear Clan ran over to Svend, who was standing still and looking at something on the ground. When he got there, he looked down and saw the stable keep. The poor man was cut in half as his blood and entrails were mixed in with the surrounding mud.

"Who could have done this?" Svend asked.

Toke looked up and examined the area again. He looked down at the mutilated stable keep, then up again at the cattle that roamed everywhere *except* the stables. Multiple cattle had rope attached to them. He never put rope around his cattle. He looked down at the stable keep again. The wounds around his torso and waist were too messy to be done by blade. The realization hit him.

"It is a distraction..." Toke said. His eyes widened, and he turned around. "HELGA!"

*

Helga slowly approached the docks and noticed the hooded figure moving in one of the longboats.

"Who goes there?!" she yelled out to the silhouette that instantly stopped moving.

She pulled out her golden seax and readied herself. The shadow then slowly stepped out of the boat and made its way towards her.

"Helga, it is just I," the man said, stepping close enough to be seen under the glow of torchlight. "Sorry for the disturbance. I just wanted to make sure my fishing gear was ready for the morning's trip!"

"Aelred," Helga stared at the man and slightly disarmed herself. "Quite a strange task to be handling in a storm like this, no?"

"Ah," the man replied, shrugging his shoulders. "Thor can try to scare me all he wishes. I am not afraid!"

Helga nodded cautiously. "Who said you could fish in the longboat tomorrow? Did we not gift you your very own fishing boat?"

"That you did. To which, by the way, I am extremely grateful," he replied, nearing her. "But Jarl Toke gave me permission to use one of these fine ships to get towards the deeper water. I can catch greater quantities there!"

"Did you not hear the screams?" she asked.

"Screams? No, no. The only sound I could hear was that of the waves hitting the side of the ship," he laughed, then looked up into the sky. "Try all you want, Thor! You will not get me!"

"Hm," she grunted, looking around. "Where are the guards that patrol this area?"

"I am not sure," Aelred said, his face looked of confusion. "I have not seen anyone in some time!"

His charming and energetic tone always made her a bit uneasy, but her husband trusted the man, so she felt she had no reason not to trust him. She watched his movements. He was getting closer and closer to her. She replied by gripping the seax at her hip a bit tighter.

"HELGA!" The two of them heard in the distance.

Helga turned to look in the direction the voice called from and then felt a sharp pain in her stomach. She felt the blood seep out of the corner of her mouth as she turned back and saw Aelred staring her in the eyes with rage.

A smile cracked his face as he pulled his own knife from her belly.

"Insignificant cow," he mumbled to her before stabbing her again. His eyes lit up. "Whoa! You are pregnant?!" he said, smiling. "Congratulations! Did I ever tell you that my wife and I were actually trying for another child when your people raped and murdered her and the rest of my family?"

He stabbed the knife in her stomach again and again until he could feel the baby that was inside of her.

"You get no sympathy from me, Helga. I had my wife and children stolen before my very eyes. Your husband will feel the same pain."

He pulled the knife from her and watched her fall to the ground. The man held the baby in his arms and then heard the voices of those rushing towards him get closer and closer. He looked down once more and picked up Helga's golden seax and put it in his belt.

"You would not mind if I took this, right? I mean, I do not think you will need it very much longer! Goodbye, Helga!" Aelred said before running to the longboat and detaching the rope that held the ship to the dock. He then jumped in, quickly raised the sail and, just like that, he was gone.

Toke and Svend arrived at the docks a few moments later and saw the scene that lay before them.

"H...Helga?" Toke said softly. His heart shattered at the thought. He ran to her and dropped to his knees and grabbed her cold, lifeless hands. The pool of blood mixed with the surrounding mud and rain. "No...no...NO!" The roar of anger that he released could have been mistaken for a thunderclap from the storm. Svend looked into the distance and saw a longboat leaving Sten and into the open waters.

"HELP!" a voice called out from the ship. "Toke! Help me!"

"Is that Aelred? They have captured him!" Svend said.

"READY THE SHIPS! WE ARE HUNTING!" Toke roared with spit flying out from his mouth. Snot coming off of the tip of his nose.

On the boat, Aelred continued to scream his lying cries for help before turning his attention to the baby that sat lifeless.

"Well, I am sorry to do this, but you would undoubtably grow up to be a monster just like the rest of them. I wonder how many families and good people of god I am saving by doing this."

The man then stepped over to the baby, picked it up, and without hesitation, threw it into the water. He whistled to himself a happy little tune as the strong wind of the passing storm caught the sail, sending him back towards England.

II

The Fenlands

The large man felt the blood stream that sat in the corner of his mouth dry up and crust. He used his giant paw to wipe it away but was unsuccessful, as it had crusted in his furry black beard. He had spent the last nine months trying to survive; using everything he could to hunt, kill, and eat his way through the hills and forests of England. However, scavenging for food in the wilderness was something he had not done in some time. The man was used to his warriors hunting and preparing him feasts. Thus, living off the land the way he had caused him to lose a significant amount of weight.

The now skinny, decently cut and well-muscled man attempted to stay away from any sort of civilization. He believed that by being a Norseman, he might not get anywhere but an early grave if he met the wrong people. Especially since England was still trying to rebuild itself. He spent the cold end of last winter hiding in a cave along the southern coastline. The spring picking off travelers on the road to Sussex and taking their belongings. He spent the summer building himself a small cabin that was eventually burned to ash when the folks of Sussex hired somebody to do so.

Now, it was September and the large man had just finished hunting down and killing the man that was hired to burn down his small cabin. The dry, crusted blood that sat upon his face was not his own.

The man was now on his way towards the Fenlands, a marshy swamp-like region located in east England. He had heard it wasn't very populated, as the marshlands made it hard to build any sort of civilization there.

However, the stories of the people that *did* live there could've frightened even that of the gods themselves. The rumor was that a group of people, known as Druids, resided in the area. They lived in a village that was made of wood and sat high on stilts due to the constant rising and lowering of the water levels. Small elevated bridges separated the huts.

The stories said that the Druids often dressed in clothes with fur and bone. They practiced magic and other dark rituals and believed in sacrificing people, oftentimes their own members. It wasn't for their god. They didn't believe in a godly figure. They believed in spirits and demons. If you were sacrificed or lived a life dedicated to your Druidic family, then you would be able to live as a spirit. Free to go anywhere in the world and live among other spirits. However, if you denied your Druidic family or hesitated if you were picked to be sacrificed, you would become a demon. Becoming a demon meant that you would be confined in the darkest depths of the earth where you would be stuck in isolation, forever attempting to claw your way back to life but never succeeding.

Rumors or not, the muscular Norseman knew there were people there. People that could give him what he wanted. He packed up his things and proceeded on his path towards the Fenlands. Towards the home of the Druids.

*

One brisk fall night, the Norseman set up camp outside the marshlands. The tall grass could be seen just a few feet away from him. The sun was setting as the chilled air blew through his long black beard and hair, making them flutter. He thought about the man that took everything from him. The young warrior that broke his face in. The one that he hoped was long dead. The one that he hoped was destroyed, thanks to Aelred.

But he knew this wasn't true. In his time robbing and killing those on the road to Sussex, he had heard talk of a new king in England. One that was on the younger side but wished for prosperity and peace. The former king Alfred's son that wished for a peaceful and one true kingdom of England. The large Norseman had also heard about the alliances the young king had already made. One was the Celtic people in Scotland, another was to the people of Paris, and another was to the king of the Norse people.

He knew that the young Norseman, Njal Tokeson, had won the battle against Aelred. But that did not stop him from wishing among the stars and praying to his gods that the boy would not last. The sparks from his small fire cracked and popped, which pulled the man out of his trance. He looked up into the virgin night sky until he heard another crack. This time, it wasn't from the fire. He looked down and noticed that he was now surrounded. People dressed in fur clothing with animal skulls as masks quietly exited the long grass, their weapons also made from bone, pointing directly at him.

Chills crawled up his spine, but he sat there calmly, staring straight into the flames of his campfire.

"If you wish to kill me, all I ask is that you do it quickly," the Norseman said.

Suddenly, the people stopped in their tracks, and a toned and tall man exited the grass. He was wearing a deer skull on his face that still featured the antlers. He was unarmed as he stared at the Norseman that sat before him. The two of them meeting each other's gaze. After a moment, the tall man pulled his mask off and set it down at his side, showcasing a middle-aged blonde man. His face was not hardened or fearsome, no. It was a kind face. One with beaming blue eyes.

"Now, what exactly makes a man look death in the eyes and say, 'take me?'" the man asked. His voice was calm and soothing.

"Hm," the Norseman replied, denying to answer.

"I think I know," the man said. "I can see the pain in your eyes. You have a story to tell, no doubt."

"You do not know a thing about me," the Norseman said.

"I think it may be because you remind me of me. A man that has had everything taken from him. *Stolen* from him. And with no idea how to get it back, you come here...

expecting death." The Norseman widened his eyes. "I understand your pain," the man from the marshlands continued. "I too had to deal with the wrath of those who did not believe in me. But I found my way and now I lead my people."

"Good for you..." the Norseman said, returning to his stern look.

"What is your name?" the man asked, sitting down across from the fire.

"Torin... Of the Eagle Clan."

"Torin," the man repeated. "Are you as strong as your name perceives you?"

"I am that and *stronger*," Torin said, a vein popping out of his neck as he finally looked up into the other man's eyes.

"So, then what happened to your face?" the man from the marshlands asked as he examined the permanent bruises, broken nose and slightly out-of-place jaw that could be seen even under the cover of his giant black beard.

"My people betrayed me. I am strong, but one man is never enough for an entire village."

"I beg to differ," the man said, which instantly caught a look of anger from Torin. "My people hated me. I am originally from Ireland, where my people lived in isolation. I was always treated with disrespect. Being pushed around every day and laughed at by the bonfires every night. Well, fate had decided to give me a bit of luck in the form of a woman. We married after a couple months and my path had finally looked like it was changing. That is until my woman decided to be unfaithful to me with the leader of my people. I was filled with hate and rage and tried to handle things the easy way by stealing my leader's horse. But I was caught and imprisoned. I used my wits to escape and snuck into his bedchamber, where my woman lied alone... naked. The rage I felt that day was like nothing I have felt before."

"What did you do?" Torin asked.

"I killed her and fled here. Like you, I was unwanted everywhere I went. Until my sorrows brought me here. To the Fenlands, where I met more people who have also been thrown aside, waiting to be feasted upon by the rats of this world."

"And the point?" Torin said, sounding unimpressed.

"My point is," the man continued. "I see a bit of myself in you. That look in your eyes is the same one I had years ago. I see sadness and pain behind them. But I also see the anger and rage. The *value* of those emotions. And those in my community believe that vengeance is a way of life. If someone has wronged you, it is only right that you wrong them back. And we have the necessary tools and skills to do so."

"Are you asking me to join your community?" Torin asked, looking back to the flames.

"I am not going to tell you that you are one of us because you have yet to prove yourself. However, it is at least a chance that I can offer you. Perhaps the last one you will ever get. A chance to *belong* somewhere."

"I do belong somewhere... Eaglecrest, upon my throne."

"If you become one of us, you will have the full weight of the Druids behind you on your journey for revenge. That is what we do. You will, however, have the responsibility to help when it comes time for another's revenge."

"Hm," Torin said, stroking his long beard. "Tell me more."

III

A Peaceful Time

The air was wet, and the leaves began to show signs of their transformation to red and yellow. Njal Tokeson was riding his giant brown steed through the forest road that led to London. Halfdan Blood-Wolf was following close behind, as well as three other members from the Eagle Clan. Everyone was dawning their respective colors proudly.

The members of the Eagle Clan had on leather armor and blue and black cloaks. Their wooden and iron shields painted the same colors, and each featured paintings of eagles on them in traditional Norse artwork.

Njal had pieces of iron armor on his shoulders, fore-arms, and hands as the rest of him was covered in black leather armor with pieces of green and black robing. His bear cloak had been repaired, courtesy of his queen, Frigyth, and was fluttering behind him. His sword, 'The Call of the King' was sitting on his side now, sheathed at his belt. Njal's head was shaved on both sides as the blonde hair on the top of his head turned into a braid on the back that bounced on his shoulder. His blonde beard was trimmed down to a goatee.

Halfdan wore black leather armor and a black cloak to showcase he belonged to not one clan but to one people. The Norse people. He carried a long axe that sat upon his back and two hand-axes sat in his belt. His hair was dark, well groomed, and flowed down to his shoulders. His beard was shaved off completely as he showed off his mid-life wrinkles.

The group of warriors noticed the giant city of London in the distance and readied themselves for their arrival. The fog weaved through the giant towers and the gray sky matched the color of the high reaching walls that surrounded the city.

Once they arrived at the main gates, the guards opened the towering doors immediately. Without slowing down, Njal and his companions entered the city limits. The smell of shite entered their nostrils. People were hunched over and coughing. Some were pissing and throwing up in the middle of the street. Houses were collapsed and they could hear people screaming and children crying. Njal hated this part of the city. He knew that some work was being done to improve the living situation, but it was still quite sad to see. Especially since the rain had been bad the last couple months to which Njal could see the repercussions of that. Some streets were flooded and the homes on those streets were sunken into the ground.

The companions eventually made it to the second gates. The walls that blocked off the poverty section of the city and the upper class. Just like the first time, the guards opened the gates, and the warriors entered without slowing their steeds down. Inside the second set of walls were cobblestone streets and green patches of grass. Buildings that released steam, allowing those inside to stay warm. People were outside shopping at the market, wearing bright colors, and laughing together as families and friends. It was a complete night and day difference.

This was Njal's fifth time in London and Halfdan's third. Neither of them enjoyed the city, but they had to do what they had to do. They turned down a street that led to an enormous castle, then crossed a stone bridge that led to it, nodding a hello to the guards as they passed them.

Once they got to the main gates of the castle, they reared their horses off to the side and hitched them. A man dressed in a leather and silver armor dawning the colors of red and black greeted them.

"Njal and Halfdan!" the man began watching them dismount. "It is a pleasure to see you again!" He had a giant sword sheathed at his waist.

"Aye," Njal said, his voice a bit raspy. "How are you today, Almund?" He reached his hand out, to which the commander of the royal guard met it.

"Cannot complain. Edward is looking forward to speaking with you, I know," Almund said before running his hand through his brown hair, pushing it out of his eyes.

"And us, him," Halfdan said as they all walked inside the front gates. The remaining members of the Eagle Clan sat behind with the horses as the rain began to pick up.

As the large doors shut behind them, the sound echoed for a moment throughout the massive corridors of the castle. Almund led the two Norsemen for what seemed like a long while into the throne room, where the new King Edward sat upon his throne. He was a young man with blonde hair that curled around his golden crown.

"Ah, there they are!" Edward said with a brilliant smile as he jumped up from his large chair. "How was the journey here, good?" He hugged them both, and they hugged back.

"It was swell, Edward!" Halfdan said. "But please tell me you have some of that wonderful wine you gave me the last time I was here."

"Of course. Did you really believe I would hold out on you like that? Here, come with me," Edward said as he began leading the group out to the shaded courtyard in the back. "I had three bottles made just for you to take back to Eaglecrest, Halfdan."

"Ah, beautiful!" the berserker said as he walked over to the table that featured three large bottles of wine on them.

The courtyard was filled with cobblestone pathways and well-trimmed hedges, as well as a few trees whose leaves were also changing colors.

"How have things been since the last time we saw you, Edward?" Njal asked, pouring himself a cup of wine.

"Well, I had a skirmish breakout in the middle of the streets the other day. Old Order loyalists dressed in black and silver. But Almund and the rest of my guard made quick work of them. Other than that, it has been quite peaceful. I am attempting to help the more financial deprived areas in the city, but they are overrun with bandits and I do not have enough men to rid the area of that. I figured that when I received the crown again, things would have at least been a little like when my father reigned. But it is proving to be a bigger problem than I had first expected."

"If you need any help from us, remember, we are willing and able," Njal said, taking another sip of wine and hearing the rain patter on the areas of stone that were not shaded.

"And you have my thanks," Edward said. "What of Eaglecrest? Have you had any more arrivals?"

"Eaglecrest has become a sanctuary for my people, and I have you to thank for that. We have been able to expand a bit, but we will not touch the small valley as we have discussed."

"I am only king because of you and your people. If you end up needing more land for your people, I would be happy to offer some. Especially since we took back the old mining village of Gulgruve."

Halfdan gritted his teeth, but kept his mouth shut.

"Thank you. I will let you know if the need arises."

"So, tell me, how are the new arrivals?" Edward asked, sipping more wine. "Any interesting newcomers?"

"There have just been those who have lost their way. Those who do not share a clan with any others. Those who had nothing left and nowhere else to go. Some are bread makers, others are skalds. Nobody that poses a threat to our alliance. They are just people."

"I am less worried about our alliance, Njal, as it is a strong one. I am more worried about those who may try to take the power from you since not every one of your people are fond of the idea that you strive for."

"Do not worry about that, Edward." Njal cleared his

throat. "Worst possibility, I kill whoever tries. And with my council including Jarl Knud, Jarl Sigrid, Halfdan and Frigyth, I am not worried."

"Fair enough," Edward said, smiling. "Speaking of which, how is the lovely Frigyth?"

"She is well!" Njal said, practically glowing. "We are actually trying for a child."

"Congratulations, my friend!" Edward said, lifting his cup up. The other two men raised theirs into his, making a clank sound. They all drank after. "And Halfdan, what of you and Ingrid?"

"She is hearty, my friend!" Halfdan said, wine dripping from the sides of his mouth. "I believe I am quite in love with her."

"That is fantastic news!" Edward said. "Shall you get married?"

"Um..." Halfdan stuttered and burped.

"Careful, Halfdan," Njal began with a smile showing. "Anymore wine and you will not be able to ride home!"

They all laughed.

"As much as I enjoy going over glad tidings with you both, we *do* need to discuss some things that require a more serious tone."

"I understand," Njal said, his smile fading.

"Come, let us go inside," Edward said, leading the two back inside the main castle corridor.

*

Edward led Njal and Halfdan into a decently large but dark room. Inside, there was a large wooden table and stained glass over all the windows. Candles lit up the surrounding shelves. The men all gathered around the table as serious looks graced their faces. They looked upon a large map of England that was spread out below them.

"My alliances with the other cities seem to get more and more fragile as the days pass. Mostly due to land orders and submission. People have not had one king in quite some time and Aelred *did* give the other Lords land and power to rule. So, getting these new ones in line has been a bit harder."

"It is an odd thing, is it not?" Njal began shaking his head. "The man who ruled with fear is actually missed by some."

"Quite a few, in fact," Edward said.

"What is your plan?" Halfdan asked.

"Well, first we have to look at the problem. The biggest problems are with Winchester, Leicester and Nottingham. Winchester's Lord, obviously being Eacnung's son himself, was bound to have problems. But they are upset because Aelred allowed them to make and keep all of their coin to themselves. Now that I am asking for some of their financials to help *all* of England, they are upset."

"That little snot," Halfdan said, referring to Eacnung's son, Cerdic.

"I actually understand their frustrations," Edward said. "When my father was king, he used to tax the bloody hell out of everyone in order to keep a powerful army. These cities are afraid that I will do the same."

"So, what are you to do?" Njal asked.

"I think the only thing for me to do is attempt to hold the peace long enough to show them that I really *do* wish the best for England. I will send the money that I receive from everyone and use it for the better. Not only will I use it to repair buildings, but I will also be offering more patrols of the roads to limit bandit problems. All the issues that need fixing will also increase job opportunities for everyone, which may create less homeless civilians."

"Alright, but what if Cerdic decides that he needs special treatment?" Njal asked. "Since under Aelred's rule, Winchester became the richest city in England."

"They will receive no special treatment just because they whine. I am taxing them the same as everyone else and they even have more to spare."

"What if the other cities get word of that? Then they begin to ask why not just tax Winchester more, since they have more to spare?" Halfdan asked.

"Again, it all comes down to fairness and patience. Once I show the people that their money is going to good use, I believe things will get better."

"Alright," Njal said, pursing his lips. "What of the other two cities that will not fall in line?"

"Leicester is where Orvyn the Young ruled. He never had a chance to put his unachievable rules in place since he died on the battlefield. But it did win him the people's favor and his skills won over Aelred's. Orvyn died letting the people believe he could achieve complete peace *and* freedom to do anything they wish. Including kill and rape without consequences. Or that fact that he told them food would be free on Sunday's due to gods will. Or that whores would be free every first four days of the week. He got them all to love him. With his plans, they would have plummeted into a state of poverty in a matter of weeks."

"Aye," Halfdan interrupted. "That little bastard was cocky, but he was charming."

Njal cracked a smile when he remembered how Knud said the charming Lord died a squealing weasel. He continued to look at the map.

"With Leicester, I am going to have to speak with their new lord, Eadburg, about maintaining peace during this change and creating new obtainable goals for the city. He is an older and stubborn man, but he has wisdom. He will listen."

"Good," Njal said, stroking his goatee. "What of Nottingham?"

"Uhtric is their new lord. He is a respectable man that was actually elected in by the people. However, he is pushing more religion than anything. His wish is that the city of Nottingham will back out of any military agreements and become a kingdom of strictly godly worship."

"So, if you were to call on him for help in a battle setting, he would decline?" Halfdan asked, to which Edward nodded his head. "What an arse."

"What are you to do about him?" Njal asked.

"I am going to tell him no. I can offer him supplies and money to build churches and other religious buildings because godly worship is also important to me. However, in return, if he wishes to keep this alliance, he needs to vow that in a time of need, he will send military forces to help."

"Sounds like a good plan, Edward," Njal said as he heard the rain smacking against the stained-glass windows.

"It is quite nasty outside," Edward said. "Please, be my guests tonight. I have plenty of rooms for you both and the warriors that accompanied you."

"We appreciate the offer, but to be quite honest with you, sleeping in the same castle that once belonged to the man that killed my family does not sit right with me. We will stay at the Blacksteel inn by the gates."

"I understand," Edward said. "Would you at least stay for dinner?"

Njal looked over and Halfdan and smiled.

"I think we can do that."

IV

Eaglecrest

The morning dew collected on the roofs of the houses and the red and orange leaves of the trees in the courtyard. A dense fog from the night prior had dissipated, leaving only a light gray overcast above. The streets were busying with people as the news had spread of a large storm that was on its way. It was early in the fall, so no snow would be possible, but being on the coast during a heavy rainstorm would, of course, bring the tide in.

Quite a bit had occurred and changed in Eaglecrest over the last nine months. Among the changes was Njal's wish to expand Eaglecrest beyond its walls. New homes and businesses were built along the roads to Demut and Muspel, the homes of the Horse and Fire Clan. However, during the spring, a heavy rainstorm rolled in and washed away three new houses, killing one person in the process. Because of this, Njal had put together a group of people that built a small wooden barrier that, well, wouldn't stop the tide from coming in. But it *would* be the difference between flooding the village and dealing with a little water here and there.

On this particular day, Frigyth was walking through the streets, people stepping out of their way for her. A smile graced her face as she passed the villagers, her wavy brown hair bounced upon her shoulders. She was heading to the top of the walls by the front gate to see if she could spot the storm, her signature red cloak flapping in the breeze behind her. As she got to the top, she looked out into the endless ocean. The sea was already restless as the wind began to pick up.

She then looked at the buildings that populated the roads to the other villages along the coast and just smiled for a moment. There was a sense of pride. She thought back to everything that lead to this point. Back to the night she spent with Njal Tokeson in the cell the night before he met her father. The night before everything changed. Now, because of their efforts, Eaglecrest was a sanctuary for all Norse people that just needed a home.

The witch, Ingrid, had become the village's seer and Halfdan led the personal guard for Njal. Frigyth was loved by most, but tolerated by all. Sure, some didn't like the idea of their queen being an Englishwoman, but they eventually got over the idea. Especially because she would be fair in all the public hearings she would sit in on and would help anywhere she could around the village. It was hard not to like a queen who spent more time in the streets and with her people than on her throne.

As for the king, Njal did a lot of traveling. He wished more than anything to be home with his wife and friends, but after Aelred's death, England was in ruin. The cities had no one to rule them, and riots and bandit raids plagued the country. However, Njal and Birstain, Frigyth's father, helped put the pieces back together in any way they could. For starters, they sent groups of their warriors to bandit camps and rid the world of them. While that occurred, the two men searched for Edward, the son of King Alfred, who ruled before Aelred. It took a while but Birstain had heard of a young man living in isolation up north who resembled the old king's son. Njal and Birstain made the long journey and found him in his cabin. They told him of the events that occurred and that England needed a king. Edward, being extremely grateful, hastened to return to power and solve the country's troubles.

Frigyth broke from her recap of the last nine months and looked towards the valley. She noticed the dark, bumbling clouds heading their way. Lightning stuck inside them and the thunder roared throughout the valley shortly after. Her heart forced her to look towards the main road as she hoped to see Njal riding back with Halfdan and the others.

"I am sure they will be back shortly, my queen," a guard watching next to her said, as if he could read her thoughts.

"I know. It will take a lot more than the might of Thor to kill my Bear King," she replied as small raindrops began to patter against the surrounding walls. "We best take cover soon."

"Aye," the guard replied, stepping over to the large horn that sat at the corner of the wall. He blew inside, causing a loud sound to echo across the entire coastline. Everyone looked up at the sky and then proceeded to head inside their homes. Well, except for the guards who walked over the small wooden shading Njal had built for them to take cover in case of heavy rain, snowfall, or scorching heat.

Frigyth began walking down the stairs as her mind filled with worry. She knew her king would return to her, but that never stopped her mind from racing. Realizing that she was with him through all of his troubles and worries in an attempt to gain the kingdom they earned through blood, sweat and tears. It saddened her to think that she was not with him in his attempt to make a better England.

She walked through the streets that were becoming less busy by the second. Once she arrived at the front doors to the Great Hall, she said hello to the guards and entered the enormous building. She walked over to the crackling fire pit and looked down into the flames. She couldn't escape her mind and her racing thoughts. The heavy rain slapping against the wooden roof of the building broke her free of her trance and she looked up. Behind the fire pit sat Ivar's hand-axe. It was mounted on the wall in honor of the fallen friend.

"I hope you are dining well in Odin's Hall," she said softly, examining the blade of the weapon.

The one thing that Frigyth loved about being queen was that she had no shortage of literature. She made an effort to read any and every saga, tale, poem, even children's book she could in an attempt to feel closer to the people she now led. Besides, every time she read something, she would feel that sense of nostalgia that reminded her of her mother. Sometimes when she read the text of the stories, she could hear her mother's voice reading to her. It was a strange sensation. She was sad those days were gone, but she was happy that they had happened.

Frigyth stepped away from the fire pit and headed to her bedchamber. As she entered, her eyes scanned around the room at all of Njal's missing armor and weaponry. Whenever he left, his missing presence would leave behind a void. The absence of his belongings from the room would multiply that void.

The rain got even louder as it smacked against the roof of the Great Hall. She began to undress, but before she even took her boots off, she heard the guard's horn from outside. She hurried to her feet and ran out of the bedchamber, her boots loud against the wooden floorboards until she ran out of the large building. A waterfall of heavy rain struck her in the face and had created a muddy mess of the streets. She didn't mind too much as she hurried to the front gates. When she arrived, she put a hand above her eyes in order to shield herself from the rain and looked up at the wall. She heard the guard yell, "RIDERS!"

That wasn't the call for when Njal came back and that wasn't the call for when Jarl Sigrid or Jarl Knud would visit. Frigyth moved her hand back to her side as the rain smacked against her red hood. She reached down and felt that her sword was with her. She stepped closer to the gates and called up to the guard.

"Who is it?" she asked.

"This damned rain will not let us see!" the guard yelled back over. "They need to get closer!"

After a few moments, the guard was able to see that riders were carrying banners. Banners of green and brown. The guard peered back over the gate, looking down at his queen.

"They are from Birmingham!" he yelled as lightning struck behind him.

"Let them in!" Frigyth yelled, feeling a bit of sadness in her heart that it was not her king but curiousness as to why men of her fathers were there.

The gates slowly opened, showcasing five riders dressed in green and brown trotting their horses inside. They came to a halt a good five feet in front of Frigyth. The lead rider jumped off his horse and grabbed the reins. He approached the queen.

"Lady Frigyth!" the man yelled, trying to talk over the heavy rain. "I bring news from your father! He wishes to discuss some things with you!"

"Well, is he with you?" she asked, examining the other four riders.

"No," the man exclaimed. "Is there a place we can go that might be a little less wet?"

"Come with me. The rest of your men can sit the storm out in the alehouse. Make sure they dawn their colors proudly as my people are kind to those from Birmingham," Frigyth hollered over the rain. "The stable keep will tend to your horses."

*

Inside the Great Hall now, the man looked around, rain dripping off of his clothes onto the floor. Frigyth stepped into a room and poured two horns of ale and brought them out, handing one to the man.

"Here, sit," Frigyth said, gesturing towards a chair and a table. Once they sat down, the man smiled brightly. His teeth were as white as snow and his brown beard trimmed perfectly. His brown hair was slicked back and his eyes were brown. He was very handsome indeed.

"Much appreciated. I am Sir Wigberht and I was sent by your father."

"Spare me the small talk, Sir Wigberht. Why did my father send you here?" Frigyth asked, taking a large gulp of ale.

"Straight to the point, I see. Well, he wishes to speak with you in person. There are some matters he needs to discuss with you. Royal matters, in fact," Wigberht said.

"Royal matters? Is he remarrying?" Frigyth asked. "If so, I do not intend to go back just for that."

"No," Wigberht said, his eyes pointing down at his horn of ale. "I do not believe I am entitled to say, but I do believe that you must go. Matters are quite... urgent."

"Wigberht, I am queen of this village. I have plenty of responsibilities here, so whatever it is, I need you to..."

"Your father is dying."

Frigyth's eyes widened.

"W...what? From what?" she asked in disbelief.

"We believe it is the rot. The sickness has riddled his body and his insides. It spread fast and no amount of healing has been able to help him in even the slightest amount. We believe he will not make it to spring."

Frigyth put her hand over her mouth as a tear shed from the corner of her eye.

"I will make preparations immediately."

*

The witch's hut was a bit far from the gates of Eagle-crest. The young woman wished to continue her practices in dark magic and her continued chanting and screaming would haunt and frighten quite a lot of people. So, her hut sat in the hills by the clearing where Njal and Aelred had their first 'meeting.'

Frigyth was bracing the elements as the light gray thunderclouds had now faded to a dark gray. Night was close, but the rain persisted. The queen walked through the heavy rain up the hill until the ground evened out. The heavily forested area around her offered a bit of coverage from the rain, and her red hood was offering a bit more. She peered her head up and noticed the multiple bone charms and skulls of animals that were hanging on the trees.

After a walking a few more feet in the mud and rain, she saw the witch's hut in all of its glory. There were small candled lanterns hanging outside as the smell of garlic filled the air. Frigyth stepped up to the hut's door and knocked on it three times.

"Ingrid? It is I, Frigyth," she said, shivering a bit. "I would like to speak with you."

After a brief moment of nothing but the rain answering her plea, the door opened, showcasing Ingrid and her tattooed body. She was in brown pants and a leather top that only covered her chest. Her tattoos of Norse knotwork style bands connected from her feet all the way up her torso and stopped at her neck. Her white hair was braided down the back as she greeted Frigyth with a smile.

"Well, hello, Frigyth!" she said happily. "Come inside. Let us get you out of the rain."

"Thank you," Frigyth said with sadness in her voice.

"Come, sit. I was just making some tea. Would you like a cup?"

"I would appreciate that," Frigyth said, sitting down next to the fire.

"You know," Ingrid started saying from the other room. "Halfdan told me that you and Njal wish to build a home up here in the hills as well. A little place to get away from the burdens of ruling." She grabbed the small pot from over the small fire in the kitchen and poured the hot liquid into two cups made from bone. The inside of the cups were coated with different herbs and spices which mixed as the hot water was poured inside. The witch grabbed the two cups and brought them to the other room. "I personally think that would be a great idea. We could all..."

Ingrid looked at Frigyth. Her smile faded away.

"The redness in your face is not from the cold weather, is it?" the witch asked.

Frigyth shook her head 'no' and began crying into her hands. Ingrid jumped over to her and held her in her arms.

"What is it? What is wrong?" she asked.

"It is my father... he is dying," Frigyth said, sniffling. "I must go and see him before he passes."

"I am so sorry... What exactly is he dying from? Perhaps I can help," Ingrid asked, already turning her head in different directions, looking around her hut for ingredients.

"His body is rotting. Apparently quite quickly."

Ingrid's eyes stopped looking around suddenly and looked at the ground instead.

"I...I hope you know there is not a... there is not a cure for the rotting..." Ingrid said. "As much as I have looked, I..."

"I know, Ingrid..." Frigyth said, crying some more. She

knew. The rot was a vicious and quick illness that destroys its victims within months. "That is not why I have come here."

"Alright, what can I help you with then?" Ingrid asked, her eyebrows creasing, showing a face of hurt and sadness.

"As much as I wished he would return today, the storm is obviously going to stop Njal from getting here for another day or so. But I need to leave for Birmingham with the men my father sent."

"Of course," Ingrid said, waiting for Frigyth to finish her request.

"Could you look out for Eaglecrest until Njal returns?" Frigyth asked.

"Yes. Absolutely," Ingrid said sincerely. "It would be my honor. You go and spend time with your father. I am sure Njal would understand."

"Thank you," Frigyth said before giving Ingrid a great big hug. "And please do not tell Njal of this. I will speak to him about it when I return."

"I..." Ingrid paused. "I understand."

The wind howled as the rain continued to show its wrath on the outside world.

V

❧

A Bear Returns Home

It was in the cold first light of day that Njal could see the wooden walls of the village on the coast. His home. The lanterns and torches that hung on the surrounding buildings could be seen as they still glowed brightly underneath a twilight sky. The salt scent of the sea filled his nostrils while the slight sounds of the water pushing and pulling on the shore hit his eardrums.

Njal galloped his giant brown horse through the tree line and out onto the sandy last stretch of road before the main gates. Halfdan was right behind his friend, with his black cloak fluttering behind him. They could tell from the soft mud like sand beneath them that a storm had passed through. Perhaps the same storm that kept the small party of warriors in London the prior evening. And just like Njal and Halfdan, the three other members of the Eagle clan couldn't wait to get home and see their families again.

The last ten years were hard for the Norse people. So much time spent apart and always wondering if they would see their loved ones again. Now, with everyone together, it was almost hard to get used to not having to worry about the Lords of England. Every single waking moment away from their loved ones felt like twenty lifetimes.

Njal could feel the passion fire in his heart build up. The long wait to see his lovely queen, Frigyth, was almost over. He had spent a lot of time away from her due to his attempts to rebuild a better world, so he tried to cherish every moment he had with her.

His eyes peered over to the massive wall of fog that sat on the sea. He exhaled softly and closed his eyes. He could see the Bear with its glowing golden runes carved into its white fur. The connection he felt to the Land of the Spirits was stronger than it ever had been. Thanks to the witch, Ingrid.

The last few months, he had continued his spiritual practicing with Ingrid, which allowed him to speak in the Land of the Spirits and navigate it without worry. Ingrid even led him to the Lost Plane, where the spirits who get trapped there cannot pass to either Hel or Valhalla. Njal did not like that area. While the rest of the land was beautiful and featured a calming presence, the Lost Plane was dark, full of black rock and red, glowing runes that floated around like snowflakes. Dark clouds dawned over the entire area and the continued sound of the spirits moaning and screaming could frighten that of even Odin.

Njal questioned Ingrid on whether those were the spirits that she steals for her power. *"Aye,"* she had said. *"If I did not take them and put them to good use, they would walk the*

Soul Road for all of eternity. I can at least give them a meaningful purpose." Njal could understand that. Especially after he saw the Soul Road. It was definitely not a place you would want to be stuck on.

Njal opened his eyes and, after a few more moments, made eye contact with the guard on the top of the main gate into Eaglecrest. He graced him with a smile. The guard turned around, announced the king's arrival loudly for everyone to hear, then the gates opened, allowing the riders inside.

Njal hurried his horse over to the stables and took notice of the small groups of villagers that were on the streets meeting his eyes with their own. He thanked the stable keep as he hitched his horse and stepped down. Halfdan and the other three warriors did the same. Njal and Halfdan thanked their companions. They then watched them run to their families that had exited their homes quickly after hearing the horn of arrival.

Njal smiled as they began their own way towards the Great Hall. Those who were out on the streets in the early morning greeted their king with cheerful looks and glad tidings. He greeted them back and eventually made his way through the streets and into the Great Hall. He expected to see his beautiful queen sitting on the throne, but instead, there was nobody but him inside.

"Frigyth?" he called out, Halfdan entering behind him, his own face twisting at the absence of the queen on the throne.

"She must be out and about, right?" Halfdan said, putting his large bag that held the three bottles of wine from King Edward on the table.

"No, if she were out there, the people would have

said something to us," Njal said, a bit of worry creeping into his mind.

They both heard a crashing noise in the room behind the throne, and both warriors drew their respective weapons immediately.

"Who goes there?" Njal shouted.

After a few moments, a woman's voice could be heard.

"Njal? Oh, I will be right out!" the woman said, her voice muffled by the walls.

"That is Ingrid's voice," Halfdan said, putting his giant axe behind his back again.

After a few more moments, the witch walked out from behind the throne, where she had dirt all over her face.

"Sorry about that," she said, wiping her face off using a small cloth. "Some angry spirits wished to have a little chat, and I ended up knocking over a shelve in the back. I apologize. I will fix it shortly."

Halfdan smiled. He loved to listen to her speak about her supernatural life, but to be honest, he had no idea what in Odin's name she was talking about. He ran up to her and lifted her up, spun her around a few times, and kissed her. She laughed and kissed him back while Njal couldn't help but smile. But then reality set back in.

"Ingrid, what are you doing in here? It is not that you are not allowed to be here, it is just... Where is Frigyth?" Njal asked with seriousness in his face.

"I know, Njal. She had to return to Birmingham and left me in charge until you got back."

Njal's face twisted.

"Why did she return to Birmingham while I was away?"

"I promised her I would not say anything, but you are my king. And to be honest, it is quite the secret."

Both men awaited the witch's next words.

"Birstain is dying, Njal," Ingrid said while both men's faces filled with shock and awe. "Some men arrived and informed her of the news."

"What do you mean he is dying? Have they asked for your medicine?" Njal asked as he began pacing around the Great Hall, the floorboards creaking underneath his boots.

"There is no cure for the rot, I am afraid," Ingrid said, her voice saddened.

Njal stopped pacing and dropped his head. "Why would Birstain not tell me this news?" Njal asked, looking over at Halfdan.

"Well, Njal," he replied. "He had just told his own daughter. I am sure he wishes to keep it a secret for as long as possible."

"Damnit," Njal mumbled as he dropped his head again. "I best travel to Birmingham quickly once Frigyth returns. I need to find another Lord there."

"Unless," Halfdan began cautiously. "Death might not be all Birstain wished to speak to her about."

Njal's eyes widened.

*

The gates of Birmingham were open, as they always were. Allowing people to come and go as they please. Frigyth's sadness followed her around like a sack full of boulders as she followed Sir Wigberht on her steed. No part of her trip back to

Birmingham made her feel nostalgic about her first journey to Eaglecrest with Njal. Her mind was full of different thoughts. She passed through what used to be Gulgruve, which was now under Edward's control. She passed through the small village where they met Halfdan. They passed through the road where they had their first conflict with Ulf and then met Ingrid deep within the woods. She even passed the old remains of Alvin's farm, which were still there.

Birstain had asked Njal if he wished to clear the area of the debris, but Njal declined. He said he wished for that area to remain Alvin's farm even in the state it was in.

Frigyth entered through the massive stone walls of Birmingham as the sun attempted to peek behind the gray clouds. Wigberht kept looking back to make sure that Frigyth was behind him. He rode his horse proudly, and he was very confident. His shoulders were always back and his head was always held high. His long brown hair slicked back like each strand was glued together. He seemed a proud man. One of great confidence and courage.

"Welcome home, m'lady," Wigberht said as the group rode inside the walls.

Frigyth didn't reply.

After riding through the city streets, and passing Ivar's old alehouse, they arrived at the main castle gates where everyone stepped off their horses. After hitching their horses to the post outside, they made their way inside the towering structure. The large wooden doors creaked open, showcasing the massive but empty throne room where, in fact, nobody sat upon the throne. That struck Frigyth hard. If her father was so sick that he couldn't even be on his throne, then his time must be short.

Wigberht led her back into the corridors of the castle. With each step, Frigyth felt her anxiety rise. What would her father look like? Was she ready to see him in his state? She followed Wigberht until they reached a room where, before he opened the door, he put his hand on her shoulder and looked at her with creased eyebrows.

"He does not look like how he used to, Frigyth. Please try to stay strong for him while he graces his eyes upon you. He needs to know that you are alright."

She nodded her head as she tried to swallow the frog in her throat.

Wigberht opened the wooden door and let Frigyth walk in before closing it behind her, leaving only her and her father in the room. Her eyes saw, but her mind had not fully processed the scene before her. Her father lay still on his bed and looked as though he had third-degree burns across his body. His body was truly just rotting away. His hair was gone and his eyes were sunken into his skull.

Frigyth put her hand over her mouth and tried to stop the tears from flowing. She sniffled once, which her father heard, and he slowly opened his eyes. When he saw her standing in his room, his mouth transformed into a smile. As large a smile he could still make.

She instantly pulled her hand down and wiped a tear away before forcing a smile and nearing closer to his bed.

"Hello, father," she said, her smile struggling to stay on her face.

"My...my Frigyth," he said. His voice was raspy. He sounded as though somebody had ripped out his vocal cords.

She sat on the edge of his bed, to which he lifted his hand up. It shook wildly before she took it and held it.

"I... I am sorry you... have to see me... this way," he coughed.

"Do not apologize, father," she whispered. "I am just happy to see you at all."

"Oh, my daughter," he said, smiling.

She gripped his hand tighter, and a tear dripped from her eye. "Father, why would you not tell me of your sickness until now? I would have been here in a moment if I had known sooner. I could have helped you prepare. We could have found healers. We could have..."

"Nonsense," Birstain coughed again. "You are a queen... you had more... important things to do."

"Oh, father," Frigyth said, her smile now gone.

"I... I am going to see... your mother..." he said, smiling, a tear falling from the corner of his eye. "I cannot... wait."

"She will be proud of you, father. I know this because *I* am proud of you. You helped us make a better England for all," she wiped a tear from her face again.

"You and...Njal did that..." he coughed again; a bit of blood dripped from the corner of his mouth. "Which is why... what I am about to... ask you... is going to hurt me..."

Frigyth listened but felt the fear build up inside her. Part of her knew what he was going to ask. And she knew that she would be vile if she refused her father's dying wish.

"I want you... to become... Lord of B... Birmingham,"

he said softly. "You are...built for this... to lead... Nobody better can take... my place."

She dropped her head. "You are asking me to give up my husband. You are asking me to abandon everything I helped build."

"Njal... has led his people... to prosperity... you can do the same with... yours."

"I am not sure what to say, father," she said, her mind racing.

"Take some... time..." he struggled to say. "You are meant... for this... Frig..." he went limp and his eyes closed.

Frigyth's eyes widened as she said, "Father?"

After no response, she quickly yelled for Wigberht, who then charged into the room and ran over to his bedside. He put his fingers on Birstain's neck, checking his pulse while Frigyth let her tears flow.

After a few moments, Wigberht said, "He is alive, he is alright. He just fell into a slumber is all."

Frigyth sighed in relief and looked upon her father's unconscious body. Wigberht noticed her and slowly stepped to her. He wrapped his arms around her and she him. She spent the next moments crying in his arms.

*

Njal was walking along the road from Eaglecrest to Muspel with the sea on his left. The buildings that now sat alongside the wooden plank and cobblestone roads were large houses or shops and businesses. The coastline from Demut to Muspel was a busying community now, and it sure acted like it. The community was a combination of the three established villages and a high number of unaffiliated Norsemen. The coastline now held over a thousand Norse people.

Misty rain made the afternoon feel like a brisk and gray morning as Njal said hello to everyone he passed. He walked alone almost every time he went to visit the other Jarls. It wasn't because they spoke about things that not even Halfdan could know about, no; it was because Njal wished for Halfdan to spend his free time with the woman he loved. Njal wished he could spend more time with his love, but he knew the burden of leading was a heavy one to bear and he didn't wish for his friend to bear it with him.

After about half an hour, Njal could see the faded glow of the lanterns and torches that graced Muspel's walls. He could smell the stench of oils and fire as he got closer. The guard that was sitting on top of the gates took notice of the king making his way towards the village of the Fire Clan and he called down to open the gates.

The large and heavy gates made from stone opened extremely slowly, but once they were open, Njal made his way through. Into the village that was built into part of the coastal cliff-side.

"Hello, sir," one guard said as he watched the large Norse king enter. The guard was dressed in black and red leather armor with pieces of blackened iron covering the vital areas. He held a spear with an obsidian tip and a wooden shield with iron reinforcement.

"Greetings," Njal replied, his bear fur cloak fluttering behind him. "Is Jarl Knud in the Great Hall?"

"Aye," the guard said back.

Njal then began his trek through the village of Muspel. He passed the new buildings made from iron as well as the famous blacksmiths. The heat that radiated off of the furnaces that were scattered throughout the village made sweat bead on Njal's face. It was an entirely different world in Muspel. As the children in Eaglecrest were running around playing with their toys made from wood, the children in Muspel would play with fire and learn how to forge weapons. Njal believed in learning survival skills as a child, but he also believed in peace. And when you live in total peace, children can enjoy their childhoods.

Njal eventually made it to the large courtyard where the statue of Odin sat. Behind the statue was the even larger statue of Surtr, the Fire Giant and protector of Muspelheim, one of the nine realms.

Njal passed the statues and eventually made it to the front door of the towering Great Hall. There, he knocked on the door three times, then proceeded to open it. Inside, Jarl Knud was sitting on his throne, speaking to three warriors that were dressed in dark blue and white leather armor. As soon as Njal walked in, everyone else's eyes darted towards the Bear King.

"Oh, I am sorry," Njal said, taking a step back. "Am I interrupting?"

Knud, who was dressed in black leather armor with a fur topped black cloak behind him, stood up from his throne and held his hand up towards Njal.

"No, no," he said. "We are just finishing up our trading discussions." He pointed his attention back towards the warriors and nodded his head in agreement. "I will agree to those terms as long as the Jarl can agree to mine."

The three warriors bowed their heads before turning around and heading for the door to which Njal stepped out of their way. The warriors completely disregarded him as they walked by and exited the Great Hall.

"I apologize about that. We were not supposed to go that long," Knud said, stepping away from his throne and approaching a table which held some wine. "Wine?"

"Who were those men?" Njal asked as he approached Knud, who then handed him a cup of wine before pouring his own.

"Warriors from Iceland, actually. I met with their Jarl a few weeks back when one of their ships wrecked upon the shore to the south of us by the cliffs due to a storm. But ever since Gulgruve fell because of Aelred, and of course is now back in the possession of the Englishmen, I have found the need for oil and other volcanic materials. As it turns out, Iceland has plenty of that to offer. So, I am now trading with them."

"I do not mind you trading with them at all, Knud, but why not tell me of your contact over there?" Njal asked before drinking his wine in one full go.

"With all due respect, my king, I *did* intend to use their alliance for my clan's personal gain only. I know it may come off as selfish, but we need oil. We need material to make our armor and weapons and if we shared Iceland's resources with everyone else in this now massive village that we created, then there would not be much of a Fire Clan anymore."

"I can understand that. The seizing of Gulgruve was not just Edward's idea, but also Birstain's. It helped show the people of England that we are willing to give back what we 'stole.' It adds a layer of trust in our people, even at the cost of losing a major resource outpost. I will allow you to continue your trade with Iceland, as it really does not affect anyone else. Nobody needs those resources as much as you, I know this. And maybe, they can offer us some help in the future. Keep them on good terms."

"I intend to, my king," Knud said before bowing his head. "You have my thanks."

"Please," Njal began. "You know I do not think of you as a servant or anything lower than me. You are a Jarl, Knud. Please, call me by my name."

"I often forget," Knud said before taking both cups and filling them up with more wine. "Now, what is it you have come here to see me for, Njal?"

"Well," Njal said, receiving his horn. "Birstain is dying, Knud. His body is rotting and Frigyth has gone to see him. I wished to talk this over with Halfdan, but I want to give him his time of relaxation with Ingrid. I was hoping you would be able to offer guidance."

"That is unfortunate news. But of course," Knud said. "Come, let us sit down." Knud led Njal to a small room off to the side of the throne room where a small round table and two chairs sat. The two men sat down and drank some more wine before beginning their discussion. "Who gave you the news about Birstain?"

"Ingrid, she was put in charge by Frigyth when she left. That was also before I had returned from my business in London. Apparently, some men came and told her of the news.

She left and I have not heard anything since. My biggest worry is not anything other than what her father might ask her to do."

"And what might that be?" Knud asked.

"I fear that he will ask her to become the next Lord of Birmingham. Perhaps that is selfish of me, but I cannot hold my true feelings back."

"It is unfortunate that Birstain is dying, but it happens to us all at some point. But you must question yourself. Why exactly are you worried about him asking her of that, Njal?" Knud said, sipping a bit more of his wine as the fire pit crackled in the background.

"Because… I am afraid that she might consider it," Njal said before sipping some more wine. "I suppose I believed she was happy here. I know I have not been around much for her, but she is still in a position of power. She leads a people and they all have come to love and respect her. We are trying for a child, Knud. If she leaves for Birmingham, that is no longer a reality."

"Maybe she does not care for a position of power. Maybe she cares about being with you; in a place where she feels as though she belongs. She obviously still feels a bit out of place here, but who would not? Nine months is not much time to get used to a new people and with the one she followed here gone for a decent amount of time; I cannot say I do not blame her for considering it. That is, if she even is considering it, of course."

Njal felt a quick spark of anger at Knud's words, but it quickly faded as he understood it as well. He loved his queen and he need to be there for her just as much as he was for England or his people. Not allowing her to join him on his quests for a better England was like putting her in a box alone. He realized that now.

"You are right, Knud," he said before slamming the last of the wine in his cup and placing it on the table. "I will speak to her when she returns."

"Good, my friend," Knud said, smiling a bit before crossing one leg over the other. "But she must be the one to tell you. It is her problem... her heartbreak. She will tell you when the time is right. But do not worry too much about why she is there because we are not even sure he asked her that question. It could just be a simple goodbye for all we know. But her heart *will* be broken, Njal," he said as his smile faded. "If you are not there for her during that time, you will lose her. I hope you know that."

"I do," Njal said, standing up and bowing his head a bit. "I will see you again soon."

Knud bowed his head back from his seated position as he watched Njal walk towards the door of the Great Hall and exit the building.

*

As Njal walked back from Muspel, the sky became clear. Gray clouds began to part as beams of sunlight shined through. The Bear King walked past all the buildings he did before and sighed. He thought about Knud's words. How Frigyth most likely felt and how she would feel once her father died. It was a hard truth to swallow, but he had no choice. He realized that when he believed he was protecting her by leaving her in Eaglecrest, he may have been pushing her away. He was being too protective.

You will lose her

Knud's words repeated in his head repeatedly.

I will never lose her

His thoughts continued racing around his head as he approached the docks of Eaglecrest. Suddenly, he heard a commotion that pulled him out of his trance. He looked up and noticed an enormous crowd surrounding a giant longboat that looked to have recently docked. Norsemen were arriving in Eaglecrest almost every day, but only a few came by ship. Most were people that lost their way across England. A few arrived from Scotland and a few from Norway. But most arrivals didn't cause such a commotion, and this ship was massive. Njal creased his eyebrows in confusion at the site and his mind began to race when he was able to see the color of the sails of the ship.

Green and black; the colors of the Bear Clan.

Njal's walk became a jog, then a sprint. He hurried himself to the docks, where he began running through the crowd of people. Pushing each one aside until he got to the front. There, he saw around twenty warriors, all dawning the same colors of the sail.

One of them was very tall and built like a mountain. He looked to be on the younger side and had a blonde braid that graced his shoulder. His cloak was green and black and he held a large sword at his side. He looked just like...

Njal.

Njal was in shock at the sight of this man. He could feel the runes of his spirit form pulsating brightly. He continued to look at the man until the man made eye contact with him. Half of his face was scarred. From what was undetermined, but the man smiled with his white teeth when he noticed Njal staring back at him.

The man walked towards the edge of the boat, which made the people of Eaglecrest back up, leaving only Njal on the dock. The man jumped off of the boat and onto the dock and walked right up to Njal's face. They stared at each other in the eyes.

The man smiled widely and reached his hand out.

"Nice to finally meet you... brother," the man said as he gripped Njal's forearm.

VI

The Druids of the
Fenlands

Torin was following the mysterious group of people through the marshlands. Water splashing all over their feet. The tall grass showcasing false ground below them as the sun began to set behind the horizon. Suddenly, Torin's foot was sucked into the mud, which caused him to stumble a bit.

"Shite!" he yelped.

"You need to learn how to walk through the Fenlands, my friend," the lead Druid said, watching the Norseman struggle.

"This damned mud! How do any of you walk through this?" Torin asked, attempting to pull his foot out of the sloppy earth.

The Druid laughed as the rest of his people passed the two and continued straight. "I will teach you a few things while they head on home. The first being, stay on the hard ground. There is always a slight path of hardened dirt that will support you. Do not walk fully into the tall grass because that is where the mud is the worst. You can tell when the ground is wet and slimy and you can tell when the ground is not. Therefore, stay where it is not."

"But you led me through the tall grass when there was a path we could have followed. So, what exactly is the right answer?" Torin struggled to say calmly.

"Exactly, because I find that the best way to learn is through experience. And now that you have experienced Fenland mud, you will know to stay away from it. It is very important to know which ground you can walk on and which ground will bring you an easy death."

Torin didn't like it, but he agreed. He thought back to when he was a part of Ragnar's army. He could see the madness in his king's mind when no one else could. One day, he told everyone that he and the rest of his clan were leaving and that everyone should follow him instead. But when nobody else followed and Ragnar's army was massacred in Paris, Torin slept good at night knowing that those who chose not to follow him in abandoning Ragnar would regret their decision. They learned because of their experiences. Torin respected the way this Druid was attempting to teach him.

"So," the man began. "When you are stuck in a bind like this, you need to move your leg in a circular motion at the ankle. This will spread the mud out around your foot, which will allow for an easier escape from it. Try it."

Sure enough, Torin did exactly what the Druid said

and after a few moments, his foot came free. Torin almost cracked a smile.

"Good!" the Druid said. "Now that you are free, let us go meet the rest of the family."

The man began to walk away as Torin followed. "What is your name?" the Norseman asked.

"Ah, silly me, I forgot I have not told you yet," the man said, laughing. "I am Cathbad Conchobar, at your service. Well, actually, not really, since I am the leader of these fine people. But in a way we do lead each other here."

"What do you mean?" Torin asked.

"You will see soon enough," Cathbad said.

*

After the sun had completely disappeared and the stars began to flicker above them, the two men found themselves nearing an area that featured glistening torches and lanterns.

"We are here," Cathbad said with a smile.

The two eventually entered a large clearing where they saw a village on stilts and the swampy water below it. There were wooden huts all connected by wooden bridges and people dressed in fur and bones were walking around on them. Those who weren't walking on them were sitting by small campfires in clearings nearby.

"Ugh!" Torin shouted suddenly. "What...what is that?" Torin felt a burning sensation in his mind. He put a hand to his head.

"Hm," Cathbad said before turning around and looking at his new companion. "You are sensitive to magic?"

"I...I..." he replied, falling to one knee.

"Well, that in fact answers my question," Cathbad said, turning his attention back towards his village. "That is good. It will make you strong here. The pain will pass. Just focus on your thoughts. Focus on the journey you took to get here. The anger and the rage that you feel. Do not let anything slow you down."

Torin struggled and gritted his teeth. He opened his eyes and stood up strongly. The pain simmered down to a slightly annoying headache. Torin stood there and looked at Cathbad. He nodded his head.

"Good," Cathbad said, smiling. "Very, very good."

Torin then continued to follow Cathbad through the dirt and mud underbelly of the village until a small staircase made of wood led them up to the main part of the village. The two kept walking until Cathbad opened the door to a small hut and smiled.

"This will be your room, Torin," he said happily. "Your training, as well as your testing, will begin tomorrow. I will bring you an herb for that nasty headache you have that shall allow you to sleep. I cannot, however, promise that the headache will not return by morning."

"That is fine. I will master this feeling, but I just need some sleep tonight," Torin said before entering his hut. He ripped off his clothes and crawled into the bed that was laying inside as Cathbad left. This was the first time in a long time that he was able to sleep in a bed. It felt amazing. After a few moments, Cathbad returned holding a bowl of a greenish brown liquid and neared Torin with it.

"Drink this," he said before pouring some into Torin's mouth.

"What... what is happening here?" Torin asked after drinking the entire bowl.

"Well," Cathbad began. "You are sensitive to magic. That is good for us and also you, but because we have so much magic here, I am sure the pain is unbearable. What you felt was the curse we put on our village. Its meaning is to ward away travelers by making them uncomfortable. But to those with spiritual attachment, like you, it is painful and grueling to endure."

"Magic... does not exist..." Torin said. "Only the gods... their power cannot be wielded by people of Midgard."

"As a matter of fact, my friend. Magic does exist, and it has nothing to do with powers from the gods. It has to do with the plants and animals of this world. The energy of this world. It has to do with the power of those who wield it. You will learn tomorrow what true magic is. Now, get some sleep."

Cathbad watched as the Norseman's eyes went to the back of his head and immediately fell limp in his bed. The Druid leader smiled as he exited the hut.

*

The next day, Torin awoke with his head pulsating with immense pain. He grunted as he flipped his legs so that he was sitting on the edge of the bed. He put his hand on his head as he grunted again.

"Torin, are you awake?" a voice said from outside the hut. Then, without any room for an answer, Cathbad swung the wooden door open and greeted Torin. "Well, hello there, sunshine!" Torin squinted as he looked up at the Druid, then looked around him to try to find his clothes. "No, no," Cathbad said. "We threw those nasty clothes of yours out because they were absolute filth! We brought you something a little cleaner."

At the snap of his fingers, three women that only wore a thin sheet that covered below their waist and had tattoos everywhere else came into the hut holding different items of clothing. Torin looked shocked at first, but decided to go along with it. One woman helped him up onto his feet while another began to put brown wool pants on him. Another put a brown wool tunic on over him and the last woman had pieces of animal bones in her hands. She quickly picked up and strapped a large femur type bone around his forearm using brown leather straps. Then, all three women reached behind them and pulled out a small container of a black liquid. They all dipped two fingers into the containers and raised their fingers towards the Norseman's face. One spread it across one side of his cheek and the other woman spread it on the other cheek. The last woman spread the liquid down the middle of the man's face until it reached his black beard.

Torin's headache immediately went away. "W...What did you do? What is this shite?"

Cathbad snapped his fingers again and the women all left, leaving only him and the Norseman left.

"I told you, our magic stems from this world. There is so much to be had and yet so much we have not even tapped into yet. As I said before, some are more sensitive to it than others, and from what we have seen so far, you are one of the more sensitive types. I am very excited to begin our training."

"I will take your word for it." And what is this bone for?"

Torin asked, gesturing to his forearm. "I have seen the majority of you wearing bones; why?"

"I guess we can begin here," Cathbad said, pacing. "These bones that we wear are to show how many acts of courage and bravery you have offered to the Druids. To your family. Everyone begins with just one, but you gain one more every time you help someone in their quest for revenge or our quest for expansion. Let's say somebody wishes to kill a small force of bandits to the east of us and they call on members of our family to help them. If you decide to help and you come back, then you will receive a bone. It shows us that no matter how different we all look on the outside, inside we are all just a pile of bone. We are one and the same. We are a family. Does that make sense?"

"Aye," Torin said slowly. "I wish for my vengeance."

"I am aware, but as I said earlier, you are not yet one of us. You need to prove yourself. Train in our ways and help the rest of our people and eventually, you will have what you need for your vengeance."

"But Njal is becoming more powerful by the day," Torin said, approaching Cathbad. "If we do not kill him soon, we may have to defeat all of England to even get to him! No amount of magic can do that."

"Oh, but Torin," Cathbad said, putting his hand on the Norseman's shoulder. "It most definitely can."

*

Torin approached a large clearing of dirt and sand. The giant surrounding blades of tall grass fluttered in the breeze. Also circling him were around twenty Druids dressed in their fur clothing and pieces of bone attached to their various body parts. The sun sat high in the sky as the morning dew faded with the early autumn heat.

"Well," Cathbad said as he approached the center of the clearing. "What a beautiful day it is to start our newcomer's training! I sense great power in this man and he shall become a fantastic ally for us in the near future!" The crowd of Druids all cheered. "But alas, this man needs to prove his worth to us. He needs to showcase that he believes in our values. And one of those values is that we fear nothing. So, let us see what he fears."

I fear nothing.

Torin gritted his teeth and looked around as the Druids quieted themselves. He then set his focus on Cathbad and squinted his eyes.

"Now," Cathbad began. "I want you to kill me."

Torin's eyes widened and his focus faded.

"What?" he asked. He felt the hilt of his new bone sword at his side, a gift from Cathbad.

"Kill me," Cathbad said as he stood still, no weapons upon him.

Torin looked around at the Druids that surrounded him. Their eyes were all glued to him and their silence allowed nothing to be heard besides the breezy whispers of the tall grass. The Norseman unsheathed the sword made of bone and readied his feet.

He looked at his new acquaintance, now opponent, and figured that he had to make the first move. So, after a few moments of waiting, Torin charged at Cathbad. The leader of the Druids didn't move. In fact, he wasn't phased at all and even gave Torin a small smirk as he got closer. Then, right at the last second, Cathbad reached into a pouch that sat on his belt and threw down a large handful of powder and stepped out of the way.

Torin ran through the large green cloud and tripped and fell onto his knees. He shook his head and looked up. His eyes widened as the entire world transformed around him. The sky turned pitch black as each blade of the surrounding grass grew into giant dead trees where the branches looked like the bony hands of an elderly woman. The crowd of Druids transformed into dark shadows with glowing green eyes and large antlers growing at their heads. Black mist flowing off of each one like snow off a mountain's peak. Torin's eyes widened as he kept looking around him until he saw Cathbad turning into a giant with the head of a deer skull.

Torin yelped and fell onto his back as the giant approached him.

"What...What is this sorcery?" Torin screamed.

The giant towered over him. Black shadowy dust was misting off the giant as well and its eyes glowed a bright yellow. Torin stared the giant in the eyes and gritted his teeth. The giant swung its massive hand down towards Torin, who quickly rolled out of the way. The large hand met the dirt, causing shadowy dust to fly high into the air. Torin readied himself in a defensive stance and waited for the next attack. The giant swung its hand again to which Torin jumped over but was met with the other hand, sending him onto his back in a cloud of smoke. Torin got back to his feet and spit off to his side.

"I fear no man... I fear no monster," he said as he reached for the sword that was lying on the ground next to him.

He gripped the leather hilt and charged towards the giant. The giant roared and began swinging its massive hand at the Norseman. Torin waited until the hand was close enough and when it was, he swung his sword. The blade went right through the shadowy hand and the giant, cutting it off completely.

The giant screeched and fell to its knees. Torin stood tall and raised his sword high. He roared as he swung it down, slicing right through the giant diagonally. And with one last explosion of black dust, the sky became blue again. The shadowy crowd became their former Druidic selves, and the giant morphed back into Cathbad, who was on his knees. A line of blood was seeping down his arm. Torin stood above the leader of the Druids and put his blade made from bone against his neck.

Cathbad looked up into the Norseman's eyes and smiled. "Incredible... Nobody has completed the test on their first attempt before. Although you still have much to learn, you may very well become the best of us — Torin of the Eagle clan."

Torin lowered his sword as a small smile graced his face.

VII

Tokeson

"What the Hel are you talking about?" Njal asked the stranger on the docks. "You are not my kin. I have no kin left."

"Look at us! We look like the same man! Well, despite my scar, thanks to that ol' bastard Aelred," the stranger said, laughing a bit.

"No, no, no," Njal said, walking away. "I do not believe this. I never had a brother. There is no way."

"But there is, my brother!"

Njal turned around instantly. "Do *not* call me that!"

The stranger put his hands up in an attempt to calm the king.

"Listen," he began as seagulls cawed above. "I have been waiting to meet you for a very long time, Njal. Me and my people have been in hiding in Norway, waiting for an opportunity to sail here. Aelred's destruction of our people made it impossible and the bastards that remain in Norway would keep us in the mountains. But we heard the news of your successes, and we felt it was the right time to pack up and move to the new and mighty village of Eaglecrest!"

His followers that remained on the massive longboat cheered proudly.

"Aelred informed me that he killed the child that was in my mother's womb... If you truly are my kin, and not an imposter, how did you survive?" Njal asked this question as he thought back to the information Aelred had told him in the clearing. About *how* he killed his unborn sibling. He wished to see if this stranger had a similar story.

"Aelred killed our mother when I was in her belly. He tore me out of her and threw me into the sea." Njal's eyes widened. "By the allfather's might and with a heart smelted from pure fire, I survived the icy depths as I was pulled from the abyss by the woman who raised me; Tora. She was attempting to use the storm as cover while she stole a few livestock animals from Sten, but she witnessed everything happen. Tora proceeded to jump in and race to save me. She found me on the brink of death as my face was graced with this nasty scar. But I survived. I was then raised as hers in a small village of nomads in the high plains. She told me the story of my mother on the day of my thirteenth winter. However, she also stated that my father, King of Sten and leader of the mighty Bear Clan, had also been slain. When I could not bear that my father would have been bested by some English fisherman, I set out for Sten myself. When I arrived, I noticed a band of bandits had inhabited what remained of our home. I returned to my village and informed the people that I would retake Sten. These mighty people that have accompanied me followed me to rid our home of the virus that inhabited there.”

“You retook Sten?” Njal asked intently, a fire sparked inside of his soul.

“Aye,” the stranger said. “Only to reclaim it for the Bear Clan... Our clan. These people behind me are members of ours now. Once we heard of the rumors of the one true king of our people had risen up and not only united the clans in England but rid Midgard of that nasty bastard, Aelred, we had to see for ourselves. Seeing that the true king is my mighty big brother, Njal, makes my heart glow brightly.”

“What is your name?” Njal asked after a slight pause.

“I am Alf Tokeson.”

Njal’s spark of fire dimmed when he saw Alf bow his head to him. There was to be no battle between them. This Alf man arrived and spoke of his family, and his intentions did not seem ill. Njal was aware that if Alf truly was his brother, he would have the same birthright as him. However, at first glance, that didn’t seem like what he was after. Njal knew he needed to keep his guard up, though.

“Njal!” a voice said behind him. He turned to look and saw none other than Halfdan approaching, an enormous axe being held in both of his hands. “What is going on down here? Is everything alright?” the berserker asked.

“Aye,” Njal said, looking at Alf cautiously. “Halfdan, I would like for you to meet my, uh... brother.”

Halfdan’s eyes widened. “I was unaware you had any blood kin left, Njal.” Halfdan said, his eyebrow creasing.

"Neither was I, my friend," Njal said. "But, um, Half-dan, this is Alf. Alf, this is my shield mate, Halfdan Blood-Wolf."

"Halfdan Blood-Wolf?" Alf asked, surprised. "The berserker that fought alongside Ragnar Lothbrok! Njal, even sharing a horn of mead with this elite warrior, is a saga in itself! How do you do, friend?" He said, reaching his arm out. Halfdan swung his in as well and they clasped each other's forearms.

"Hm," Halfdan said, looking into Alf's eyes. "I may like this man already, Njal!"

"Ha ha!" Alf laughed heartily. "Is there a place where me and my warriors can drink our bellies full of mead tonight?"

"Of course," Njal said, still a bit cautious. "We shall hold a feast in the longhouse tonight."

Everyone cheered loudly as Njal and Halfdan shared a cautious smile.

*

That night, the stars were out, and the joyous festivities were in full swing. People were flyting, drinking, singing, humping, and dancing to their heart's content. Njal and Halfdan sat alongside one another in the longhouse as they ate their roasted boar and drank their wine, curtesy of King Edward. Alf and the rest of his band of warriors were dancing around in a circle in front of the large and ever stretching table. Njal and Halfdan were seated in their chairs as they watched the group of new arrivals intently.

"What do you think about him, Halfdan?" Njal asked as he leaned over to his friend. "Do you believe he could really be my brother?"

Halfdan sighed. "I believe you are allowed to feel

cautious since he just walked in here and said that. But to be honest, you both look identical. I mean, other than that nasty scar on his face. But if he really is your brother, this could be a major blessing. You could have a piece of your family back. Your clan, too."

"Aye, but he did say that these warriors were not born into the clan. They were nomads in the high plains back in Norway. Even if he is a true warrior of the Bear Clan, the rest of them are not." Njal said before taking a sip of wine.

"Aye, but what does it matter?" Halfdan asked, which surprised Njal. "I mean, think about it. You have already changed how we live for the survival of our people. Eagle Clan members living with Horse Clan members and Horse Clan members living amongst Fire Clan members. Every one of them is living with other Norse people who have lost their clans and families entirely. Why not let these warriors of his believe they are members of your clan? If what they say is true, and they took back Sten, then I think they most likely earned it, you know?"

"You have made a great deal of points, Halfdan. Perhaps I shall give this man a chance."

"I mean, what is the worst that can happen?" Halfdan said, shrugging his shoulders. "If he turns out to be a liar, we will just kill him."

Njal chuckled.

That night, the entirety of Eaglecrest, Muspel, and even Demut celebrated and feasted until the next day's twilight.

*

Alf awoke to the splashing of water drenching his entire body.

"What?! Who goes there? I will stab you!" he shouted as he jumped to his feet.

"Whoa, whoa, whoa, there," Njal said with a smile on his face.

Alf wiped his eyes and saw his brother standing before him. He sighed with relief and began laughing. "Jotun's balls! Do not startle me like that, brother!" he exclaimed. "What a night that was, though. Am I right?!"

Halfdan was standing behind Njal and laughed. "You realize you slept in pig shite, yes?"

Alf nodded his head and pursed his lips. "Eh, still not as rotten smelling as that woman I humped last night!"

Both Njal and Halfdan gave looks of disgust.

"Alright, well, I thought it be best that you come and hunt with us this morning," Njal said as he handed his brother a spear. "Take this. You must understand that everyone pitches in around here so that we can all enjoy this life we have made for ourselves. First, we will enter through the valley and up the backwoods path towards Gulgruve. There should be a number of deer and rabbit that we can eat. If we are lucky, maybe another boar."

"Ah, I would love to, brother!" he said happily. "Let us go!" Alf gripped the spear and began walking towards the front gates of Eaglecrest. "Oh, wait. My apologies! You are the king of our people. I shall follow you!"

Njal was quite surprised by the energy the man had, especially after the night that he had. But he went along with it. Both Njal and Halfdan walked in front of Alf as the three of them left the village through the main gates and ventured out into the world.

"Is this your first time in England, Alf?" Halfdan asked.

"Aye," Alf replied, smiling. "I been in Norway my entire life. But I heard some stories about England that made me wish to visit. And not only because our people are here."

"Is that right?" Njal asked. "What sort of stories?"

"Well, there was a traveler to Sten a few winters back. An old bastard, but strong. He had a strange accent and I come to find out he journeyed to Sten from England! He said he was exiled by Aelred for harboring coin when he owed taxes. Well, due to the old man's courage and grit, and the fact that he was so old he probably would not survive a journey somewhere else, we took him in. He told us all about the never-ending hills, the endless waves of grain fields, and the towering cliffs along the coastline." Alf paused for a moment and looked around him. He took a deep breath in and exhaled. "Aye, I am quite excited to see this land."

They followed the dirt road up through the valley until Alf began to sing a happy little tune.

Felt her breast upon my hand,
Heard the sea upon my ears!
Why ye be cryin' son, wipe those little tears!

I be a man from Jorvik,
My beard be long and so!
My woman makes me lovesick,
So, she has got to go!

OHHH
I never been with a foreign gal but I...

"Gods..." Halfdan said quietly to Njal while Alf finished the song in the background. "This man is starting to get on my nerves." He turned around instantly and stared at Alf. "HEY! You are going to scare the animals away, you damned fool!"

Alf scoffed and said, "I know how to balance fun and hunting, Halfdan. Why are you all so serious here? You won this land in combat fair and square! Should you not be happy?"

"We are quite happy, Alf," Njal said, turning around and looking at him in his green eyes. "But there are things we must do. Things that require all the thinking that is available in our minds. We are attempting to make a better England for all people and it has proven harder than we imagined. So, if you would like to stay here and be at my side, I am going to need you to stop doing things that will make you sleep in the pig-pen. Aye?"

"I understand," Alf said. "I am just happy to see some-body I am kin with. Actual blood kin. You got to live a bit in mothers' presence and some in fathers. I did not get to live even a moment's worth in either of their presence, so being able to spend time with you just makes me feel joyous. I apologize."

Njal creased his eyebrows. If this truly was his brother, then it would be the only blood kin he had left, too. A piece of him hurt at the way he had just talked to Alf. If the story he told was true, then he had a very hard life as well. One that did not deserve to be discarded but deserved to be heard. Listened to and believed. Especially by what could very well be his actual brother.

"It is alright. I suppose I could raise my spirits as well," Njal said with a crack of a smile. "Come, let us go hunt."

The three of them continued their way up the road until the sand that surrounded them became grass, which then turned into trees. After a few more moments of walking, Njal turned to the left and stepped off of the main road and onto a small pathway that was overgrown with blades of grass.

"Was Gulgruve actually real?" Alf asked.

"Aye," Njal said back. "It was very real. I heard the stories, but did not believe it either until we saw it on our way to Eaglecrest for the first time."

"Wow, the tales I have heard of Jarl Bjork and his miners," Alf said, looking up into the trees. "You know, it was said that Jarl Bjork was the son of a Jotun! That he stood as tall as a tree and was as big as a mountain."

"We were there when it fell, sadly," Halfdan said coldly.

"Wait, really?" Alf asked, drawing his attention back in front of him, his smile fading.

"Aye, we were attempting to get help from them, but Aelred beat us there, set a trap for Jarl Bjork, and we had to escape. That is when Njal killed Dodson of Canterbury," Halfdan said.

"Hm, I have not heard of him," Alf said. "Was he one of the lords here?"

"Aye," Halfdan said. "One of the most intimidating, too. But once Njal kicked him off the cliff and his body splat against the ground in front of Aelred, oh you best believe that put the fear of the Christian god in Aelred's eye."

"Amazing," Alf said as he stepped over a fallen branch. "So, wait, before you became this 'Lord Slaying Bear King,' what happened?"

"What do you mean?" Njal asked, still focused on the path before him.

"Well, before the battle with Aelred, but after the fall of Sten."

Njal stepped over a bush as he began. "I came over here for my...our, father's vengeance, but I did not get far as I was captured and sent into slavery. The man who bought me was named Alvin. He was a kind soul that ended up raising me as his own son in the city of Birmingham. However, about a year ago now, he was murdered by some bandits and the Lord of Birmingham decided to throw me in jail for hunting down his murderers. That is when they discovered my identity and Aelred became desperate to finish his quest to destroy us all. I ran away with the lord's daughter and we met Halfdan and another Norseman, Ivar, along the way. All four of us fought our way through England until we reached Eaglecrest, where we had to rid the village of Jarl Torin. Once I bested him in combat, we united with the other clans and ended up defeating Aelred. Now we are here."

"By Odin's one eye," Alf said, shocked. "What of the Lord of Birmingham? And his daughter? What of your friend Ivar? Why has not he joined us on this hunting trip?"

"Because he is dead," Halfdan said sternly.

"Torin killed him," Njal said. "The Lord of Birmingham

ended up betraying Aelred due to some personal reasons, and Frigyth, his daughter, is my wife and the queen of Eaglecrest."

"It is sad to hear about your friend, Ivar, but I am joyous to hear you have a queen! Where is she? Why was she not feasting with us last night?"

"Because she had some business to attend to in Birmingham," Njal said. "She will be back soon and you can meet her."

"I would very much like to!" Alf said, but then pausing. "But she is an Englishwoman?"

Njal felt a brisk chill of wind that tingled in his spine. "Aye, shall that be a problem?"

"No, no, not at all," Alf said. "Just, I was not aware that an Englishwoman could be queen of our people."

"Well, now you are aware," Halfdan said coldly. His first impression of Alf wasn't a bad one, but the more he was around him, the more he found himself not wanting to be around him. It wasn't really anything he said, he just seemed to be a bit immature. Granted, he was quite young.

"I am not trying to be cold with the next words I speak, Alf," Njal began. "But father taught me the new way of our people. One that relied on expansion and allies instead of raiding and taking. A way that we can still please our gods but will allow us to build. We must be open to letting people in. We must be open to peace. So, aye, Frigyth is an Englishwoman, and she is my queen. Just about everyone in Eaglecrest loves her, as well."

"Hm," Alf said. Halfdan turned his head and gave the

man an awful stare before turning his head back towards Njal. "What of you, then, berserker?" Alf asked, noticing the stare.

"What about me?" Halfdan said, annoyed.

"Do you have a woman?"

"Aye," he replied sternly. "She is a witch. The seer of our village."

"Your seer is also a witch? And *that's* who you are humpin'?" Alf said with a little laugh behind it.

Halfdan turned around and grabbed the man by the collar of his green tunic. "You best leave her out of your mouth, aye?"

"I meant no harm by it, my friend," Alf said without any worry or fear. "I am just surprised, that is all." Halfdan let go and continued in front of Njal. "I only mean that because my wish is to meet a fine Norse woman that plays no part in magic. Only glory and has great skill with iron."

"Shhh!" Njal said as he got down in a crouched position. He gripped the wooden shaft of his spear tightly in his right hand. Halfdan followed, as did Alf. Njal pointed with the tip of his spear deep into the forested area as the other two squinted their eyes to see what their leader could.

Once their eyes focused in on the beast, they were able to tell that it was a big meaty boar, minding its own business around fifty yards away. Njal slowly began crouch walking towards the boar when he felt the shaft of Alf's spear block him from going any further. Njal turned his head and looked at his brother, who smiled back at him. Alf winked and raised to his feet as he felt the spear within his hands. Each wooden splinter stabbing into his fingers, making its own grip. He raised it and cocked his arm back. Njal and Halfdan shared a look of disbelief as Alf took one step and swung his arm forward, releasing the spear.

It was like the whole world stopped as the spear traveled quickly and precisely through the air. Whistling as it flew. Then, in a moment, the lethal end of the spear hit its target, sending the boar flying back a few feet as the spear sat lodged in its side.

"What the..." Halfdan began saying as Njal started laughing.

"That was incredible, Alf! Where did you learn to throw a spear like that?"

"I trained myself as well as the other warriors in our clan, brother! We are fierce and wish to be a part of your community!" Alf said happily.

"Keep it up, and you got yourself a deal," Njal said with his eyebrows raised. "Let us go see your award!"

Halfdan, although impressed by the spear throw, was feeling a bit strange about this man. His skills were excellent. But he seemed quite immature. Immaturity can be forgiven often. But sometimes it can lead someone to do horrible things. Halfdan held his tongue and decided that having a man like this on their side, and it being Njal's blood kin, is a good thing and that any doubt he had was probably just due to the man's loud mouth.

The three warriors stood up and walked towards the dead boar. When they arrived, Alf grabbed the shaft of his spear and pulled it out, making a crunching sound. "That is a fat one. We shall feast well tonight!"

Njal put his hand on Alf's shoulder and said, "Of that, I have no doubt, *brother*."

*

That night, the village of Eaglecrest feasted again. This time, the main course was the massive and fatty boar that Alf skewered with his spear. Everyone was laughing and dancing as the stars lit up under the fresh autumn night sky. A crisp breeze was in the air as the fire lights from bonfires could be seen from far away.

Inside the longhouse, things were pretty much the same as the night before. Except for the fact that Halfdan was seated at his seat on the long table alone as he watched Alf and Njal dance together in a circle of villagers. The skalds were singing songs and drums were banging rapidly as the two brothers laughed at one another.

"Let us place a wager," Alf said, panting as he hurried his feet.

"What do you have in mind?" Njal asked, breath also short.

"Whoever cannot keep up with the Skald's tune has to drink six horns of mead back-to-back!" Alf said happily.

"You are on, brother!" Njal replied. "Skald!"

The Skald stopped playing his music and singing his song. The villagers stopped dancing and Halfdan watched intently from his seat.

"Quicken the song please," Alf said. "We wish to see who is the faster brother!"

The Skald nodded his head and began to sing slowly. Njal and Alf looked at each other with smirks on their faces.

They both took a step forward, then one backward. Each movement going with the Skald's song. The song began to speed up just a tad. Njal nodded his head as if to say he knew he was winning. Alf replied by shaking his head no. After a few more steps, the Skald's song sped up to an extremely fast pace. Njal and Alf quickly danced around in a circle, staring at one another. Njal began to clap his hands to the beat as he high stepped. Alf laughed as the song started to become a little too quick.

"I got you now, brother!" Njal shouted, the villagers all laughing as they clapped to the beat.

"Not if I have anything to... Whoa!" Alf missed his step and went tumbling to the ground.

The villagers all clapped and cheered as Njal laughed and approached his brother. He reached his hand down and Alf grabbed it with a smile across his face.

"Give it up for my brother, everyone!" Njal said, which received a thunderous applause from the villagers.

"No, no," Alf replied. "Give it up for your king! A man that can dance as well as he fights!"

Everyone went crazy.

Halfdan looked at Alf with squinted eyes but thought back to his previous thought. If Njal's blood brother was here, then there was truly nothing to worry about. Nothing to run from and nobody to fight. As he watched the two head over to a barrel of ale to see Alf hold up his end of the wager, Halfdan thought about the benefits of this.

He loved Njal like a loyal brother, but his time accompanying his king on their journeys across England took time away from what he really dreamed of; a quiet life with Ingrid.

Before Njal met him, Halfdan spent his days drinking in that alehouse, hoping for another chance at an explosive saga. One that would be sung in alehouses for years to come. But after the battle for Eaglecrest, he found himself wishing for nothing more than to have a son and teach him what he knew. And Alf seemed to be his ticket to that life.

He figured that if Alf became Njal's shield mate, he would be able to live out the dream he now had in his head. Of course he would always love Njal. He would fight for him, even *die* for him. But he was alright with leaving the heavy lifting to Alf, if that is what Njal decided in the near future.

"My brother!" Njal said after Alf downed his third horn of ale. "Come with me. I wish to share something with you!"

"I have three more horns to go," Alf said, words slurring.

"Never mind the other three, come on," Njal said, laughing.

Alf agreed with a smile on his face and followed Njal out of the longhouse. The two stumbled and said hello to everyone in their path until they exited the village gates and headed down to the beach. The tide flooded their brown wool boots, but they didn't care. Njal instantly sat down with a sigh, paying no mind to the water that was now soaking his brown pants and white tunic. Alf followed his brother's actions.

"Alf," Njal began. "Tell me of Norway."

"Norway is not bad, brother! Everything is pretty much the same," he belched. "I have not seen much of England yet, but I would be lying if I said I did not miss home."

"I understand," Njal said. "How is Sten?"

"Sten was home to us for a long time. We rebuilt a lot of it. Actually, expanded into the mountains."

"Really?" Njal said in disbelief. "That is quite... wait. *Was?*"

"Aye," Alf said, belching again. "It was stolen from us by riders a winter ago. We were pushed back into the high plains, and that is where we heard of your victories here."

"Riders?" Njal asked, concerned. "Who were they?"

"They were Norsemen, that is certain. Not sure who, though. I could not see as they forced us to leave quickly, and they were wearing iron helms." Alf said.

Njal squinted his eyes and looked out upon the darkness of the ocean. The stars sparkling above it. There were more Norsemen out there. And they *stole* Sten. Njal's proper home. It made him angry. Until Alf brought him out of his trance.

"Can you tell me a bit about our parents?" Alf asked. His voice sounded sad. Lonely.

Njal paused a moment, letting his blood cool. He closed his eyes, a sense of calmness overcoming him. "Of course," Njal said, bringing his attention back toward his brother. "Mother was a lovely woman. She was fierce... dangerous to anyone who opposed her or father. She was kind... I remember her warmth. Her..." he paused. "You know what? The older I become, the less I remember of her." He took a deep breath before continuing. "Father, on the other hand, well, he was everything to me. To Sten. He fought hard when he needed to, but he always chose an alternate way of dealing with problems. Discussions, physical challenges, or coin. He was wise. Driven on the protection of our people rather than sending them to Valhalla."

"He solved problems with physical challenges... but it was not fighting?" Alf asked, a bit confused.

"No," Njal laughed. "Father tried to please the gods in ways that did not involve violence unless it was absolutely necessary. You see, the thing about the gods is that they only die when people do not believe in them anymore. Father kept them alive by settling debates with axe-throwing contests or games of flyting, or even fishing competitions. In every one of them, he would start with a ritual and an offering to the gods. Each challenge would be in the name of one of the gods."

"Interesting," Alf said, stroking his beard. "I always thought he was this great violent warrior."

Njal scoffed. "He *was* that! But he had something that was much better than any other king we have ever had. Wisdom of *how* and *when* to use violence."

"I wish I could have met him. The fall of Sten was not until I was six winters old."

"So, why did the woman who found you not give you back to our father in Sten?"

"Tora could not have children. It was something Loki cursed her with, so when she found me, she raised me to be her own. When she finally informed me of my blood kin, I was angry at first. I was furious..." Alf paused. "But once I realized that *she* was the one who cared for me, I decided that she was enough for me. Everything I learned until that point, I learned from her."

"I can understand that," Njal said, looking forward out into the ever-extending ocean. "The man that took me in, Alvin. I loved him like a father."

"Even though he owned you like property?" Alf asked.

"He never made me do anything I would not want to. I mean, sure, there were chores to be done, but I never minded doing those since he would do them right next to me. He fed me until my belly was full, allowed me to explore and hunt for wood-trolls and frost-jotuns. In fact, he even blessed me with the sword I wield today."

"Hm," Alf began. "So, even though we were not raised together, we had similar childhoods. Being raised by other people instead of our parents."

"Aye," Njal said, nodding his head. "What ever happened to Tora?"

"She is still alive," Alf said. "But when we decided to take Sten for ourselves, I told her that it could become the new home of our people. She looked at me in the eyes and told me no. She said that her home was in the high plains, but it was time for me to find my own. The place where I belonged."

"Have you seen her since that moment?" Njal asked.

"Aye, she visited once. The entire village did, in fact. But that was the last time."

Njal nodded his head as he looked out into the ever-expanding sea before him.

"You know what I think, brother?" Alf asked after a moment. "I think that we, as cubs and as full-grown bears, we require a place to belong. There is nothing wrong with it, it is just we... we need family. Whether that be our blood kin or those we meet along the way, we just need people to love."

Njal thought hard about his brother's words. He looked high up into the sky and thought about Frigyth and

Halfdan. Ivar and Alvin. They were the only people he ever let in. It was time to let his blood brother in, too.

"Listen to me, Alf," Njal said, putting his hand on his brother's shoulder. "I wish for you to be by my side. I know we got off on the wrong foot, but it was because of my inability to trust. There has been so much betrayal in my lifetime. Things I hold attachment to are stripped away from me without hesitation. But here is the thing: I am going to trust you. I believe you are telling the truth about what happened when you were young. I believe you have good intentions here. So... would you care to stay here in Eaglecrest with me and help me create a better world for our people?"

"Brother," Alf said with a tear forming in his eye. "It would be my undying honor."

The two brothers eventually fell into a deep slumber as the tide swallowed their feet in the sand. The midnight sun glowed over the joyous village of Eaglecrest.

*

BOOM!

The Bear awoke to the sound of thunder. He got to his paws and looked around quickly. Shadows were lurking behind trees in the darkness of night. The Bear's runes that were carved into his fur now shined a bright blue. He began pacing back and forth, looking at the shadows that watched him with great focus. His jowls raised up, showcasing his teeth, as he released a deep and raspy growl.

CAW!

The Bear heard behind him. He twisted his massive

body until he saw that of a large Raven that was perched on a tree stump before him. It cawed again as the Bear approached it.

BOOM!

With the flash of a lightning strike, the Raven was now a man cloaked in black robes with a long gray beard flowing out at the bottom of the dark hood. He held a golden spear in his right hand. The Bear stared at the man and waited for him to speak.

"Njal Tokeson..." the man said, loud and deep. His voice echoing throughout the world.

"Odin..." the Bear replied. "I was wondering when I would see you again."

"You must be careful, young one. Dark forces are at play here, dark forces indeed," Odin said, his head still lowered.

"What forces? If you are aware of them, why not tell me so I can put a stop to them?" the Bear asked. "Please tell me it has nothing to do with my brother."

"As of now, the arrival of your brother spun a thread of fate that leads to glad tidings. It is the man in the swamps that I fear for you and the rest of my people."

"Man in the swamps?" The Bear sat and thought for a moment before he understood. "Torin? Is he coming back?"

"Watch with a keen eye of your surroundings, Njal. The thread you are walking is spun into paths that even I cannot see. The decisions you make over the next few months will help decide which thread is yours, and which is the man that is sitting next to you on the beach. If you do not make the proper decisions, my entire people could be annihilated."

"I understand and will heed your warning..." the Bear

said. "But wait, I must ask. Is this man Alf... is he truly my brother?"

"He is, Njal. Everything he has told you so far is the truth. I just wish I could see what is fated. Although my people are thriving, thanks to you, I still feel weak. Everything is cloudy. The Nine Realms feel cold. I fear Fimbulvetr may be upon us. You must keep your head up and your sword ready for whatever may come your way."

With another flash of lighting, Njal awoke wildly on the beach to the sound of the guard at the main gate blowing his horn of arrival.

VIII

The Englishwoman and the Northman

Njal entered through the large wooden gates of Eaglecrest as the sun crawled its way up over the horizon. He noticed a crowd of people surrounding somebody, which caused Njal's spirits to rise. He then pushed and bumped his way through the crowd until he saw her.

His eyes lit up at the sight of her signature red cloak and her shoulder-length brown hair.

"How was Birmingham?!" a member from the crowd yelled.

"Did you have to fight anyone?" a woman asked from behind a few other people.

Frigyth looked around until she locked eyes with Njal. Her beloved king. Her bear. He was standing a few feet in front of her. His enormous smile and creased eyebrows made it aware to absolutely everyone how much he had missed her. She approached him slowly, and he grabbed her soft hands.

"My queen," he whispered in her ear. "How much I have missed you..."

Her piercing blue eyes looked into his. Her brown hair waved to the top of her shoulders. "I missed you, too," she said before embracing him with all of her. Her arms wrapped around his massive shoulders and her lips met his. The hair from his mustache tickling her a bit.

Everyone that surrounded them cheered before one man jokingly yelled, "Hey! Get back to your business and let the two lovers be!"

Frigyth broke away first due to curiosity. It wasn't Halfdan's voice, as she knew well what he sounded like. As the crowd faded away, she looked behind her king and noticed a man that looked very similar to her lover. He was broad shouldered and blonde; his eyes were green and his face featured a massive scar, although his expression showed that he looked to be a kind soul. He seemed to be some winters younger than the two of them.

"Njal, who is that?" Frigyth asked, gesturing behind him.

Njal smiled and turned around while putting his hand behind Frigyth's back. "My love, I would like for you to meet my brother."

Her eyes widened. "I... I was not aware that you had a brother."

"Neither was I," Njal said, watching Alf approach. "This is Alf. He arrived here while you were away on that large longboat that rests by the docks."

"Well, it is a pleasure to meet you, Alf," Frigyth said, reaching her hand out.

"The pleasure is all mine," Alf said before taking her hand, bowing, and then kissing it. "I am honored to meet the Queen of Eaglecrest and my brother's woman." He paused for a moment as his eyes examined her. "Wow, he was not jesting about your beauty, either! It matches that of Freyja!"

"Well," Frigyth said, taken aback by his forwardness. "Thank you."

Njal smiled as happy thoughts fluttered through his mind.

*

"How do you know that he is your brother and not just some random man claiming that to earn your favor and achieve more power?" Frigyth asked as the fire crackled in the throne room of the Great Hall. Only she and Njal were present.

"I held the same fears until I remembered what Aelred said to me on the battlefield. He told me that he enjoyed killing my mother, father, and ripping the baby out of my mother's belly," Njal said as his voice carried through the empty building. "This man had the same story!"

"But that does not explain how he could have survived all of that," Frigyth said. "No babe has that much strength."

"Nordic babes do..." Njal said, to which Frigyth scoffed jokingly. "His story lines up, Frigyth. He took back Sten from bandits, then heard of our victory here."

"To possibly receive *more* power, no?" Frigyth asked, pacing.

"Listen," Njal began. "I will choose to trust him because he is my blood kin. Odin told me so. And while our values and personalities might be a bit different, I feel as though I can teach him to act like we do and to see the goal that we have for this world. Then perhaps he can take over. Maybe... maybe I can spend more time here; with you." Njal walked up behind her and put his hands on her stomach. He kissed the back of her neck. "You are my home, Frigyth. You are the love of my life. I wish to start a family with you and live out the rest of my days loving you and the child we inevitably bring into this world."

She smiled at that and put her hands on top of his. "I would like nothing more for that either, Njal." A few moments passed with them holding each other before Frigyth spoke again. "But that does not mean we can allow ourselves to be blind by further schemes. Whether Odin says so or not."

Njal sighed and released her. He walked over to his throne and put his hand on the Norse knotwork carved armrest. He examined each etching in the chair. "You know," he began. "I had to watch my father die. I had to watch Alvin die. I had to watch Ulf die. Everyone I ever held close in my life has been killed. Now, I have people that I call my family. You, Halfdan, Knud, Ingrid, even Sigrid. But this man is my actual *blood*, Frigyth. He comes to my door and just wishes to spend time with me here. He wishes to spend time in the presence of his brother. I do not understand why that is such a hard thing to grasp."

Frigyth put her head down, then lifted it back up as she approached her king. "I am sorry. Please, I just... I just wish for you to be careful." She grabbed his waist and turned him around so that he looked at her. "I only want the best for you and if we do not keep our eyes open, even when something seems amazing, we allow it to have the chance to bite us when we are not looking. Your father did the same thing with Aelred, did he not?"

That truth hurt Njal's heart, but she was right. "You are correct. Just like you always are." He brushed a wave of her brown hair from her face and kissed her soft lips before pulling away and stomping towards the front door of the Great Hall. "But Aelred was not of my father's blood."

*

That night, the village of Eaglecrest was quiet. After a couple of days of constant feasting, everyone was looking to relax and spend the night in peace and quiet. Well, except for a few people who filled the alehouses and drank to their heart's content. One of these people, being Jarl Sigrid of the Horse Clan. After the battle with Aelred, she had been hurt so badly that Ingrid informed Njal she was going to die. But one day, her fever chilled and her wounds began to heal. Ingrid called it a miracle.

During the battle, though, Demut, the home of the Horse Clan, was completely ransacked and burned to the ground by Eacnung's men. When Njal informed Sigrid of this when she woke up, he told her that he was already in the process of rebuilding and making Demut better and larger than it already was.

Sigrid, although happy that Aelred was defeated and was pleased with the alliance, was extremely angry when she found out that Halfdan let Torin out of his cell and wished to kill him in the hills which ultimately lead to his escape. Sigrid wanted Halfdan to pay for that, but Njal stepped in and told her no. After that, Sigrid mostly spent her time in Demut and the surrounding alehouses. She would only ever come to Eaglecrest if Njal absolutely needed her, or she needed him. Or, on nights like this, when most people would be asleep, she would come to the Eaglecrest alehouses because they had the best ale.

That night, Sigrid walked in through the door of the alehouse and headed to the bar. The barmaid saw Sigrid enter wearing a white shirt and brown pants with brown boots. Her sword strapped to her waist and her blonde hair braided down to her chest.

"Good evening, Sigrid!" the barmaid said happily. "The same tonight?"

"Aye," Sigrid replied while sitting on a chair at the bar.

"Did you see the Lady Frigyth is back from her trip to Birmingham?" the barmaid asked as she filled up a horn of ale.

"Hm," Sigrid grunted, not caring in the slightest.

She looked around and took in the sight of the few people that were dancing and drinking themselves into oblivion. Her eyes eventually caught that of a man that was sitting by himself at the table in the corner. He was smiling as he, too watched the people dance. His horn of mead looked to be empty.

"Njal?" Sigrid said to herself out loud.

"No," the barmaid said, taking notice and looking at Sigrid. "That be Alf Tokeson. Njal's long-lost brother."

"Alf?" Sigrid said to herself. "I was not aware that Njal had a brother."

"Neither was he, apparently," the barmaid laughed.

"When did he arrive?" Sigrid asked as she received her drinking horn.

"Just the other day, actually. Him and Njal were spending almost every moment together until Frigyth returned from Birmingham this morning."

"Hm," Sigrid said, clearing her throat. "Get him another horn of mead; on me."

"You betcha!" the barmaid said happily.

After a few moments, Sigrid watched the large woman fill up the horn and head over to Alf. She met his eyes when the barmaid pointed over to her as she handed him the horn. Sigrid smiled and looked away. Alf couldn't believe it and he grabbed the horn and stood up. He walked straight up to the bar and sat down next to Sigrid.

"So," he began as he looked at her. "Who might you be?"

"I am Sigrid," she said, turning and meeting his eyes. They were green like the forest. "Jarl of the Horse Clan in Demut."

Alf's eyes lit up. "Jarl Sigrid... What an honor," he said, bowing his head. "I am Alf..."

"Tokeson," she said, cutting him off. "I am aware. And what brings you here to Eaglecrest, Alf Tokeson?"

"I came to spend time with my brother," he said. "His victory has become known far and wide, so once I knew he was here, I had to come."

"I can understand that," Sigrid said, sipping her mead. "Eaglecrest has become a home to many Norsemen."

"Aye," Alf replied. "I am enjoying it here."

"Where were you before you sailed here?" Sigrid asked.

"I was back in Norway. I honestly believed we were the last remaining Norsemen other than Jarl Torin. But I was not going to sail all this way for Torin." Alf looked away and spoke under his breath. "No good betraying bastard."

"I am glad you also dislike Torin," Sigrid said. "He bullied my clan for years. It was nice to finally defeat him and put him in his place."

"I heard. But what ever happened to him?" Alf asked.

"Oh," Sigrid said in a condescending tone. "Did your brother not tell you?"

"No," Alf said, genuinely confused. "What?"

"After Njal defeated Torin in a challenge for the throne, he decided not to kill him and instead throw him in a cell. Well, Halfdan took Torin out of the cell and into the woods without Njal's say and was going to kill him. But apparently, he got distracted and Torin escaped. Now, we are not sure where he is."

"Was Halfdan punished for that? That is a pretty major offense, no?" Alf asked.

"Of course it is, but no," Sigrid scoffed. "Njal just slapped him on the wrist and called it a day."

"Hm," Alf said. "That is strange. But what of you?" Alf asked. "I did not see you at the feasts we had the last two nights. I am aware that Jarl Knud usually stays with his people but..."

"We all feast in our own ways, Alf," she said, taking another sip. She noticed he hadn't touched his yet. "Why have you not yet accepted my gift?" she asked, gesturing towards the drink.

"I am sorry. I meant no disrespect," he said with kind eyes. "I just... I am very honored to meet you, and when my belly becomes full of mead, I often act a fool. Especially because I like to..." he stopped himself.

"Like to, what?" Sigrid asked with a little smirk.

"I become a little too forward with the womenfolk. I act like a dog that will tear apart its evening meal," he said nervously, laughing before stopping himself as he realized what he said was a bit strange.

"And why is that such a problem?" she asked, smiling as she put her hand on his thigh.

He looked at her for a moment. She bit her lip and moved her hand upwards on his thigh. He began pounding the horn full of mead.

*

Njal awoke in his bed with Frigyth by his side. Her bare back showcased a few scars that she had earned from her journey with Njal to stop Aelred. The Bear King sat there for a moment, staring at them as he sighed. He didn't like to see her hurt, but he knew she was strong enough to take it. Then the realization set in that he had not spoken to her about her father. Their minds were on the arrival of Alf and each other. He touched her back with his giant rough hand and felt her breathe. She was still asleep.

He then decided to stand up and head to his dresser, where he pulled out some black pants, black boots, and a gray wool tunic. His large hands grabbed 'The Call of the King' and secured it to his waist. He gave Frigyth one last look before he exited his bedchamber in the Great Hall.

He then proceeded to leave the building entirely as he made his way down to the market to grab some breakfast for his queen. The air was cooler that morning. A chilling breeze could be felt as people along the main street were lighting fires by their shops and tents. Njal liked walking through the market in the mornings. He was able to greet everyone and feel the morning chill on his face. He liked the cold, as it reminded him of Norway. Of Sten.

"Balig," Njal said, approaching one of the tents with a smile gracing his face. "How are you on this fine but awfully chilly morning?"

A tall man with a massive gut greeted him back with a smile. "Njal! I suppose the frost jotuns have paid us a visit early! What can I do you for?"

"Aye," Njal said cheerfully. "How is business?"

"Ah," the man replied. "I cannot complain. I am excited for the harvest festival to arrive. Just need to take my mind off things." Balig gave a laugh of sadness. He was a good fighter. He survived the battle with Aelred and killed fifteen soldiers all by himself. However, his wife was killed during the battle.

"I understand," Njal said. "If there is anything I can do for you, you let me know, aye?"

"I appreciate that, my king," Balig said. "Can I get you anything?"

"Aye, I would like to have a few eggs and some bread as well as..."

Njal was interrupted by the sound of the horn that sat upon the main gate.

"Riders!" the guards on top of the walls yelled.

"Shite," Njal said to himself. "Odin keeps life surprising; I suppose."

"That he does," Balig said, obviously nervous. The arrival

horn reminded him of the battle with Aelred. The day he lost everything.

"Do not worry, Balig," Njal said. "It is probably nothing. You have a good day, alright?" He then began a slight jog to the gates. People that stood along the street murmured as he passed them. "Who is it?" he called up to the guards at the gate.

"Five men, sir. They are flying King Edward's banner!" the guard called back down.

"Let them in," Njal commanded. He stood off to the side and waited for the gates to open. Once they did, the five riders headed inside and greeted Njal with a nod. They jumped off their horses and approached the king of the Norsemen. Their leather and silver armor covered their entire body, minus the head. One of them was dressed more officially than the others as he had a cloak behind him dawning the colors of England.

"Almund," Njal said, recognizing him. "What are you doing here? Not that you are not welcome, but..."

"It is good to see you, friend," Almund said with a smile as he reached his arm out. Njal clasped his forearm in return. "Is there a place we can talk where it is not so cold out here?"

"Aye," Njal said, beginning to lead Almund. "Come, we can speak in the Great Hall. Will your men be joining us?"

"No, they will stay with the horses," Almund said following, the fall breeze causing his cloak to flutter behind him. "Will the lady Frigyth be joining us?"

"If she is awake from her slumber, aye," Njal said. "She had just returned from a trip to Birmingham."

"Birmingham? Why is that, if I might ask?" Almund asked.

Njal realized that not only did Birstain not tell him, but he also didn't tell his new king either. He realized he needed to stay tight-lipped about the subject. At least for now.

"Just to visit her father. She had not seen him in a while."

"To be honest with you, Njal, neither has the king. In fact, we have not heard from Birstain or his men in a long time. You would tell us if you knew of any sort of rebellion, would you not?"

"Rebellion? Gods, Almund, Birstain and I helped put Edward in that throne. The last thing we would do is attempt to take him out of it. Birstain has his own city to run. If you absolutely needed him, he would answer the call, I am sure."

Almund sighed with relief as the two then entered the Great Hall. Inside, Frigyth stood wearing a white shirt, black pants, and black boots. Her hair was a bit messy, but she didn't care.

"Oh," Njal said, seeing her. "I am sorry, my love. I was heading down to grab you breakfast when Almund here showed up at our gates. He said he has something he needs to speak to me about."

"That is quite alright," Frigyth said, wiping her eye of sleep. "Shall I be present for this meeting?"

"If you would like, my love," Njal said.

"Where shall we sit then?" Frigyth asked with a smile.

The three of them headed to a room off to the side of the throne room where a table sat with a few chairs. They all sat down and waited for Almund to begin.

"I do not want to take too much of your time," he began. "But King Edward has a proposition for you, if you would be so inclined as to accept."

"Well," Njal said with a slight smirk. "What is it?"

"You are aware that the mining village known as Gulgruve has been under the king's control for the last five months and has been used for trade and things of that nature, yes?"

"Of course," Njal said, now extremely curious.

"Unfortunately, news was received three days ago that a group of bandits had attacked and defeated the men we had there. They now hold Gulgruve and the king, well, he wishes for you to help and get it back for him."

Njal's eyes widened.

*

"So, that is basically all," Njal said to everyone that was sitting at the table. Across from him and Frigyth sat Halfdan, Knud, Sigrid, and Alf. "We were tasked with taking Gulgruve back for Edward."

It was very quiet for a moment. Everyone stared at Njal and he looked back at them. The glow from the candles made their shadows flicker on the wooden walls of the Great Hall.

"I think we should," Halfdan said, drawing the attention of everyone at the table. "Think about it. Our people lost Gulgruve once, right? We owe it to Jarl Bjork and his miners to take it back."

"But if we earn it back, we would just be giving it back to the Englishmen," Sigrid blurted out. "We do all of the work with none of the reward in this situation."

"Our reward, Sigrid," Njal said, which made her look at him with a dirty glance. "Is peace and a powerful alliance with Edward. I feel as though that is most important. And if we do this favor for him, he will owe us one in the future."

Alf looked at his brother, obviously wishing to speak his mind.

"I agree with Njal," Knud spoke up. "We have built ourselves a pleasant community here and while Gulgruve falling back into our control would serve our people greatly, the alliance between us and Edward is vital to ensure we do not have another war on our hands."

"But if we take it back for them," Sigrid said. "Then we are just a tool to be used in Edward's game. He will believe that he can just call on us for help every time he needs something done. Why will the pup not use his own men?"

"Because, from what Njal has told me of his meeting in London," Frigyth interrupted. "Edward's men are elsewhere. The new Lords are not cooperating very well, so he calls onto us. He now must keep a feeble alliance with some of the other cities while clearing his own of bandits and old order loyalists that are running rampant. He does not have enough men to spare to send to Gulgruve."

Sigrid looked over at Frigyth with a nasty look. "Oh, I get it," she said. "The Englishwoman trying to give more power to her people." She scoffed. "Tell me, do you wish for your father to be made Lord of Gulgruve, too?"

"THAT IS ENOUGH!" Njal shouted as he shot out of his chair and slammed his hands on his table. "Sigrid! I do not know what your problem has become, but after everything we have done for you, you choose to torment us over the mistake of letting Torin escape. Was that the most important thing to you? Our people are prospering, our lands have expanded, our lives are better. You would think that would be enough, but no, you wish to *only* think about Torin, who, by the way, IS NOT HERE!"

Sigrid kept quiet and looked away.

"No," Njal said again, ice in his voice. "I will not have you sit here like a spoiled child and insult my queen because of your inability to move on."

Sigrid scoffed again and stood up as she began walking away when Alf decided to speak up.

"When you take land," he said. "You get it. You do not *give* it." Everyone looked over at him. "Right? Is that not how it has worked forever with our people?"

"Alf..." Njal said, sitting back down. "I do not wish to dismiss your point, but as I said before, we do things differently here. Father taught me as a child that we need to focus more on expansion if we wish for our people to survive. No more stealing and raiding. I told you this."

"But how does that honor the gods?" Alf asked.

"I told you how," Njal said, looking down at the table.

"But how do we know it even works?" Alf asked. "It is not like you have just spoken to Odin and asked him if that was alright."

Everyone stared at Alf like they all had something to say. Alf took notice and looked at them all back.

"What?" he asked.

"I have spoken to the gods," Njal said. "I am somehow able to walk into the Land of the Spirits without trouble. It is a place where I and everyone else who walks there takes the form of an animal of some kind. The world is essentially the branches of

Yggdrasil, the world tree. It is an area where those who walk can speak to the gods..."

Alf's eyes widened, and he turned to look at everyone else's reaction. Even Sigrid, who was standing by the door. She nodded her head in confirmation. "I do not believe this," Alf said. "You all know of this power?"

Everyone nodded.

"Alf, the only ones here that can walk this land in between are me and Ingrid. In fact, she is the one who taught me how to navigate it carefully. Without her help, we could have lost Halfdan long ago. It took a while for me to understand it, but I have practiced it enough to where I can now speak to the gods. And Odin agrees with us."

"What I am about to say, I really mean no offense, brother. I hope you understand that. But how are the people of Eaglecrest supposed to know that you mean true? That this is not just a way of you to keep the people in check by using the fear of the allfather."

Everyone felt a chill at that. Alf had no worries when it came to expressing the thoughts that fell into his mind. Everyone turned to Njal to see what his reaction would be.

"I understand your fears," Njal said calmly. "In fact, I have had this conversation with both Sigrid and Knud. But here is the reality of the situation. Odin told me how the gods only survive when there are people that believe in them. Meaning, if Aelred succeeded in killing every Norseman in Midgard, then there we be nobody left to believe in the gods, which would ultimately leave them dead and forgotten."

"I understand," Alf said. "So, by listening to father's

new take on our ways, it should allow our people to keep living, which would allow the gods to keep living."

"Aye," Njal said, nodding his head.

"Alright," Alf said with a smile. "I apologize for my hesitation. This is all just very new to me. For expansion then!"

Everyone cheered. When they did, Sigrid decided to leave the room. As she was leaving, she heard the cheers stop when Alf's voice could be heard saying, "But I think we should take Gulgruve." Sigrid stopped in her tracks...smiling. Everyone in the room went quiet.

"What do you mean?" Halfdan asked. "We just told you we wish to expand, not fight a war. Especially with England again."

"It would not be a war, Halfdan Blood-Wolf," Alf said. "Frigyth said it herself. Edward does not have enough men to spare for a fight with some bandits, let alone his strongest allies. Sure, it would put some distrust between Njal and Edward, but in the end, I actually believe it would earn us respect. Because if Sigrid is right and Edward is just using us and our strength to carry out his dirty work, then he will keep calling on us for that. And if we wait to take a stand against him until he has enough men to fight us, it could turn ugly. If we stand up against him now, when he does not have enough men to spare, he will learn quickly he cannot use us like tools. I say we take back Gulgruve and keep it for ourselves. It was ours to begin with. It should be ours again."

Njal sat there in thought. He looked at the flame of a candle and watched it flicker.

"But the other side of that coin could be that it

weakens our alliance with the man that now rules this land," Halfdan said.

"I have one more question…" Alf asked, to which everyone raised their heads and looked at him, even Njal. "Why did you decide to put Edward in charge? Why did you not take the throne of England yourself, Njal?" Everyone looked at their king. "I mean, would that not be the ultimate expansion? Making England the new Norway would be a pretty fantastic way of not only pleasing our gods, but allowing for more land for our people to be free."

"But what of the English people? Should we have killed them all?" Frigyth asked with a bit of an attitude.

"No, my queen," Alf said, shaking his head. "It could have been the same as now. We are able to coexist with your people, no problem. You are our queen, for Odin's sake. But I believe the real problem is *your* people. I will tell you why Njal decided not to be king in England. It was because your people would have lost their bloody minds. There would have been a revolution every single day. Expansion would not have lasted with Njal on the throne because the people of England are a virus and do not want to see anyone else on top except for themselves. Even if it is the best course of action for both of our people. I have seen the way the people around here look at you, lady Frigyth. We have all accepted you as our queen. But tell me, if the roles were reversed, would your people ever accept one of us in a leadership role?"

Frigyth had nothing to say.

"I say," Alf continued. "We take back Gulgruve and keep it.

That is the least the Englishmen can offer us. After all, it was our people who took back their country from that bastard, Aelred."

Both Frigyth and Halfdan looked at one another with worry. They could see that Njal was thinking hard about what his brother was saying. Knud sat there in his chair, stroking his beard in thought, too.

"We will take Gulgruve back from the bandits..." Njal began. "And I will come to a decision once we have achieved our goal."

IX

New Lives

Green smoke and gas surrounded Torin. He gripped the hilt of his sword made from a deer's femur bone tighter. He looked around at all angles and noticed the shadows looking at him. Their glowing green eyes and the dark cosmic dust flying off of them like snowdrifts on a mountain peak. The Norseman growled and readied his feet. A thin shadow that stood before him morphed its cloudy self into a giant. The antlers that protruded from its skull of a face were huge. Just like the crowds of shadows that watched, waves of smoke and shadow continued to sweep off of the beast, showing that it wasn't made of flesh and bone.

Then, at once, all of the surrounding shadows charged at Torin with everything they had. Five from behind him, five in front of him, and the enormous giant. Torin ducked underneath an attack from one shadow before quickly jumping over the attack of another. He punched one in the face with his hand, to which the shadow then disappeared in a cloud of black dust. Torin spun around and swung his bone sword, slicing through two more shadows, turning them both to dust. Three more were coming for him up high, so he rolled in between them and hopped back to his feet on the other side. He swiped his sword beneath two of them, sending them to the ground where he swung his sword sideways, turning the two into gaseous clouds.

He reacted quickly as the third shadow attacked. Torin used the hilt of his sword and crunched the shadow's face. He then swung his sword diagonally, slicing the shadow into a dusty cloud. The final four shadows were huddled together by the giant. Torin squinted his eyes and readied his attack. He did not wait for the giant or the other shadows to attack first as he began to move his large feet forward. His strong and muscled legs pushed the ground beneath him harder and harder with each step until he got around five feet from the giant. That's when Torin used the strength of his legs to push off the ground and send him flying into the air. He roared as his bone sword went right into the skull face of the giant.

It went down with a roar as Torin rolled off the dead giant and back onto his feet, the body of the dead beast fading into dust behind him. The other shadows were hesitant to attack, so Torin wasted no time in attacking them first. He chased two down and sliced them up with no problem. The other two tried to get him while he was distracted, but he knew better. He jumped away from them and then back in between them where he spun around with his sword swinging wildly, slicing them both into clouds of dust with one blow.

As Torin stood there, sweat dripping from his face, the word became light again. The gas faded, and the shadows turned back into people. Everyone of them was on the ground in pain with bruises and minor cuts. Torin's sword of bone turned back into a dull stick. The giant turned back into Cathbad, who was attempting to get to his feet.

"You are..." he said, grunting as he stood up. "An excellent fighter, Torin."

"My thanks," he replied. "I hope I did not hurt any of you beyond repair."

"No, no," Cathbad said, approaching his new friend. "You defeated us all without any of us even touching you. We deserve our pain." Torin smiled at that. "You have come a long way in a short time, Torin. I am very impressed with the way you are able to master your fears."

"I am not afraid of anything," Torin said, his smile fading.

"Well," Cathbad said with a look of disbelief. "Of course you are."

"No, I am not," Torin said, annoyed.

"Well, I hate to break it to you, but that is not how that gas works. That ingredients in the powder we throw down before starting the test brings out your worst fears. It is a test to see if you can master your fears and destroy them. We all must do it. Mine was the fear of loneliness after I arrived here. I had to learn how to be fine with only myself present." Torin stayed quiet. "I think that you have no problem with the physical side of things. However, we must train more mentally."

"What do you mean?"

"Come with me," Cathbad said, walking away.

"Wait, the village is back that way," Torin said, pointing toward the village.

"Exactly," Cathbad said back. "We are not going to the village. Not yet. We are going to see someone."

Torin shook his head and began jogging to catch up to Cathbad.

"Who are we to see?"

"We Druids rely on magic. Our magic comes from the Earth that you stand on and is not given to us by a higher power. We worship the forces of this land, as you already know, and we have somebody who teaches us. As I said before, there are those who are more sensitive to the magic of this world and there are those who have no sensitivity at all. Why? We do not know. But we have come to the conclusion that those who are more sensitive are the most powerful. And the one we are off to see, well, it is somebody who, like you, has a powerful connection to magic."

"So, what is this person going to teach me?" Torin asked.

"How to use it properly."

The two of them continued through the marshy landscape for a while until they reached a small but tall shack that sat underneath a few dead trees. Immediately, Torin felt a horrible, painful sensation shoot throughout his mind. He screamed as he fell down to his knees. Cathbad looked down at him and smirked.

"Torin," he began. "You need to focus. Learn to push the pain to the back of your mind. Push it as far back as it can go. Take deep breaths and feel the magic flow through you. *Feel it, Torin! Feel the magic!*"

"AHHHHH!" Torin screamed louder. It felt like his veins froze over with ice and his eyes burned with fire. His head felt as though somebody had smashed it with a hammer continuously but he just wouldn't die.

But he listened to Cathbad's words. To focus on pushing the pain further and further down his subconscious mind. As he did this, images of his time with Ragnar's army flashed in his head. He remembered everything. Raiding and pillaging everywhere and anywhere. Images of himself speaking his mind before traveling back to England before Ragnar's army was demolished in Paris. He then remembered the smell of cooked bacon at the fisherman's house. He remembered tearing the clothes off of the woman he saw inside the home before taking his turn. He remembered the look on the Englishman's face when he saw them. Then, images of the Englishman's face when he rose to power and tried to take Eaglecrest for the first time. Torin remembered... Torin remembered how he created Aelred.

Torin remembered Njal's face when they fought. He remembered the look was the same as the one on Aelred's. That look of rage and hate. So much built up inside his soul and releasing onto Torin. He realized he had that same rage and hate inside of him, too.

It needed to be let out.

Not at just any time, though. It needed to be controlled. Used as a weapon, just as Njal had.

His pain began to fade. He pushed it away. Shoved it back inside of himself. He slowly opened his eyes and saw

Cathbad's hand in front of him. Torin took it and was raised to his feet.

"Are you alright now, my friend?" Cathbad asked as the wind picked up. Dark clouds started to threaten the sky.

"Aye. What was that?" Torin asked, shaking his head.

"That was the curse," Cathbad said.

"Another curse?" Torin sighed.

"Yes," he smiled. "The ones we have on our more 'special' structures are the ones that are *meant* to be harmful to those who do not know our ways. Now that you have confronted your demons, you are able to enter."

"I did... I saw..."

"I do not wish to know," Cathbad said, putting his hand up. "Your demons are only yours to bear. You are almost a one of us now. Everything from this point on, we will bear together. But none of your past life will be relevant to us now."

"Alright..." Torin said, looking at the building in front of him. The scent of garlic and onions struck his nostrils. It was so strong he could almost taste them on his tongue.

"Now," Cathbad said. "Let us see, Elhhere."

*

The two entered the building, which smelled like a combination of firewood and strawberries. The area was small, and vegetables and bones were scattered everywhere. One room featured an enormous cauldron with some greenish blue liquid steaming inside. Another room held a small mountain of bones of all kinds. Another room featured a table that held jars full of fingers, eyes, rat tails, and other unknown body parts. The room that Cathbad led Torin into wasn't really a room. Rather, a small area where a cellar door sat below them.

"After you," Cathbad said with a smile.

Torin didn't hesitate as he grabbed the handle on the cellar door and lifted it up. A foul and disgusting smell struck his nose instantly. He looked at Cathbad once more before descending the ladder into the room. Once his feet hit the ground, he noticed a deep and dark tunnel that led to another room in the distance. The room was lit up with candlelight and was the only source of light in the tunnel. Torin looked back up at Cathbad, who then smiled and quickly shut the cellar door.

"Hey, wait!" Torin yelled.

"I will wait for you outside!" Cathbad said from the other side of the door.

"Shite..." Torin said before looking down the tunnel again.

He began walking through the long corridor to the room that sat in the distance. It felt like a long time before he finally got there. Each footstep echoed throughout.

Once he arrived at the room, he looked inside and noticed a line of candles on both sides of him. They were leading him to another room in the distance. He followed the line of candles through three other and vastly different rooms.

One room was filled with a glowing red liquid that seeped down the cobblestone walls and into jars and glasses. Another one was full of flowers. They were not pretty red roses, no; they were evil looking. More thorns than pedals and they all held a foul-smelling scent. The last room was full of pumpkins and candles. It was dark in there, but he could hear the faint screams of something somewhere in that small room.

The lines of candles eventually led to the biggest room yet. Candles of all shapes and sizes were everywhere, and a woman sat in the middle of them in the center of the area. Her legs were crossed and her eyes closed. Tattoos filled every inch of her body from her waist up to her bare chest and up to her neck. The designs of the tattoos were like nothing Torin had ever seen before. She opened her eyes and looked at Torin as he entered the room.

"Well, hello, there," she said. Her voice was raspy. She looked to be middle-aged, but her voice sounded like that of an old woman.

"Hello," Torin said cautiously. "You must be, Elhhere."

"I have been expecting you, Torin of the Eagle clan," she said.

"That is not who I am anymore..." Torin said, dropping his head.

"And that is the reason for you being here, yes? You have lost everything and so when Cathbad found you, you wished for him to kill you so you could enter your Valhalla, yes?"

Torin's eyes widened. "How much do you know about me?"

"I know that you wish to kill Njal Tokeson. The new leader of the Norse people. I know you feel responsible under your cold and hard shield for the rise of Aelred and what he did to your people. You feel as though you created him. It was only right for you to destroy him, yes? But Njal beat you to it so you hate him for that even more."

"I wish to destroy Njal Tokeson and take my life back."

"You would do such a thing even though Njal has proven to be the better leader for your people?"

"Njal is a liar!" Torin said, biting his teeth. "Not only to my people, but to himself. He is going to be overthrown and he will lose it all. It may seem better now, but it will not stay that way for long. This I know."

"But what of Cathbad?"

"What of him?" Torin asked, creasing his eyebrows.

"Cathbad sees you as a man that could help lead the Druids to something better. He feels as though instead of setting out on this path of revenge, you can let your people be and instead take the mantle of a Druid. Retire the Norse gods and embrace the Druidic way of life. You have a gift for magic. This I knew since you stepped into the Fenlands. I can sense it. But you wish to live in the past when you could have a strong future here with us."

Torin lowered his head. He thought about it for a moment. Something inside of him wished to do exactly what Elhhere was saying. But he couldn't leave his gods behind. Not when he spent so much of his life trying to please them. Trying to enter Valhalla.

"Why can I not have both?" Torin asked, looking up into the woman's darkly shaded eyes. "Why can I not stay here with these people and also have my revenge against the boy, Njal?"

"That is a very dangerous path to walk on, I am afraid. If you become one of the Druids, they would not hesitate to help you on your quest, such is our custom. However, you would likely get them and yourself killed due to Njal's sizable force of power versus ours."

"Njal does not have the power and magic that I have seen in these people's arsenal."

"Njal is closer to the Norse gods than you would like to believe. He can travel the Nine Realms and speak to them. He has also earned their favor. It would not only be a fight between the two peoples, but the two cultures. You must think hard on this, Torin. It is a decision that will have massive consequences."

"How do you know of my gods?" Torin asked. "Cathbad does not believe in them. So, why do you?"

"Because *I* know they exist," she replied. "But that does not mean he needs to know."

"So, you are just lying to him?" Torin scoffed.

"Is it lying if you were never asked?" Elhhere asked.

"Hm," Torin said. "I will think on your words, witch. I will heed them, but I cannot promise anything. I have my own saga to write. Whether I am alone in achieving it or not, it will be completed with me fulfilling my revenge. I will continue to train and help these people of the Fenlands, but in the end, my saga ends with Njal Tokeson dying by my blade."

*

"I do not know, Halfdan," Frigyth said as she paced back and forth through the Great Hall. Her footsteps echoing on the floorboards. "It feels as though Alf's arrival might bring worse events onto us. Perhaps I am being paranoid, but there is something about him I do not like. Am I wrong for thinking this? Am I a horrible wife to my husband?"

Halfdan's eyebrows creased with worry. He stood up

from his chair. The sound of the wood leg scraping the ground echoed throughout the empty hall. He put his hand on her shoulder and stopped her from pacing. He stared into her blue eyes.

"You are not as wrong as you think you are. Your mistrust is not misplaced, dear Frigyth. I feel the same way. However, Njal thought the same as well. Until a certain point. When you were gone in Birmingham, we held a feast due to Alf's arrival. We celebrated as though he was Njal's brother and even then, as we sat upon the table in the longhouse, Njal leaned over and asked me if he could trust him. I told him that he should." Frigyth looked at him with wide eyes. "As much as we do not trust the boy, we must understand that it may be due to our experiences in life. Nothing has ever been as good as it seemed and so we do not trust this man who just randomly showed up here and said he was Njal's brother. But what if that *is* the truth? While the man is young and immature, he does seem like he means well."

Frigyth dropped her head. "I am just being selfish. I have not been able to spend much time with Njal since we won our battle against Aelred. And with what I learned in Birmingham, I... I only wish to be by his side more..."

"What news came from Birmingham, dear Frigyth? If you do not mind me asking," Halfdan asked. He knew the answer, but he figured that if she hadn't told anyone, it may be better to share the burden with him than no one at all.

She broke away and walked over towards the fire pit. She looked inside the flames as she spoke. "My father is dying... he asked me to be the next Lord of Birmingham once he passes."

"Oh, Frigyth..." Halfdan said, sounding convincingly shocked. "Does Njal know of this?"

"No," she said, wiping a tear from her cheek before turning to face Halfdan again. "I have not told him as of yet. The news of his brother seems to be the only thing that has taken hold of our thoughts. Now, with the Gulgruve discussion, there just... there is no time. I do not wish to flood his mind with further pointless thoughts of Birmingham when he has his plate full already."

"That is not a pointless thought, my queen," Halfdan said. "I know Njal. All he wishes is for a life with you. I know he would drop everything for you."

"Perhaps," she said, pausing. "But not his brother..."

Halfdan pondered that for a moment. Although Njal mistrusted Alf at the beginning, he had grown fond of his brother. In fact, that night, the two of them were scouting Gulgruve by themselves. Seeing how many bandits there were and how they acted. How they fought and so on and so forth. Halfdan knew that Njal cared about family more than anything. And as long as Alf didn't give him a reason not to trust him, then he would trust him for as long as they lived.

"Are you considering your father's wishes?"

Frigyth dropped her head and sighed. "He said that they are my people and that they would be in good hands with me as their leader. That *I* was meant to lead them."

"I do agree that you would make a fine leader of your people, Frigyth. But what are you to do?"

"I do not know," she said before sighing. "Njal and I wish to have a child. We wish for all of this work in England to be over with so we can enjoy our life together. I feel so selfish for saying this but, with Alf here now, I am not sure we will ever get that time."

Halfdan sighed. "I understand." Frigyth looked up at him with a confused look. She obviously didn't expect to hear that reaction from him. "I know he loves you and I know he would die for you. But these people are not your own. As much as they have adopted you as one of them, I can see within your eyes that you still feel like an outcast. I wish that would change because we all do love you, dear Frigyth. But I know the only reason you came here in the first place was because of Njal and avenging your mother. Now that the latter is complete, you only remain because of Njal and with the arrival of Alf, you fear that you will *always* be an outcast."

Frigyth shed another tear. Halfdan was right. She had plenty of things she needed to ponder and question in the near future. She walked up to her friend and hugged him. He hugged her back and smiled.

"Just know," he said. "The whatever you do chose, you will always be welcome here, Frigyth. You are family to us."

She cried harder and hugged him tighter.

*

Njal and Alf were making their way through the wooded pathway towards Gulgruve. Both men were wearing their usual gear. Alf was wearing brown leather armor and a green and black cloak that fluttered behind him. His sword was sitting at his side and his blond braid at his shoulder. Njal was wearing his black leather armor and his blackened iron bracers. 'The Call of the King' sat at his side and his bear cloak sat upon his shoulders. The sun was beginning to set behind the horizon now as a dark blue hue sat above them and a deep orange glow sat to the right of them.

"You brought the torches, yes?" Njal asked his brother.

"Aye," Alf replied with a smile. "It is becoming quite dark. How are we to survey them?"

"We still have a bit of light left," Njal began. "And I am sure they have torches inside the village. Besides, we are almost there."

The two brothers continued their way up the steepest part of the hill. The last bit before they reached the overlook of the village. A place Njal knew quite well.

"Hey, brother?" Alf asked as he stepped over a bush.

"Yes, Alf?"

"How did it feel to kill Aelred? Did it make the pain stop?"

Njal sighed at himself. He never really had time to think about it. Whether he felt happier after beheading the Englishman.

"To be honest, brother... no. He told me before I killed him that nothing would be able to bring my family back and, sadly, he was right. The feeling of their losses still hits like a sword to the heart. But I suppose what I realized is that I was not doing it for me. I was doing it for *them*. The man who stole their lives deserved to have his stolen, too."

"Hm," Alf said, agreeing. "I am surprised that father did not attempt to avenge mother with the full might of the Norsemen behind him. He was king, after all."

"Well, he tried," Njal said, feeling the nip of the

autumn night in the air. "Aelred faked his kidnapping so father was not quite sure who did it until he found mother's golden seax in London."

"Mother had a golden seax?" Alf asked, like he knew something. His brother could also sense it.

"Aye. Have you seen it?" Njal asked, stopping in his tracks. He turned and faced his brother.

"Aye," Alf nodded. "I seen it with my own eyes in a fire pit of one of the burned down houses in Sten when we were rebuilding."

"It is still there? Did you retrieve it?" Njal asked, concerned.

"Aye, we put it in the Great Hall after it was finished. I am assuming one of the riders that arrived and took Sten from us must have it by now."

"Damnit..." Njal said to himself. "Remind me when we are done with this that we need to find out who took Sten. Whoever it is, I need that seax. For mother's sake."

Njal's mind raced. This Sten issue was becoming a bit larger every passing day. Once Gulgruve was liberated, Njal could turn his attention to Sten and the Norsemen who stole it.

"I understand, Njal. We will focus on that task in the coming days. I promise," Alf said as he saw his brother begin walking up the path again. Alf was silent for a moment and began thinking about their most recent discussion back in the Great Hall. "I do wish to apologize for my outburst back there during our meeting. I did not mean to question you about your ability to travel in between realms. I have just never heard of that before."

"Neither did I, Alf. But it is alright. I understand your hesitation."

"So, you really can do it, huh? Travel in between worlds and speak with the gods."

"Aye," Njal said as he noticed the summit of the hill before him. "Odin speaks with me occasionally about our people."

"Fascinating. Have you met any of the other gods?"

"No," Njal said as he looked around at the tall pine trees that swarmed around him. "Only Odin. I believe the Realm I am in currently is Asgard, although I am not entirely sure. It feels a bit different from how it usually does."

"Why not just ask Ingrid?" Alf asked as he stepped over a large rock. "I am sure she knows."

"I do not doubt it, brother," Njal began. "But she does not tell me too much. She says that the Land of the Spirits is kind of all the Realms together, so it does not really matter. It is as if each realm is being held together by Yggdrasil, the World Tree. Go too far one way and you will be in another one. She has taught me much, but states that I must learn certain things for myself."

"So, how many realms can you say you have certainly been to?"

"I believe three," Njal said. "Asgard is where I usually am. Its glistening and forested. The bright sunshine feels warm and homelike. I have been to Muspelheim and the glowing red runes and the fire that lies inside. It is where the beginning of the Soul Road lies. If you follow that all the way through Muspelheim, you reach Helheim, which I have only seen the outside of. Other than that, I have touched the ground in Svartalfheim, but I have not met any of the dwarves."

"Interesting," Alf said, trying to envision it all. "What do you speak to Odin about other than our people? Anything?"

"My fate."

"Your fate? Have the Norns told you how your saga will end?"

"No, they have not. In fact, even the Allfather cannot see. He says there are multiple threads that are being woven and I must choose the correct one in order to stay on course. Apparently, some of them are not so good and can lead us to destruction."

"Guess you have to be careful then," Alf said. "So, Sigrid was telling me all about the old Jarl of the Eagle clan. What was his name, Torin? She told me how Halfdan let him..."

"Sigrid has been upset about Halfdan's mistake for a long time now. It would be wise for her to get over it."

"Why would you punish Sigrid for holding a grudge, but not Halfdan for releasing a prisoner? Especially one that, from what I have heard, is sort of unhinged and could prove to be a significant problem."

"Sigrid is not being punished. Every time she acts like a spoiled brat, I will speak to her as such. But if she speaks to me as an ally and her friend, then I will respect her. And also, because Torin killed a good friend and companion of ours right in front of Halfdan. His revenge blinded him just like how I was and our father before us. I promised everyone that we would hunt down Torin as soon as England was in a stable place, which, as of right now, it is not."

"I understand," Alf said, as a brisk breeze hit his face.

"You know, I would be happy to join you on your quest to hunt down that bastard!"

"I would quite like that, brother," Njal said. "Also, are you and Sigrid...together?"

"Aye, we have been humping," Alf said, laughing. "She is a hearty woman, Njal! Her beauty stands unmatched and her personality is strong and stonewalled!"

"I am happy you are hitting it off with her," Njal said, smiling. "You both deserve happiness."

The two men finally reached the summit of the hill that overlooked Gulgruve, the mining village that was now crawling with bandits. The sun was still offering a dark blue and purple light.

"Whoa," Alf said as he saw the village below him and the ever-stretching hills that continued miles behind it. "This country is beautiful."

"Aye," Njal said. "Come, there is a small cliff down a ways that will give us a better advantage."

"How do you know this path so well?" Alf asked.

"This is the path we took when Gulgruve fell. And this cliff I am taking you to was where the Lord Dodson stood with his men. That is where I killed him. When so much happens to you within a short amount of time, it is quite hard to forget."

Alf felt a chill rise in his spine.

*

The sun had come over the horizon now as a gigantic wall of fog sat on the ocean. A chill was in the air, which let everyone know that a storm was on its way. The question of whether it would be rain or snow was still being pondered since it was now the beginning of October. The horn that sat on the top of the front gate of Eaglecrest blew, signaling the arrival of Njal and Alf, who had returned from their scouting trip.

Once they entered, Knud and Sigrid were standing by the stables, waiting to meet them. Knud, wearing his regular black leather armor, smiled at both of them while Sigrid, who was wearing just a tunic and brown pants, only smiled at Alf. She paid no mind to Njal. The two brothers jumped off their horses and approached their companions.

"Hello, Knud," Njal said. "How are you this morning?"

"Cold," he said, smiling back and clasping Njal's forearm. "I take it the trip went well?"

The two turned to look at Alf and Sigrid, who were kissing wildly in front of everyone. She slammed her hand upon his privates and bit his lip as she pulled away.

"Knud and Njal can take over strategy. You and I will go play," she said as she looked at Njal with annoyance and smiled at Knud before walking away, pulling Alf with her. "Call us when it is time to bloody our swords," she yelled back behind her.

"I do not understand why she is still so upset," Njal said, watching the two fade into the morning crowd of the Eaglecrest market. "She needs to stop her immaturity or we shall have actual problems."

"Well, you best do something before your brother falls too hard for her. Otherwise, that can cause a divide," Knud said, Njal grunting in agreement. "What of Gulgruve, though?"

"Oh yes," Njal said, turning his attention back to Knud. "Where is Almund? He should be here for this."

"Somebody fetch the Englishman!" Knud yelled out into the streets of Eaglecrest. "Shall we meet you in the Great Hall?"

"Aye," Njal said. "I will get Halfdan and Frigyth."

The two clasped forearms again before preparing for their meeting.

*

"Alright," Njal said as he looked at the two empty chairs in the Great Hall. "I suppose since Alf is too busy humping Sigrid, it will be just us. Almund, you can take one of those empty seats if you would like."

Sitting in the room now was Knud, Halfdan, Frigyth, Almund and Njal.

"What did the village look like, Njal?" Halfdan asked.

"Well, the Englishmen have done some rebuilding in the past months, that is for sure. The walls have practically been built to what they were, and some have even been expanded upon. The fallen towers are now cleared and the buildings inside have been repaired. However, I could see where the bandits got in. There is a section of the wall to the south that has not been covered. One night, the guards must have gotten sloppy, and the bandits took the village under the cover of night."

"Idiots," Knud said under his breath. "What of the bandits? What are their numbers and how do they seem?"

"We counted around thirty of them outside the mines, and they seem like decent fighters. There could obviously be more inside the mines, which is something we need to prepare for. But I will not lie to you, a bit of a chill climbed up my spine as we observed them," Njal said, shaking his head. "There was an enormous pile of blackened ash off to the side."

"They burned the Englishmen," Knud said. "What else?"

"Well, they were painting on the walls of the homes and other buildings inside."

"Painting?" Knud asked.

"Symbols of all kinds in red and black," Njal said coldly, the fire pit crackling in the background.

"Runes?" Knud asked.

"No, I have not seen these symbols before. I am not sure what any of them mean, but they all got down on their knees and chanted some words. It was quite an interesting ritual we witnessed."

"Almund, do you know of any sort of Englishmen that sound like they fit the description?" Knud asked, stroking his chin.

"No," Almund said. "They most certainly are not Englishmen. And if they are, then they are none I know of."

"That was not even the worst part," Njal said, everyone looking at him with curiosity and worry. "They entered a building and came out holding a blonde woman and stripped her down to nothing. As the rest of them got down to their knees, one of them tied the woman to a wooden post. They spoke some words, then cut her heart out and lit her remains on fire. I have not seen anything quite like it before."

Everyone's eyes widened at that and said nothing.

"However," Njal said, putting his hands up. "Before everyone starts to worry, we did see them train a bit after their ritual. And while yes, they are 'decent' fighters, they are nothing compared to us. At least, that is what it seemed. It looks as though their fighting style is to just swing their weapon wildly, so any bit of real training should over-match them without much trouble."

"So, what is the plan, then?" Frigyth asked. "How many warriors do we need?"

"I say we take around thirty as well. I would like for Halfdan, Knud, Alf, Almund, and Sigrid to join me..."

"Wait," Frigyth said. "I am coming with you, too."

"No, my love, I need somebody to watch the village while we are..."

"Ingrid can watch the village just fine," Frigyth said, standing up from her chair. "I am coming with you and that is final. I am tired of not being able to join you on your quests and journeys. My life is not going to end with me dying on an oversized chair. Do you understand me?"

Everyone looked at Njal as he stared at Frigyth with wide eyes. It was a moment before he spoke. "Alright, my love. You can join me. I just wish for you to be careful..."

"I can take care of myself," she said as she stormed out of the small room.

"I apologize everyone," Njal sighed as he looked around the room. "We will set off for the attack tomorrow morning before dawn. So, spend the rest of the day preparing and get five or ten of your best fighters. Knud, if you could speak to Sigrid, that would help. I will speak to Frigyth and try to put her in better spirits."

They all nodded their heads as they got up to their feet and went their separate ways. Halfdan stayed behind for a moment to speak to Njal.

"Do you need me in there with you, my friend?" the berserker asked.

"No," Njal said calmly. "I just do not want to put her in harm's way, you know?"

"We are Norsemen, Njal," Halfdan said. "Harm's way *is* our way."

"It is not supposed to be anymore," Njal said, lowering his eyes.

"I know," Halfdan said. "But I do think it is important for you to include Frigyth on your travels a bit more. She is strong. She survived a war."

"I almost lost her three times on that journey," Njal said. "I would not be able to live with myself if I allowed her to fight, and she is killed."

"But keeping her locked away is going to push her away from you, brother," Halfdan said with a sad smile. "Just think of my words, please."

"I will," Njal said.

"Do you wish for me to ask Ingrid for her help? It sounds like there may be some magical elements to these bandits. She could perhaps help us."

"Like Frigyth, I would not wish to put your woman in danger. We can manage, Halfdan."

"Alright," he said with a look of understanding. "Let me know when it is time to leave. I will be ready."

"Thank you, friend," Njal said, clasping Halfdan's forearm.

"And hey," Halfdan said before leaving. "Take it easy

on her, alright?" He gestured towards the bedchamber. "She is going through a lot. You know this."

Njal nodded his head but felt sadness. He wondered to himself why she hadn't told him much of her pain. Granted, they didn't have too much time together since she returned, but he could feel her sadness and wished that she would tell him of it.

Does she not trust me anymore?

He knocked on the door of the bedchamber.

"Come in," he heard his queen's voice from behind the door.

Njal entered and saw her sitting on the edge of the bed. She looked at him with her giant and pure blue eyes. He walked over to her and sat down next to her. He put his hand on her thigh and sighed.

"I am sorry, my love," he said. "I really meant no disrespect. I only wish for you to be safe. It is selfish of me to do so because I am essentially locking you in a cage. I just would not know what to do with myself if I lost you."

She turned her head and looked at him. "I know...but at some point, Njal, you have to realize that it is *my* choice. Not yours. I can decide what to do with my life and if I wish to run into battle with you, then let me. Because like you, I would not know what to do with myself if I lost *you*. The only difference is, when you leave, I must sit here in silence with people that are not my own and hope to god that you come back to me. That is a pain unlike anything else, and I wish to be free of it. At least on the battlefield, I can look out for you."

"I am sorry, I did not mean to put you through a pain like that," Njal said, creasing his eyebrows and using a hand to brush the hair behind her ear. "I was not aware, and I feel like a fool."

"It is alright, but I am coming," she said to him. "I need to."

"I understand," he said.

He leaned in and his lips met hers. She moved a hand onto his thigh and raised it until she met his groin. The two rolled back onto their bed as the thunder from an arriving storm cracked the sky open.

X

The Battle of Gulgruve

At twilight the next day, a giant wave of fog swallowed the entirety of England. Under a darkened blue sky, a mist like rain followed as the warriors of Eaglecrest were preparing to set off on their journey to retake Gulgruve.

Njal was preparing his giant brown horse as he was dressed in his black leather armor with his signature bear cloak strapped to his back. 'The Call of the King' sat proudly on his waist as his blond braid sat upon his shoulder. He held a wooden shield with the Nordic painting of a bear on the face.

Frigyth was standing next to him, preparing her athletic white horse next to the stables. She was also in black leather armor. She had pieces of iron stitched into parts of the armor like the heart and stomach. Her signature red cloak was strapped to her shoulders. Her new silver sword that she had the blacksmith forge when she became queen sat at her side. She was holding her red and black wooden shield that Ivar had gotten her and her shoulder-length brown wavy hair sat nicely under her red hood.

Halfdan wore black leather armor made specifically by Knud. Volcanic material was stitched throughout. It was meant to allow Halfdan to be hit several times when he was in his berserker trance without any repercussions afterwards when the berserker wore off. His large two-handed axe sat on his back over his black cloak. His black leather belt held four hand-axes in front and a seax behind.

Knud wore his regular black armor with his red and black cloak on his back. His large black sword sat firmly in its sheathe on his waist. He also held a black and red wooden shield. He brought around ten of his men, all of whom were dawning the colors of the Fire Clan proudly.

Sigrid arrived a bit later than everyone else, with Alf at her side, along with five other members of the Horse Clan. She was dressed in lighter brown leather armor and her blonde braid bounced with every step her horse took. She held a spear behind her and a large wooden shield. Her men were wearing tunics and pants with small leather pieces covering the more vital areas of their bodies. Njal shook his head at that. He remembered back to when he saw their battle attire before the fight with Aelred and thought about how idiotic it was, but hey, so is playing with fire, right?

Alf wore his brown leather armor and a cloak colored a dark green. He had an iron helm hooked to the side of his belt that featured two large horns stemming from the top. He held a large steel sword and two seaxs that were all sheathed in their respected spots on his belt. His large green and brown wooden shield that featured the knotwork painting of a bear on it sat at his back. His beard was becoming longer as each day passed by. He greeted everyone with an enormous smile.

Almund and the three Englishmen he brought alongside to fight were also gearing up. They were dawning the colors red and black, the new colors of England. They all wore dark brown leather armor with iron pieces attached to the shoulders and chest and they had full iron helms strapped to their belts. Their swords were giant, and their wooden shields were a rectangular shape instead of the Nordic circle.

Everyone hopped on their respected horses. The rain started coming down a bit harder as there was now more solidity in the raindrops. The dirt roads started to morph into mud, which wasn't ideal.

"Who is ready to take back Gulgruve?" Alf asked everyone happily as he sat on his brown horse.

"AYE!" the companions shouted in unison.

Njal looked at everyone and smiled. They had ten men from the Fire Clan, five men from the Horse Clan, three men from Edward's army, not including Almund, and five more from Eaglecrest. Everyone together equaled thirty, so it should be a fair fight in terms of numbers.

"I am so proud of you all," Njal said to everyone, the large gates of Eaglecrest opening behind him. "We have come so far since Aelred. I am proud to call you all my family." Alf pulled his sword from his sheathe and raised it in the air. They all did the same with smiles on their faces, and Njal smiled wider. "Now, let us fight for a better England!"

Njal turned his horse and galloped out of the front gates towards the valley, his horse's hooves picking up chunks of mud with each step. The rest of them followed and, just like that, they were off to Gulgruve to retake it for Edward.

But Alf's suggestion on what to do with the village still floated around Njal's mind like a fly.

*

"Njal," Alf began as they sat upon the little rocky cliff overlooking the village. The same cliff where Njal killed Dodson. "Have you given much thought to my proposition?"

Njal continued to look over the cliff, down onto the bandits and the village. The sun was now over the horizon, but covered as the fog and rain remained.

"Aye, I have," he said.

"And?" Alf asked quietly, looking around. Everyone else was hitching their horses to the trees and preparing to go the rest of the way on foot. "What are you to do?"

"I am not sure," Njal said, keeping his eyes locked onto the village below. "I believe you made a good point, brother. However, I know Edward would be very upset and it could ruin our alliance with them."

"But Edward *needs* you. He needs us. He would understand why we would only take Gulgruve for ourselves since it was once ours."

"Aye," Njal said, wiping the rain off of his forehead. "But it could also turn him into another Aelred. It is a decision that cannot be made lightly."

"I agree," Alf said. "Whatever you decide, I will stand by you."

"Good," Njal said with a smile, now looking at his kin. He put his hand on Alf's shoulder. "I am happy to call you my brother."

"And I you," Alf replied happily.

"But what is this thing with Sigrid?" Njal asked with a smirk. "Is she to be your wife?"

"Ah," Alf said playfully pushing Njal's arm away. "I do not know. She is strong and smart. She can hold a grudge, though, that is certain."

Njal laughed. "I am glad you are able to see that."

Frigyth and Halfdan stood back a ways and watched the two brothers laughing and horse playing.

"Have you spoken to Njal about your father?" Halfdan asked quietly.

"No, not yet," Frigyth said. "I think the time will be right when we are done here."

"I do not think there will ever be a *right* time, dear Frigyth," Halfdan said, clearing his throat. "I think Njal is actually considering reclaiming Gulgruve for our people. That means things will just become more complicated here."

"Perhaps you are right," she said after taking a moment to contemplate what her friend had said. "I will speak to him tonight. It must wait until after the battle."

"I agree. But how are you doing with it?" Halfdan asked her.

"What do you mean?" she asked, now looking at him in his eyes.

"I mean, how are you coping with the news?" Halfdan's tone was soft and sincere.

"I..." Frigyth stuttered and sighed. "I have not given too much thought to the whole thing, to be quite honest. Not as much as I should be. I have thought more on who will take over as Lord more than the thought of me losing my father. Maybe it is because I am selfish, or maybe it is because I do not want to believe he will be gone soon. I am scared and sad at the same time, but I cannot afford to be. It would not be right to the people of Eaglecrest, nor the people of Birmingham."

"It is alright to feel pain, Frigyth," Halfdan said, putting his hand on her shoulder. "And do not be afraid to think about yourself once in a while. You need to look out for yourself first and foremost because you have a kind heart and that heart will benefit everyone from both of our cultures. But if your heart is broken or you do not allow yourself to feel pain, you will not only hurt yourself but everyone around you."

"You are right..." Frigyth said, sighing again. "How do you know so much about this?"

"When I was following Ragnar, I would have done anything for him. I was a few years younger than Njal is now and so I looked up to him like he was my father. He was strong and smart, always put the village before himself. He was the king of our people, yes, but he acted as though he was one of us. The same level as us. Not proud or bashful. But calm and col-lected; fair. But one day, it all changed. Why? I do not know. But Ragnar changed his entire personality. Instead of being happy and laughing with the rest of us, he would hide away in his bedchamber. Instead of feasting with us at the table, he would sit at his throne and say nothing. I do not know what it was he was going through, but he declared war on the world. And eventually, that war got a lot of us killed and scattered the rest. That is, until Toke was able to pick up the pieces. And then... well, you know the rest."

Frigyth looked at him with wide eyes as he cleared his throat.

"After Ragnar was killed, I came to England in search of his sons. I figured that they would be around with some of Ragnar's old allies, but I was wrong. That was around the time the Lords of England began to murder my people. I had nowhere to run. My mind filled up with so much rage and anger and I had nobody to talk to. Nobody that could help me through that anger. And because of that, one night at the alehouse in the town where you met me, there was a man who would not stop calling me heathen. He continued to push and harass me until I decided to leave. Well, the man followed me and pushed me down into the mud. And just like that, all of that rage and anger came out onto that man. I turned him into mush. All because I had nobody to share my pain with."

"I... I did not know that," Frigyth said with her mouth open in a gasp.

"Even though the bastard deserved it, killing him haunted me most nights until I met you and Njal. After that, I have never had the urge to do anything like that to another person. Well, unless I take my potion, that is," he said, chuckling.

"I understand, Halfdan," Frigyth said, turning her attention towards Njal and his brother.

"Our people have an interesting way of life," Halfdan began. "One that is fun to learn, no doubt. But even in our vast and ever-expanding differences, we are still the same as you and your people. We bleed the same blood and we live in the same world. So, Frigyth, please. Take the time you need to heal your heart. It is important for everyone. And please, talk to your husband."

"I will," she replied as the sky above them cracked open with a lightning strike and thunder that followed shortly behind. "I promise."

*

About an hour later, Njal was leading his warriors down the hillside towards the rear of Gulgruve; towards the opening in the walls. Njal felt a bit of nostalgia as he approached the fallen walls. His mind ran through the events that transpired during his first visit to the mining village. The anger he felt when he had to choose his path over that of saving Jarl Bjork. Who knows what thread the Norns of Fate would have spun if Njal decided to take that path?

Once they hit the bottom of the hill, Njal looked back at his followers and smiled. He nodded his head at them before he crouched down behind the stone walls of the massive village. The bandits that they were about to fight did not know much about security, as there were no fighters or guards on top of the repaired walls. Njal creased his eyebrows at that, but it did allow them to close in. Perhaps it was because the village was awfully big and having to guard every corner of it with an estimated thirty bandits would prove to be a challenging task. Or perhaps there was something more valuable to guard.

Njal crouch-walked his way around the walls until they reached the section that was still being rebuilt. The section with a giant hole that could allow anybody to enter. He held his hand up, which told everyone to stop and remain quiet. Njal then peeked his head around the corner of the cobblestone. At first glance, he could make out ten or so bandits that were just walking around or moving debris and other supplies.

Njal's eyebrows creased with confusion when he noticed their apparel. Black fur clothing and red paint that was lined across all of their bodies. They held hand-axes, seaxs, and swords. Some were holding wooden Norse style shields. Their bodies were painted black and featured a red painting on it, although Njal couldn't make out what the painting was from that distance.

Their hair was long and braided. The men had long beards, and the woman had black eye shadow on making them look like their eyes were sunken into the depths of their skull. Njal turned his head back towards his warriors and whispered quietly.

"They are Norse..."

Everyone looked at Njal with confused looks.

"Do you see what clan they belong to?" Alf whispered.

Njal shook his head and proceeded to unsheathe his sword.

"Time to find out," he said as he stood up and turned the corner, making his way into the village.

His eyebrows creased as he walked in, gripping his sword and shield. He walked through the mist-like rain as thunder clapped above him. Everyone else did the same and followed close behind. Njal's strong and prideful walk turned into a slight jog. The first three bandits stood around fifteen yards in front of him. When they noticed a large band of warriors running at them with their weapons in hand, they dropped what they were doing and began to yell. Soon, everyone in the bandit camp was screaming their heads off with a disturbing and screech like battle-cry.

Njal roared his own battle-cry in response, spit flying out of his mouth, as he began sprinting at his opponents. Nothing but bloodlust filled his mind. No worries, no politics, no fear, just battle.

The first bandit, a man with a red beard and black eye shadow, swung his sword at the Bear King but missed when Njal jumped out of the way. Njal jumped back, closer to the man and swung his sword quickly, slicing the man's head clean off in a geyser of blood. His back was now to a woman bandit that stood behind him, so Njal raised his sword over his head so that the blade was behind him. 'The Call of the King' blocked her blade and sent sparks flying. Njal smiled, realizing he guessed her next move correctly. He then turned around in one swift motion and caught the woman's jaw with the iron rim of his shield. He then followed it up with his sword and sliced the woman diagonally, her innards spilled out on the ground in front of her.

Njal continued his attack forward as bandits began to come from all sides. Knud used his sword to block an axe attack from a woman bandit who wasn't wearing much clothing. She was painted red and black from the waist up and screamed like a demon. Knud kicked her knee in and proceeded to step up calmly behind her and run his blade across her neck, spilling blood everywhere. Two other bandits, both men, jumped onto Knud until one of them was speared in the neck by Sigrid, who was running on foot by her fellow Jarl.

Sigrid was then quickly surrounded by five other

bandits as she crouched in a battle position and held her spear tightly. One bandit smiled at her with yellow teeth.

"Ugly as a goats scrotum, the lot of you," Sigrid said at the sight of the bandits licking their lips as they were certain they had her pinned down. "Do you have me, my love?" she called out.

Suddenly, one of the bandits saw the blade of a sword burst out from his chest in an explosion of blood. The sky cracked open with thunder as the other bandits turned their attention to their fallen comrade and the man who killed him, Alf.

"Of course, I have you," Alf said with a smile. "Now, let us rid these bastards of their life-blood."

The two went back-to-back. Slicing and cutting the bandits down without trouble. Sigrid stabbed her spear at a bandit who was jumping in mid-air at Alf. Alf sliced open a bandit that was running behind Sigrid. They looked out for one another, their bond growing fast in such a short time. It was a bond even the gods could see was strong...

On the other side of the battlefield, Halfdan and Almund were fighting four more bandits. Three men and one woman. The three men were giant and shirtless and wielding large two-hand axes. The woman was agile and carried two seaxs. Almund used his giant silver sword to block a blow by one of the giant axes, but it left him a bit off balance. Halfdan swung his own axe at one of the large men, but the blade missed and stuck itself into the dirt. Halfdan looked up and noticed the man sending his own axe down, so he jumped away from the axe, leaving his own stuck in the mud. He then rolled over to the other side of his axe, pulled it out of the earth and swung it upwards, quickly lodging the lethal end into the large man's lower jaw.

The woman quickly jumped at Halfdan and grabbed onto his black cloak. He tried to get her off him, but she was holding on for dear life. It became harder to get the woman off his back as she raised and stabbed one of her seaxs into his back. Halfdan roared loudly and tried to grab her from behind him, but she was too quick. She stabbed him again with her other seax in the shoulder blade. The berserker growled with pain but was able to reach behind him, grab one of her forearms, and throw her over his head. He felt one of the seaxs still in his back, but he looked at the woman in front of him and realized she held the other. He readied his axe. She screamed wildly and charged at him. The woman leaped in the air, trying to come down onto Halfdan, but he gripped his axe and swung it sideways, catching the leaping woman in the side in mid-air. She slammed into the ground with Halfdan's axe lodged in her side. She twitched a few more times before Halfdan kicked her in the face, breaking her neck. He pulled his axe out from her torso with a crunching sound.

"Fuckin' banshee..." he said as he spit on her body. Blood began to leak from his wounds.

Almund used his sword to finish off one of the larger bandits. The bandit swung his axe down onto Almund, but he rolled away, then swung his sword upward, slicing the man into two. Blood and innards were everywhere.

Frigyth was against three bandits herself. Two women and one man. She readied her sword for another attack, but felt the blade miss as it cut through air instead of her target. The man before her grabbed her by the neck and began to raise her high into the air.

"He will enjoy you," the bandit said while smiling,

showcasing black and rotting teeth. The women behind him smiled and laughed. The black soot around their eyes made them that much whiter and horrifying.

Frigyth, however, still gripped her sword when she cocked her arm back. She sent the pointed end of her sword right through the man's neck. Blood burst out of the back as the women screamed. The man's grip on Frigyth loosened as he fell to the ground. She landed on her feet and smiled up at the women.

"Care to join your friend?" she asked as she walked towards them.

One of the women charged quickly and swung her seax, but Frigyth blocked without trouble and sliced the woman behind her knee in a splash of blood, sending her to the ground. Frigyth quickly blocked the other woman's hand-axe with her shield and punched her in the face. The woman that was on the ground, however, grabbed Frigyth's cloak and pulled her down onto her back and into the mud. Frigyth dropped her sword and shield in the process. The woman then crawled up onto Frigyth and tried sending her seax down. Her attack missed as Frigyth turned her head to the side and felt the mud that flew up from the blade that struck the earth instead. The woman tried pulling her seax out of the ground, but Frigyth head-butted the woman, sending her onto her back. Frigyth quickly rose to her feet, grabbing the seax in the process, and jumped on the woman with the cut knee. Without hesitation, she used the seax to slice the woman's throat clean open. She then dropped the seax and picked her sword and shield back up off the ground.

The other woman watched in horror, then screamed

wildly before throwing her hand-axe right at Frigyth. It hit Frigyth in the chest hard and sent her down on her back. She felt the loss of breath, but was relieved when she was able to find it. She looked up and noticed the little iron chest piece in her armor did its job and stopped the hand-axe from piercing anything vital. The woman roared angrily at her failure as Frigyth rose back to her feet.

"Alright, bitch. If that is how we are going to play it," Frigyth said as she charged the now disarmed woman.

The woman tried to use her long fingernails to do some kind of damage but was unsuccessful as Frigyth dodged and swung her sword upwards, slicing the woman's hand off completely. A fountain of blood sprayed out as the woman looked in disbelief before Frigyth ran her blade into the woman's chest, silencing her screams.

Close by, Njal slammed the rim of his shield into the side of a bandit's head, crushing his skull in. He looked up and noticed that six of the bandits were grouping together for a small shield wall. He could see their black painted shields and the red painting on them.

They were in the shape of a spiral...

Njal looked around him and noticed everyone fighting their own battles.

"Knud!" Njal called out.

Knud looked up and then back to the bandit he was fighting. He blocked a hand-axe with his shield, but the lethal end sent wooden splinters everywhere. Knud lowered the shield, bringing the bandit's weapon with it as it was still lodged in the shield, as he then stabbed his sword right through the off-balanced bandit's head.

Knud pulled his sword out of his enemy's face with a crunch, then jogged over to Njal, assessing the situation in front of him. Thunder cracked loudly above.

"Yes, Njal?" he asked, catching his breath.

"It seems as though our enemies wish to fight us with a shield wall. Since everyone is a little busy right about now, would you care to show them how Surtr fights his enemies?"

"That, I can do," Knud said before reaching behind him. He pulled out a small black container and popped the cap off. He poured the thick black liquid all over his blade, then put the container behind him again. The Jarl of the Fire Clan then slid the edge of his blade across his obsidian bracer, creating a shower of sparks. Some of the fire lights landed on the blade and it caught fire in an instant. Knud's sword was now engulfed in flames.

The six bandits in the shield wall all looked at each other with worry. They couldn't believe their eyes. Knud readied his broken shield in one hand and his flaming sword in the other before walking calmly towards the shield wall. The bandits were in shock at the single man with the flaming sword that was coming their way. They readied their own weapons and prepared for anything.

Knud's walk became a jog, which became a sprint. His eyebrows creased angrily and his mouth unleashed a roar of battle. He lowered himself a little, which showed the shield wall he was going low. They all bent down a bit, but to their surprise, Knud extended his legs at the last moment and leaped over the top of the bandits. He hit the ground behind them and rolled. As the bandits turned around, the middle two had noticed they had black liquid on them.

Knud only used a small amount of oil from the container to light his sword. He also never put the lid back on when he put it behind his back again.

The bandits looked down and noticed the same black liquid on the ground in front of them that was in a line that led to Knud. Who then smiled and touched his flaming sword to the substance. No amount of rain could stop the eruption of fire that followed, which began burning the bandits. The fire gripped onto their fur clothing until the flames completely overtook them.

The shield wall was now broken. The other four bandits, two on each side of their burning comrades, watched in horror. Suddenly, one of the bandit's throat was slit by a long steel sword. The bandit's body hit the muddy ground showcasing Njal Tokeson standing behind him.

After a moment of shock, the other bandit tried to act quickly, but Njal was too fast and swung his shield upwards, breaking the bandit's jaw with the rim. The bandit flew into the air before hitting the ground as Njal raised his sword up; the blade pointed downwards. Suddenly, the blade came down hard and entered the bandit's neck, killing him.

Knud used the distraction and shot at the other two bandits. He swung his flaming sword diagonally, which sliced one bandit in two. Both halves of his body caught fire. The other bandit swung his sword at Knud, but the Fire Jarl blocked it with his shield, another piece breaking off. The bandit pulled his weapon back and tried again, again, and again, but was blocked each time. Knud's shield was breaking further with each strike from the bandit as wooden splinters went flying.

Knud breathed out calmly and counted the moments between each strike. The bandit would attack with the same amount of time between one swing and the next. So, when Knud realized the exact moment the bandit would strike next, he pushed what remained of his shield up into the strike, parrying the bandit and making him stunned. Knud then lowered his shield and swung his sword sideways, slicing the bandit's head clean off.

Knud looked down at his destroyed shield before realizing it was too broken to do anything for him now. He threw it off to the side before he and Njal shared a look of appreciation and impressiveness towards one another.

Suddenly, an extremely loud roar came from inside the mines. Everyone on the battlefield stopped their fighting. The bandits were losing badly, but once the sound of the roar hit their ears, they stopped, dropped their weapons, lowered their heads and took a knee.

Njal looked around with confusion at every remaining bandit that was following the same pattern. He shared a look with Frigyth and Halfdan, then another with Alf, and even Sigrid. Their personal problems did not matter on the field of battle. Especially when an unknown threat potentially entered the fray.

Suddenly, the sounds of running footsteps could be heard echoing inside the mines. Njal began jogging back towards his warriors. Their numbers were now around twenty-five thanks to a couple of bandits overpowering some people from Eaglecrest and one from the Fire Clan.

"Everyone, regroup!" Njal called out. The footsteps in the mines made it seem like there were around forty more bandits, at least. "Kill the ones you see in front of you. Do not be fooled by their pathetic kneeling!"

Everyone who had a bandit kneeling in front of them looked down and raised their weapons. They brought them down hard, killing the remaining bandits in the village. The bandits did not care. They just stayed still and let it happen.

The companions then ran over to Njal, who was standing in front of a large cave-like entrance to the mine. They all looked inside the dark black hole that was carved into the side of the hill with great worry and confusion.

"If you do not have a shield," Njal called out to his people. "Grab one of theirs...SHIELD WALL!"

Everyone either raised their own shield or picked up one from a dead bandit before stepping up next to Njal and raising their weapons. Halfdan and Frigyth stood next to Njal on his right as Alf and Sigrid stood next to Njal on his left. Knud stood next to Frigyth and Almund stood next to Sigrid.

Suddenly, a shadowy wave could be seen inside the cave. Everyone squinted their eyes. Eventually, the wave exited the cave and entered the light of day, showcasing around fifty bandits. They all held shields and weapons and were running right towards the shield wall.

Everyone quickly planted their feet firmly into the muddy ground and prepared for the collision. Their swords, spears, and axes were all pointed outwards, waiting to strike true.

"This place belongs to OUR people!" Njal called out so everyone could hear him. "It is time we take it back!"

Everyone gave a quick and low chant.

"HOO!" they yelled while slamming their weapons on their shields, making a loud clanking sound.

"HOO!" they all yelled again and made the same gesture with their weapons as the bandits got closer.

Then, the bandits screamed wildly as they leaped for the shield wall. But Njal called out a command and the only greeting the front line of the bandits got was the shields of their opponents shooting out and striking them in the face and or body and throwing them onto their backs. The Norsemen pulled their shields back and stabbed the bandits that were hurt on the ground before returning to their shield wall stance.

The next line of bandits attempted the same as the first, but after a command from Njal, they met the same fate. The third line of bandits learned from the first two but they began tripping over the bodies of their fallen comrades in front of them, allowing for easier kills.

Eventually, the bandits stopped charging at the shield wall. They stood back, and some of them even ran back into the cave.

"They are retreating!" Halfdan said happily.

"They are hiding something in that mine," Alf said coldly. "What, I do not know. But they know they cannot beat us. Those that are returning inside are not retreating from us.

They are trying to escape with whatever they hold so valuable inside."

The same giant roar inside the mine echoed throughout the village and the surrounding valley before the bandit force in front of them began escaping inside the hill.

"Good, they know we have won," Halfdan said happily.

Alf looked at Njal and shook his head. "We cannot let them escape. They will just come back here or hide in the mine. Instead of dealing with them later, let us deal with them now."

Njal looked forward again, into the large, almost never-ending dark cavern that sat before him.

"Njal," Halfdan said with a shocked look on his face. "You cannot be considering this. They are retreating. Leaving in order to hold on to what they still have!"

"We must rid them of this place, permanently," Alf said.

"We have already won!" Halfdan pleaded. "The fight is over; we do not have to lose any more men!"

"If any more of us die, they will drink with Odin in Valhalla," Alf said to Njal. "You would have led them to a beautiful death."

"This goes against the change you were fighting for, Njal!" Halfdan said to his friend. "They are a group of Norse who have not yet changed. Give them the chance to!"

"They are nothing but pigs who thought they could take from you," Alf said. "Take from us! Gulgruve belongs to us, Njal. It belongs to our people."

"Do not listen to him, Njal," Halfdan said, grunting

as more blood leaked from his wounds. "It goes against our hope for change!"

"But the hope for change does not mean we will be walked upon. Whether it be by these bandits or Edward himself... Gulgruve is ours, Njal," Alf said, gritting his teeth.

Njal thought about each option. If he let the bandits escape through the mine and out somewhere else, it would just mean that they could attack another time. If he gave Gulgruve back to Edward, then the new king might think of Njal as his new errand boy. Njal didn't like that. He closed his eyes and remembered what Odin had told him. This must be one of the crossroad decisions that would change his fate. He had to think carefully. As he thought deeper and harder, his choice became clear.

"Alf... with me," Njal said coldly as he walked away from the rest of the shield wall and towards the dark entrance to the mine. Alf quickly jogged after Njal until he caught up with him. Sigrid followed the same.

"What are they doing?" Almund asked, with shock on his face.

"They are going in there to finish them off," Frigyth said with her head down. She then looked at Halfdan. He looked back at her and shrugged his shoulders with a look of sadness on his face. Njal chose his brother over him. While he slightly expected that to happen, seeing it play out the way it did hurt him deeply. It cut worse than the wounds on his back. Njal's decision also made one for Halfdan.

The berserker broke away from the shield wall and ran

after his king, but before he could get halfway to them, Frigyth called for him. She left the wall and chased after her friend.

"Halfdan, what are you doing?" Frigyth asked.

"This will be my last fight at Njal's side... perhaps my last one at all. I will be there for him until it is finished."

Frigyth's eyes widened. "Your last fight? What... what do you mean?"

"Njal's decision to enter that mine was not just about the bandits that reside inside. He will choose to keep Gulgruve for our people, which will cause distrust between Edward and us." Halfdan's eyes met the muddy earth beneath him. "It has also shown that he does not need me anymore. I have been thinking about leaving for a while now. Living with Ingrid in isolation," he smiled at Frigyth as he thought of the future. Then his face turned stern. "Njal is showing the same signs that Ragnar did. I cannot see another friend go down that path."

Halfdan gripped his hand-axe and shield from a fallen bandit tightly. He then charged inside the mine after Njal while Frigyth thought hard about his words. After a few moments, she could hear screams and sounds of weapons clashing together inside. She then turned her attention back towards the remaining members of the shield wall and approached them.

"What is going on?" Almund asked.

Frigyth took a deep breath and looked at the Englishman. "Njal is going to keep Gulgruve. This is the only location that we will ever do this to, but it is too important to our people. Bring this news to Edward, but please let him know that this is no act of war. It is an act of justice. We fought for this village and we earned it. Our alliance remains strong."

Almund couldn't believe the words coming out of the queen's mouth.

"Edward will not like this..." he muttered.

"We are aware," Frigyth said. "But he must accept that this village belonged to us and, in the grand scheme of things, is not much of an asking. Especially since we earned it back with our forces and we are not a group of bandits, but instead powerful allies to the crown. Let it be known that by allowing us to have this village back, it will create more trust between us."

"Understood..." Almund said before turning around and leaving with his men.

Frigyth then turned her attention to Knud, who stood there with a disappointed look on his face.

"Knud, are there any exits out of the mine besides the ones here?" she asked. "Maybe some that we do not know of? I only ask because you used to deal and trade with Jarl Bjork before he died."

Knud looked at her piercingly blue eyes. He couldn't tell what she was thinking, but she was his queen. He had to answer truthfully.

"Aye," he said. "The other side of this hill... there are three other exits. Two lead towards the cliffs to the south and one leads to the swamps to the northwest. Do you wish to send our men there so we can stop the remaining bandits?"

"No," Frigyth said to Knud's surprise. "I do not share this view with my husband. I thought it right to leave them to their escape. We beat them and showed our strength. We do not need to hunt and kill the remaining survivors."

"I share your beliefs as well," Knud said. "What shall

we do? Njal will expect me to know of the other exits and be there to ambush the fleeting bandits."

"Return to Eaglecrest," she said. "I will stay and wait for my husband."

"I will stay with you," Knud said. "The rest of you, return to your homes!" he yelled as he looked at the rest of the warriors behind him.

They all hesitated at first but then began to make their way towards the broken wall they entered the village through.

"Njal will not be happy," Knud said. "Especially if he decides to keep Gulgruve like you theorize."

"His decision has been made already. When he returns, I will talk to him," Frigyth said as the screams and sounds of battle from inside the mine got louder.

XI

Consequences

About an hour had passed by as Frigyth noticed the four warriors exiting the mine. They were all covered in so much blood it was like they had been painted red. No smiles graced their faces, and no words were spoken among them. Frigyth could tell their pursuit did not go the way they had wished. Njal finally approached Frigyth as his face was graced with a look of confusion. He then shared the same look with Knud.

"Where is everyone?" he asked in a sour tone.

"I sent them home," Frigyth said back. Her hands were shaking. The rain had stopped, but the overcast remained. The high noon temperature was still ice cold as winter began to tease itself upon the land.

"Why would you ever do such a thing?" Njal asked. "Did I ever give the order to do that?"

"No, you did not," Sigrid said, staring at Frigyth. She looked at her with a disgusting smile.

"Knud," Njal said, looking at him. "You used to make dealings with Jarl Bjork and this village. Were you aware that there were other exits to the mine? Because one moment, we were slaughtering them and then the next, they were gone. They were able to escape with whatever it was they were guarding. For the life of me, I could not understand why you, a man who obviously knew about the exits, would not inform me of that information. Or, if you were aware, would be waiting on the other side of those exits to cut them off. So, tell me, why is it that I find you here, alone, with my wife?"

"Njal, I figured..."

"Figured what, exactly?" Njal asked. "I cannot believe one of my most trusted allies would..."

"It was me," Frigyth said.

Njal looked at her with wide eyes. "What was you?"

"I ordered Knud to stay here before I sent everyone home."

"Why?" Njal said coldly.

"Because, Njal!" Frigyth now pleaded. "We had already won! Gulgruve was ours again! What the hell are you doing hunting the rest of them down and slaughtering them like animals?"

"How dare you speak to your king like that!" Alf said with genuine shock.

"Shut up, you filthy bastard," Frigyth said sharply. Alf held his tongue.

"I do not need to explain myself to you, Frigyth," Njal said. "I did what was best for our people."

"Our people? Or Alf?" she asked sternly.

"What the Hel is that supposed to mean?" Njal asked, obviously taken aback.

"Ever since he has been here, you have not acted like yourself. You are making decisions that you would not normally make. It is like you replaced your father's inner voice with Alf's. He did not grow up with your father's teachings. He is changing you back to what you and your father wished to change. And justifying killing at entire group of people because you think it better that they all die than have a chance to change sounds an awful lot like Aelred."

Njal swung his hand out and struck Frigyth across the face. She stumbled but didn't fall. He looked at her with wide eyes, as did Halfdan.

"What are you doing?!" Halfdan yelled as he dropped his weapons and ran to Frigyth. He put his hands on her shoulders and asked if she was alright. "What is the matter with you?!" he shouted as he looked at Njal.

Njal looked down at his hand and watched it shake. "I...I did not mean to."

"Njal..." Frigyth said. A line of blood trickled from the corner of her mouth. Both of their worlds shattered. "You are on your own..."

Halfdan looked at Njal with a look of shock before he began leading Frigyth away from them.

After a few moments, Alf approached Njal and put his hand on his shoulder. "I am sorry, brother. But you know that what we did was right. It gives you more power, and this village belongs to us. They will come to understand in time."

"Plus," Sigrid said. "You need a woman that *likes* to be struck like that."

Alf smiled back at her before the two walked away.

Njal felt nothing in his heart. No joy from winning the battle. No glory, no pride, and no love. He felt numb. Striking the woman he loved... Even he couldn't believe he was capable of doing something like that.

*

That night, back in Eaglecrest, the cold began to grip itself around the village. Njal was inside the Great Hall, sitting on his knotwork carved throne. His head was rested on his hand as he was in deep thought. The emptiness of the Hall filled him up with lonely thoughts that raced and raced, throwing his mind further into a deep void.

The events of the day replayed in his mind. He remembered returning home with Alf, Sigrid, and Knud after Gulgruve. No words were spoken by anyone on the trip home besides Alf and Sigrid, and they mostly talked about how they were going straight to the bedchamber when they arrived. Sure enough, when they did return to Eaglecrest's gates, Alf and Sigrid went towards Demut, the home of the Horse Clan. Knud said a quick goodbye and returned to Muspel.

You will lose her.

Knud's words kept rotating in Njal's mind repeatedly.

More images filled his mind. Njal had asked the guards where everyone was, to which he received his answer. Halfdan was with Ingrid, getting help for his back. He apparently needed help walking through the gates as his adrenalin wore off. Frigyth went with him, so Njal went to the Great Hall and waited to see if any of them would pay him a visit afterwards.

As his mind caught up to where he was now, lost in thought, he closed his eyes tightly and returned to the Land of the Sprits. The Bear woke up in the middle of a clearing. The night sky was flickering with stars above. The smell of fresh flowers and recently fallen rain struck his nostrils. He was in Asgard, the home of the gods. The Bear heard the caw of a Raven and he turned around and looked up. A sudden strike from a lightning bolt hit the ground, turning the Raven into the hooded man who held a golden spear.

"Odin..." The Bear began.

No words from the allfather.

"Did I choose the correct path?" the Bear asked.

The god looked down onto the Bear and said nothing for a long moment.

"Your choices have thrown your fate into a wild and tangled mess, Njal Tokeson. Perhaps I misplaced my trust in you. Perhaps there is another that can lead my people to prosperity. Perhaps I was wrong."

The Bear could not speak. He could not think. Those words felt like a sharp pain stabbing him in the heart.

"But..."

"I will always appreciate your sacrifices in fighting against Aelred and building a new home, but it seems as though your time of having my favor... is no more."

The Bear was filled with a rushing wave of sadness and anger.

"You must go now," Odin interrupted the Bear's feeling. "There are some who wish to speak to you."

Then, another lightning strike and Njal was thrown from the Land of the Sprits and back into reality. Where Halfdan and Ingrid were standing, waiting in front of him. Ingrid looked a bit sad while Halfdan looked angry.

"I am sorry," Njal said, his hand on his head for a moment. "I was just..."

"We know," Ingrid said, knowing exactly where he just was.

"Right..." Njal said, his tone sad.

A few moments passed where nobody said anything. Ingrid then looked at the two of them.

"I will leave you both," Ingrid said before turning her attention to Halfdan. "I will be waiting outside, my beloved."

He nodded, but kept his eye contact with Njal. They both waited until Ingrid turned, bowed her head at Njal, then walked out of the front door. Once the wooden door shut behind her...

"Halfdan, I..."

"Enough," Halfdan replied. "I am done, Njal. I often forget that you are still just a young man. So much left to learn. While I am deeply thankful for you helping me further my saga and find my Ingrid for me, I will not be a part of this any longer."

"I admit my wrongs, Halfdan. I should not have struck Frigyth. That fact will forever haunt me. But you must know that I thought about our people when I chose to go after those bandits."

Halfdan laughed sadly. "You have ambition and you are brave. But you are also a blind man, Njal Tokeson."

"Look, I am trying to apologize, but I will not have you come in here and belittle me like this. We can have a civil discussion about my wrongs and my decisions, but I will not tolerate this."

"You are not aware of how similar you and Ragnar are," Halfdan said, a sad look on his face.

"What is that supposed to mean?" Njal asked angrily.

"He was a very flawed man, but one I loved and cherished until he led us to our demise."

"Is that what you think of me? You believe I will lead us to our demise? No man is unflawed, Halfdan. I made mistakes, but it is not to say I cannot fix them. Be *better* from them."

"What of Alf?"

"What about him?" Njal asked, his face twisting.

"How can you not admit that ever since he arrived here, he has changed the way you think and process things? You know he believes in the old ways and your idea of changing his mind was to let him sit in on our meetings, but what it *actually* did was change yours. Taking Gulgruve back for ourselves when we had the responsibility to put England back together shows how immature you..."

"GODS, ENOUGH OF THIS!" Njal roared as he shot to his feet. "You continue to call me these names when you released Torin! Especially after I specifically told you to leave him alone until *after* the battle! I let you go unpunished, but now you are punishing me!" Njal took a breath and sat down in his throne again. "You were mad at me, I know that. For locking Torin away when he killed Ivar. But you *knew* my reasons! Now, you see me making mistakes, but you decide to insult me. Verbally torture me over them. Can we not talk about them like men? Like friends?"

Halfdan was taken aback by that. He realized he was being unfair to his friend that was obviously going through a hard time as well.

"Njal, I..."

"Unless you never truly were my friend..." Njal said, heartbroken. "You just used me to further your own saga."

"Njal, you know that is not true!" Halfdan pleaded.

"I need you to leave," Njal said, a tear forming in his eye. "If this is how it is going to be from you, I want you out of here."

Halfdan dropped his head. "I am doing so."

Njal watched as Halfdan turned around and walked out of the Great Hall. He took notice of Halfdan's last words before the door shut. But they weren't directed at Njal. It was somebody else that was standing outside. After a brief moment of silence, the door opened and Frigyth walked in. She was dressed in the same attire she wore earlier that day for the battle.

Njal jumped out of his throne and began walking towards her.

"Frigyth! Oh, I am so..."

"Stop," she said, to which his smile faded and he stopped walking. "I have some things I wish to speak with you about, Njal."

"Alright, we can talk, but I really wish to tell you something first," he said. She nodded, allowing him to go first. "I wish to apologize for my behavior on the battlefield earlier today. I do not know what came over me. You know that I never wish to see you hurt and to see that happen by my own hand... I just... I have some things I need to figure out and I should not have taken them out on you. Please... please see how sorry I am."

"I can see, Njal," she replied sincerely. "Trust that I know that is not who you are as a person and as a man. However, it is how I see Alf. And I think he is not good to have at your side. I..."

"Does nobody wish for me to be happy?" Njal interrupted, sighing. "Is nobody happy that I have my brother? I mean, what am I supposed to do? Push him away to keep all of you? Or push all of you away to keep him? I DO NOT KNOW WHAT I AM TO DO!"

"It is a hard choice but one that you have to make. Alf will change what you have been fighting for. We supported your first dream, but we will not support his. England itself will not support his. I am sorry, Njal."

"Have you completely lost trust in me, Frigyth? You do not believe I will do the right thing anymore; you do not tell me of your pain. What am I even doing as your husband if you cannot even share with me the news of your father?"

Frigyth's eyes widened.

"No, that is not..."

"Ingrid informed me on the night I returned to Eaglecrest. I needed to know you were alright and you never even told me about him. Why have you lost this trust in me?"

"Njal, I wished to tell you," she said sadly. "That is what I was coming to do..."

"But why not earlier? We are supposed to be man and

wife. King and queen. Shield mates. What have I done for you to misplace your trust in me?"

"I wished to tell you when things began to settle down. When your mind could be on me and not England or your brother or..."

"Gods, here we go again! Why does everyone hate my brother?" Njal snapped. "For Odin's sake, he has not been here for long and you all despise him!"

"Because he is a horrible influence on you, Njal! He is changing who you are! Please listen to my words!"

"I have had enough, Frigyth," Njal began as he walked back towards his throne. "You either stay here and live with me *and* my brother and continue to rule at my side and we can discuss things together or you do not. I will not rid my life of my blood kin to keep you and I will not rid you to keep him. It should not have to be this way."

Frigyth thought hard. The silence of the Great Hall was endless, other than the crackle of the fire pit. With Alf at Njal's side, things would never be the same again. Things would never be well again, at least in her eyes. They would just continue to fall. But she knew she couldn't ask her husband to let go of his brother. That would be unfair to him. Especially because she still loved him deeply. She figured the best thing for him and for her... was to let him go.

As Njal looked at the knotwork carved throne, he heard Frigyth's words from behind him. He then shed a tear as he heard her footsteps and the sound of the door to the Great Hall closing behind her. He gripped the throne tightly in his hand, then fell to the floor and broke down, sobbing. Alone in the Great Hall and its high reaching ceiling, Frigyth's words repeated in his head.

I am leaving to become Lord of Birmingham once my father passes. You will have a continued alliance with us, but our marriage is no more. I love you, Njal, and I always will. But this is the right choice for us in the long run. I do not belong here. Perhaps in another life...

Njal's sobbing grew louder. Knud's words struck true...

You will lose her...

You will lose her...

You HAVE lost her...

XII

Ari

"Damnit!" Torin yelped as he sliced his thumb open on his knife. "What kind of bone is this?"

"You have to be patient, my friend," Cathbad said, laughing a bit. "Small and simple slices with the knife are the only way that bone will sharpen."

"I still do not understand why you are having me make a knife with a knife," Torin said before sucking the blood from his thumb.

"Because we need more knives. There is not enough for everyone to have, so we must make some by using bones. If you sharpen them correctly, they can be as strong as an iron blade." Torin sighed before going back to work on the bone knife. "Remember, you are not a Jarl here, Torin. You must do things that benefit us just as much as they could benefit you. If some need more food than others, you may have to go hunting with the chance that you may not receive much on your own plate. If somebody needs a weapon, you might have to forge one with nothing but your hands and even then, you may not get to use it. Being a part of this community is about sticking together. That is what makes us strong."

"I understand," Torin said, nodding his head. "I will keep trying."

"I know you will," Cathbad said with a smile on his face. He looked up into the morning sky and felt the chill in the air. "How was Elhhere this morning?"

"Not too bad," Torin said as he continued to cut the bone. "I am learning a bit more about this magic shite. You know, at first, I thought you were all mad. But now, I am enjoying this side of the world."

Cathbad laughed. "How are the lessons going? What have you learned so far?"

"Just a couple of things. For starters, I have learned about what plants and herbs can make a Teine. I have also learned about how meditation can not only heal wounds but create a stronger bond with the energy of the world."

Cathbad chuckled. "What do you think of a Teine? Pretty wonderful weapon, would you not agree?"

"Well, I have only learned how to make one. I have not used one as of yet," Torin said with a smirk.

"Well, remind me to show you how it's done later. Perhaps this evening when we are finished with our lessons here."

"I like the sound of that," Torin said.

"So, was there ever a woman at your side?" Cathbad asked.

Torin looked up at the sun, which was now slowly

fading behind a wall of low and dark clouds. "There was one," he said softly before going back to his carving.

"Oh," Cathbad said, looking at the man. "Do tell."

"Her name was Olga. I met her when I was but a boy. She was the daughter of a family friend. I used to spend all of my time with her hunting for trolls, fighting invisible frost Jotuns, and spying on people in our village."

"I like that!" Cathbad said with a smile. "What ever happened to this Olga?"

"Well, we continued our friendship until it turned into a passionate love when we had sixteen winters at our backs. We could not get enough of each other. Every single moment of every day, I spent with her."

He stopped carving and looked up at the sky again.

"That is until Ragnar Lothbrok arrived in our village and said he needed raiders for his journey to England. And Olga knew how long I had dreamed of being a raider, so she had no issues with me leaving. Then I spoke to Ragnar, and he said he wanted to bring all of those who volunteered on a hunting trip high in the mountains. It was going to be a test of sorts to see which of us were strong enough to go with him. Well, the snow came down hard one day up there and I lost my footing. I fell down a cliff and broke my leg. I knew everyone thought I was dead, so I did not spend any time crying for help. I fixed myself a splint for my leg before coming face to face with a Lynx. A truly fascinating and beautiful creature. I fought and killed the cat with my bare hands. After a month of surviving, I eventually found my way down the mountain. I was excited to finally be back home." Torin's smile faded. "Until I came to find that Ragnar had left already.

Cathbad's face dropped as Torin continued.

"I went to find Olga and... I had learned that in my absence, a man from Ragnar's army mistook her for a whore. He forced himself upon her and she fought back hard. She even scratched one of his eyes out. But unfortunately, he was able to overpower her. And he choked her to death."

Cathbad's eyes were wet with tears. "I am... truly sorry, Torin."

"I then stole a boat and a hand-axe and sailed to England myself. I nursed my leg back to normal on that boat and I hunted down Ragnar's army. They made camp in Norwich and when I arrived, I walked right through that army, acting as one of them, until I found the man with one eye. I sat down next to him at the campfire and told a fake story about raiding a village. I asked him how he lost his eye and he told the truth. He said he 'humped a bitch to death' during a raid, and she got his eye before he could finish. While everyone laughed, I sat there and asked what her name was. He was obviously confused and said he did not know. I told him what her name was. I continued to tell him over and over as I pulled my hand-axe out and chopped the lethal end into the man until he was a bleeding pile of shite. Ragnar's men pulled me off the dead man and brought me to the king himself. I told him my story, and he said that he would like to have me as a part of his army."

"You are a vigorous man, Torin. And you fight for revenge. We will get you yours against the Bear King. This I promise..."

Suddenly, two Druids came out of the tall grass with spears in their hands.

"What is it?" Cathbad asked.

"Ari has returned from her mission and wishes to speak with you at once."

Cathbad's face hardened.

"Alright. Torin," he said. "Let us go. I would like for you to sit in on this meeting."

Torin nodded as he stabbed the sharpened bone into the dirt and put his knife behind his back in the sheathe hung on his belt. The four of them walked in silence a short distance until they returned to the village. The blue morning sky was becoming a dark gray now. Thunder rumbled in the distance. The two men followed the other Druids up the wooden stairs.

They opened the door to the main hut and stepped inside. A woman in gray robes with blonde hair was sitting in a chair by the fire pit. She shot up once she noticed Cathbad enter the room.

"Cathbad!" she exclaimed. "We need to kill them! Kill them all!"

"Whoa, whoa, whoa, Ari," he said, putting his hands up in an attempt to calm her. "Let us sit down and you can tell me of your mission."

Cathbad and Ari sat down at a large wooden table while Torin stood there not knowing what to do. Cathbad noticed.

"Come," he said, waving the Norseman over. "Sit down with us."

Torin did so.

"Ari, this is Torin. He is a strong Norseman that is hoping to become one of us. So far, he is doing a fantastic job! Anyway, he is going to sit in on this meeting with us, so please share with us what you must about your mission." Ari nodded her head at the now sitting Torin. "Actually, let me catch him up first. So, Ari here was going undercover as a Christian in the small town known as Wolves Hollow. It is this fancy little town on the edge of the river where a massive temple sits on a hill! Anyway, we sent her and her friend Fionn there to see if they would pose a threat to us. Believe it or not, some of these Christians like to worship in peace and we do not care much about them. But then there are others that try to find anyone who does not follow their god and they attempt to forcefully make them. We have had problems with those types of Christians in the past, so Ari and Fionn were supposed to disguise themselves as regulars at the temple and see which kind they were."

"And they were a bunch of bastards!" Ari yelled, slamming her fist on the table. "A gust of wind blew Fionn's robe up and one man saw her tattoos on her legs. We did not notice anything strange until they broke in while we were sleeping and dragged us out of bed. They ripped our robes off and saw all of her markings. Those lying pigs called her a witch and tied her up on a stake. They made me watch as they... they burned her alive! I can still hear her screams ringing in my head. I tried to fight back, but I was beaten. I suppose because I did not have any markings, they decided to just throw me in a cell. When I awoke the next morning to a guard telling me they were going to hang me, I told him I would hump him since it was probably the last time I ever would. Believe it or not, he entered the cell, and I killed him, took the keys, and escaped with only my robe. Which, by the way, get this thing off of me!"

She stood up and ripped the robe off of herself. Torin looked at her and felt warm. Her naked body reminded him of Olga's back when he was a young man. This woman's beauty amazed him.

"I am saddened to hear about Fionn's death," Cathbad said. "Let us make preparations and we shall burn their town to the ground. Torin, would you like to lead the attack?"

"No!" Ari exclaimed. "I wish to lead! I wish to watch as that priest's life floods from his body."

"How about we both lead?" Torin said, instantly receiving the eyes of the other two in the room. "I see rage inside of you that reminds me of the rage inside of myself. If we put our heads together, I do not think anything would stop us."

Ari looked at the Norseman with squinted eyes, and then her face returned to normal. "Alright, fine. Let us go. I do not have much to lose, anyway."

"Ah ha!" Cathbad said. "I like this!"

"Well, Norseman," Ari began. "What would be your plan for infiltrating their town?"

"What sort of defenses do they have?"

"None. The village is wide open," she said. "They have about twenty armed guards, but that is all. They do have one captain, though. He is a massive bastard, but I only ever saw him guarding the head priest."

"Really? That is all?" Torin asked.

"Yes, they are supposed to be just a town of worship.

Turns out they are far from. They use their power to torture the people of the town and they call it 'Gods Will.'"

"Well, that will bite them in the arse," Torin said. "Without many guards, it means we can either attack them head on or we can sneak through at night and kill them silently. And if this captain guards the head priest, then Ari, you can go for the priest to get your revenge. I will take care of the captain."

Ari gave a little smirk to the man she had just met.

"Hm," she said. "I like this man, Cathbad. Where did you say you found him?"

"The southern border of the Fenlands. You and him will have to talk sometime. Your pasts are not so different."

The three of them smiled.

*

"WHAT THE HEL!" Torin yelled as he jumped from his bed, ice cold water soaking him completely. He looked up to see Ari standing there, laughing hysterically. She was wearing a deerskin hide that covered her chest and below her waist. She had quite a few animal bones strapped to her arm. A long femur type bone strapped to her forearm and the rest of her hand and fingers were covered in tiny bones. It almost looked as though the skin was removed from her right elbow all the way up to the tips of her fingers.

"Wake up!" she said, still laughing. "If we are to fight together on the battlefield, I want to hunt with you. Or do some training, whichever you prefer."

"Is sleep not an option?" Torin said, shaking his wet hair, droplets of water flying around. "Alright, fine. Let us hunt. I have not killed anything in a while anyway." Torin ripped his wet tunic off and threw it aside, slapping against the wooden floor. He stood up a few inches away from her and was a good foot taller.

"Ooh," she said, looking into his eyes. "I like the fierceness. Come on, let us go."

She instantly turned around and walked out of Torin's hut.

"Wait! I..." Torin watched her close the wooden door behind her. "Need another shirt..."

*

After a few moments, Torin walked down the wooden stairs of the village that stood upon stilts down to the swamplike ground beneath it. Ari stood on a solid dirt patch where a tent and remnants of a campfire sat. She had a silver sword resting in a sheathe at her hip, a knife and a seax at her back, and a bow and quiver wrapped around her shoulder.

"There he is," she said, seeing the man walk down the steps. "I see you found a dryer shirt."

He chuckled as he noticed her attire. "We best be hunting trolls with a sword like that. Is that an Englishman's blade?"

"Aye," she said, looking down at it then back up to him. "I stole it off a blacksmith's tent in Birmingham a long time ago."

"Birmingham? Is that where you are from?" Torin asked.

"We can talk about things like that later. First, I want to see what kind of skills you have."

"Alright, just tell me what to kill," he said strongly.

Ari squinted her eyes for a moment, then smirked and immediately took off running, her blonde hair flying behind her in the crisp autumn breeze. Torin's eyes widened as he stood there shocked. After a brief pause, he took off after her. His body was toned now. His time spent on the road shredded the ale and overabundance of fat and meat from his diet, causing him to become quite skinny. But in his time spent with the Druids of the Fenlands and his constant physical and mental training, it didn't take long for the muscle to build and the tone to set in. He was a beast of a man now, one that was hell bent on revenge against the man that took his throne.

His legs kept pumping into the dirt and mud as he chased Ari through the pathway between the tall grass. He remembered Cathbad's words about how to navigate through the tall grass without getting sucked in by the mud, allowing for an easy kill. The Norseman jumped through the grass and stepped on the solid dirt until he almost caught her. He was closing in on her like a lion would a gazelle. Right at the last second, he leaped to tackle her, but she ducked. Torin noticed in midair how the tall grass had stopped and the ground below him began to lower. His eyes widened as he realized she had just led him to a steep hill and made him jump off of it.

He screamed as he came flying towards the ground. He hit the dirt hard, causing a cloud of dust to fly up. His body kept rolling and tumbling around until the hill evened out a few feet later.

"Ugh," he grunted as he looked up at Ari, who was still on top of the hill, laughing.

"You are fast, Torin, I will give you that. Unfortunately,

I am smarter!" she said with an enormous smile on her face. "First lesson, always be aware of your surroundings! If you can lead your opponent to an area that you are familiar with, you can lead them right into your trap."

"Hm," Torin said before spitting dirt and getting back to his feet. "Impressive."

"Now," she said as she approached him. "Time for weapons training."

"I think I know how to handle a weapon, Ari," he said.

"I know, but we are going to hunt. I would like to see what you are made of."

"Finally," Torin said with a smile from ear to ear.

*

The two of them ran through the Fenlands until they exited the swamp and traveled up a high reaching hill. It took them all day to do so as the sun was finally beginning to set. The sunset gave everything an orange glow as Ari and Torin were crouched behind some moss-covered rocks at the summit of the hill.

"It is beautiful up here, is it not?" Ari asked as she looked at the view. She could see from the Fenlands to London's tall reaching towers all the way to the ocean and the sun that had set behind it in the distance.

"Aye," Torin said. His hands still itching to see a deer or boar or something.

"So, Cathbad said he found you on the border of the Fenlands. What exactly were you doing there?" she asked, now looking at him. The scowl on his face seemed to be a hard and impenetrable shell. But Ari felt a warm feeling inside when she knew there was more to him. A mystery that she wished to solve.

He hesitated a moment before speaking.

"I had nowhere else to go," he finally said.

"Well, that makes us alike," she said as she turned her gaze towards the ocean.

"Oh, yeah? How so?" he paused briefly, then sat up and looked at her. "What exactly brought *you* to the Druids?"

"You first," she said to him with a sad smile.

"Alright," he said before taking a moment to speak.

It was a hard topic to speak about. Having one life taken from you so abruptly and finding another. It definitely takes a toll on someone.

"I fought with Ragnar Lothbrok," he began. "I was with him in his pointless sieges and raids that got a *lot* of my people killed. And while dying is the way of my people, many of us wish to die with purpose. I could see that if we kept following the man as he became mad, he would lead us all to a pointless death. I was the only one to speak out, and I left. A number of others followed me to the coast, where we set up our village. I was king of my people for a long time. That is until that little bastard Njal Tokeson showed up. He took it from me. Everything I lived for, everything I fought for, everything I *killed* for... gone."

Ari looked at him with creased eyebrows and a look of sadness. "I am sorry, Torin. Is that how you got all of those scars?"

Torin felt a bit embarrassed, as he had not seen what his face looked like in a long while. He knew he had a scar where

Njal broke his jaw with the rim of his shield because he could feel it. But he wasn't aware he had anymore on his face.

"Do my scars frighten you?" he asked.

"No, no, not at all," she said. "All scars have a story to them. Each one its own saga and I wanted to know the story behind yours, that is all."

"I understand," he said with a small smile at Ari's honesty.

"So, how did you find Cathbad?" Ari asked, forgetting the scar question, as it obviously cut too deep.

"After my demise, I was captured by my own people," Halfdan said as he looked out at the sunset. "Thanks to the hulking oaf that is Njal's friend, I escaped captivity. After spending nine months on the roads, I came to the realization that my death would not have a purpose. Everything I worked for to change back in Ragnar's army, it was just going to happen to me anyway. So, I decided to travel to the Fenlands in hope that the Druids would kill me quickly. Or at least use me for a sacrifice so my death could at least have a purpose for somebody else."

"But instead, you found a new purpose, yes?" she asked, watching the sun finally set behind the horizon.

"Exactly," he said. "I am assuming the same goes with you?"

She turned her attention back towards Torin and then down at her boots. "Yeah, you could say that."

"Would you like to tell me your story?" Torin asked. "I would love to hear it."

"Why not?" she asked herself before clearing her throat. She brushed a blonde strand of her hair behind her ear.

"I was born in Birmingham to loving parents. My mother used to take me to the market every morning and my father would take me fishing every evening. I had a best friend that I would spend the afternoons with and we would always cause trouble. You know, either mess around with the guards or sneak into an alehouse to see what it was like inside. Nothing too wild. But one day, we grabbed some carrots from a basket in the market and threw them at some guards. It was hilarious until we got caught doing it. The guards took us to the Lord, and he forbid me to see my friend from that point on. I did not accept the punishment, so I snuck out of my parent's home and tried to sneak into my friend's window. But when I got there, she was so afraid of her father that she called for the guards herself. They took me and the Lord exiled my family and I from Birmingham. Because of me, we had no food, nowhere to sleep, no weapons to defend ourselves. I snuck inside the walls one night without my parents knowing and stole this sword from the blacksmith. My father was so mad."

She laughed, a tear streaming from her eye before her face twisted in sadness.

"It was not long before some bandits attacked us on the road to London and killed my parents in front of me. Those same bastards took me and beat and raped me. That lasted six years until I learned everything from them. I learned how they lived, hunted, and fought. And one night, one of them wanted to take his turn with me, but I decided I would rather die than be taken advantage of again. So, I used what I learned and killed him using my bare hands and teeth. I was able to find my sword in a nearby chest, and I used it to kill the entire camp all by myself.

I let the rage from those six years build up to the point where it all released onto those poor bastards."

Torin was speechless.

"Turns out, one of the bandits also stole from the Druids and on that night, they were preparing to take their revenge. Instead, they watched me do it all myself and Cathbad exited the darkness and told me I could rest now as I had a new home."

"That is... quite the story, Ari. I am sorry that happened."

"Ah, it is quite alright. It led me to who I am today. I would not change a thing."

"Why would the Lord of Birmingham do that?" Torin asked. "You were just children. Children are mischievous."

"Well, I guess I forgot to mention that my friend was his daughter. He thought I was being a bad influence on her."

Torin's eyes widened, and he said nothing for a moment.

"What exactly was your friend's name?"

"Frigyth," she replied.

"Ari, I believe there is a reason we found each other..."

"Oh, yeah?" she said with a smile and a chuckle. "And what reason would that be?"

"Frigyth is Njal Tokeson's wife."

Her face turned serious.

*

THUNK

"Ah ha!" Torin called out as he watched his hand-axe meet its mark. The boar fell to its side with a thud and Ari yelped with excitement.

"Quite the throw there, Torin!" she shouted.

"My thanks," he said, rotating his arm, stretching it. "I am happy to know my arm is still what it used to be."

The two of them approached their prey under the cover of nightfall. They looked down at the beast, which was still huffing and puffing, the hand-axe lodged in its side. Ari pulled out a seax from her belt and nudged it at Torin.

"You do the honors," he said to her. "We need to share this win."

"Suit yourself," Ari shrugged as she spun the seax in her hand and proceeded to slice the boar across its neck, putting it out of its misery.

"Cathbad will be pleased, no?"

"Absolutely," she replied as she wiped the blade of the seax off and put it back in her leather belt. "However, I think he will be more pleased about the bond we created since we met. He is always telling us that by working together, we can accomplish anything."

"Well, I think he may be right about that," Torin said with a smile on his face. His beard was getting longer and mangier.

"You should shave when we get back," she said with a smile.

"Why is that?" he replied, a little self-conscious now. "Not a supporter of the beard?"

"I think I would be if it were more well-groomed," she laughed.

"Fair enough," he said, smiling. "Let us get this boar back home. Then we can talk about my beard."

She grinned as she watched him pull the hand-axe out of the boar's side with a crunch. He then lifted the beast up and over his shoulder. They began walking back down the hill towards the village. Both held large smiles on their faces, although they didn't say too much to one another on the journey back. Each one of them had a warm feeling inside. One that neither of them had felt in some time.

Torin thought back to the way he felt when Ari talked about his beard and, before that, his scars. He felt a sense of self-consciousness for both. But why? His entire life as a Jarl, he never cared about what anyone thought of his appearance. Why did he now care what she thought?

Once they arrived at the village, the other Druids noticed the fat animal that was slung over Torin's shoulder and they erupted in a cheer. Cathbad heard the noise and exited his hut and looked down. He smiled, too.

"The mighty duo have returned with dinner!" he hollered loudly so that everyone could hear him. "Start a fire, gather around, and let us eat and enjoy this glorious night!"

Everyone did just that. Songs were sung, dances were had, and laughter could be heard for miles. Everyone was able to eat some of the fatty boar, and Torin and Ari couldn't stop smiling at one another. This newfound friendship was special, at least to the two of them. It was something that Torin had been searching a long time for. A sense of companionship. A sense of belonging. A sense of home.

"Torin!" Cathbad called out, obviously drunk. "Come, I wish to show you something."

Torin gave Ari one last smiling look from across the dancing circle before approaching Cathbad.

"What is it?" he asked.

"See how the bonfire is becoming dim? We need to liven it back up."

"Would you like me to gather more wood?" Torin asked as he examined the bonfire.

"Nonsense!" Cathbad said as he put his arm around Torin's shoulder. He then reached behind his back and pulled something from there. He then showed it to Torin. It was a small gray sack that was held together by some brown string. "I told you I would let you use one later."

"A Teine!" Torin said as he grew visibly happy. He grabbed the Teine from Cathbad's hand and looked at him again. "Are you sure? This is not going to burn anyone, is it?"

"No, of course not!" he said before turning his attention to everyone in the village. "TEINE!" he shouted. Everyone heard him and began running far away, every one of them laughing as they did so.

Cathbad nodded to Torin. The Norseman then grabbed the Teine and felt the sack of herbs and powder in his hand. So much power in such a little bag. He then readied his arm, stepped forward, and threw the Teine inside the dying bonfire. It took about three brief moments before the fire exploded, sending flames high into the air and sparks everywhere else. The forceful wave of heat hit Torin like a wall, and he flew back onto the ground.

He grunted before he glanced up. The bonfire was well lit again. After a long moment, the silence was broken by a wave of cheers from the Druids. Every one of them coming back to the area and dancing like nothing happened.

Torin looked with wide eyes at the power he just wielded. And it was only to give more life to the bonfire. He couldn't imagine what that little bag could do in a battle setting.

Cathbad approached him and smiled.

"Great job, my friend," he said. "How was your first time throwing a Teine?"

"It was absolutely fantastic," Torin replied, a smile from ear to ear.

Later that evening, everyone fell asleep with either dreams of glad tidings in their heads or they were too drunk to dream at all. Torin was inside his hut alone as the small fire pit crackled in the background. He had a silver plate sat up on a wooden table and he looked at himself through it. He felt younger and looked it, too. His fat cheeks were now small enough to show off his cheekbones. The bags under his eyes were non-existent. He quickly pulled his tunic off and looked at his upper body. He was now a mass of chiseled muscle. His shoulders were broad as boulders, his biceps looked like mountains, and his pecs were as defined as they could be.

After admiring himself a bit in the mirror, he focused on all of the scars he had. The ones all over his upper body, from fists and knifes to shields and swords. Then his eyes went back to his face. He looked at the scar where his jaw was broken by the rim of Njal's shield during their duel. It was mostly covered by his beard. He thought back to the feeling of self-consciousness and decided to not shave. That is until he examined his beard a bit more and noticed how matted with dirt and mud it had become. Not even a wash could fix that.

He sighed as he figured his beard would always grow back and pulled out his small knife and watched himself closely in the mirror. He grabbed some of his beard and cut a piece off using the blade of the knife. He continued until he accidentally pricked himself with the blade.

"Shite!" he yelped.

He looked down at the blade and heard the door open behind him. His eyes darted back up into the silver plate mirror, where he could see someone standing behind him. It was a slim woman's naked body. She held scars on her as well. Torin watched her in the mirror get closer and closer to him until he felt her hand touch his cheek and neck from behind. She lifted his chin upwards so that he was looking at her in the eyes as she stood above him.

"Ari," he said.

"Let me," she said with a smile. She grabbed the knife from his hands and began smoothly cutting his beard.

"I do not know if you wish to see the scar hiding beneath my..."

"Shhh," she whispered. "If you keep talking, I might cut you."

He smiled and sealed his lips. He let her finish cutting his beard until it was nothing but a small stubble.

"There," she said, stepping away, admiring her work. "I am done."

He looked at himself in the mirror again and saw the scar in all of its glory. It stretched from the top of his cheek down to his neck and looked like somebody welded his jaw back together.

"I look hideous..." he said.

She wrapped her hands around his shoulders and continued rubbing.

"I think you look strong. You look like a man that looks out for his people. Like a man that fights for what he believes in and does not let anyone tell him otherwise."

She moved herself so that she was facing him. She then sat down on his lap; her legs wrapped around his torso. She felt the scar with her hand and leaned in. Her lips meeting his. Their lips continued to lock until he put his hand behind her neck and pulled her closer. He then grabbed her legs and stood up, carrying her with him as he walked to the bed.

XIII

Those Who Fight Alone

The cold emptiness of the Great Hall was overbearing. No more laughs from Halfdan or the loving embrace from Frigyth. Everyone had gone. Alf and Sigrid were staying together in Demut and Knud was back in Muspel with his people. A few weeks had passed and Njal spiraled into a great depression.

Although the winter months were incoming and the days were shorter, the duration of each day felt long to Njal. The emptiness and pure sadness that he felt at every waking moment was just too much to bear. He spent his days locked inside and stopped showing his face to get even food or water for himself. Nobody had seen him in days. His beard was long, the hair on his head was growing out, and his body felt weak.

Our marriage is over...

Frigyth's words would not stop echoing in his head. Everything he had fought for up until that point felt meaningless without his companions by his side. He hadn't even been able to escape his loneliness and visit the nine realms. After his final meeting with Odin, he had lost the ability to travel there.

Suddenly, a knock at the door took him out of his trance. He looked around as a quick sting of anxiety met his mind. He hadn't had a visitor in quite some time.

"Who is it?" he grumbled under his breath.

The door opened. He didn't even bother to sit up in his throne when Knud entered the room. He was dressed in his black leather armor and with his black and red cloak flapping behind him. His heavy black boots made a loud sound against the floorboards with each step he took as he neared his king.

"Almund is back," he said before stopping close to the throne. "He keeps asking about Gulgruve. Edward is not happy."

"This is the same message you have brought me three times in the last two weeks," Njal replied. "Nothing changed. Tell him to leave us alone."

Knud sighed and pursed his lips at Njal. "I cannot do that."

"Are you disobeying an order?" Njal asked while sitting up in his throne.

"As a matter of fact, I am. I am acting the same way Halfdan would have if he had seen you like this. I gave you time to grieve, but now this is too much."

"What? Too sad to watch me decay in my loneliness and sadness?" Njal mocked. "And if you had not noticed, Halfdan is no longer here."

"No, he is not, and it is time to get over that fact."

"How dare you!" Njal shouted as he shot up out of his throne.

"No!" Knud yelled back, staring his king in the eyes. "How dare you sit on your arse while our people still need their leader! Their king! This is exactly what Torin did, and it turned us into sheep! You taught us how to come back from that. How to rise up and fight for what we believe in. It is an unfortunate fact that Halfdan and Frigyth left your side, but they did. There is no changing the past and you must move forward."

"Your words of wisdom cannot heal the pain that I have felt, Knud. Everyone that I have ever loved has either died or left me. Other than Alf, I am alone in this village."

"Fine," Knud said, annoyed. "But there is somebody here to see you and you best be prepared for the conversation, as it may not be a pleasant one."

"Tell them to piss off, whoever it is!" Njal yelled at Knud as he watched him leave. The Great Hall was silent again for a brief moment until the doors flew open and around eight English soldiers entered, dawning the colors of London. Almund was leading in his armor with another man next to him.

It was King Edward himself.

And he did not look happy.

Njal's eyes widened.

"Edward, what are you doing here?" Njal asked, shocked, as the Englishmen stopped and stared up at the Bear King.

"I am here, because you would not come to me since I had called to you many times before. I am also aware that our alliance goes both ways and since I had you journey to London so many times, I figured it was only fair for me to make the trip here to Eaglecrest. I believe that was the statement you were attempting to make in keeping Gulgruve, yes?"

"The statement I was attempting to make was showing you that we cannot be your lap dogs. We are our own people and we did not trade Aelred for another king that would treat us like slaves."

"You see, that is the problem," Edward said, sounding a bit disappointed. "It was never about that. I would have taken Gulgruve back for my people myself if I had had the proper forces to spare. But I had informed you when you were last in London where my forces were. Besides, I thought we were in an alliance. If you needed men of mine to help you with your cause, I would have done what I could and provided the necessary men for you because that is how alliances work."

"But how was I to know that you would not have just taken advantage of us like that?"

"Was it not you who found me in the north? Was it not you who put your trust in me and gave me back my crown? Was it not you that I let into my home and spoke about all of my weaknesses with? I believed that you had as much trust in me as I had in you. And if you did not trust me fully, then why put the crown back on my head?"

"I…"

"I know some events have occurred that made trusting not one of your strengths, but you need to learn to trust again. I still wish to keep our alliance, but *you* need to decide whether that will happen or not. We must speak about Gulgruve, but I will give you time to think on what I said. I am returning to

London and am giving you one week. If you do not show up by sundown, I will know our alliance is over and we will have no choice but to go to war. Understood?"

Njal didn't like to be threatened. The fire in his heart sparked and began to burn. He began to snarl and show a look of anger. Then, a quick flicker of the Bear in the Land of the Spirits showed in his mind. The surprise of that calmed the fire down in his heart, and he looked up at Edward. He took a moment to speak.

"War will not be necessary. I have been but a fool, Edward," Njal said, shaking his head. The flashes of the Land of the Spirits were painful, and his head began to throb. "Our alliance is still strong. There have been some major changes in my life and I am struggling to keep up with them all. I am sorry. I will see you in London in one week to discuss Gulgruve and its future."

Edward nodded his head, then turned and walked out of the doors of the Great Hall with the rest of his men. Njal grunted and put his hand on his head in an attempt to numb the pain. More flashes of the Bear and more flashes of pain occurring more frequently until... nothing.

Darkness.

Emptiness.

Loneliness.

The sound of birds chirping. The sound of whispering pine trees. The feeling of warmth and peace. The Bear opened its eyes and saw the sun high in the sky. Purple runes floated around him as he peered his head around, examining his surroundings.

The forest's pine trees stood tall and the mountain

range in the distance had strokes of snow blowing off the peaks. The Bear stood up and yawned, its large jowls flapping in the process. He looked in the opposite direction of the mountains and saw the massive branches of a tree reaching high in the sky in the distance. It was very far away, but the Bear could see that its branches were stretching higher in the air than the mountains did. The Bear took off running towards the tree for a better look. He dodged through the forest until he came to a stop at a cliff that overlooked a glade that seemed like it stretched forever. And in the middle of the glade sat the entirety of the giant tree.

"Yggdrasil..." the Bear said to himself.

It heard the caw of a Raven to his right and turned his attention in that direction. He began trotting along the cliff side, trying to hear the cawing again. Closer and closer, the cawing became.

Suddenly, the Bear entered another clearing and saw the Raven perched on a branch. The bird of prey was looking at something else and paid no mind to the Bear. The Bear was confused and approached cautiously.

"HISSSSS..."

The sound of a snake pierced the Bear's ears and sent Njal back to reality.

*

"TORIN!" Njal shouted as he shot out of his throne. "No, no, no!"

With no idea how long he had been away from reality for, he hurried to his bedchamber and began putting his gear on. His black leather armor and his iron bracers and black boots.

Followed by his bear skin cloak as he strapped 'The Call of the King' to his hip.

He jogged out of the room, then out of the Great Hall. The cold, early winter air hit him in the face like a block of ice. He hurried down the slight hill towards the main gates. Everyone he passed was looking at him with wide eyes, as they had not seen their king in some time.

"Where is Knud?!" Njal shouted up to the guards at the gate.

"He is over by the market, sir!" the guard yelled down.

Njal turned and sprinted towards the market and examined everyone in his path. He was searching for Knud's black armor and red cloak. There were so many people out at the market that it was hard to find him. Especially because everyone had turned their attention to Njal.

"KNUD!" Njal yelled. "Where is Knud?!"

He looked around frantically until he heard a voice behind him.

"So, the Bear leaves his cave."

Njal turned quickly and saw Knud standing there behind him with an unimpressed look on his face.

"Knud, we must speak. I..."

"No," Knud interrupted. "What you must do first is explain to your people why you have not showed your face in weeks."

The people in the market had all stopped their shopping and other various activities to watch their king and the Fire Jarl speak.

Njal felt strange at first. Having little to no human

contact for a few weeks and then suddenly having hundreds of eyes glued to him caused his anxiety to increase. However, he knew Knud was right. The people needed to understand what was going on. The rumors they spread and the worrisome theories had run their course. It was time to set the records straight. Njal turned and looked at what seemed like the entire village now before he walked over to one of the tents in the market. He stood on a wooden table so that everyone would be able to see him.

"People of Eaglecrest!" Njal began. "I am sorry for my absence. Things have been a bit hard recently, and I have needed some time to accept it all. Halfdan and Ingrid have left to live on their own. And the queen, Frigyth, well, as you might have already guessed, is no longer your queen. She is following in her father's footsteps and is to become Lord of Birmingham. As I am sure you noticed, King Edward visited us and spoke to me about our alliance. It is still strong, but we may have to give up Gulgruve to keep it that way. I..."

"Like Hel you will!" A voice called out from the crowd. Njal looked around to see who it was until he made eye contact with them. His eyes widened.

"Alf?"

"You are not going to give up Gulgruve! We fought for it; it is only right that we keep it for ourselves!"

A few people in the crowd audibly agreed.

"What is more important, brother, is that we hold our alliance with England. Edward called on us for help, and we can call on him for help if we ever require it."

"You would rather trust those bastards in London

than your own people?" Alf said angrily and even more people verbally agreed with him.

"How would you feel, Alf, if we asked him for help in retaking a land of ours and he took it for himself?"

"He did already! Gulgruve!"

"Gulgruve was not always ours and you know this... We are not even from this land. It was all theirs at one point." Njal was becoming angry now. "Even this beach was theirs."

"So was Norway, but Aelred did not care when he traveled there in an attempt to kill us all."

"I am trying to keep you all alive!" Njal shouted, looking around at everyone. "That was the whole point of fighting against Aelred! How is it that now that we have our wish, everyone wants more? And what would you do, Alf? Go to war with all of England? You sound like a blind fool!"

"I sound like a Norseman! That is what we do! We fight and take and die and end up in the Hall of the Allfather! You sound like a wimpy lap dog of an English king!" He began laughing, and so did a handful of others. "You have been wallowing in your tears inside that Hall of yours while I have been out here helping our people build and train! It is time us Norsemen become whole again!"

"SILENCE!" Njal screamed. "I will not have this. I am your king and you will respect my say, as it is the best for our people. Go back to Sigrid and shut your mouth. I know she is behind this poisoning of your mind with foul thoughts, so why not go back for more? Ever since I began listening to you, my life has become a nightmare. Not anymore. I will do what is best for my people. Not what is best for Sigrid."

Alf squinted his eyes and turned around. He and the handful of people that were cheering all left the crowd of villagers and disappeared.

"I am sorry you all had to witness that," Njal said to everyone else. "Things have been complicated, yes, but I do not wish to throw us back into a violent war. I promised you almost a year ago that if you all fought for your lives against Aelred, we could then enjoy them and live them to the fullest. I plan on keeping that promise. Just believe in me a little longer."

Everyone nodded their heads and cheered a bit for Njal. Alf heard the commotion from a distance and he squinted his eyes.

Njal got off of the desk and walked towards Knud. "I need to speak with you urgently."

"Then let us go to the Great Hall," Knud said with a smile.

*

The two men entered the extensive building and Njal immediately looked at his friend and began speaking.

"You know how I can visit the Land of the Spirits?"

"Aye," Knud said.

"Well, right around the time when both Halfdan and Frigyth left my side, Odin visited me and told me that he no longer trusts that I am the one to keep our people alive. I no longer have his favor and I can no longer walk the Nine Realms."

Knud's eyes widened.

"So, you lost Odin, too," he said sad but Njal continued.

"Well, when I was speaking with Edward, I saw flashes of the Land and when he left, I was thrown back into it. I woke up in a place that I have never seen before. I saw the entirety of Yggdrasil!"

"The World Tree…" Knud said.

"But then something darker happened. I heard the caw of Odin's Raven. I ran to it and it led me to a clearing where he was speaking with someone else. That was when I heard the hiss of a snake and was thrown back into reality."

"A snake?"

"Back when I fought Torin for his crown, I saw images of a Bear fighting a Snake. It meant that he was also in tune with the Land of the Spirits, even if he did not know it. He took the form of a snake!"

"So, that means…"

"Odin is putting his faith in Torin."

"Gods help us…"

"It was prophesied by Odin that my fate was being rewritten. He informed me that I would need to make tough choices and if I chose wrong, my life would spiral out of control."

"Looks like you chose wrong, then," Knud said, stroking his beard.

"I know, and I think it began with Gulgruve."

"Or earlier than that," Knud said.

"How so?"

"Your brother seems to believe he is king now."

"I know what he said out there was unacceptable, but I do not think he believes he is king," Njal said, sounding convinced.

"Njal, he has been informing the people of Demut that Sigrid is the new queen of our people. He has ordered to build a Great Hall there that would be double the size of this one. He and Sigrid have had meetings with those who believe in the old ways late at night about other English villages they could take without stirring up too much trouble."

Njal's head dropped, and he sighed. He wished to ask why Knud had not informed him of this, but he knew why. This was because of his grief and isolation. It caused this. Without anyone to keep Sigrid and her grudge in check, she was going to do whatever she wished, and Alf seemed to be madly in love with her. Therefore, he would follow her anywhere.

"So, perhaps it was Sigrid. Not punishing her allowed her to believe she could get away with everything and anything. My brother was not the problem. It was letting him fall for Sigrid."

"We all watched him poison your mind about Gulgruve. You never would have thought like that. You never would have struck Frigyth or let her and Halfdan go. But I have noticed all the things he is telling you are the things that Sigrid has said openly in the past. He is your kin, but something must be done. Whether it be about her, him, or them both. But something must be done."

Njal took a moment to ponder everything.

"I agree," Njal finally said. "If they keep it up, they could get more of the villagers to join them and then there will be a revolt. I just do not know if I can make the correct decision."

"How do you mean?" Knud asked.

"I did not with Sigrid, I did not with Gulgruve. I have

not been a righteous king the last few months," Njal said, his head down.

"You will make the right choices," Knud said. "I know you will."

"How so?" the king asked.

"Because you have a great heart, Njal Tokeson. And when you listen to it, amazing things can happen. When you listen to others, well, we have seen what can happen. I know he is your own kin, so whatever you do about him, it needs to be because *you* think it right."

"I appreciate that, Knud," Njal said. "Thank you."

Knud nodded his head. "It also seems we now have to worry about Torin returning for vengeance."

"You are right, Knud. Do you have any spies you can spare?"

"Of course. What is it they will be spying on?"

"I need to know if another meeting of Alf and Sigrid's takes place and where. What they are speaking of and whom they are speaking of. I will put a stop to them."

"Done."

"I also need to head to England to discuss with Edward what we will do about Gulgruve."

"And what are we to do about Gulgruve?"

"We are going to give it back to them. In return, I will ask him to widen the borders of Eaglecrest. I wish to have a bit more land. Besides, if we give up Gulgruve, that should help determine if our alliance with England is truly strong and built on trust, or if Edward is really using us."

"Agreed."

"Good, let us begin," Njal said while the fire pit crackled behind him.

XIV

Wolves Hollow

The torches lit up the Druidic village like an oasis in the endless black void of night. Everyone in the clearing was silent besides the soft ringing of some small bells by the witch Elhhere. Each Druid had their face painted either white or red and had streaks of black around their eyes. They were all dawned in ritualistic robes and had their various bones strapped to their limbs.

The Druids began to chant and hum while the Elhhere began ringing the bells a bit faster. They continued this until a man that was facing the opposite direction turned around and stared at the rest of the Druids in the clearing. He was naked, his entire body painted in black and white. His face was clean shaven and his black hair ran down to only his shoulders now. The chanting and humming stopped as the Druids looked at Torin with wide eyes.

He stared in front of him and noticed a man exit

the tall marsh grass. This man was wearing a large deer skull on his face. Massive antlers protruding from the top of the skull. His entire body was covered in animal bones. The man moved forward, passing his fellow Druids until he stood a yard away from Torin.

The Norseman kneeled down and dipped his head.

"Look at me, my friend," the man in the mask said to which Torin did. "It is time for you to move on from your past. Since the time you have arrived, you have trained and learned our ways. You have done all that I have asked and more. You have postponed your revenge for the one who stole your life from you. Now, you enter a new life. One with family and friends. One where your revenge will eventually be had. Forget your Nordic ways of life and enter your new Druidic form. I believe I speak for everyone here when I say that we are proud that you are going to become a member of this family. Your skills and sensitivity to magic will help us prosper and live long lives. From this moment on, Torin 'God-Killer' will be your new name. And as of now, you are a Druid of the Fenlands!"

Everyone began to hoot and holler as Torin got to his feet. He looked through the bone mask and into Cathbad's eyes. He couldn't help but smirk. He felt like he belonged. Elhhere approached Cathbad with a wooden bowl. A dark red liquid was inside. Cathbad grabbed the bowl and dipped three fingers inside without looking away from Torin's gaze. He reached his hand up and spread three lines of the blood down Torin's face.

Cathbad returned the bowl to the Druidic priest and both he and Torin turned towards the rest of the Druids. They raised their hands up and everyone cheered. Torin was now a part of their family. Torin smiled as he locked eyes with Ari, who was standing in the front row of the crowd. She blushed as she smirked at him.

A feast began shortly thereafter in the village's largest hut. Ari and Torin had done some more hunting for the feast earlier that day and brought back three deer and two rabbits. Cathbad had given the rabbit meat to the children and the deer to the adults. More food was given to those who would venture to Wolves Hollow the following day and fight for Ari's revenge.

Among those that were going were obviously Torin and Ari, who were sitting next to one another and smiling from ear to ear. Next up was Daegal, a young Druid with about twenty winters at his back. He was slim and had a bare face with a blond braid on top of his head. He preferred to fight from a distance, as he was very skilled with a bow.

Next to him was Golmac, who had the largest body in the entirety of the Druidic village. His pure mass made him a force to be reckoned with on the battlefield and he used a large hammer to crush his opponent's heads. He had a short temper, so if his opponent dodged his hammer too many times, he would throw it off to the side and just use his hands instead. He was only a few years older than Daegal and his hair was brown and almost always in a ponytail. His large beard stretched down to his sternum.

Finally, there was Camma. The youngest of them all, with only nineteen summers at her back, she was very skinny and very quiet. She had black hair and always had black paint around her eyes. She loved to be stealthy as she preferred to use throwing knives, daggers, and a small steel sword to eliminate her enemies.

She gave off a very intimidating and fearsome energy. Some of the Christians that joined the Druids believed she was a demon from hell that lived among them.

All of them together were to infiltrate Wolves Hollow and kill the head priest and the captain that guarded him. While that was the top priority, the secondary goal was to burn the rest of the village down without killing the civilians, only the guards that tried to stand in their way.

"So, Torin," Golmac said, smiling, his massive hand gripping a cup of mead. "How exactly are we going to get in there to-morrow?"

"Ask Ari," he replied, shrugging. "She has seen the defenses and knows how they patrol there."

"True," Golmac said. "But you are supposed to lead us on this, so we would wish to hear your plan."

"Actually, Ari and I are both leading," Torin said. Ari gave him a look as if to say she wished to know how he would answer the question, so he did. He spoke up a bit so that his companions could hear over the commotion of the feast. "We are going to arrive by the forest that sits a short distance from the village. When night falls, we will then send you, Golmac, towards the dock to cause a distraction. Get the guards' attention and once you have it, start running west towards the woods where Camma and Daegal will be waiting under the cover of darkness where you will silently kill them all. That is when Ari and I will sneak into the church and kill the priest and the captain and anyone else who gets in our way."

"Hm," Golmac mumbled. "I like it."

"Then we can round up the other priests and civilians and

tell them to follow their faith more peacefully or we will find and kill them all," Ari interrupted.

"Then burn their village to the ground?" Daegal asked.

"Then burn their village to the ground," Torin confirmed.

"Cheers to that, friends!" Golmac said while he raised his cup high in the air.

His fellow companions clinked their cups to his and cheered. The rest of the night was followed by everyone enjoying each other's company, especially Torin and Ari, who couldn't keep their hands off one another.

*

Torin awoke the next morning with Ari's head rested upon his bare chest. He looked down at her and laughed when she snored a bit. He began to think about his fate. Everything that had happened in his life that led up to that single moment. He had always known hate and revenge, but being with the Druids and with Ari, it felt like a different saga entirely. Even though he had done horrible things in his life, he felt as though he could change everything with the Druids and become a better man.

He smiled as he began to dose off again until he fell back into a deep slumber. Happy dreams danced around his mind. The feeling of his new life...

CAW!

Torin shot up out of his bed, which frightened Ari.

"Torin! What is it?" she asked, looking at him. He was covered in sweat and was breathing heavily.

"I...I am not sure," he said, trying to catch his breath. "I think I had a nightmare."

"Do you wish to talk about it?"

"I... I do not think I remember what it was."

"Alright well, just take deep breaths," she said, rubbing his bare back. "In and out until you feel better. I am right here."

"Thank you, I think I am alright, Ari," he said as he leaned over to her and kissed her soft lips. "We best get going, anyway."

She nodded, and the two got out of their bed and began to change into their gear. Each piece of brown leather armor they had held little bits of white animal fur protruding from it. They strapped their bones onto themselves and put their respected weapons onto their belts. Torin noticed Ari was securing a very nice Norse knotwork carved hand-axe to her belt.

"Where did you get that one?" he asked, examining it.

"What, this?" she said, gesturing to the axe. "It was my fathers. He won it in a bar game against a Norseman in Birmingham when I was young."

"A Norseman was allowed to play games in Birmingham?"

"Well, yeah," she said. "He used to do favors for people in Birmingham and Lord Birstain gave him his own alehouse. His name was Ivar, but most people called him Axe."

Torin's eyes widened, but he kept his tongue quiet. His mind filled with the image of him lodging his own hand-axe into Ivar's neck back in the Great Hall in Eaglecrest. The world was so big and yet at times, felt so incredibly small. Torin pushed the thought back into the depths of his mind and smiled again at Ari.

"I like it," he said. "So, since you are using that, can I borrow your silver blade?"

Ari looked at him with a smile. "What, not a fan of the bone sword?"

"No, no, I just prefer a heavier and sharper weapon."

"Of course you can," she said before she approached him. She put her hands on his shoulders and kissed him on the lips. "I am more of an axe girl, anyway."

"My thanks, Ari," Torin said.

"Now, let us go avenge Fionn," she said.

"Let us achieve your revenge, Ari," he replied.

The two of them, now fully equipped in their gear, left their hut and descended the stairs. There, the other three comrades stood, checking their gear and equipment. They were all in similar gear except for Camma. She had on black leather armor and painted her entire face with black paint and even colored her bones black. She looked extremely intimidating. Like a shadow itself, even in the morning sunlight.

"Everyone ready to go?" Torin asked with a smile.

"Absolutely!" Golmac said. "I cannot wait to pop some heads!"

"You oaf," Daegal chuckled. "You are only meant to cause a distraction, remember?"

"Eh, you know how plans go. They often never go the way they are planned!"

Daegal rolled his eyes.

"Alright, Cathbad should be down by the river with our boat," Ari said. "Let us go see him."

The rest of them nodded in agreement and began to make their way towards the river, which was about a good mile away from the village. The walk there was pretty boring. Torin grabbed Ari's hand and held it close to which Daegal sighed and rolled his eyes again.

Daegal and Ari had become members of the Druids around the same time. He was found by them when he was young, too. Cathbad had found the boy sitting under a dead tree where the rest of his family was hung on each limb. He had felt so disgusted that he asked the boy who had done that and the boy had said the butcher in the village of East Pire. Cathbad took the boy, traveled there, and killed everyone while leaving the butcher alive. That is when he beat the butcher and let the boy slide his blade across the burley man's throat.

Daegal grew up with Ari and tried to make a move on her multiple times to which she ignored or completely rejected. They have, however, remained good friends and always wished the best for one another.

"There they are!" Cathbad said as he saw the companions coming towards him. "I got your boat all ready to go."

"My thanks, good friend," Torin said with a smile. The rest of the group began throwing their equipment and other things into the boat while Torin stood by Cathbad.

"Please, try to bring that boat back in one piece," he said. "Last time I let this group go wild, they returned with holes and arrows all over it, and it is very hard for me to get boats."

"I will do my best," Torin said, laughing. "Alright, gang, let us get to it, yeah?"

He shook Cathbad's hand one last time before they all entered the boat and began to make their way downriver towards the village of Wolves Hollow.

Towards their revenge.

*

The small vessel was floating down the river steadily for the entirety of the day. The majority of it was nice. Rays of sunshine and a pleasant breeze allowed for an easy passage down the river. However, an enormous wall of fog rolled in around dusk, which didn't allow for much visibility on either side of the river. The songs and small conversations between the companions turned to silence as the breeze turned to a chill. While the world was calm and quiet, the companions began to check their surroundings, as the fog could be a brilliant cover for an ambush of any kind. Not by the guards or people of Wolves Hollow, but by any bandits or others that may wish to check the boat for silver and gold.

"Where in god's name did all of this fog come from?" Daegal asked quietly. "Ari, are we almost there?"

"We still have a bit to go," she replied.

"Well, I do not like this much," Golmac said, attempting to make out the edges of the river. "The world is so..."

"Quiet," Camma mumbled. It caught the look of everyone on the boat, as she didn't ever say much.

"What is it?" Ari asked, knowing that Camma only speaks when it's important.

"I feel something..." she said in a tone that actually sent chills down Torin's spine.

"Like what?" Daegal asked. "Something here?"

"No," she replied. "On its way."

"What does that even mean?" Golmac asked.

"Stay quiet," Torin commanded. "Listen."

They all sat still. The only sound they could hear

was the steady water beneath them being divided by the slow-moving boat. The sun finally set, which made the sky a dim blue and the fog a bright white. It became harder and harder to see as each moment passed by.

"I saw something!" Golmac shouted. "There! In the fog!"

"Quiet you damned fool!" Daegal shouted as they all looked towards Golmac. "You are going to get us all killed."

"What did you see?" Ari asked.

"A shadow! Right over there!"

They all examined where he was pointing, but they didn't see anything.

"Alright, everyone, let us just calm ourselves," Daegal said. "It could be a bird for all we know."

"It was not..." Camma said.

"Then, Camma, please inform us what this mysterious force is that is haunting our vessel and explain why anyone out here would even want to kill us!"

Torin rolled his eyes. Daegal was starting to get on his nerves.

"Has Cathbad ever told you about the other Druidic clan from Ireland?" she asked.

"The one that he escaped from?" Ari asked.

"Aye," Camma replied. "The thing he never tells anyone is that they still hunt for him. Sometimes they..."

"There it was again!" Golmac yelled.

"You damned idiot! You are going to get us all killed!" Daegal said, slapping Golmac on the back of the head. "I swear I am going..."

Torin growled and whipped his hand around Daegal's throat and threw him down onto his back. The boat rocked back and forth due to the force. He pulled his bone knife out and placed it upon Daegal's throat.

"If I hear one more thing about Golmac come out of your mouth, I will rip you apart and feed you to whatever is hiding in this fog. Do you understand me?"

Daegal's eyes widened as he stared into the rageful eyes that looked back into his.

"Alright... I understand..." he whimpered.

Torin let go of Daegal and sat back down. Everyone stared at him. He was so angry and then, in a split second, so calm. Torin saw the eyes that looked at him and he decided to speak.

"If we fight each other, we are not strong," he began. "If there truly is something hiding in this fog, we need to keep our eyes open on the enemy, not each other. Understand?"

Everyone nodded their heads. Torin gave Golmac a wink. He understood Golmac as a man. A man that would never hurt nor lay a harmful hand on the ones he called family. But if someone were to mess with his family, he had every physical attribute to crush them. He wasn't the sharpest sword in the armory, sure, but he didn't need to be smart and Torin saw that. Golmac was an arrow that he could aim. So, he found it best to keep his spirits high and his mind clear.

"Camma, do you really think it is the other Druids?" Torin asked, changing the subject.

"Hm," she nodded.

"I wonder why they would be all the way out here?" Golmac asked.

"Wolves Hollow does sit on the river. And this river stretches all the way to the north coast. It is possible they could just be following it," Ari said.

"Well, with it getting as dark as it is and with this fog, they cannot see us just as much as we cannot see them," Torin said. "We need to stay quiet. Everyone, if you see anymore shadows, snap your fingers once."

They all nodded their heads and sat still. The Druids readied their respective weapons and watched from all angles.

Calm.

Quiet.

Peaceful.

The next few moments were nothing but that. That is until...

Snap

Torin looked towards Camma.

Snap

Torin turned back towards Golmac.

Snap

He looked at Ari. He then also saw a shadow in the fog.

"Steady," Torin whispered. Nightfall was gripping the world in its clutches now, only offering a dark blue hue of light. Torin closed his eyes and listened intently to the world. To every little bit of water beneath them. Every brief call from an animal or insect in the distance. Every little whisper of wind. Every little footstep of somebody running straight for them then leaping off the side of the river bank.

Torin whipped himself around, swinging his sword, slicing through the person's torso in midair. The person's two halves, blood, and innards plopped into the river, making a loud sound. At that moment, shadows showed themselves on both sides of the river bank, all holding weapons. Some jumped into the river and charged after the boat from all sides.

Daegal struck first as he launched an arrow from his bow, killing one attacker. Ari used her hand-axe and lodged the lethal end into another man's skull. Camma stood up in the boat and began throwing her knives into the bodies of the men.

Torin looked around at the attackers for any sort of information about who they were based on their clothing. From what he could make out in the dim light and fog, they wore black clothing, masks made from skulls, and the collars of their armor was lined with large black feathers.

It appeared that Camma was right. The attackers looked like Druids.

An arrow flew right past Ari's head and lodged itself in the back of the boat.

"Daegal! Shoot the archers on the bank!" Torin shouted.

He did just that. He began releasing arrow after arrow at the men. Golmac stood up and gripped his giant hammer. He saw a feathered Druid approaching in the river to which Golmac waited until the last second and swung his hammer, taking the Druid's head clean off.

Suddenly, a Druid shot up from the side of the boat, grabbed Ari with both hands, and pulled her down into the water with him.

"Ari!" Torin shouted before leaping off the side of the

boat after her. He continued towards the shallow area of the river where he gripped his sword tightly and noticed two Druids in front of him. Torin dodged one of their swings and swiped their leg with his own sword, cutting it off. He readied his sword for the next Druid and swung it. His opponent met his blade with his own and the two began fighting. Torin swung his sword in different ways, but the Druid blocked them all.

The Druid then grabbed Torin's hand, stopping his attack, and swiped Torin's leg out from under him using the back of his sword. Torin splashed around in the water attempting to get to his feet, but his opponent was too fast and jumped on him, attempting to keep him under water.

As the Druid kept Torin submerged under the water, his mind raced. He thought about his life as he struggled to breathe. As each moment passed, he felt weaker and weaker. The world around him grew dark.

CAW!

Suddenly, Torin's eyes opened under water and he grabbed the man's hands and pulled them off him. He stood up slowly and looked at the Druid in his eyes. He roared loudly and proceeded to bite the Druid's jugular and pulled it off. Blood sprayed everywhere as Torin threw the Druid down, splashing into the river. He spit the man's jugular into the water.

"FUCK YOU!" he roared at the lifeless body.

He looked up to try and see Ari, but he couldn't see anything. It had become dark now. He could hear the shouting of his companions on the boat behind him as they continued to fight. Torin closed his eyes again and calmed his mind. He was able to push the sound of his companions fighting behind him out of his head and focus on light splashing in front of him. He opened his eyes and continued straight.

Ari was being dragged by a Druid in the river. Every time she tried to fight back; another Druid that was there would punch her in the face. They brought her to the river bank and threw her down onto her back. She tried to get up but was met with a fist, knocking her back down, dazed. They both looked at her and smiled.

Suddenly, the blade of a sword exploded through one of the Druid's faces. The sword was pulled back and swiped across the other one's neck, almost to the bone. The two fell to the ground and showcased a bloodied and dripping wet Torin behind them. He kneeled down and put his hand behind Ari's head.

"Are you alright?" he asked.

She nodded and smiled through the pain. "Yeah, they hit like a pair of sissies." He smiled and helped her to her feet. "We need to get back to the boat. They might need us."

"I know, let us go," Torin said.

The two of them ran alongside the river bank as it was faster than running back into the water. They could hear a commotion in the distance. More fighting and shouting. The pair continued until, judging by how close the shouting was, they were upon their friends.

"I cannot see anything!" Golmac shouted.

"None of us can, you idiot!" Daegal yelled back.

The last two Druids jumped out of the water and onto the boat. They stood there with their weapons ready on one side while the other three companions stood on the other side.

"What is it you want from us?" Daegal asked.

"Cathbad is to return to us and face the consequences for his actions," one of the Druids said in a hissing tone.

"That is not going to happen," Daegal replied, readying his weapon.

"Well, he will just have to mourn you then," the feathered Druid said.

Right before they all clashed, hands popped out of the water, grabbing the two Druids legs. They were then pulled down into the river to which both Torin and Ari used their weapons to slice their throats. After they were done, they climbed back onto the boat, breathing heavily.

"Well, that was eventful!" Daegal laughed before being punched hard in the face by Torin.

"What the fuck did I tell you?" Torin shouted, adrenaline obviously pumping through his veins. "Just because I was not here, that gives you the right to call your brother in arms an idiot?"

"I... I am sorry," Daegal sputtered.

"Sorry is not *good* enough!" Torin yelled. "Next time I hear you call him, or anyone of us idiots or any other name that is not our own, I will personally stab you and watch the lifeblood pour out from the wound and wrap itself around my blade."

Daegal nodded and Torin got off of him. He went and sat down on the other side of the boat with Ari. Everyone stayed quiet after that. The boat kept moving down the river as bodies of Druids floated in the water behind them.

"We will speak to Cathbad when we return home," Torin said. "As of now, let us stay focused on Wolves Hollow."

*

"We are here," Ari said as she could see the mass glow of torches trying to shine through the dense fog in the distance.

"Good," Torin replied. "Let us make shore by those trees over there. I am assuming that is the forest just before Wolves Hollow, so not only are we closer to our target, but it also allows for suitable cover."

Camma and Golmac reached down and grabbed two small oars and began rowing. The boat turned until it made landfall underneath some willow trees by the water. The group stayed quiet as they all grabbed their gear and exited the boat. Torin got to the entrance of the forest first and waited for everyone to join him. Ari was next. She smiled and grabbed Torin's hand as they awaited the others.

"Are you ready?" he asked as he smiled.

"Of course," she said. "But I wanted to ask; do you think you should maybe take it a little easy on Daegal? I mean, I agree he needs to be humbled, but I do not know if someone should be killed for that."

"Ari, when one of your shield mates acts as though they are better than you, that can cause mistrust, which can lead to death for everyone. By acting as though he is the leader, Daegal puts us in danger of failing this mission. Or even worse, leads us all to an early death. I believe that those who act that way must be punished. And if they continue to act that way, should be killed which may actually *save* lives."

Ari nodded her head but inside, she was offput by that. She felt a little strange. But once the other three made their way to them, that feeling subsided.

"Alright, remember the plan," Torin began. "Golmac will sneak to the docks, cause a distraction and lead the guards that follow to this here forest. That is where Camma and Daegal will be waiting to dispatch them all. While all of this is happening, Ari and I will head up towards the temple and kill any who stand in our way. Once we are all done, you three will meet up with us at the top by the temple. There, we can make a decision on what to do about the rest of the village."

"My vote is to burn it to the ground," Golmac shrugged. "I mean, from what Ari told us, these people are not even real Christians."

"Well, what they believe they are doing is an act of god. But I had a little read of their Holy book and nothing in it says they should burn women alive due to a marking of another religion," Ari said.

"You can read?" Golmac asked.

She laughed and nudged his arm.

"Alright, let us get to work," Torin said before taking one last look at the group. "See you three at the temple."

The two groups went their separate ways. Torin and Ari headed to the right towards the top of the village where the temple stood. Camma, Daegal, and Golmac went straight and followed the river towards the lower section of the village by the docks, where Golmac would make his move.

With them being alone now, Torin and Ari could have a private conversation.

"We do not have much time before dawn," Ari started. "Those Druids slowed us down."

"I am itching to speak to Cathbad about that," Torin

said. "I doubt they are going to stop their search anytime soon. Especially because we did not have enough time to clean up the river of their dead. The rest of them will come upon the mess we made."

Ari felt a bit strange at that. Cleaning up the battle-field? Hiding dead? With that thought being in his mind, it had meant he had done that before. With whom exactly was the question. But after a few moments, she brushed it off again.

"I would like to be present for that conversation," she said.

"Of course," Torin replied as he led her through the trees. The fog was so dense it felt like walking through a wall of mist.

"Do you think they will be fine down there by themselves?"

"I do not know, Ari, they are your friends," Torin said monotone.

"I trust them. I just wish to know your thoughts on them."

A light rain began to patter against the surrounding forest. Torin stayed a bit quiet for a moment and sighed.

"I like Golmac and Camma. Daegal is not showing he can be reliable, even though his skill with a bow is quite impressive."

Ari nodded her head and decided to change the subject. "We can use this rain to our advantage, no?"

"That was my plan. I do not know how Golmac is going to distract the guards, but I hope he is smart enough to not use the lanterns and torches in the rain."

The two of them continued on their path towards the temple, which sat on the hill above the rest of the village. Down by the docks, their companions began their part of the plan.

*

"Alright, so how are you going to distract them, Golmac?" Daegal asked. "I think we should discuss it before you go out there with your pants down and fling your cock around."

"I will use one of their torches to light some of their boats on fire," Golmac said. He was eyeing the lanterns that were hung on the buildings and wooden posts that surrounded the dock.

"Bad idea," Camma said, looking up into the foggy night sky.

"And why is that?" Daegal asked.

"Rain is coming. Can you not smell it?"

Daegal sniffed in the night air and looked at her like she was crazy. "No, I only smell that of a dead animal somewhere in these woods. Oh, wait, that is just Golmac."

"Hey, do not make me call for Torin," Golmac chuckled.

Daegal put his head down and snarled a bit before spitting. "Fine, I agree. I say we use fire, Golmac."

Camma shrugged her shoulders.

Suddenly, muted voices could be heard approaching the docks. Daegal thumped his chest, to which Golmac and Camma both dropped into a crouch. After a brief moment, they noticed three guards dressed in leather and iron armor and white and red cloaks that flowed behind them. The guards all had large silver swords strapped to their leather belts. They were all talking about the head priest, but the Druids couldn't hear exactly what.

Daegal turned and looked at his companions.

"Alright, Golmac, there are lanterns lined up on those posts. We can throw something in the water and turn their attention to the river and that will allow you to..." he stopped as the sound of rain patting against the wooden boards of the dock struck his eardrums. He turned towards Camma, who shrugged her shoulders again. Daegal rolled his eyes and looked back at Golmac. "On second thought, how about we just kill them?"

Daegal stood to his feet and readied his bow. He pulled an arrow out from the quiver on his back and loaded it. "When I say, Golmac, run in there and kill the last one."

"But there are three of them," Golmac said.

"Exactly," Daegal smiled. He pointed the arrow at the furthest guard. He inhaled and held his breath for a brief moment before exhaling and releasing the arrow. "Now," he whispered as the arrow traveled so quickly through the air that it went straight through the guard's neck and out the other side. The guard grabbed his leaking neck as he fell to his knees and then down onto his back. Daegal made sure there was enough time that the other guards would see it, then call for help so that the temple would be unguarded. That's exactly what happened as he loaded another arrow and aimed it at the guard, who began the call for help.

"HELP! We need help down by the docks! We are under..."

The guard's voice stopped as an arrow went straight through his mouth and out the other side. The last guard looked around quickly and saw a large bumbling man running straight out of the woods with a hammer in hand and a deer skull as a mask. The guard readied his sword and swung diagonally. Golmac dodged shockingly quick for a big man and swung his hammer over his head, coming down on the guard's head, exploding it like a melon.

An arrow flew right past Golmac's head, and he looked up towards the temple where a few other guards were running down the hill. The large man turned towards the forest where Daegal and Camma were waiting in the darkness and took off in that direction.

The guards were not far behind and chased after him through the tree line of the forest. The misty rain made it hard for them to see or hear. They began to slow down, as they couldn't find the large man anywhere. The five guards kept trying to see within the darkness until one of them collapsed.

They all turned their attention to their fallen comrade and noticed he had a small knife sticking out of the side of his head. One of the guards tried to yell when he was cut short by a knife being thrown through the air and striking him in the throat.

Another guard was struck with an arrow straight in the head. Golmac appeared out of nowhere and swung his hammer sideways at another guard, snapping the man's neck. Camma jumped out of the shadows like a demon dressed in all black. She grabbed the guard's hair from behind, pulled his head back, and slid her knife across his neck, killing him.

The three Druids stood there and looked at each other.

"Good work, everyone," Daegal said. "Now, we just have to..."

He was interrupted as the sound of church bells struck their eardrums. They all turned their attention towards the temple.

*

Torin and Ari sat still in the cover of the tree line as they watched three guards run towards the docks. Ari looked at Torin and smiled. The temple was in sight and now there were no more guards to stop the two from reaching it. Torin examined the height of the temple in awe for a moment before returning to reality. The building had a large high reaching tower, and the steeple was just as tall. A large cross sat on top.

"Alright, let us go," Torin said as he pulled his sword from its sheathe, the ringing echoing softly. He crouch-walked his way out of the forest and into the light of the lanterns. Onto the stone pathway that led to the church.

Ari was close behind, holding her knotwork carved hand-axe tightly. The two of them continued until they reached the massive wooden and black iron lined front doors of the building.

Torin looked at Ari one more time, to which she smiled and said, "For Fionn."

"For Fionn," he replied.

They both pushed open the doors, which creaked continuously until they were all the way open, showcasing the interior of the temple. Inside, pews were lined up alongside a long stretching red carpet that let to the altar. Candles were lit up at different tables throughout the large room. Giant banners with crosses hung from the stone walls.

Standing at the altar was a thin, bald man wearing a brown robe with a wooden cross at his neck. He was talking to another man in similar attire. Both priests quickly looked towards the entrance.

"Is that him?" Torin asked, pointing the tip of his sword at the man standing upon the altar.

"Aye," Ari said before meeting the priest's gaze. "Hey! Remember me?"

"You blasphemous she-demon!" the man called down. "What is the meaning of this? Where are my guards?" His eyes widened, and he began to look around frantically. "Guards! Guards!"

"Quit your squealing," Torin shouted. "Your guards are occupied at the moment. Besides, we only wish to have a little talk."

The two of them began to walk forward towards the altar. The other priest attempted to leave, but Torin grunted a sound and pointed his sword at him, which stopped the priest in his tracks.

The Druids both stopped at the foot of the stairs that led to the altar and looked up at the two bald men for a moment before speaking.

"Remember that woman that you killed for having a marking? Well, she was my friend," Ari began.

"I know she was your friend. I remember how much you screamed and cried when she was sent to hell."

Ari gritted her teeth but stayed calm.

"This is a Christian priest?" Torin asked before

chuckling. "I have met some Christians before and they do not act like this! This is laughable to me."

"WHAT DO YOU KNOW OF THE CHRISTIAN FAITH, HEATHEN!"

"Well, for starters, I know that your god does not wish for you to burn people alive just for a simple tattoo."

"A tattoo of *your* faith!" the head priest yelled.

"Are people not allowed to change? Can they not be converted? Is that not what your god actually *wishes* for you to do?" Torin asked. "I am starting to believe that you all just use your 'faith' to do whatever you please."

"Our god, heathen, has specifically called onto me to show the people of this valley that they can find solace in god's teachings," the priest said. His pride was unmatched. "He speaks to me and tells me that only I can save these people. That only I have the power to save us all!"

"And when did you make all of that up? Was it just a random thought? Was it in a dream? Or...?" Torin said, smirking.

Ari let out a slight laugh.

"I will hear no more of this!" the head priest roared. "Go fetch the captain!"

The other priest didn't hesitate as he attempted to run down the stairs right by the Druids. However, Torin immediately stuck his sword out and pierced the chest of the priest. He stared into the poor man's eyes as blood began to stream out of his mouth. The Norseman smiled and pulled his sword out with a crunch, dropping the man dead in front of him.

"You monstrous h..."

"I know how you spend your time 'worshiping' here,"

Ari began. "Raping women and beating the townsfolk for any money they have left. You are thugs that do not deserve the power you hold. God does not want that. In fact, I am sure he will thank us for ridding the world of you."

"You disgusting bitch!" the priest yelled.

"You pathetic little man-child," Ari replied calmly. "Fionn was a kind girl. We were sent here to see what kind of Christians you were. Would you be the kind to worship in peace and we gladly leave alone? Or would you be the kind that use god as an excuse to do whatever you wish? Those are the ones that have caused problems for my people in the past. We do not like them very much."

Ari gripped her hand-axe tightly and readied for an attack.

Suddenly, Torin felt a painful sensation at his side and he began flying through the air and crashing into some pews in a cloud of splinters and dust. Ari quickly turned around and saw a large man, a few heads taller than Torin, wearing gold plated armor and a feather on his helm. He was holding a large hammer. He grabbed her by the neck and began lifting her high in the air. She tried to break free, blasting her forearms against his, but to no avail.

"What exactly did you think was going to happen, you filthy whore?" the captain asked behind his gold-plated helm. "You thought you could just walk in here and kill my employer without any trouble?"

"A little bit... yeah," Ari struggled to say.

A silver blade grated past the captain's side, causing sparks to fly. The large man didn't even have to look to know that Torin had gotten up and tried to attack from behind. But thanks to his golden armor plating, he remained unharmed.

Torin had never seen armor like this. He was used to the lighter leather armors, but not this. The gold plates of the captain's armor covered up practically every inch of the man.

The captain turned around quickly, using Ari as a weapon as he launched her into Torin, and the two of them flew back into some more pews, breaking them.

"Fuckin' pathetic, the lot of you!" the captain laughed. He turned back towards the priest and whispered. "Get out of here. I can handle them."

Torin was getting to his feet as he looked over at Ari.

"Are you alright?" he asked her.

"Aye," she grunted, holding her neck, which was red. She looked up towards the captain and saw the head priest running out the back door of the temple. "Shit! We cannot let him get away."

"Listen, this man cannot cover the entirety of this place. I will go to one side of the church and you the other. He will naturally come to me and let you go after that bastard."

"Why do you think he will go towards you?" Ari asked, gripping her hand-axe.

"Just look at the bastard. He is big and dumb and will probably think I am more of a threat to the man that pays him than you. Even though we both know it is about even," Torin laughed as he gripped his sword tighter. The sound of the church bells struck Wolves Hollow like crackling thunder.

Must be the priest.

"You think you can take him on alone?" Ari asked.

"Aye," he replied. "I know I am not fated to die today."

"I will see you when this is over then," Ari said, smiling before leaping into action. She took the left side of the church while Torin went to the right. Just as he had said, the captain turned his attention towards Torin without hesitation.

Torin watched the large man walk at a quick pace but was able to see Ari make it to the back door and exit the room, following where the head priest had just gone.

"Just you and me then, you thick headed bastard," Torin growled.

The captain roared and swung his large hammer over his head. Torin jumped out of the way as the hammer met a pew behind him, smashing it into a pile of splinters. The Druid rolled quickly so that he was behind the captain and swung his sword diagonally. But just as before, his blade slid itself off the armor plating, creating a shower of sparks. The captain quickly swung the back of his hand upwards, catching Torin right in the jaw, sending him flying onto his back.

The captain walked over as Torin tried to catch his breath and readied his hammer for another strike. Torin's eyes widened as the head of the hammer came swinging down, looking for a killing blow. But he worked up enough gumption to roll away as he felt the hammer meet the floor next to him where he was previously laying. He then shot up and swung his sword sideways, attempting to cut the captain's throat, but to no results, as there was armor plating there too.

"Shit," Torin mumbled under his breath before he realized the captain's hammer's head was stuck in the wooden floorboards of the church. His eyes lit up with hope. He sheathed his sword quickly and took a few steps back. That's when he charged at the captain, who was attempting to free his hammer. He jumped up and drop-kicked the captain in his chest, pushing him away from his hammer and leaving him a little dazed. Torin noticed the golden-mail under his arms and realized that's where he could strike true. Sure enough, he jumped to his feet quickly and gripped the hilt of his sword. In one swift motion, he pulled it out and stabbed upwards into the armpit of the captain.

Torin quickly pulled his sword out and watched the blood spray out from the giant man. The captain tried to swing a few more times at the Druid before falling to his knees. Torin then grabbed the man's helm and ripped it off, showcasing an older, green-eyed man with red hair. The man looked up into his opponent's eyes with sadness.

"Hm, figured a man with your size and confidence to look much more mighty," Torin said as he placed the tip of his sword at the captain's Adam's apple. "But no, just another pathetic aresling to add to my endless list of those I send to the Soul Road."

Torin punched his silver blade forward, running it through and out the back of the captain's neck. The man's eyes widened as his life came to an end. Torin pulled his blade out and kicked the man's body to the ground with a loud thud.

"Now burn in your hell."

*

Ari busted through the back door of the temple, her brow sweating. Her eyes were examining every turn the head priest could have gone on that cold, rainy night in Wolves Hollow. When she couldn't find him, she cursed herself, then looked down. She noticed the cobblestone path went only one way, down towards the rest of the village and the docks. There was also a muddy path that went in the other direction, but to where it would lead, she didn't know. She examined the mud to see if she could make out any tracks, especially recent ones that looked as though a man was running through the mud. She couldn't make anything out other than some old horse tracks along with a donkey and maybe a dog or two.

"So, you went down to try and find your guards then," Ari whispered to herself. She then took off running down the cobblestone path. She peered into every open window of every house she passed by on her way down.

As she came into full view of the rest of the village, including the docks, from the top of the hill where she stood, she didn't see anything. Not even her companions and the distraction they were supposed to create. However, no guards could be seen, therefore she trusted that her friends got the job done.

Ari squinted her eyes as she tried to examine the houses that surrounded her, to see if any lanterns or candle lights were on inside. She also tried to listen over the sound of the misty rain to hear any commotion in the houses. She slowly walked through the street, but couldn't hear anything. As she walked by one home, however, her eyes caught somebody looking behind the animal pelt that was strung in front of their window, acting as cover from the rain.

It was a woman, shivering cold and featuring a black eye. Her other eye was wide as she stared at Ari with fear. Or was it salvation?

"I am not going to hurt you," Ari said softly but still gripping her hand-axe. "I only want the priest."

The woman nodded and pointed with her finger at the house that was opposite of hers. Ari turned her head to look at the home, which didn't have any candles, torches, or lanterns on. Ari smiled as she turned back towards the woman in the home.

"You have my thanks. Do not worry, you are free now. You can do as you please. Leave this village or stay and make it a better one. Either way, you are free."

The woman mouthed the words 'thank you' as she watched in awe as Ari turned her attention towards the other house. The woman stared as Ari used her shoulder to break in the wooden door and enter, fading into the darkness of the home.

Once inside, Ari looked around, her defenses up, hand-axe ready to strike.

"I know you are in here, you limey bastard!" she shouted. "Come out and face me! You had no problem dragging me and Fionn through your streets. Your true self was shown that day! Why hide now?"

Moments of silence followed by some noises of a struggle upstairs in the attic. Ari rushed up the stairs until she was met with the sight of the priest. He was hiding behind a young woman, his knife graced upon her throat. The woman was crying as she looked down where a young man, presumably her husband, was grunting and holding his stomach, which was leaking blood onto the floor.

"Stop!" the priest screamed; snot bubbled out of his nose. "Not another step or I kill her!"

Ari stopped her charge and considered all of her options.

"Really? You would take shelter from these people and then attack them? God, you are pathetic," Ari said, shaking her head.

"I SWEAR IT!" the priest bellowed as he tightened his grip on the knife. The woman yelped as the blade cut her neck a bit. A dot of blood seeped out.

"Alright," Ari said, realizing she couldn't mess around. "What can I do so that you leave these people alone?"

"You put down your weapon and... and you leave, leave this village! Then and *only* then will I release this woman and her husband!"

"Listen, this man will not last much longer. You stabbed him pretty good. He needs a healer now. If you truly value god and his teachings, you will stop this nonsense and help me help them," Ari said, dropping her arm from attack position.

"Fuck off!" the priest screamed.

Ari closed her eyes in anger. The priest valued his life more than anything. She wished that she was wrong, at least a little, in thinking he wasn't a man of god. But this proved that she was right. There wasn't much she could do for the young couple because the priest needed to die. She couldn't leave and allow him to do the same thing over again to even more people. The Druidic way of life had taught her that revenge was what was important. By killing the priest, even if he killed the young couple, she would be avenging them as well and saving everyone else in the village.

"If you kill that woman, there will be absolutely

nothing left to stop me from lodging my hand-axe deep into your skull, sending you to hell," she said as she readied her weapon. She then looked at the woman and gave her a look of sincerity. "I will avenge you. I promise."

The woman began to cry but nodded her head as she started mumbling a prayer.

Ari took one step forward.

"Stop it!" the priest yelled.

"Why? I have nothing left. You have taken all that I have left," Ari said while looking at the woman. "You have taken everything that everyone has left to spare here. And you need to die."

The woman looked at Ari and stopped praying as she began to realize. Ari took another step before setting her feet. One forward and one back. Her hand-axe in prime position.

"I only did as god commanded!"

"You can keep telling yourself that falsehood," Ari said. "NOW!"

The woman quickly moved her head to her left, to which Ari stepped into her throw as she released the hand-axe from her hand. The weapon took no time reaching its target as it blew through the air and the lethal end crunched itself in the priest's face. The force was so great that it launched him backwards and out the window behind him and onto the cobblestone street below with a plop.

The woman instantly ran over to her husband, who was bleeding out. She looked up at Ari with a trickle of blood coming down her neck.

"Thank you," the woman said, crying. "Can you please help him?"

"I will do my best," Ari replied.

*

Torin exited the temple and began walking the cobblestone path until he was able to see the silhouettes of three different shaped figures. He knew it was his fellow Druidic companions.

"Damn," Golmac said when he could make out Torin, who was bruised and a little bloody. "Good fight?"

Torin nodded his head.

"Where is Ari?" Daegal asked, which immediately got a hard and stern look from Torin.

"She went after the priest. Let us look around."

The three of them began walking through the cobblestone streets looking for any sign of their companion or her bald adversary. It wasn't long before Golmac shouted for everyone to meet up at his location. When they all arrived, they noticed the body of the priest on the ground with Ari's hand-axe lodged in his skull. They then heard the sound of a man screaming in pain, which caused their eyes to shoot upwards towards the attic of the home they were beside.

Without any hesitation, Torin blasted through the doors of the home and charged upstairs with every intention of helping kill whoever Ari was fighting. Once he reached the attic, he had his sword raised and ready to strike until he realized what he was looking at.

"Torin! I need your help," Ari shouted as she pressed her hands on the abdomen wound of a man who was laying down, screaming in pain. The man's wife was kneeling next to him, tears streaming out of her eyes. "The priest had stabbed this man," Ari said as she watched Torin sheathe his sword and approach them.

Torin examined the wound for a moment before he looked at Ari. He shook his head, to which Ari dropped hers. The woman grabbed Torin by the collar and began begging.

"Help him! Help my husband, please!"

"I am sorry, the wound is too deep. If we try to take him anywhere, he will bleed out within the moment. If he stays here, we can at least offer you a goodbye," Torin said, surprisingly soft-spoken.

Ari's prior concerns about him were put aside when she noticed his compassion towards the couple. She looked down at the man once more and noticed his life was fading away. His head slumped back and his eyes stared straight up at the ceiling.

Torin looked down, then back to the woman. "You should speak swiftly..."

The woman cried even harder as she grabbed her husband's hands and looked at him in the eyes. "I am so sorry I could not be stronger for you," she said while getting choked up. "Please know that I love you... Forever and always."

Ari and Torin both dropped their heads in sadness... pain. Saying goodbye was no stranger to them. Watching somebody else say it was almost as painful. They knew of the years to come after of trying to find a new purpose. A new reason for existing.

The man coughed; his skin was as white as snow.

"You are my life," he coughed again, blood trickled down his mouth. "I will see you soon. I love... I love y..."

The man's body went lifeless.

"No, no!" the woman screamed. Torin grabbed her and held her in his arms. She gripped onto him and unleashed the pain of her loss on the entire village of Wolves Hollow. Ari sat there in sadness over the incident.

The companions looked at each other from down below and dropped their heads in honor. It was unspoken, but understood by everyone that there would be no burning of the village. It was clear now that the people there were hostages of a false promise. Hostages that were now free.

The woman's screams of loss haunted the surrounding forest and hills of England. However, the one causing the pain would soon be a forgotten memory. The people of Wolves Hollow could now create a better place to live. Where everyone could live in peace and quiet on the riverside.

XV

❦

True Intentions

The night air was frosty and calm as the stars shined brightly above the village of Eaglecrest. The hour was late as villagers were either asleep or sat in the dining rooms of their homes drinking ale. A fresh sheet of snow had dropped during the day, creating a brisk evening.

Despite the cold, a few villagers remained out on the streets. One of them, a large Norseman, who was walking on the cobblestone streets with a hood over his head and a sword at his hip. A warm cloak was wrapped around him, and each breath created a puff of smoke. He was walking steadily; calmly. After a short time, he passed by a few men who were drunk off their arses.

"Want a sip of this ale?" asked one of the men before belching. "It will keep you warm tonight!"

The Norseman shook his head no, then continued down the pathway until he reached a small alehouse right next to the walls of Demut, the village of the Horse Clan. The small building did not have any of their lanterns on and looked dead from the outside. The man turned and looked around one last time. Nobody was watching and the drunkards from earlier were pushing each other around now. No way they were paying attention to the man.

He then proceeded to enter the building, and he closed the door behind him. He took his hood off and looked around. It was completely dark other than one table with two candles sitting at the center, offering a dim light. A woman was sitting there with two other men. The woman smiled as she noticed the Norseman approaching their table.

"Alf!" she said happily. "I am glad you could make it. I have not seen you in some time. I know you have been busy..."

"Of course, Sigrid. I would not miss this for the world," Alf replied. "Especially after what happened a few days ago."

"Oh? And what would that be?" Sigrid asked.

"I need some mead first," he said while he took off his cloak and threw it on another table.

Sigrid snapped her fingers and the bar maid hurried over with another round of mead horns for the table. Everyone took their drinks and Sigrid snapped again. The bar maid then ran back over and hid behind the bar.

Alf sat down and sighed as he did it.

"My brother finally exited his cave the other day," he began, to which everyone looked at him with wide eyes. "Apparently, King Edward actually showed up here and had to kick his arse into shape, but evidently, it worked, as Njal was outside enjoying the fresh air." Annoyance could be heard in his voice.

"Did you speak with him?" one member of the Horse Clan asked. He was a thinner man with a patchy brown beard.

"Aye," Alf replied. "I told him he was a fool and a poor leader for entering hibernation without warning."

"You said that to him? In front of everyone there?" Sigrid asked. "He did not punish you at all?"

"No," Alf laughed. "Sigrid, you told me of his need to grab onto any sort of 'family' and hold them close. He did not punish Halfdan, and he did not punish you. He sure as Hel was not going to punish me, either."

"Fair enough," she replied before taking a gulp of her drink.

"Sigrid, tell him what we were just talking about," the other Horse Clan member said.

She sighed and looked at him with a worried look.

"What is it?" Alf asked cautiously.

"Well, I know we have not fully discussed what to do about your brother because I know that you *did* in fact come all this way to see him and your intentions were pure."

"Yes, go on," Alf commanded.

"You then realized what kind of a man he was. You learned that he is not fit to lead our people due to his passive attitude towards problems. The leader of our people must rule strongly and create a life for his people. He also cannot take any shite from anyone who tries to disrupt that life."

"I know of all this. What is the point?" Alf asked.

"While I appreciate the rebuilding your brother has done for my village and our people, I believe that somewhere down the road, we will all fall due to his inexperience. His immaturity shows itself greatly. I believe it is due to his age."

"But you and I are also young like him," Alf said. "What is the difference?"

"I have been leading my people since my father died when I was but a child. You have been leading your people around Norway since *you* were a child. He was working as a slave to a farmer until about a winter ago."

Alf dropped his head. "What exactly are you asking of me, Sigrid?"

"I wish to rid the throne of Njal Tokeson."

Alf's eyes widened, and he looked at her with shock. "You want to kill my brother?"

"No, no, no," Sigrid said. "But we have been ruling the people here in his absence very well. The idea of putting the Great Hall in Demut is a wise choice. You have been training the people to fight when he trained them to build. We both agree that the old ways are better. I used to think Toke was wise, but I have come to realize that he was a fool and Njal is following in those footsteps. So, while we do not have to kill Njal, I think we need to put you on the throne instead."

"You are asking me to betray my brother. My own blood."

"You called him out in front of everyone in Eaglecrest today. This means that you are also hitting your breaking point with him. I hit mine when he decided to let Halfdan go unpunished for letting Torin go free."

"I agree that he is not acting as a wise king, but he is my brother. I am allowed to speak about him the way I have. Besides, in his absence, and with Halfdan gone, somebody needed to take his place, which is what I decided to do. But do you know how long I thought I was the only person left from my family? I thought I was the sole heir to the throne. A throne I did not even know existed anymore. When I heard he was alive and that he killed Aelred, my heart was set on finding him. My ambition for the throne sunk into the abyss of my mind. As much as I am angry with him for how he has handled things, I do not wish to kill him and I *will* not. Do you understand me?"

Sigrid rolled her eyes and sighed.

"These meetings are for ranting about the state of our home," Alf continued. "They are not for treasonous conversations."

"Here is how things are going to work out if we do nothing," Sigrid began. "Njal will give Gulgruve back to Edward, which will allow Edward to think that we will do whatever he wishes. Once that happens, he will steal more and more from us until there is nothing left. Not only that, but I can guarantee that Torin is out there somewhere plotting his revenge against Njal. However, if we rise up and overthrow Njal, we can put our foot down and tell Edward that Gulgruve is ours. He will have no choice but to listen and perhaps give us even more land. Then, we can keep Njal in a cell until Torin comes here. Then, instead of destroying the village, they can have another proper one-on-one fight and be done with it."

Alf dropped his head. He was happy to have finally met his brother, but he had grown to be quite angry with him. A king cannot afford to feel emotions like Njal had been. It affects everyone else that lives in the village. Since Njal's isolation, Alf helped with the training of younger warriors. He also began overseeing preparations for a new war room and housing in the forest to the north by Demut. And truth be told, he liked being in a leadership role. He felt it suited him nicely.

Maybe Eaglecrest would thrive under my rule.

But I would need to rid the throne of my brother.

I do not know if I can do that.

Sigrid put her hand on his thigh and another one on his cheek and turned his head so that she was looking at him. She kissed him once on the lips, then broke away, her forehead touching his.

"I want you to be my king, Alf. I want to rule alongside you and have ten sons. I wish to live the rest of my saga with you at my side," Sigrid whispered.

He grabbed her by the back of the neck and pulled her close. Their lips locking repeatedly.

He broke away.

"Alright..." he said, his breathing heavy. "I will do what I must to preserve this village."

The two of them kissed passionately while the two members of the Horse Clan cheered and banged their drinks together, mead splashing over the rim of the horn.

On the outside of the alehouse, the drunkards that Alf passed on his way to the alehouse were sitting up against the side of the building. Their ears were pushed up against the wooden walls in an attempt to hear everything. Once they got that verbal confirmation from Alf, they knew what they needed to do. They pulled away from the side of the building and looked at each other with great worry.

"We need to tell Knud," one of them said.

"What exactly do we tell him?" the other asked, shocked by what he had just heard.

"We tell him the truth. Alf Tokeson and Jarl Sigrid are plotting to overthrow the king..."

*

A week's journey came to an end as Njal was riding his horse through the streets of London. Word had spread that Njal and the Norsemen retook the village of Gulgruve for themselves, so the people of London looked upon the Bear King with wide and cautious eyes. None of them knowing whether there were more Norsemen hiding in the shadows, ready to strike and take London next.

Njal galloped through the streets and passed the wide eyes without much care. His mind was on other things; Where Halfdan was, if he was alright, and living the happy life he wanted to with Ingrid. He thought back to their time on the battlefield when Lord Halig was standing over Halfdan, readying his large hammer. Njal thought that was the end of his friendship with the berserker. That is, until Ingrid's arrow pierced the large Lord of England and saved Halfdan's life. Njal realized that Ingrid could protect Halfdan when he could not. It was a sad feeling, but a necessary one.

His mind then shifted focus to the love of his life, Frigyth. The woman that started this all. He realized that if he did not see Frigyth behind the alehouse that day in Birmingham, none of this would have occurred. He probably would have still been a slave to Alvin. Or perhaps, due to Alvin's old age, Njal would have been running the farm all by himself at this point.

While that seemed like a semi-pleasant thought, he knew it wasn't the reality of the situation. He knew that by thinking too much on false realities, it would take his focus off what really mattered.

The fact and the matter was that he was the king of his people and since his brother arrived on the docks that day, every good relationship he had was ruined. Although blood kin is important to him, he realized that his brother was not worth losing everything else over. Especially because he had fought tooth and nail for it all. It wouldn't be fair to himself. But more importantly, it wouldn't be fair to the people that he was now leading. Those who entrusted their lives to him. And he knew that now more than ever.

He thought back to Frigyth again. What she might have been up to. If she still loved him. If Birstain had been taken by the rot already. Was she already the Lord there? He didn't know, but he forced his mind to think of other things. Even thinking of a life without Frigyth made his heart hurt. His blood boiled, and a frog formed in his throat. He was angry and sad at the same time. Without his lovely wife and his mighty best friend, a void was created in his heart. One that he wasn't sure how to fill.

Njal slowed his horse down as he approached the castle gates. He saw Almund and two other soldiers in leather armor and their red cloaks standing there. He stopped his horse, hopped off, and hitched it to a post before walking over to Almund.

"Almund, a pleasure to see you again," Njal said.

"Mm hm," Almund replied, turning and leading Njal to the inside of the castle.

Njal sensed his anger, but he understood it. He wished to keep this alliance, so everything needed to be put on the table. No more hiding. No more secrets. Just honesty from this point on.

The entire walk to the throne room was quiet. Each footstep echoed throughout the long and ever-expanding hallways of the castle. When they entered the throne room, Edward was sitting on his large chair with a cup of wine in his hand. He had a fur cloak that was pinned on by a golden broach. His hair was slicked back and his face was unamused.

The other soldiers stood back by the doors while Almund and Njal continued their walk until they reached the foot of the stairs that led to the throne. They stopped and Njal looked up into the eyes of the King of England.

"King Edward, I..." Njal began before being interrupted.

"Njal Tokeson... I am quite joyous to see you arrive here. Especially after our most recent conversation," Edward said.

"Listen, I just wish to be honest," Njal said, looking at both Edward and Almund. "I have some things I wish to explain."

"I am listening," Edward said.

"When I met Aelred on the battlefield, he told me he ripped a child out of my mother's womb and threw it into the ocean. Well, that child survived by the power of the gods and arrived in Eaglecrest in the form of my brother, Alf."

Both Edward and Almund's eyes widened as Njal continued.

"I was hesitant at first in listening to anything he had to say, but eventually, I came to trust him. To think of him as my brother. He was raised in a different kind of world than I was. One where he was not aware of our father's teachings. He still held onto the old way of Norse life and I trusted him enough to where, because I did, my mind was poisoned. He made me believe you were trying to steal everything from us. He made me push my best friend away. He even made me strike the love of my life..." he broke off for a moment but then continued.

"The point being, I should not have listened to him despite our shared blood. I need to show those who create problems, despite my relationship with them, that there are consequences. That is why I have acted the way I have. But I have come to realize that nothing will be done with me sitting in isolation. I need to right my wrongs. And that starts here, with you, Edward."

Edward was silent for a moment but then stood up and walked down the stairs of the throne so that he was meeting Njal's eye level.

"Thank you for your honesty, Njal Tokeson. I forgive you, and our alliance can remain strong. I am sorry for what you are going through, but I hope you understand that you have a friend in me. Anytime you need me, even if it is to share a drink and speak of our woes, I will gladly answer that call."

Njal reached his arm out but Edward reached his arms around and hugged Njal. It surprised the Norseman, but he felt good. He needed that. It didn't matter who it was from, but he needed that sort of embrace after he believed nobody loved him anymore. Edward broke away and looked at the Bear King in the eyes.

"Without your efforts against Aelred, I would still have been living in my exile and for that, I thank you deeply."

"Of course," Njal said. "But as you looked out for your people in coming to Eaglecrest and confronting me, I must also do the same."

Edward creased his eyebrows. "What do you have in mind?"

"While I am here to give back full control of Gulgruve to you and your people, I do not believe that the land that we have is enough. We wish to expand and we wish to do it peacefully. My father had the idea of Englishmen and Norsemen coexisting and I wish to believe in that idea as well."

"That can be done," Edward said without any hesitation. "I truly wish to keep this alliance going and I want you to be king of your people. How about the entirety of the valley up to the borders of Gulgruve?" Njal's eyes widened. "And to top it all off, let us make Gulgruve belong to both of our people. It can be a safe place for everyone. I can send men to rule there, but we can build housing for your people. Does that sound like a plan?"

"Absolutely," Njal said, surprised by the offer. "This will undoubtably make my people happy."

"And what of your brother? Do you think this will make him happy?"

Njal's face hardened. "I am not sure. I am afraid I may have to confront him, depending on something that Knud is doing for me."

"Well, remember, if you need my help, I am able and willing."

"You have my undying gratitude, Edward."
Edward nodded his head.

"Now, let us get some wine before you return home," Edward said with a smile.

*

Knud was relaxing in Muspel's Great Hall by himself in the late hours of the night. He was sitting naked in a large wooden tub with warm water filled to the top as he held a large horn of wine. His breathing was slowed and his eyes shut. His mind was in the middle of processing trading negotiations with men in Ireland. They wished to exchange weapons and armor for oils and volcanic materials. However, Knud believed that Eaglecrest was home to some of the best blacksmiths in all of Midgard since its expansion. And getting a hold of those volcanic materials and oils was hard, since he had to receive them from villages in Iceland. Therefore, Knud thought the trade was a bad one. He began to think of what else he would wish to trade his clan's valuables for that Eaglecrest or Demut or Muspel didn't already have. Before he could even consider any options, there were three knocks at the door.

"Uh, yes, what is it?" Knud shouted.

"The men wish to speak with you urgently," the guard said from across the door.

"Can it wait a few more moments?"

"It is about the spies, sir," the guard said from the other side of the door.

"Oh, well come in," Knud said.

A guard entered the room and noticed Knud in his vulnerable state, but didn't care much.

"So?" Knud asked from his tub.

"The spies are waiting for you out in the throne room. They have some... uneasy news."

"Let me dress. I will be there momentarily."

The guard nodded before he exited the room. Knud then stood up, downed the rest of his wine, and headed over to where his clothes were. He put on his black pants, black wool tunic, and black boots before securing his black leather vest and pinning his black and red cloak onto his shoulders.

He walked out of the washroom and into the throne room, where two young Norsemen were standing. They were dressed like drunkards. Their hair was messy, their clothes torn, and dirt covered areas of their bodies. Muspel was not known for their spying, which, according to Knud, meant they were *very* good at spying.

"What is this news you bring me, gentlemen?" Knud asked as he approached them. He didn't sit in his throne, but stood eye level with the two.

"Sir, we followed Alf Tokeson down to an alehouse by Demut. Inside, he met with Jarl Sigrid and two of her men. They spoke about Njal and..." one of them started.

"They are planning to overthrow him and put Alf in charge," the other finished.

"Are they planning to kill him?" Knud asked, stroking his beard.

"No. Sigrid believes that Torin is out there plotting his revenge, so they wish to keep Njal alive. When the time comes, they can just give Njal to Torin in order to avoid war."

Knud thought back to what Njal had told him before he left for London. About what he saw in the Land of the

Spirits. It was very troublesome but something they could not think about at the moment. Torin wasn't forgotten, though; he had been in the back of everyone's mind.

"Damn," Knud mumbled. "Then that is all we need to make an arrest. But how did Alf seem this time around? Last time you said Sigrid was picking on him a bit and that he essentially rolled over and showed his belly to her."

"Alf seemed hesitant," one spy said. "I really do not think he wishes for this. Aye, he was angry that Njal spent weeks in isolation, but who was not? Now that Njal is out and traveling to London and participating in his kingly duties again, I believe Alf would rather spend his time fighting alongside his brother rather than fighting against him."

"I see your point and I agree," Knud said. "I had a similar theory. I believe Sigrid is poisoning Alf's mind like Alf poisoned Njal's in his decisions. But due to Sigrid's position as Jarl, we must make the arrest against Alf. We shall wait another week so Njal can be present for it. Keep spying on their meetings. Tell me if there are any details on the matter at hand."

"What about Sigrid?" one of the spies asked. "She seems to be the true cause of all of these problems."

"We must take her away from Alf," Knud said. "Remove her from the area, but nothing more."

"We? You are to come with us during the arrest?" the other asked.

"Of course," Knud said. "I have seen the two of them fight together on the battlefield. They are fantastic. We will attempt to do this the easy way."

"Fire?" one spy asked.

"Fire," Knud confirmed.

*

Another week had gone by and nothing had really changed. Alf visited Sigrid and the two men from the Horse Clan at the same alehouse every night. They were ironing out a plan to overthrow Njal in the near future. Those were often deeper conversations, but on this particular morning, the companions were full of glad tidings.

A little brush stroke of orange could be seen over the horizon. The twilight sky showed the stars flickering high above and the cosmic dust of the milky way was still present.

Alf was mildly drunk and walking towards Demut's front gates with Sigrid under his arm. The two other men from the Horse Clan were walking behind them, laughing about something one of them said.

The plan, on the other hand, was one that didn't include the death of Njal, but rather put him in chains and behind the bars of a cell. Alf didn't like the thought of going against his brother, but after seeing how immature he was in the role of a leader, he felt he had no other choice.

His silver lining was that he found love in the process, though. In the form of Sigrid. Her blonde hair and the feeling of her warm body in Alf's arms made him feel at home. In his mind, she was a wild horse. One that could never be tamed but one that, for some reason, decided to let him ride.

He felt a happiness come over him. His woman under his arm, his friends behind him, and a home full of his own people. Alf also hoped that Njal would understand one day. Part of him dreamed that when Torin arrived at their gates, he could release his brother from his cell and they could fight Torin together. Back-to-back, shield to shield. Like proper brothers.

Alf then started to plan his idea to marry Sigrid in his head. Where it would take place, when it would, and who all would be present. He was excited. When all the drama was over and he could finally relax and start a...

WOOSH!

A wall of fire erupted around the four of them, causing them all to quickly spring into action. They all unsheathed their respected weapons and pointed them at the flames. They shouted to one another in confusion before a voice was heard from beyond the flames.

"Alf Tokeson," the voice began. "You are hereby being arrested for the attempted plot to overthrow your brother and the rightful king of our people! Jarl Sigrid, you and your men put down your weapons and we will not have to bring you in as well!"

"Who is that?" Alf asked, sweat forming on his brow.

"It is Knud," she said to him. "What the Hel do you think you are doing, Knud?" she shouted.

"We have become aware of your traitorous conversations and have no other option but to bring in Alf!" Knud shouted, still unseen behind the towering flames.

"Then you best arrest everyone here in the village because I can bet they have all had the same conversations!" Alf yelled.

"If anyone had formed an actual plan like you, I would have known about it! Put down your weapons and this will go no further than it needs to!"

"I still cannot believe you are taking his side, Knud!" Sigrid hollered. "He is going to destroy us all with his immaturity and lack of experience!"

"Njal has done more for this village and our people than you, and I, or anyone else has combined! The fact that you wish to betray him due to feeling pain and suffering for losing his wife is monstrous, Sigrid!"

"Enough of this! Try to take us in, but we shall have no other option but to fight back!" Alf said.

"If you wish to spill blood, that is on you!" Knud said. He turned to his men, which were about ten in numbers, and told them to enter the flames. Their heavy wool armor allowed them to brace the flames without much trouble. Five of them entered the wall of fire with their iron and obsidian weapons drawn. The second they did, Alf, Sigrid, and the other two men sprang into action. They all attempted to swing their swords and kill the Muspel soldiers, but to no avail. Their swords would strike the multiple layers of wool but wouldn't cut through, as it was too thick. This allowed the soldiers to have a simple attempt to grab the companions.

One of them put his arms around Sigrid, trying to stop her from fighting, but it made her fight even harder. The soldier kept his grip, lifted her up and jumped out of the wall of flames. Alf saw it and roared loudly into the sky. He gripped his sword and examined the wool armor of the Muspel soldiers. He could pick out where their weak points were. Neck, groin, and joints. Each of those spots were only covered with chain mail. While Alf realized it was probably steel lined mail, he didn't much care. It was still breakable.

He pulled his sword back and pointed the tip forward, aiming at a soldier's neck. The soldier attempted to grab Alf but Alf pushed his arms forward, hands strong on the hilt of his sword. The tip punched through the mail as the blade slid throughout the soldier's neck until the tip burst out the other side in an explosion of blood.

Knud saw it all from the other side of the flames and grew angry.

"I have had enough! Beat them! And if you have to, kill them!" he shouted at his men.

One soldier then reached out and grabbed one man from Demut's neck. The soldier pulled his sword back and swung it forward, straight into the chest of the poor man.

The other Horse Clan member's eyes went wide. He screamed loudly and charged the soldier who did it, but he felt a hand grab his hair from behind him. He attempted to turn around, but before he could, the soldier who grabbed him from behind reached around with his sword and sliced the man's neck wide open.

Alf quickly jumped to the soldier who did it and plunged his sword straight into his armpit. Once he pulled his sword out, leaving the soldier to bleed out, he charged the remaining soldier inside the inferno. His sword worked swiftly as he dodged an attack, then swung upwards, his blade lodging itself into the groin of the soldier, making him scream in agony. Alf pulled his sword out and watched the soldier drop to his knees, where he swung his sword sideways in one swift motion, removing the soldier's head.

Alf then roared and jumped out of the wall of fire. The

cloak he was wearing for anonymity began to burn. He growled like a wolf as he stood, crouched with his sword drawn, staring at Knud and the remaining soldiers. Without looking away, he grabbed his burning cloak up by the shoulder and ripped it off, showcasing Alf Tokeson and all his primal glory.

"Where is she?!" he roared as he foamed at the mouth. A vein pulsating at the side of his head.

"Away from you," Knud said. "Which is better for all of us."

Alf screamed and charged at Knud, who was standing behind two of his soldiers. These soldiers were dressed in black leather armor. One of the soldiers attempted to push Alf, but he whiffed as Alf dodged. He was very light on his feet. Alf then swung his sword upwards, cutting straight through the neck of the soldier. The other one tried too, but Alf was too quick. He shoved his sword directly through the head of the soldier.

He pulled his blade out with a crunch and growled as he looked at Knud. "You will not take her away from me!"

"Your love for her is misguided, Alf," Knud began, as he unsheathed his long, black sword and pointed it at his ravenous opponent. "Her hatred towards Njal stems from her attraction towards him. He rejected her many times and then you showed up. She does not see Alf Tokeson when she looks at you. She sees Njal."

"Liar!"

"I would not lie to you, Alf! She is plaguing your mind! Making you turn on your brother! Look at how you are acting! This is blasphemous!"

The bass in Alf's roar that followed matched that of

thunder. He jumped to Kund, who quickly dodged the attack. Alf landed on his face before quickly rolling back up onto his feet, sword still drawn. Knud realized Alf's anger made him sloppy.

"If you would come in and speak about this issue, then I will let you see her again. But if battle is what you wish to have, then battle is what you will receive," Knud said calmly as he gripped his sword strongly.

Alf charged again, this time a lot less maniacal and more relaxed. Knud realized that Alf was a quick learner. He swung his sword diagonally, which Alf quickly jumped away from, then jumped back and swung his own blade. Knud had to raise his sword quickly, which he did, as he blocked the attack with his own sword, sending sparks flying. The two of them continued pushing on their swords, trying to get the better of the other.

Suddenly, a voice shouted from behind the two men.

"That is enough!"

The two men broke away and looked towards the voice.

It was the Bear King himself, Njal Tokeson. His bear cloak fluttering behind him in the morning air. 'The Call of the King' was held in his right hand.

"Brother! This piece of shite betrayed us! He has attacked me and has taken Sigrid! He wishes to steal the crown from you!" Alf shouted.

Njal's face did not change expressions. "Odd choice to choose your own plans when pinning wrongfulness onto someone else, is it not?" he said. Alf's face went stern and angry again as he realized his brother wasn't falling for it. "Do you understand how happy I was?" Njal asked. "My brother was *alive*. The dreams of us fighting side by side occurred in my head every night. I was excited. But it turns out that ever since I began trusting you, I lost everything in my life. My best friend, my queen! Hel, listening to you almost destroyed our alliance with the King of England! You have ruined everything since your arrival, Alf. And the way you spoke to me in the market the other day confirmed my earlier suspicions. You are hereby arrested and are to be thrown in a cell."

"You sorry excuse for a king!" Alf shouted, his façade no longer present. "I did not wish to listen to Sigrid's ideas at first, but now I can see they were justified! You will doom us all! You are weak! You are..."

A fist met Alf's cheek and knocked him straight out. Knud was standing over him with a stern look on his face.

"Quiet yourself, boy..." he said coldly.

Njal sheathed his sword and approached Knud. He noticed that dozens of villagers had been watching.

"Go back to your morning, everyone," Njal said. "We will handle it all." He then stood next to Knud, both of them looking down at Alf. "Where is Sigrid?"

"Wherever you wish for her to be," Knud said.

"Take her to Muspel. I want her far from her clan members," Njal said. "I will take Alf to the Great Hall in Eagle-crest. There, I will tie him up and speak to him about his plan. But Knud, whatever you do, do not kill or let Sigrid go. I sense as though she has something to do with my brother's actions."

"I could not agree more," Knud nodded. "There will be eyes on her at all times. What of her people, though?"

"I will speak with them directly. Tell them that their Jarl was a traitor. If there will be any more traitorous actions, they will be punishable by death. I am done playing games here. I should have killed Torin when I had the chance. I should have punished Halfdan for letting him go. I need to be a powerful king. I am tired of being walked over due to my kindness."

"Good. The makings of a wise king," Knud said with a smirk. "What of Edward and our alliance? Did your trip go well?"

Njal looked at Knud and smiled. "We have a strong ally in Edward."

"Good," Knud said. "Let us keep it that way."

XVI

The Lord of Birmingham

Frigyth was walking down the hallway of her old home, the stone castle that stood tall on the Northside of Birmingham. She thought about the last few weeks of her life since she left Njal and Eaglecrest behind. The first few days, she did not sleep. The anxiety of leaving Njal alone to deal with his brother in Eaglecrest seemed like a selfish decision. But after some more thought, she felt as though she had to be selfish. As much as she tried, Eaglecrest just didn't feel like home. Surrounded by people who were so much different from her. She grew up hearing her mother tell her stories of the Norse people and she fell in love with them. She dreamed of being on the battlefield with them, living among them, seeing what freedom was like. But now that she was able to live it all, she realized that the Nordic way of life wasn't for her.

The first week of being back home, she spent a lot of

time in her room or visiting her father, as she missed Eaglecrest and Njal. But strangely, that didn't last very long. The second week, she woke up with a smile on her face. Sure, she still missed Njal, but she was happier. In fact, she spent the days with the people of Birmingham. Walking around the markets and playing with a group of children she would see outside an alehouse every night while their parents drank inside. She would also see her father every single day and talk to him as much as she could.

During the second week, Frigyth also began spending a lot of time with Sir Wigberht. He was always at her side and she his. They would go fishing with one another or spend time walking through the city and helping people in need. Wigberht was always trying to help people, no matter the size of the problem that needed solving. It was an admirable quality, to say the least. He would ask Frigyth to dinner every night for an actual date, to which she always said no with a smile. But Wigberht's spirits never broke and towards the end of the second week home, she finally said yes.

He took her out to Ivar's old alehouse, The Ironside, which was now called Dragon's Inn. They danced, laughed, and drank until the sun came up. At the break of dawn, she led Wigberht to the old ruins where she took Njal when they first met. Up there, all she could think about was Njal. She remembered when she knew she liked the Norseman. She then remembered seeing the smoke and hearing the screams of those below signifying the burning of Alvin's farm. She realized while she sat there on that hill that she never really got to see Njal in a relaxed state. When she first met him, he was just a young Norseman who worked for an old farmer. She only got to see one full day of him without any stress or worry. Every day after that, was spent surviving and fighting, which was then followed up with him traveling across England, which left her lonely.

She knew it wasn't easy on Njal to try to balance her and his people, but she felt as though that was something a king needed to do. As she sat there with Wigberht, she looked at the ruins and felt a bit of shame that she brought the Englishman to the same ruins. She dropped her head and shed a tear. That is, until Wigberht moved closer to her, touched her chin with his thumb and he turned her head to him. He wiped the tears off of her cheek and moved in to kiss her. Frigyth let him and their lips locked. It was hard for her at first. She wanted to feel Njal's lips on hers instead. The tickle of his blond beard. But after a few more moments, she decided that this was to be her fate. She was to become Lord of Birmingham once her father passed, and she knew that Njal was never going to stop being king and living in Eaglecrest with his people. This was it. Wigberht was who she was choosing.

Was it quick? Absolutely, and she knew it too. But while it didn't necessarily feel right, it did feel like the best logical option for her.

The two of them began to take off their clothes as the sun slowly crawled its way up the horizon and back into the sky.

Frigyth's thoughts on the recap of the last three weeks ended as she made her way to her father's bedchamber. She knocked on the door three times before pushing it open. Inside, the healer was there. She was giving Birstain some medicine to reduce his fever and cough.

"How is everything today, Bertha?" Frigyth asked.

Bertha was a slim woman that looked to be in her fortieth year. "I am alright," she said. "Your father, however, he..."

Frigyth nodded her head and felt a frog in her throat. "I know," she said. "Do you mind if I get a few moments alone with him today?"

"Of course, m'lady," Bertha said before standing up then walking towards the door. She stopped as she was next to Frigyth, though. "I would say he has about a week or two left. Treat every moment you get with him as it is his last," she whispered. She walked out of the room, closing the door behind her, leaving Frigyth alone with her father.

She examined him as she slowly approached his bedside. He had a part of his old green expressionless mask from his time with The Lords of England covering his face. He had lost an eye and a leg recently due to the rot and he didn't wish to have his daughter, or anyone else for that matter, see his scarred face when they came to visit.

"Hello, father," Frigyth said as she touched his hand. "How are you today?"

"My daughter..." Birstain struggled to say the words. "You look so beautiful. You look just like your mother." Frigyth smiled as a tear streamed down the side of her cheek. She wiped it quickly. "I get to see her soon..."

"I know you do, father," Frigyth said, trying to hold all of her emotions back.

He sat his head up as much as he could in his condition and looked over at his daughter. The side of his face that wasn't covered by the mask showed a look of worry. "Do you... do you think she will be happy to see me?"

"Of course she will. She will be so proud of what you did. You fought for me and avenged her."

He rested his head again and sighed. "I am so tired, Frigyth."

Frigyth broke down crying as she gripped his hand a bit harder. "Whenever you are ready to go, father."

"You will lead them... Frigyth... you will lead our people to prosperity. More... than I ever could..."

"I love you, father," she said.

"I love... you, too," he said before falling asleep.

Frigyth cried more now. Her father was still alive, but at what cost? He was miserable and hated that people had to look at him that way. She had thought about asking Bertha to end it, but she couldn't bring herself to do so. It was selfish to keep him alive, but she needed him. She wasn't ready to say goodbye. But is anyone ever truly ready?

*

That night, Frigyth was changing in her room. She still didn't wear dresses or anything related to them. That was the one thing that stuck from living among the Norsemen. She threw on her black boots, her black leather pants, her white shirt and her big black leather belt, which held her sword. She finished off the outfit by securing her signature red cloak onto her shoulders.

Suddenly, there was a knock at her room door.

"Come in," she said as she tied her brown leather gauntlets around her wrists.

Wigberht opened the door and entered the room. He was wearing a blue tunic with brown pants. He also had his sword attached to his belt. He rarely knew what a night with Frigyth would turn into, so he dressed for a nice dinner which could be interrupted by fighting or chasing a bandit at any moment. He saw her, examined her attire, and smiled.

"Well, I hope this means we are hunting for trolls or something exciting!" he said, laughing.

"No, no," she said. "I actually have to train some of the guards after we eat tonight."

"Aw," Wigberht said, frowning. "But tonight is date night."

Frigyth shrugged and approached the Englishman. She put her arms around his neck and he put his hands on her waist. "I am sorry," she said. "But my father will be passing soon. I need to do 'Lord things' now."

"I completely understand," he said sincerely. "Let us go have a nice dinner, then."

"Sounds good," she said, smiling then kissing him.

The two of them exited the room, Frigyth holding onto his arm. They passed by a few guards who all said hello then went out of the main castle doors and down the path towards the inn where they would be eating dinner. The sun was setting, which created a beautiful golden light throughout the city.

"I know it is not something you wish to think about," Wigberht started, looking at the cobblestone path they were walking on. "But is any part of you excited to rule here?"

Frigyth looked around the town. A few guards were lighting lanterns as the city prepared for nighttime. Some children were playing with wooden swords nearby. People were talking and laughing while eating and shopkeepers were closing their stores for the day.

"Yes," she said with a smile. "I actually am. This was and always will be my home. I think I have had enough adventuring in my life."

"Well, surely that is not true, considering every date night ends up in an adventure in some form or another," he said, chuckling.

"I meant like, across the country or open seas type of adventuring," she said, giving him a nudge. "I suppose I should have worded it as 'I have seen enough bloodshed and war for my lifetime.'"

"But you train as though you will see another war," Wigberht said.

"I think it is because I have a feeling that I *will* be seeing another one at some point in my life. And I..." she broke off.

"What is it?" he asked as she stopped walking and he looked at her. She looked back up at him and smiled.

"It is nothing," she said. "Let us get there soon. I am quite hungry."

"Alright, my darling," Wigberht said as he took her arm in his again. "Onward!" he shouted jokingly.

*

Frigyth awoke with crusted eyes as the sun shined through her window. Winter was in full swing now as a late-night storm rolled in and stretched a thin sheet of snow across the city. She stretched and sat up so that her legs were hanging off the bed. She thought back to the night before. It was a good one. A date night she probably would not forget anytime soon.

It had now been six weeks now since she left Njal's side. Her father was still hanging onto his life, but she knew it could be any day now. She was a bit happy that the last few visits she had with him; he was spryer and even acted like his old self before Aelred. She realized since she had been home, she couldn't dwell on things she couldn't control, so she chose to enjoy the time her father had left instead of crying about it.

Suddenly, she felt a bit strange and held her stomach.

"What the f..." she said before her eyes went wide and she ran towards her window, where she stuck her head out and threw up. Her eyes stayed wide as she turned back into her room. She immediately thought about Njal. They had been trying to conceive a child, but it wasn't working for months. What were the odds that after she and Wigberht spent only a few nights together that she would now be pregnant? She shook the thought off and prepared herself for the day. Besides, it was probably due to the anxiety she had about becoming Lord of Birmingham, right?

Right?

*

About three days later, every day had been started by a similar result. Throwing up outside of her window. Frigyth knew deep down what was happening, but she didn't wish to tell anybody. Not even Wigberht. Not yet.

She hurried as she got dressed and immediately her stomach began to growl.

I need some bloody food.

She exited the castle and headed down to the market. A brisk and snowy morning greeted her. She said hello to everyone that was sitting at their tents in the market before she stopped at a kind old man named Emrys' shop. There, she picked out some carrots and a nicely cooked salmon. She thanked old Emrys and began walking towards the training grounds, snow crunching beneath her feet.

She ate as she walked and by the time she arrived there; the food was all gone. She noticed a few of the guards were sitting and talking, not focused on the training battle that was being had. Frigyth squinted her eyes and approached the men.

"Having a delightful conversation, are we?" she asked with a creased eyebrow. The guards jumped to their feet and grabbed their wooden swords.

"Sorry, m'lady!" one guard shouted as he stood at attention.

"Apologies!" the other one said. "It will not happen again!"

Frigyth told them she was going to sit there and watch them fight. To which they did. She watched the fight play out, but her mind was on other things. Including asking Bertha the healer for advice and confirmation of prior suspicions.

*

"You are with child," Bertha said happily.

"Fuck..." Frigyth said, to which Bertha's smile faded.

"Is this not a happy moment?" Bertha asked. "I thought you would have been more pleased. Especially since you told me of your troubles with conceiving a child."

"I should be happier, yes," Frigyth began. "But it is a bit hard to get it through my head."

"Why is that, m'lady?"

"I tried for months with Njal and there was no result," Frigyth began. "Now, I start seeing Wigberht and suddenly, it works? I am pregnant?"

"Well," Bertha started. "If I were you, I would think of it as the Lord's way of showing you that you made the right decision to come here. He does not always speak loudly, but to me, this is shouting to you that you made the correct choice."

Frigyth wasn't as religious as she once was, but she did believe in fate. She became happy after hearing those words from Bertha. Nobody had told her that she made the right choice in coming to Birmingham. Sure, she said it to herself multiple times, but she didn't actually believe it. But those words from Bertha. They warmed her soul.

"There is that smile," Bertha said happily. "You are to be a mother and the new lord of Birmingham soon. This is a joyous moment. Please, enjoy it."

"I need to find Wigberht," Frigyth said, tears filling her eyes.

XVII

The Past Catches Quickly

The docks were still wet from the rain that had passed through. Streaks of dark orange could be seen from the east as the sun was trying to crawl its way into the sky. Torin, Ari, Daegal, and Golmac were all standing close to the woman who had just lost her husband. They were all watching Camma chant some words into the sky as she blessed the small boat where the woman's dead husband's body was wrapped in a blanket.

The woman started to sob more as she embraced Ari. The Druidic woman, while surprised by the quick embrace, hugged the woman back and held her. She thought back to when she lost her parents. That cold and empty feeling of your entire life being thrown into shambles was one that Ari knew well. This woman was on a path now. One that didn't include the quiet life she envisioned with her husband. One that neither Ari, Torin or any of the other Druids could walk her through. This was her new journey, and she had to walk it herself.

Camma stopped chanting and looked over at Golmac and reached her hand out. The giant Druid sniffled and approached her. He then gave her a torch that was unlit. Camma gripped the wood of the torch and said something to the sky. She then pulled out one of her small knives from her belt and scrapped the blade across her forearm, which had a small piece of steel attached to the leather gauntlet. Sparks flew and caught the hemp wrapping around the tip of the torch, setting it ablaze.

Camma then chanted another line into the sky before she carefully set the torch in the small fisherman's boat. The branches and other kindling inside the vessel began to catch on fire and the woman's howling got louder as she held onto Ari tighter.

Golmac approached the boat and with a sad look on his face, he pushed it into the current of the river without much trouble. The boat began floating down the watercourse as the Druids and the woman watched. Every one of them was silent other than the grieving woman, who stayed in her sobbing state for a long time.

They stayed there with her for a little while longer until some civilians of the town came down to the docks to join them all. Several of them approached and thanked the Druids for ridding Wolves Hollow of the horrible men that were in charge. The other townspeople approached and embraced the woman.

Torin saw that they weren't needed anymore, so he looked at his companions and told them that it was time to go. Ari was a little hesitant as a part of her wanted to make sure the woman was alright. That is when a little old lady saw the worried look on her face and approached her.

"Do not worry," she said. "We will take care of her. I promise."

As the rest of the Druids began making their way back towards their own boat, Ari decided to speak to the villagers.

"All of you are free now," she said proudly. "You are free to make this village a quiet farm, a busying community, or even a proper place of godly worship. But please, look out for one another. Your lives are in each other's hands now. Stay strong."

Ari smiled at them before turning and running after the rest of her group. Once she caught up to them, she noticed that Golmac was already putting their boat back into the water. She smiled at Torin and he did the same. He reached out his hand, and she grabbed it. They descended the little hill and got into the boat with the rest of the Druids.

"I am happy that we decided not to burn the village down," Golmac said as he used the oar to push away from the riverbank. "Those people need that town. It seems like everyone there was being held hostage."

"I am also glad that we did what we did," Ari started. "Their captivity was something I was blind to in my time here. We helped those people have a chance at a better life."

"I agree," Torin replied. "It is a shame that the woman lost her husband, though. She seemed kind."

"Kind, rageful or evil," Daegal interrupted, not meeting Torin's eyeline. "It always hurts when you lose someone, no matter who you are."

Torin squinted at the young man but didn't pay

much attention to it. He was contributing to the conversation, after all.

"Aye," Torin replied, grabbing the other oar. "When we get back, I will speak with Cathbad about our successes here. But first I wish to ask about the Druids that raided us. They wanted him dead, and they were going to kill us to get to him. If there is a threat to us, we need to know everything about it."

"I agree," Ari said as she watched Golmac and Torin pushing and pulling their oars in the water. "They were just watching the river. And how did they even know that we were there? Was it just by chance?"

"Maybe," Torin said, feeling the current push against the boat as they headed upstream. "They could have just been following the river and then one of them spotted us and told their friends. Or maybe our village has a spy."

"A spy?" Golmac asked. "But who would be stupid enough to cross Cathbad? Or you? Or me, for that matter?"

"Coin is a powerful tool, Golmac," Torin said. "If you have enough of it, you can pretty much make anyone do whatever you want them to."

The Druids all stayed quiet and pondered the question for a moment.

"I am not sure a spy is the answer," Camma said, which caught the attention of everyone. "I fear something dark is coming. Something dark, indeed. We are fated to face it."

Everyone felt chills crawl up their spine as the boat made its way back towards the Fenlands.

*

The smell of bonfires crackling, meat roasting, and

vegetables boiling filled the air as the fishing boat made landfall on the riverbank. The sun was starting to set as the journey back to the Fenlands took a bit longer since they were going upstream.

"Smells as though they started the feast already," Daegal said, sniffing the air. Golmac quickly hopped out of the boat and started rushing towards the village. His shoulder brushed Daegal as he ran by. "Hey!" he yelled, but then looked at Torin. Daegal dropped his head and said no more.

"I feel a chill in the air," Torin said. "Could be a storm soon."

"More rain?" Ari asked.

"No," Torin said. "I sense snow."

"Great," Camma said as she walked by and made her way towards the village.

Torin smiled at that.

"Shall we, then?" Torin asked Ari as he reached out for her hand.

She smiled and nodded, grabbing his rough hand. With only Daegal behind them, they began following their Druidic comrades up the pathway that divided the tall grass and led to the village. About halfway up the path, they noticed Cathbad standing there with a smile on his face.

"Already starting the feast, eh?" Torin asked with a smirk.

"I spoke to Elhhere. She had said that you would all arrive today, so I prepared a feast so that you could all eat your hearts out when you arrived."

"Thank you, Cathbad," Ari said. "But there is..."

Torin put his hand up, interrupting her. "You go on and enjoy the feast, Ari. I will speak to Cathbad about what we need to."

Cathbad raised his eyebrow as he heard that.

"I wanted to be a part of the conversation," Ari said.

Torin leaned in and whispered to her, "I promise I will tell you everything. I need to handle this my way."

Cathbad then watched Ari kiss Torin before heading off into the village.

"Hello, Daegal," Cathbad said as he watched the young Druid say nothing and walk towards the village, leaving only Torin and him behind. "Is... everything alright?"

"Aye," Torin said. "Daegal needed to be taught a few things on the journey."

"Like?" Cathbad asked as the two slowly began walking back towards the village.

"He is going to get him and his shield mates killed someday if he does not cool that fiery head of his."

"How do you mean?"

"He continuously made fun of Golmac and called him harsh names. In my experience, continued verbal attacks like that will get yourself killed by either the one you are attacking or you will create a division of trust within the companion. If nobody trusts anybody, then you will be annihilated on the battlefield."

"I agree, friend," Cathbad said as the village came into view now. People were out dancing around a massive bonfire. Others were playing drums and singing songs.

"They are all very skilled," Torin said. "I mean that. They just need a bit more maturing."

"I agree. Otherwise, the mission went well, I am assuming?"

"The priest was a piece of shite and we had a funeral for a woman's husband there. The captain hid behind his armor and that still could not save him from my blade, so I would say it was not bad. We did what we had to do."

"You decided to leave Wolves Hollow standing, then?"

"Aye, we made the choice to let the townsfolk decide what kind of village they wished to live in."

"Good," Cathbad said. "You are becoming quite the leader. I am happy to call you my friend," he put his hand on Torin's shoulder. "Now, shall we eat?"

"Not quite yet," Torin said. "Can we go to your hut? There is something I wish to discuss in private."

Cathbad raised his eyebrow again, but nodded. He felt a bit of anxiety travel throughout his body. The two men passed through the village and smiled at everyone who was having a grand time. They then walked up the wooden stairs towards Cathbad's hut. Once they entered, Cathbad approached his small table and chairs he had set up and sat down, gesturing Torin to do the same.

"So, what seems to be the issue?" Cathbad asked.

"Well, we were attacked on the river."

"By whom?"

Torin paused a moment and examined Cathbad's facial features. He attempted to see if his friend already knew the answer to the question he was asking, but it had seemed like he hadn't.

"A group of Druids, actually. They were covered in feathers." There it was. Torin could see his friend's eyes widen and his throat tighten. "They said they were looking for you."

Cathbad said nothing for a few moments. His eyes met the table.

"Did you kill them?" he finally asked.

"As many as we could see," Torin replied. "The fog was heavy and night was approaching. I am assuming that this is the clan you left in Ireland?"

"Yes," he replied, sounding disappointed in himself. "I am so very sorry. I have put you and everyone else in danger. They should not have been able to find me."

"Listen," Torin said as he sat up. "This is my family now. If I did not think so, I would not have helped fight those bastards off. I truly think of you as my friend and I hope you know that I would be proud to stand by you as we kill those bastards."

Cathbad looked up into Torin's eyes. He could see the truth in them. The changed man.

"I appreciate that, Torin. You have come a long way since we met. I promise we will achieve your revenge."

Torin sat back in his chair and smiled. "You know, I am starting to not want it as much anymore. My time here; it feels like another lifetime for me. One where I can start over and not worry about my past. I have forgotten my gods. Perhaps they never existed. I just wish to stay here and live among my people now. Fighting for their survival."

"That brings great joy to my heart. I know Ari would love that, too. I see you both have become quite fond of one another. I am so very happy for you both."

"Thank you, brother," Torin said. "She makes my life worth living now." Cathbad smiled at that. "But please, tell me how we can stop this other clan from finding us."

"Where exactly were you when they attacked?"

"About halfway to Wolves Hollow, maybe closer. The fog was heavy. But I do believe they are following the river. And once they find out that the group that attacked us is dead, they will send more to that location."

"Unless..." Cathbad said, a chill was sent across his body.

"Unless, what?"

"The bodies would float downstream... Straight to..."

Torin's eyes widened at the realization. "Straight to Wolves Hollow."

*

A woman was being ripped open by a sword made of black steel. Sparks and flames flew high into the air, making the village itself look like a torch. People were screaming and running for their lives. Another woman was running before being struck with an arrow right through her neck.

A man in black leather armor with large black feathers protruding from the collar walked forward. The skull of a wolf was sat upon his head like a mask. He calmly made his way through the burning village without any worry. His finger nails on his right hand were long and sharp. They were at least four inches in length and were splinted my iron rods. He was examining the work of his people and was pleased. He fluttered his long nails together, making a horrifying sound that matched the screams of the burning villagers.

He noticed a young villager approach him with a pitchfork. The Druidic man quickly dodged the attack and grabbed the attacker's neck with his right hand. The villager screamed. The Druid then used his sharpened nails to pierce the man's neck causing his scream to turn into a muffled gurgling sound. Blood streamed from the holes in his neck and his mouth.

The man threw the body to the side and stood there menacingly, blood dripping from his hand as he watched the flames engulf Wolves Hollow, burning it to cinder.

*

"Who exactly are we dealing with here?" Torin asked, the muffled sounds of a feast happening outside.

"His name is Ruadan the Silent. He was born with black hair which turned red when he was but five winters old. The witches of the village said that was due to the magical power developing inside him. He became the leader of my old Druidic clan in Ireland due to him challenging the heir and killing him for the throne. He is a pure animal like no other, and I was a fool for wronging him. His weapon of choice is not a sword. The finger nails on his right hand are long and he has them splinted with iron so they do not break. He silences screams by using his nails to tear the throats out of his victims. He is quick on his feet like a wolf and he howls during battle. He is not right in the head."

"And now he is after us," Torin said, stroking his chin. All he felt was stubble.

"I could find him, and perhaps challenge him to a fight."

"No," Torin said sternly. "If he wins, then there is no reason he would not come down here and destroy everything you built so that you leave no legacy at all. We cannot lose you before our fight with him."

"Then we take the fight to him," Cathbad said. "We can send scouts to seek him out. Maybe find where they have camps and dispose of them one by one."

"We would have to be extremely careful, though," Torin said, staring at the flame of the candle burning on the table, the wax dripping down the side. "If he catches wind of where the scouts are coming from, he could track us all the way back here."

"We send the scouts to the hills. Keep them away for a couple of days."

"It is risky, brother. That much, I know. This could go wrong in a number of ways."

"We must know where their village is and how close to us they really are," Cathbad said. "We shall send scouts, have them come back and tell us what they know, then we quickly attack with our full might. Their camp will not stand a chance."

"That leaves our village open for anyone to take. Then, after one fight, we would just have to return home to another one."

"Then what do you propose we do?" Cathbad asked, hand on chin.

"If this Ruadan the Silent wants you, let us give him what he asks. We make our location known."

"Are you mad?"

"Hear me out," Torin said, sitting up in his chair. He thought back to how Ari had made him jump off the small hill when he first met her. "We know these lands better than anyone else, right? We set up traps and push them into the mud. There, we can dispose of him and his men quickly without the danger of any of us falling. I say we tell him where we are when we are ready. Once he marches here, we trap him."

Cathbad sat in thought for a moment. "I like it."

"Good," Torin said. "We can discuss more of this tomorrow. I am quite famished."

"Of course, my friend. Let us fill your belly with mead and food."

The two of them got to their feet and clasped forearms. A feast was to be had.

*

Torin felt the sweat drip on his brow as the flames of the bonfire raged before him. His feet moved quickly as he clung to Ari's hand. He quickly stopped and spun her around as the drums banged loudly behind them. She laughed as he almost tripped over another Druid's feet.

"Sorry, friend," he said to the Druid who was so drunk he didn't even notice.

Ari laughed at that. The drums stopped and Cathbad approached the bonfire.

"Alright, everyone! Gather around! Take a seat if you need a breather!" he said loudly for everyone to hear. Everyone took their seats and panted as he stood tall above them. "I hope you are all enjoying the feast." Everyone cheered at that. "Good!

Good. I wanted to say a few words about the ones who we are celebrating tonight. Starting with Ari here. When we found her, I knew she was going to be a force to be reckoned with. She killed an entire camp of slimy bastards without our help. Look at you now. A fierce warrior who knows no bounds. I could not be more proud of you."

Everyone cheered for her. Torin gave her a kiss on the cheek as Cathbad continued.

"Next, I want to appreciate Camma. I know you rarely have much to say, but when you do, it is always worth listening to. You are smart and cunning. You walk a thin line between mystical and reality and we are all thankful you are on our side."

Everyone cheered. Camma even grinned at those words.

"Golmac! The big troll of a man! I hope you eat until you cannot move anymore tonight because I have come to the realization that the bigger you get, the more of a threat you are to our enemies! So, please, someone keep feeding him!"

Everyone laughed and slapped their knees so hard at that, including Golmac. In fact, he might've had the largest smile there.

"Daegal!" Cathbad said as he looked around for him while everyone was settling down. "Where is Daegal?" Everyone began looking, but couldn't find him.

"Perhaps he went to bed early?" Ari said, trying to look around.

"Well, even if he is not partaking in the feast, I would like to thank him. He has much yet to learn, but he is somebody that I can see growing into quite the warrior. I hope he can hear this because I wish for him to know how much we all appreciate him and his potential."

Torin looked around once more. He didn't like that Daegal wasn't at the feast. He had dealt with mutinies before. The thought of him heading back to his hut and being attacked by Daegal filled his mind. That was a thought that could make any man sober.

"And finally," Cathbad said. "Our newest arrival Torin. My dear friend. My brother. That day I found you on the border of the Fenlands, I could not help but see myself in you. A man who had lost everything and was just about to give up, but was graced with a new opportunity. A new place to belong. A new family."

Everyone cheered.

"Now, not only do we have what very well may be the greatest fighter to ever join us, but we have a leader. Someone to depend on and rely on when things get tough. A man that will tell you the truth as straight as an arrow. We thank you for joining us, Torin."

Torin smiled at Cathbad and then at the rest of the village. He then stood up and looked at them all.

"Thank you. Thank you to every single one of you for allowing me to be who I truly am. I have a new life here. I have found love here," he said while Ari smiled and blushed. "I have found friends and family alike. So, again, thank you for helping me find where I truly belong."

Everyone clapped and cheered.

"Now!" Cathbad shouted. "Let us drink!"

The village broke into a wild frenzy. Dancing, drinking,

laughing, and singing. Torin danced with Ari a bit more before deciding it was time for him to turn in. Ari said she would come to bed with him, but he declined. It wasn't that he didn't want her to, but it was more because he felt as though he needed to watch out for Daegal. That thought continued to race around his head. If the young Druid truly was attempting to try something, the last thing Torin wanted was to put Ari in danger. So, he kissed Ari on the lips and told her to continue dancing and that he would see her in the morning. He looked over to Camma and Golmac and told them to keep an eye on Ari as she was very drunk. They obviously said yes, and Torin began his walk back to his hut.

He walked up the wooden stairs and across the pathway until he reached his hut. His eyes scanned every possible spot where Daegal could be hiding.

Nothing.

Inside, his hut seemed quiet. The muffled sounds of the feast were the only things he could hear. Three small candles were lit on a table, offering dim light. Torin stood in the middle of the room and continued to look around. When he decided that Daegal was not inside, he began to take off his clothes.

But before he could take off more than just his leather belt, he heard the caw of a raven. It caught him by surprise as he spun toward the sound, but he couldn't see anything.

"Hm," he said to himself.

WACK!

Torin jumped and grabbed his sword from his bed and un-sheathed it. He pointed it directly at the door where the sound came from.

"What the..."

WACK!

Another smack against the door, causing Torin to jump again. He then slowly approached the door and heard another smack against it. Then another. And another. Soon, it was rapidly pounding against his door so loudly that Torin couldn't even hear his own thoughts.

BANG!

The door broke from its lock and flew inwards, causing Torin to have to jump out of the way. He looked up to see dozens of ravens flying inside his hut. They were swarming around him and cawing repeatedly. Torin held his arm up in defense until the raven's circular swam grew smaller and smaller until they just disappeared. Torin looked up at what remained. An old man in a black and blue robe holding a golden staff. His long gray beard exited the darkness of his hood.

"Wha...what?" Torin struggled to say as his eyes widened. "Who are..."

"I think you know exactly who I am, Torin," the man said. He then used his vacant hand and pulled his hood down, showcasing the rugged old face and eye patch covering one eye.

"Odin?"

"Aye," Odin said. "Because of your adversary, Njal, people believe in me enough that I have enough power to speak to you face to face. Usually, we would have to speak as though we did before in the, what do you all call it? 'The Land of the Spirits?'"

"We have not spoken before?" Torin said as he got to his feet.

Odin sighed. "Of course, you do not remember. Asgard does not come as easy to you as it does to Njal."

"Njal has visited... Asgard? The Land of the Gods?"

"Aye," Odin said while stroking his beard. "Quite a few times, actually. Well, the wilds, at least."

"Why have you come to visit me?" Torin asked, wiping the sweat from his forehead.

"Because I wish to discuss something with you. I am aware that you have decided to stop living for me and the other gods, but I have come to ask for your help."

"What could the allfather possibly need my help for?"

"Exactly what I needed Njal's help for."

Torin pondered what he said, but he also couldn't figure out if he was dreaming or was too drunk or anything other than what was actually happening.

"I had given Njal everything I could offer him on his journey to defeating Aelred. I had given him my favor. I made it so that when his friend was struck with an arrow, there were the proper items nearby to help him. I made it so that it snowed heavily on the battlefield in Eaglecrest so that it would be easier for my people to fight the Englishman in. I also gave him *just* enough power so that he could defeat you."

Torin's eyes widened, but then he bit his teeth and looked away. "I do not care anymore. I am living a new life. One where I can be free of my passion for revenge."

"But Njal is failing. He has chosen family over his people and his brother will be the destruction of him and everything he has worked for. So, I have become desperate again. However, in my search for a new answer, I realized that you are one who can lead our people to prosperity."

Torin looked up at Odin with creased eyebrows. "Do you actually mean that?"

"I have come here to offer *you* my favor. I wish to put my faith in you now, Torin. And I wish to see you fulfill your task of revenge so that our people may live. Think about the life you can have. Being a leader again. The king of my people. I can teach you how to travel to Asgard and speak with me whenever you wish."

"Why me?" Torin asked.

"Because Njal's brother is too infatuated with Jarl Sigrid, which makes his judgement easily skewed. And Ragnar's son back in Norway is too prideful for himself. He is more focused on making his father proud than anything that has to do with me. You, however, have always believed in me. You disobeyed Ragnar when you saw he would get everyone killed. That is the true making of a leader. A king."

Torin was silent for a moment as he pondered the idea. "But these people here need me."

"These people will die at the hands of Ruadan the Silent. Cathbad will make a choice to give everything up to his enemy in exchange for their lives. Ruadan will not forgive Cathbad and will kill him in front of everyone before turning this village to ash. Cathbad will be the death of these people. That is, unless you do something to change that."

"How?"

"You will need these Druids to follow you. You will also need Ruadan's to join you. There is only one way to make that happen, and you will know it when you see it. And as unfortunate as it may be, you have the choice to give Ari a death at the hands of Ruadan or you can give her the life of a queen. The choice is yours."

The swarm of ravens appeared out of nowhere again and covered the god entirely until they disappeared again. Leaving Torin alone in his room. The Norseman stumbled as he stood up and approached his bed. He ripped off his tunic as he felt hot and sick. Then bile released from his mouth onto the wooden floor before he laid down in his bed. He stared up at the ceiling, pondering what he had just seen. What he had just heard.

Odin wants to give me his favor.

Odin...

The allfather.

XVIII

❧

A Lord Falls

It had now been two months since she left Njal. Frigyth and Wigberht had spent a lot of time together. They hunted for deer, they fished by the river, they walked to the beach, and basically never left each other's side. When Wigberht found out about Frigyth being pregnant with his child, he could not have been happier. He was already thinking of names for the child depending on what the sex would be, and he continued to tell Frigyth that she needed to tell her father. She did not wish to tell him yet as she wanted every hour she spent with him to be about them. Nobody more. Not even her unborn child.

Frigyth would see her father for about an hour or two every day. She would have liked for it to be more, but she had other responsibilities to tend to. Also, because her father was usually only awake that long. They would talk about things from her childhood or memories of her mother, but they always ended with Birstain's mind focusing on something else. In fact, his mind was constantly fading in and out of the conversations that sometimes, Frigyth would have to act as though she had just walked in the door even though it had already been an hour. She would have to repeat what they spoke of. However, it didn't matter to Frigyth. She wished to see her father every moment she could and if she had to repeat a story, then so be it.

On this particular day, Frigyth was out with Wigberht in the market, fetching toasted bread and cooked chicken for dinner. Her baby bump was showing and almost everyone knew of her pregnancy. Everyone except her father.

Afterwards, they continued their walk throughout the market. The dimly lit cobblestone streets featured a thin sheet of snow on them as the early winter sun began to set behind the horizon. The two lovers reached the Dragon's inn which was now run by an Englishman. There, Frigyth's mind wandered. She looked at the exact spot where she waited in the cold mist like rain for the Norseman. She remembered seeing the large blonde man coming up to her with a smile across his face. His cheeks became as red as her cloak. She remembered thinking how handsome he was. How...

"Frigyth," Wigberht said, which finally pulled Frigyth out of her trance. "Is everything alright?"

"Why, yes, of course," she replied. "I am sorry."

"It is alright," he said with a smile as he grabbed her hand. "Let us keep going then."

She looked at Wigberht as she followed him. As she examined the features on his face, her mind stopped thinking about Njal. Her heart raced as she began to think of a life with the

Englishman. A life of her ruling Birmingham and an heir already on the way. She needed to tell her father. It was time. No excuse she could think of in her mind was valid anymore, since this was the life she chose.

"I want to tell my father tonight," Frigyth said out loud.

Wigberht stopped and faced her. He pulled her close and smiled. He wrapped his arms around her and kissed her forehead.

"That is the most splendid idea, my love," he said.

Frigyth heard those words.

'My love.'

She didn't know what to make of them. Those words made her mind race again. Did she love Wigberht? She wasn't entirely sure, so she decided to stay quiet. Was she truly happy about the child? Was she happy about leaving Njal and Eaglecrest? Her happiness was all Njal and Halfdan wanted for her, so she chose this path. Perhaps this path was the most logical to her, but was it the path that would achieve that goal? The one that would make her a genuinely joyous human being? What did it mean to even be happy? She was still very confused.

But even with all the confusing thoughts that roared loudly in her head like a thunderous summer night, she knew she chose this path. She had to see where it led.

She hugged Wigberht back and said, "Let us head to the castle."

*

The entirety of the chilly walk inside the castle walls, Frigyth thought in her mind of what to say to her father. What could she say? She had never said anything about leaving Njal, as she felt it wasn't important. And her father also didn't ask. His mind was so far gone that she had to wonder if the news would even register.

Each step in those cold and empty hallways felt like a year. She held onto Wigberht, the soon to be father of her child. She thought back to what he had called her.

My love.

Her mind shifted to the night when Njal had said that to her for the first time. As soon as he said it, she couldn't wait to say it back. Their connection was real. But was her connection to Wigberht real?

It must be, she thought. There was no place for her mind to be on anything or anyone else other than that of her people.

As they finally approached the corridor of her father's room, Frigyth knocked on the wooden door and after a few brief moments, Bertha opened. Frigyth tried to greet her with a smile, but she then saw the expression on Bertha's face. It was that of sadness and heartbreak.

"Lady Frigyth..." Bertha began.

Frigyth let go of Wigberht and got close to Bertha. She didn't even try to look in the room as she locked eyes with the caretaker.

"Is he... Is my father..." she asked, trying to swallow the frog in her throat.

"Not for long, dear. You best say your goodbyes..." Bertha said, tears streaming down her cheeks.

"I thought there would be more time," Frigyth said as she peeked into the room.

"After his slight improvements, so did we all. I am so

sorry," Bertha said before leaving and walking down the castle corridor, sobbing.

"Should I... Should I join you?" Wigberht asked, a look of sincerity on his face.

"No," Frigyth said before walking inside. She wiped a tear from her cheek. "I need to say goodbye to him myself, please."

"I understand," Wigberht said as he dropped his head. "I will be in the throne room."

Frigyth turned towards the room and walked in. She could hear Wigberht's footsteps in the hallway get fainter and fainter as she looked at what was left of her father. More of his old green expressionless mask was reforged together, not allowing anyone to see anything other than the empty black voids of the mask's eyeholes.

"Oh, father," she said as she sat down on the edge of his bed.

"Daught...daughter, is that... you?" he struggled to say. "I am sorry for my... my appearance. I hate the... the order.

Tears began to stream down Frigyth's face as she listened to his breathing. His lungs sounded like they were full of fluid and his mouth dry as could be. She reached out and grabbed onto his hand.

"I am here, father," she said.

"There is not much...time left for me...I am afraid," he croaked. "I can see glimpses of your mother... she awaits me in heaven... I can see... I can see her."

"You will be with her soon. Then, you can tell her how much I love her. How much I love the both of you."

"She is... she is proud of you...Frigyth. I am... I am proud of you... the woman you became. Leader of two people."

Frigyth creased her eyebrows at that. She remembered him saying that her place was in Birmingham. With her own people. She believed that her mere presence in Birmingham had shown her father that she left the Norseman behind. Left Njal behind.

"But father... I am here. I chose *our* people."

He coughed and turned his head so that he was facing the sound of his daughter's voice. "I wish I could see you... just one last time..."

"I am here," she said, squeezing his hand. "I am proud of you, father. You betrayed Aelred and fought against his tyranny. You avenged mother. You saved me. And now, our legacy will live on."

"What... what do you mean?" he struggled to say.

"I am with child," she said with a smile, her face as red as her cloak.

Birstain made a happy gasping noise. "My beautiful daughter... is with child? What a joyous... joyous day," he said while turning his head back so that he was looking up towards the ceiling. "The child will change everything."

"Change everything?" Frigyth asked, her smile turning to a look of curiosity.

"Yes," he coughed. "A child born of both... English and Norse... What will... you name the child? I bet Njal... I bet he wishes to name it... name it Ivar."

Frigyth froze at the sound of those words. Her heart sank.

"Well, father, I don't think you..."

"Or perhaps... after his friend... Hm, what was his name?" he paused for a moment. "Ulf!"

Frigyth's heart sank.

"But father..."

"He saved you, Frigyth...Njal saved you... I would not have done anything...I was not strong. *He* saved you... he saved *our* people... he saved... saved..."

Birstain's head went limp and his mouth made a strange gurgling sound.

"Father?" Frigyth asked. Her cheeks were home to waterfalls of tears. "Father, do not leave me... please... no, no... NO!"

Frigyth's screams of agony could be heard throughout the city of Birmingham. There was no feast that night. No coronation of the next Lord. No glad tidings. The city was so silent that it felt as though it was abandoned.

And nothing but the pain of loss remained.

XIX

Brothers

Alf blinked a few times before raising his head. He awoke to the feeling of an icy breeze hitting his face and the smell of hay and dirt striking his nostrils. His back was leaned up against the wall as his eyes finally focused on the man that was standing tall in front of him. It was his brother. Alf gave a little smirk and laugh as he felt the cold iron wrapped around his wrists.

"So, this is how you treat your family, huh?" Alf said as he raised his hands as far as they could go, being chained to the wall.

"You know why you are in here, aye?" Njal asked. "I truly hope that you do. Otherwise, you would be far more stupid than I could have imagined."

"Fuck you..." Alf said sternly before spitting off to the side.

"Maybe being under all that water as a child fucked

up your mind," Njal said. Alf's eyes widened, and he tried to jump at his brother in anger, but the chains kept him down. Njal didn't even flinch.

"You know NOTHING about what I have been through!" Alf yelled.

"And you know nothing of what *I* have been through either," Njal replied calmly. "But that is hardly the point. The point is that you would rather listen to that woman than even attempt to help me through my losses. It was so easy for you to let me go while I gave everything up for you."

"You know nothing of her. Her power and independence. Her strong-willed mind and her warrior's heart. She has given me the will to live, Njal. And your decision was to take her away from me."

"Alf, I have known her longer than you. I know who she is. And while she is an impressive woman, she has poisoned your mind with false dreams. She has a grudge against me and she is using you to punish me. She has turned you against your family."

"*She* is my family now," Alf said, a tear forming in his eye. "I wished to make her my wife. I... I love her, Njal."

Njal just shook his head. "I know you do. But love is not about everything you *would* do for a person. It is about working together. It must not be one sided. She took advantage of you, brother. I am sorry, but it is the truth."

Alf began to sob as he sat down with his back against the wall again. "You are punishing me for what I did. I understand that but...but I need to see her again."

"I cannot let that happen. You decided to kill Muspel

soldiers and attack Knud when he was attempting to bring you in peacefully."

"HE ATTACKED US WITH FIRE!" Alf roared.

"He did not attack anyone until you struck the first blow. But that again is not the point. The point is that you were attempting to overthrow me as king. You actually created a plan and were openly insubordinate in the market. For that, you are going to be in here for a while."

"WHY ME?! HOW IS IT THAT I BETRAY YOUR RULE AND I GET PUNISHED BUT HALFDAN, TORIN AND SIGRID ALL GET OFF EASY?!" he shouted, spittle flying from his mouth.

"Because you were not wrong about me. I should have punished them for what they did. But instead of going behind my back, you should have spoken with me privately. Not one time in my isolation did you come to speak with me. I truly am sorry the punishments had to start off with you, but I need to become the king our people deserve. One that focuses on expansion rather than taking what we want. A selfless king. With you on the throne, you would doom us all. You would have created a war with England and put our people in harm's way. I may have inexperience at leading, but I am following our father's teachings. His legacy needs to live on. For our people's sake."

"I...I hate you. I came here expecting to fight at your side and to live with my brother, but now all I feel is hatred towards you. I... I hate you," Alf said, then looked up into his brother's eyes. "DO YOU HEAR ME?! I HATE YOU! I DESPISE YOU!"

"And I am truly sorry for that, brother. But I have

now taken responsibility for my mistakes. You obviously have not. You are lost and you will pay for your betrayal."

Njal slowly walked out of the cell and closed it behind him. Alf continued to scream and cry at the top of his lungs as Njal walked out of the corridor and up the stairs until he was at the main level of the Great Hall.

*

The small road from Eaglecrest to Muspel was busy. People were out and about, shopping, eating and drinking. Njal felt the slight briskness in the air and looked out towards the sea to his left. He saw the waves were picking up a bit, which meant a storm was coming soon.

It was midwinter now. Snow would fall occasionally, but it was nothing like the prior winter. Njal thought back to the battlefield that day. The snow definitely helped slow down Aelred's forces and gave the Norsemen a bit of an edge. But how lucky were they that the snow fell like that when it did? Njal thought about if the battle was to be held during the current winter. Would they still have won? It didn't matter anymore. The world was as it was and there was no reason to dwell on false realities.

Njal broke from his trance and noticed the villagers that crowded the streets all looked towards their king as he passed by. They all greeted him with a smile and some even said, "Good to have you back."

Njal felt a warm sensation at that. He had stepped away from his isolation almost two months ago, but he was happy that the people chose to forgive him and were still on his side. After a few more moments of walking, he smelled the stench of oil and felt the heat that radiated from Muspel's walls.

The guards saw him approaching, and they opened the gates without hesitation.

Inside, Njal walked briskly through the village until he noticed the statue of Surtr, the fire giant, standing proudly in the courtyard before the Great Hall. He approached the doors, and the guards let him in. Knud was sitting on his throne with a cup of wine in his hand.

"Njal," he said with a smile. "Welcome back to Muspel. How did the meeting with your brother go?"

"Same as before, he will not speak with me. He will not even look at me. His mind has been poisoned by Sigrid, and the distance is not helping at all like we thought it might."

"Hm," Knud said before taking a sip of wine. "Shall we speak with her?"

"Aye, it is about time I finally speak with her since her capture," Njal replied. "Take me to her."

Knud nodded and stepped up off of his throne. He waved for Njal to follow him as the two walked through a corridor that sat behind the throne. It led a ways back until the level floor turned into a decent sized set of stairs. They both walked down until they reached the bottom, which showcased three very large cells that were separated by blackened steel bars.

Inside the middle cell was Jarl Sigrid of the Horse Clan. She sat with her back against the wall and her knees up. Her arms were resting on her knees and her head was drooped.

"Sigrid," Njal said in a forceful tone.

Her head raised, and she looked at him with a smirk. Strings of her blonde hair dangled over her face.

"Oh, the big boy finally came to see me," she said in a sour tone. "Is it to speak about your brother? Or perhaps you are looking for a good humping, since your precious Frigyth left your sorry arse."

Njal stood there straight faced and unamused from the other side of the bars. "I wish to know how this started. Honestly. No jests, only the truth. How did we go from fighting Aelred and trusting each other to this feud that you will not let go? This feud that you needed to win so badly that you even turned my own brother against me."

Sigrid started laughing. "You honestly do not know? Njal, you let that bastard Torin go free. Do you know how much pain he had caused me and my clan over the years? When you arrived in Demut that day, you said you were going to handle him. That our alliance would stay strong. But once I saw you let Halfdan off with a warning, I knew Torin would never be hunted down. No matter how many times you would say, 'oh, after this meeting with Edward' or 'oh, after I travel to London for Edward.' Honestly, at one point I thought the reason you never took me up on my offers to hump was because you were too busy playing with Edward's cock. Either way, I saw you as a weak man."

"That never stopped you from trying to make advances on me, though, right?" Njal asked, his face still stern as stone.

"Well," Sigrid shrugged. "What can I say? You are quite nice to look at. But truth be told, I felt as though I was the better leader. I should have been king. Humping you would have led me to the top, where I could have led our people."

"What makes you think that even then, I would have let you lead?"

"I told you; I saw you as weak. I would have made you my bitch," she said with an evil smile.

Njal smirked in amazement at what he was hearing. He scoffed.

"Loki lives among us, I suppose," Knud said, to which Sigrid turned her attention to him.

"Do not act as though you are free of any guilt or punishment. You have been trading with the Irish and those Icelandic bastards for months without any hesitation and no permission!"

"Njal is aware of my trades and has fully supported them."

Sigrid spit at Knud from her seated position and looked towards Njal again.

"We could have let you die on that battlefield, Sigrid," Njal began. "We rebuilt your home; we kept you alive. But leading your clan without the fear of Torin was not good enough, I suppose. You tasted a bit of gold and wished for the entire chest."

"Oh, spare me your lecture, Njal. I am tired of this. You either kill me or set me free. I will not sit in this cell much longer," Sigrid said, her attitude condescending.

"You will do whatever I fucking say," Njal growled. His face a look of anger. Everything that he had gone through since the beginning of autumn was building up inside of him. He was rageful. Frustrated. And yet, his mind was clear. He knew what he had lost. Most of which he knew he probably wouldn't get back. But he knew he could still make life better for his people. One task at a time.

Sigrid was taken aback by his bluntness, but returned to her normal attitude.

"Well, where has this beast of man been? Last time I saw balls this big on you, you broke Torin's jaw in and took his village! They must have finally dropped again!"

"You are never going to see Alf again. I hope you know that."

"That is fine, as long as I have you to visit me every once in a while," she said, biting her lip jokingly.

"You really do not care about him, do you?" Njal started, but continued before she could answer. "Of course not. He was just a pawn to you, I suppose. This whole entire time, I thought Torin was the worst of the Jarls on this coast. But as it turns out, it was you I had to worry about."

Njal and Knud turned and began to walk away, back up the stairs.

"I wonder where Frigyth is? Hopefully, you strike me harder than you struck her!" Sigrid shouted as the two men continued their way up. Once they got to the top, Knud led Njal over to a table and told him to sit down. He then went and fetched two horns of wine and brought them over to the table before he sat down, too.

"Well, that was something," Knud said. "You are sure that her clan will not attack us?"

"I made it very clear to them that if any sort of mutiny forms, they will have to attack Eaglecrest and Muspel soldiers. Obviously, with the Horse Clan being the smallest of us here, I am hoping that they have their wits about them and they continue to fall in line."

"Let us hope," Knud said softly. "I do not wish to destroy one clan of our own people due to their leader's actions."

"We could leave both of them locked up for a summer. See if that does much," Njal said before taking a drink of wine.

"I was thinking more than a summer, but yes. I am happy you do not wish to kill either of them."

"I wish to punish them so they have the chance to learn from their mistakes. I will not take their lives, so they do not have that choice," Njal said before sipping his wine.

"You have learned a lot in a short amount of time," Knud said.

"Experience will do that to someone," Njal said. "Besides, if word got out that we killed Sigrid, that might spark a flame in Demut's people, and they would want to avenge her. And Alf, I mean the villagers he arrived with, as far as I know, have nothing to do with his plans. From what I can tell, he saw them living happy new lives and just let them be. But just in case..."

"I will have spies watching them," Knud said, to which Njal nodded his head. "That woman downstairs really messed with his mind," Knud chuckled before taking a sip from his horn.

"I say we let them sit in their cells a bit longer, see if anything changes. Maybe if their attitudes change, they will only have to sit in there for the rest of winter, perhaps the spring. Until then, I bring news from London."

"Oh?" Knud said. "Good news, I hope."

"Aye," Njal said. "Edward said he will give us some of his builders to help with the expansion throughout the valley."

"Well, that is quite nice," Knud said.

Suddenly, there were three knocks on the door. Both men looked with curiosity.

"Come in," Knud shouted.

A guard swung open the door and said, "Men from Birmingham have arrived in Eaglecrest. They wish to speak with the king."

Njal's heart froze at the thought of what men from Birmingham wanted. The possibility that Frigyth was among them made him jump out of his seat.

"Let us go, Knud."

"After you," the Fire Clan Jarl said as he followed his king out of the Great Hall and through the village towards Eaglecrest.

*

They jogged as they journeyed back. Dark clouds could be seen forming over the ocean to their right. The smell of sea salt filled their noses, overpowering the stench of oil, which meant they were getting closer to Eaglecrest.

Once they arrived, they saw a crowd forming in the market around somebody, obviously whoever arrived from Birmingham. Njal's heart pounded as he quickly slipped through the crowd. He lightly pushed people to the side until he got to the center of the crowd. His eyes scanned the people in front of him for a red cloak. But...

Nothing.

Three men wearing green and brown robes looked at him. One of them was wearing brown leather armor with some silver lining. His hair was slick but long. His jawline was sharp and his stubble beard looked like a shadow.

"Ah, Njal Tokeson!" the man said, making eye contact. "A pleasure it is to finally meet you."

The man stuck his arm out, and Njal clasped his forearm. "Hello there, uh…"

"The name is Sir Wigberht. Leader to the Royal Guard of Birmingham, at your service."

"What can I do for you, Wigberht?" Njal asked hesitantly.

"Well, while I am very pleased to meet you, I do bring bad news."

"Yes?"

"The Lord Birstain of Birmingham has died," Wigberht said. Murmurs in the surrounding crowd. "There is to be a funeral in five days' time, followed by the coronation of the new Lord of Birmingham."

"Which is?" a villager shouted from the crowd.

Njal felt his throat constrict. He didn't wish to hear the answer. He knew who was to be crowned, but he knew that hearing it out loud would make it that much harder.

"The Lady Frigyth!" Wigberht shouted.

Njal felt a bile rise in his throat, and he clinched his fists and swallowed it. Wigberht looked back towards Njal and put his hands on his shoulders.

"I know that you are a busy man, Njal, but the Lady Frigyth and I would love for you to come and say goodbye to an old friend while waving hello to a new Lord."

Njal nodded his head. "I will see what I can do."

"Great! See you there!" Wigberht said before jumping back onto his white stallion and calling for his other two men he was with to do the same. Once they were all mounted, they stirred their steeds into a gallop and, just like that, they exited the village walls and were on the road back to Birmingham.

The people all looked at Njal and waited for him to say something. The urge he felt to just walk away and go back to the Great Hall was strong. Knud put his hand on Njal's shoulder and whispered, "Come on, friend. Let us get out of here."

Njal thought about Alf's words. Sigrid's words. He was not going to be weak. He needed to stay strong for his people.

"No," Njal said quietly. "No!" he said louder. He then walked towards the staircase that led to the top of the wall by the front gates. He turned and looked at all the people that were gathered in the market.

"People of Eaglecrest!" Njal shouted. "As it has come as a shock to you all, it is also one for me. Frigyth is to be the new Lord of Birmingham. We will have an alliance with her, that is the most important thing. Now, everyone go back to your days. There seems to be a nasty storm coming and we must prepare accordingly."

Everyone nodded and some whoops and hollers were heard from the crowd as well before going back to their business. Njal walked down the stairs and approached Knud, who smiled in sincerity.

"Are you alright, brother?" he asked.

"Aye," Njal said, slightly nodding. "I will be. It is the way of the world." Knud clasped Njal's shoulder, and the two walked towards the Great Hall. "Time to prepare for a funeral, I suppose."

XX

A Gods Asking

Torin awoke in a cold sweat as he struggled to catch his breath for a moment. He felt how wet his tunic was, so he quickly pulled it off him and threw it across his body. It slapped against the wooden wall of his hut. He put his head in between his hands and rubbed his eyes.

Odin is real. He came to visit me and offer me more than any saga story I could have ever asked for. I earned his favor.

He flipped his legs around so that they hung off his bed. The large man then stood up and walked over to his other set of clothing, which was a brown wool tunic, black pants, and black boots. He threw those clothes on and approached the door. Once he grabbed the black iron handle, he paused for a moment and contemplated what he was going to do about the prior meeting with a god. But after a moment, he shook his head and swung open the door and was met with a powerful beam of sunlight hitting his face. His eyes squinted.

"Torin!" the big lumbering and young Druid Golmac shouted to him from across the walkway. "Beautiful day for a hunt, no?"

"That it is, Golmac," Torin said, covering his eyes from the sunlight with his hand. "But I am going to have to pass. Have you seen Ari anywhere?"

"Aye," the big man said in his fur and bone clothing. A giant hammer was strapped to his back. "She is with Cathbad in his hut."

"Thank you, friend. Have a good hunt," Torin said as he began walking toward Cathbad's hut. Golmac smiled and trotted away like there wasn't a worry in the world.

A war is brewing, friend. I hope you are ready. Not only may I need you to fight Ruadan's men, but I may need you to help me kill that bastard Njal.

Torin shook the thought off.

What am I saying... The path towards my revenge is only obtainable by dispatching Cathbad, and I cannot kill him. He saved my life. Gave me a new home. I cannot throw that away. I WILL not throw that away. This is my new life. Odin's favor or not, this is the life I wish to have.

He waved hello to every Druid he passed on his way to Cathbad's hut and once he got there, he could hear muffled yelling inside.

Ari's voice.

Torin creased an eyebrow and walked in without knocking.

He saw Cathbad sitting in his chair while Ari was standing; her face was red as she turned towards the door.

"Torin," Cathbad said, surprised. "I would have come to fetch you if I knew this conversation would have started so early this morning."

"Oh, do not act like I have ambushed you," Ari said with a stern look. "You have known about Ruadan and have not said a single thing to any of us. How many failed missions ended with Ruadan killing our people and nobody knew except you? We all just thought, 'Oh, they failed' and yet they were probably murdered because of you!"

"What, uh," Torin stuttered, trying to interject. "What seems to be the problem?"

"He wishes to speak to Ruadan one on one and either fight him or offer him part of our land," Ari said, putting her hands on her hips.

Torin turned towards Cathbad in confusion.

"I thought we had spoken about a plan," he said. "One that does not involve you dying or giving any of our lands up."

"I slept on the matter and... You do not know this man, Torin," Cathbad said, shaking his head. "He is a monster. A devil in the form of a man. He will kill us all."

"What really changed your mind?" Torin asked. "Because we have excellent fighters here. Ones that could really give it to this bastard. And if you think you would die against him in battle, then let *me* have him. I found a new life here and the last thing I am going to do is throw it away because somebody tells me to."

Even though a god told me to...

The allfather...

"Wolves Hollow has been burned to the ground," Cathbad said, catching the wide eyes of the other two in the room. "Yes, I received word this morning. Obviously, Torin, you and I thought it would happen when we were speaking last night, but... It happened. And the details of what my scouts found they... they are absolutely horrific. People were found cut in half. Limbs missing. Innards scattered everywhere, waiting for the crows to feast. Children were burned to ash. Old women were strung up with nooses on the docks. Men were found with clean claw marks at their throats. Those were the ones who Ruadan found and killed. Effigies from their clan were scattered around the ruins to show that they were the ones responsible."

"But we have all faced men like him before, no?" Torin asked. "This violence is only meant to scare us. And I..."

"I *am* scared!" Cathbad shouted. "I am horrified! He is a living nightmare!"

Torin looked at Ari with shock and worry. Not because he was worried about Ruadan, but because he was worried about how scared his leader was. He was showing weakness and Torin saw it. He thought back to Odin's words from the night before.

"It is alright, Cathbad," Ari started. "We are here for you and we can..."

"Find out if there are any of his camps nearby," Torin interrupted. His friends both looked at him. "We are going to fight. I will lead my companions into their camp and kill them all. If they have done the same to us, then we must balance the scale. We owe it to the people of that village."

"No," Cathbad said. "I will not allow it. This man could be anywhere and he is a vicious animal. Losing you all, my best fighters, would mean the end of it for us."

"It will not be. We have the skills to wipe out a camp of them. Hel, we already took out a group of them while we were stuck on a boat as they came at us from all sides. Imagine what we could do to them with *us* on the offensive."

Cathbad put his hand to his chin in thought. "I suppose I can send scouts out like we discussed. But like you said, that itself is a task with much risk. If he finds out where our scouts are coming from..."

"Well, we cannot live in fear forever," Torin said. "Forget what I said last night. And I am sorry, but it is time you face this man you have been running from for so long. There is no other choice. If you do not do this, then I will anyway."

Cathbad looked angry at first, but then his face returned to normal.

"You are right, friend," he said. "Living in fear is no life at all. I will see what I can find."

Torin nodded his head, then looked towards Ari before turning and walking out of the hut. Ari had followed him out and she got close to him as the door shut behind them. She put her hand on his face and felt the stubble. Her thumb outlined his scar on his jaw. He closed his eyes as he felt her warmth.

"What is the matter?" Ari asked, her eyebrows creased with sincerity. "I can tell something is troubling you. Please, talk to me."

Torin sighed. "I just...I wish life were easy sometimes.

I know that it is not and it never will be, but... just give me one moment of peace so I can be a happy man."

"I wish for the same, too," Ari replied. "But at least we found each other. We can face these troubles together."

"Aye," Torin said, before brushing a strand of her blonde hair behind her ear. He leaned in as his lips met hers for a moment. He pulled away with a smile on his face. "I am quite hungry. Would you care to fetch some food with me?"

"I would love to," she said happily.

*

Torin watched Ari take a large bite out of the red apple that she had gotten from the market. They were walking along the pathway through the tall grass of the Fenlands. The birds were chirping as the sun shined brightly above. Not many clouds sat in the sky and the ones that did were white and fluffy.

He couldn't help but smile at her. At her beauty. The dimples that would form when she would chew her food or her shoulder-length blonde hair. He thought it seemed blonder in the sunlight. She looked over and caught him staring.

"What?" she asked, smiling with a mouthful of apple.

"Nothing," he laughed. "Just admiring is all."

She gave him a playful punch on the shoulder. "How far do you wish to go today?"

"As far as we want," Torin said, looking up at the sky. "I like not having to worry about much."

"I agree," she said. "It is nice to enjoy the company of nature and you."

"I also agree," Torin said as he watched her throw the stem of the apple off to the side.

"It is bloody chilly, though," Ari said. "Winter needs to hurry up and end already."

"But then I will not be able to hold you in my bed anymore," Torin said.

"Oh, you better," Ari laughed.

"No, it will be too hot," Torin chuckled as he got a look from Ari. He then reached out and grabbed her hand. The two of them walked in silence for a moment, listening to the sound of the birds and their feet crunching the dirt below them with each step.

"There is not much snow here," Torin said. "I figured we would have had much by now. It is not like the coast."

"It is always too warm here in the Fenlands for snow," Ari replied. "Rain, sure. But snow? Not very often."

"I do not mind a winter like this," Torin said before he sniffed the fresh winter air.

"So, tell me about your Jarl days," Ari asked as she used her free hand to brush a strand of hair behind her ear. "You have told me about your time from before Ragnar to your time with him. Then you told me of your time from your fight with that Tokeson man until you reached us. But I would like to know what kind of ruler you were."

Torin didn't mind the question. In fact, he actually liked talking about his past. Sure, there were parts that he chose to leave out like when he raped the fisherman's wife, which ended up giving life to the monstrous leader known as Aelred. Or when he killed Njal's companion Ivar just because he said that Njal was the true king. But the other events that occurred around those bad moments, he truly enjoyed speaking of. It made him feel like he wasn't alone in the world.

Torin looked at the hand-axe in Ari's belt when she asked the question. How something like that could tie together his old life and his new one was something he thought so strange. It made him wonder if he would do all of those horrible things now after everything he had been through with the Druids. He felt as though he was an entirely different person.

"My time as a Jarl was great. I made some mistakes, but I had many successes. I fought off Aelred and his men. I had a fight with a group of Celtics that washed up on our beach. And I even traded with one of Ragnar's sons, Bjorn."

"I was not aware that they were still alive," Ari said curiously.

"Of course they are. They are quite mighty as well. However, they are all on their own adventures. After their father died, they just decided to move on. That's when Toke took over as king in Norway and everyone migrated there. Until he let a fisherman invade and kill everyone. Which is what I believe Njal will do as well sometime in the future."

"Ah, I understand," Ari said, still a bit curious. "I mean, *did* you like leading, though?"

"I did," Torin said after a moment of pondering. "But it got hard at times."

"How so?"

Torin paused.

"Well, sometimes I did not know if I made the right choice. Eventually, I will admit, I became a bit stubborn. I found that the only way to convince myself that I had made the right choices was by continuously telling myself that I was right. Sometimes I was very wrong."

"I could never lead anything," Ari said as she reached her free hand out and felt the tall blades of grass. "Too much responsibility."

"Really?" Torin asked with a smirk on his face. "I could see you becoming an outstanding leader." She looked at him like he was insane. "No, I am serious! Your determination and your grit. You are not afraid to get dirty. You are not afraid of any man or woman or beast. And you also care for people, which is a big part of it. I personally have not mastered that one, but I can see it is a skill that you were born with."

"None of that changes my mind about wanting to lead, but, well, thank you for saying those kind words," she said with a smile as she gripped his hand a bit tighter.

*

The two of them watched the sun fade behind the horizon as they were laying on a patch of grass on top of a hill. The area sat about four miles west of the Fenlands. Torin was holding Ari under his arm as she rested her head on his chest. She traced her finger around the scars she could feel through his tunic.

"Do you believe there is an afterlife?" Ari asked randomly.

Torin's mind shifted to what he saw the night prior. Meeting the allfather face to face. Odin asking him to lead the Druids against Njal in an attempt to retake the throne. He had Odin's favor. He just didn't know what to do with it.

Yet.

"Aye," Torin finally said. "I know it is wrong, but I still believe in my gods. I do not pray to them anymore or honor them in the old ways, but I do believe they are there."

"Wow, that goes against everything Cathbad taught you!" Ari said in a sarcastic tone.

"Quit that," Torin said, as they both started laughing for a moment. "What about you? Do you believe there is an afterlife?"

"I believed in the Christian god when I was young, but after everything he put me through, I do not believe in him anymore," Ari said, sounding a bit hurt. They both sat in silence for a moment before Ari continued. "If your gods are the true gods, then why would they allow for so much pain and suffering?"

"I believe that my gods try to give us the hardest challenges to overcome. Not because they are cruel, even though some are, but it is because we have to overcome those challenges in order to reach Valhalla. We must use our surroundings, our own mind and hands, and destroy whatever challenge presents itself to us. Sometimes, people cannot handle it and they do not reach Valhalla. But if you die in battle, no matter the age, as long as you are holding a weapon, the Valkyries will come down and swoop you up and carry you to Odin's Great Hall where you can drink yourself into oblivion."

"Do you think that if we were to die in battle together, they would let me in to Valhalla with you?"

"If Odin did not let you in, I would travel across the Nine Realms and pull you from Hel's gate myself."

She smiled and kissed his cheek.

They decided to spend the night on that hilltop. It was peaceful and away from everything and everyone. And as Ari fell asleep on his chest, Torin looked upon the valley of stars above him and breathed calmly. In and out. A flash of a snake coiled up in a clearing struck his mind. He snapped out of his trance and thought back to Odin's words. He pondered them for a long time until he eventually fell asleep.

*

In the cold light of the morning, Ari held Torin's hand as they approached the village in the Fenlands. As they neared closer, they could hear a commotion coming from the village.

Voices yelling.

Screaming.

Their smiles turned to looks of seriousness as they both sprung into action. They unsheathed their weapons as they sprinted towards the village. Once they got past the last bit of tall grass, the village was in full view. A crowd was formed, and they were all looking at something.

Torin shouted, "MOVE!" and the crowd split like the red sea. Once Torin arrived at the front of the crowd, he could see a man...

No, not a man.

A boy.

It was one of the village scouts. Torin recognized the boy from the village gatherings. He always held a smile and a positive attitude. But that was not the case here. The boy was crying and blood streamed from his eyes. Or the empty sockets that remained instead. The scout's hands were missing, and the wounds were black and covered in ash. On his hip, the other two scouts' heads were strapped to his belt.

Torin looked up and saw Cathbad and noticed his

look of fear. Eyes wide, neck veins bulging, and sweat pouring off his face. He was horrified. Torin looked back at the scout. He leaned down and spoke slowly.

"Hello there, son," Torin said softly. "It is Torin. Try to calm yourself. Ease your mind. Listen to the sound of my voice. Focus on each sound I speak."

"T...T...Torin?" the boy struggled to say. "I cannot see... I cannot see!"

"Easy," Torin said, trying to calm him again. The scout was only around twelve summers. "Could you tell us what happened?"

"I...we were scouting a camp... to the north of us... beyond the river and hill...and...and... the man... he came out of nowhere and killed them," the boy struggled to say. "The man with the talons of a falcon. He... he dragged me to the middle and...and he...Oh god...he took my hands! He took my eyes! He...."

Torin quickly used his sword and, in one swift motion, cut the boy's head clean off. Most of the Druids knew what he was doing, but a few others, including Cathbad, gasped and looked at Torin in shock.

"No! What did you just do?!" Cathbad shouted as he ran over to Torin.

"The boy was not going to make it," Torin said, looking at the scout's body. "His mind, as well as his body, were fractured beyond repair. I have seen it before. Rather, give them a quick death than watch them suffer through the savage pain that awaits them."

Cathbad stayed silent, as did the other Druids, who were shocked.

"Where is the camp he was speaking of?" Torin asked, still looking at the body. "Are you aware of the location?"

"No," Cathbad said, shaking his head. "Absolutely not. We are not going to..."

"How did he find their camp? How did he find his way home? Did you go and fetch him, or did they drop him off here?"

"I will never have you or anyone else be..."

"CATHBAD, JUST ANSWER THE FUCKING QUESTION!" Torin shouted with thunderous rage as he turned towards his friend.

The village was silent. All were surprised at that. So much confusion... so much fear clouding the entirety of the Fenlands.

"I sent them to the north," Cathbad said, his head down. "I went out for a walk after our conversation yesterday morning and saw a camp close by. I returned home and sent the scouts to determine what sort of camp it was. Now we know." He cleared his throat. "And the boy was found by our fishermen, and they arrived moments before you did."

"You did not check the camp yourself? You just saw there was a camp, and you decided to turn back and make your scouts do it instead?" Torin scoffed. "You sent a boy to do your job?" He gave him a horrible look of disappointment.

"I do not like the way you are speaking to me, Torin."

"I do not much care anymore," Torin said before looking around the village. He felt the eyes that were glued to him.

The fear that was spreading through the camp like smoke. Torin realized it then.

"Do they know?" he asked Cathbad quietly.

Cathbad looked at Torin. "I do not know what you..."

"You bloody fool," Torin said loudly as he scoffed and began walking away. "Camma, Golmac, Ari, and Daegal. Let us stain our weapons with their blood."

"No! You get back here this instant!" Cathbad shouted.

Torin turned around and looked at Cathbad as he walked backwards. "You cannot stop us; you will be too busy explaining to the village why you sent a boy to do a man's job." He then turned around and continued walking north towards the river.

Cathbad slowly turned back towards the villagers and saw their looks of disappointment and anger.

Ari was the first to follow Torin.

Then Camma.

Golmac followed and as he passed by Cathbad, he shook his colossal head.

Daegal stopped and looked at his leader for a moment, then began following his other companions, leaving Cathbad to face his people and explain the situation they were in.

Torin was already up by the river when his comrades eventually caught up with him.

"So, what is the plan, boss?" Golmac asked.

"I am happy you all chose to follow me," Torin said with a smirk. "We have fought and defeated these bastards before and we can do it again. However, let us not get cocky.

They have experience and they know how to use fear. Keep your heads, stay by one another, and we will be fine."

"Aye," Daegal said confidently, which Torin took as a sign of respect. He looked at him and nodded in approval.

"Our plan is to move north. They know we are coming, so keep your guard up. This could easily be a trap, so stay sharp. We will walk this path until we come into eyesight of the camp. Then we will sit until nightfall and attempt to sneak in."

"If they know we are coming and it is a trap, why would we want to spring it?" Golmac asked.

"Because they know the ones who are coming are the best fighters," Daegal spoke out. "They will want to kill us. If we find their trap, but we have one of our own, we can find their weaknesses."

"Daegal has a point," Torin said. "If we know what their trap is, it is no longer a trap and we might even be able to make it our own."

"Right," Ari said. "Let us go then."

The five of them crossed through the river as the morning sun showed its face.

*

Around midafternoon, the companions came up onto a hill where they were able to see a small walled-off camp in the distant glade below.

"I am assuming that is it," Torin said as they all stood on the hill that overlooked it.

"God... they were not even a day's march from us," Golmac said. "Imagine if we did not cross their path on the river. We may have had no idea they were this close."

"A haunting thought, indeed," Torin said. "We will camp here until nightfall. Then, we enter."

"Right," Ari said. "Everyone lay down and stay under cover. They cannot see us up here."

Torin looked at her and smiled. *Not a leader, my arse,* he thought.

The companions laid down and began surveying the camp. They were a pretty respectful distance away, but they were able to see that people were walking around inside the short wooden walls. The camp looked as though it was put together within a few days. There were some tents scattered around and the wooden walls were high enough to keep out animals and a maybe a minor attack by bandits. However, they wouldn't be able to handle anything more than that.

After a few moments of silence, Golmac looked at Torin with a saddened look on his face. Torin took notice and sat up, showing the large man that he had his full attention.

"What is it, Golmac?" Torin asked as the sun sat high in the sky behind him.

"I am just thinking about Cathbad. He was so afraid," Golmac said. Everyone else began to listen in on the conversation. Camma was still surveying the camp, but even her ears were wide open.

"Aye, he was," Torin replied. "But we have fought them and won before. I am sure we could do it again."

"That is not what he means," Daegal interrupted. His eyes were looking off into the distance. "We have all had to train and defeat challenge after challenge, all based on conquering our fears. We all assumed that because Cathbad put us through those challenges, that he had already conquered his. Now, the entire village saw that he has not. In fact, he seems more scared than anyone else. And when your 'fearless leader' shows how fearful he actually is, it can come as quite the shock."

Torin nodded his head. "Everyone is afraid of something. Sometimes we do not know what we are afraid of until it shows itself to us. Perhaps he thought he was far enough away from Ruadan that he did not have to worry about him. But the past catches up with everyone. Sometimes when we least expect it."

Everyone nodded as Torin continued.

"We can speak on Cathbad later," he said. "Let us focus on the task at hand."

After a bit of time and some more surveying, the sun started to set behind the horizon, leaving a brush stroke of orange and purple in the sky.

"Alright gang," Torin said. "What have we learned about these bastards so far?"

"We have only seen five of them down there, but there could always be more," Daegal said.

"That they do not seem to be a combative camp," Golmac began. "But that does not mean they are not."

"Good, good," Torin said as the chill air flowed through his hair.

"They have no guards, we should be able to sneak right in," Ari said with a smirk to which Torin responded with the same.

"That they may very well be using magic," Camma said coldly.

"Aye," Torin said seriously. "We need to be ready for any sort of trap that involves magic. Stay on your toes, keep your head up and your wits sharp. Let us avenge those villagers from Wolves Hollow. But most importantly, let us protect our home."

They all gave a little cheer.

"The time is almost upon us," Torin said.

*

It was nightfall. Torin had looked around at his companions and they all nodded. They walked over to a small stream that was on top of the hill they were camped at and each one dipped their fingers into some mud that surrounded the stream. They began to paint their faces so that they would be even harder to see in the dark. Camma didn't have to do anything though, as she always wore extremely dark clothing and painted her face, so she constantly looked like a shadow.

"It is time," Torin said. He unsheathed his sword and gripped it tightly. Everyone else did the same with their respective weapons. His eyes gazed at the blade of Ari's hand-axe. He shook the feeling off. "We move swiftly, we strike fast, and we leave as soon as possible. We are here to send a message. Nothing more and nothing less."

Everyone nodded in agreement. Then, Torin began to jog down the small pathway that led towards the tiny camp. He could see the orange glow of the campfires inside and, as he got closer, he could smell the scent of cooked fish and vegetables.

With his companions close behind, they finally arrived at the wooden logs that acted as a small wall. Torin could peek inside the gaps between each log. When he did, he noticed the few tents, a fire in between them, and some people standing by the fire wearing black leather with feathers. Some had feathers attached to their shoulders, some on their heads, and others had them spread out on their various limbs. He noticed how some of the Druids had more black feathers on their clothing than others did. He assumed that it was the same as the Fenlands' process with the bones. The more you have, the more you have done for the rest of the clan.

Torin put the tip of his sword in the ground as he looked at Golmac. The large man quietly approached Torin, and they both grabbed the same wooden log. After a couple nudges and pulls, the log came loose. Torin looked at the gap and realized that while everyone else could get in through there, Golmac wasn't going to fit due to his large body. He tilted his head towards another log and Golmac understood. They then grabbed the log and pulled it until that one got loose from the ground as well.

Once the gap was big enough for everyone to get in, Torin grabbed his sword, crouched down and began walking through into the camp. They approached the first tent and listened. It didn't sound like anyone was inside. Anyone awake at least.

Torin then moved up to the front of the tent. This was where he got a full wall to wall view of the camp itself. There were four tents that sat on the outer areas of the camp and three small fires lit towards the center that allowed for the Druids to cook their food or get warmer. However, Torin could only see about five Druids. And while the camp was small, it seemed big enough to hold way more than five people.

A chill rose up Torin's spine. He felt a presence. One

that he had never felt before. At least not this strong. His mind began to see glimpses of a Snake, a giant tree, and a large black Raven that flew above the Snake.

"Odin," he whispered to himself. Torin had felt that Odin was with him. With the allfather at his side, there was no way he was going to fail this mission.

"What are we doing?" Ari asked him quietly.

He turned and looked at her and smiled. "I am going to spring the trap. Stay here until you know it is time."

Ari opened her mouth, but no words could come out in time as Torin instantly shot out into the open with his blade held high. The two feathered Druids that saw him first jumped up from their campfire and tried to unsheathe their weapons. However, they were too slow. Torin quickly slashed one across the chest diagonally in a spray of blood and the other one straight down the middle of his head with a crunching sound.

Torin's companions waited by the tent as they saw the last three feathered Druids approach him. Daegal and Golmac looked at Ari with confused looks and she responded with one of her own.

Torin waited for the first Druid to swing his sword as he blocked it and used the momentum to parry the man's move. Torin quickly jumped into action and jabbed his sword forward, his blade erupting out of the Druid's back in an explosion of blood.

The next Druid tried to attack from behind, but Torin sensed it. He quickly rolled out of the way and sliced through the Druid's ankle. The man toppled over and screamed as Torin shot up so quickly with his next attack, that even when the final

Druid blocked it, it left him stunned leaving room for Torin to make two quick slashes, cutting the Druid down. He then calmly walked over to the Druid who was missing a foot and ankle, and he slowly pushed the blade of his sword into the man's chest, silencing his grunts.

Torin looked around, waiting for something. Anything at all. But his eyes were met with nothing other than an empty camp and the confused looks of his companions. His ears heard nothing other than the nighttime breeze and the crackling of the campfires. His nose smelled nothing other than fire and life blood now.

Suddenly, a whistle could be heard in the distance. It wasn't a normal whistle. It was a screeching sound. Torin heard the noise, however, and felt nothing but caution. He continued to look around, but saw nothing. He then looked over and noticed his companions. They were all holding their ears and looked to be in an immense amount of pain. Golmac was rolling around on the ground, Ari screamed in agony, Daegal was crying and even Camma was releasing a scream of her own.

Torin, however, was unaffected. He thought back to his first meeting with Elhhere. He remembered the curse that was put on her shack. The one that he had to learn to focus on other things and it would reside. He realized this must have been the plan. Trap those that attacked with a curse so they are an easier kill.

Torin heard the small gates of the camp open up and he turned to look. Inside came around twenty more Druids. They were all dressed in black and had red paint around their eyes. They all had collars made of large black feathers. Their swords were curved and the hilts black. They looked a bit different from the Druids that attacked them on the river to Wolves Hollow and even the ones Torin had just killed.

These Druids looked more elite.

They surrounded Torin and stopped moving at once with their weapons drawn. Torin steadied his feet and gripped his sword tightly. He felt the cool wind flow through his black hair. He felt his muscles twitch as they were ready to pump all the energy into his attacks. He snarled as he waited to taste his enemy's blood.

But before anything could happen, he heard the sound of some kind of metal tapping together rhythmically. The faintest sound but one that caught Torin's attention. Suddenly, two Druids stepped to the side, showcasing a man. His clothes were black. His cloak flapped behind him as he walked forward. His face was covered by the skull of a wolf. The tapping of metal was clear now. Torin looked down at the man's right hand and saw his long nails. They were splinted with iron, so when he tapped them together, they would make a fluttering sound.

The man approached Torin but stopped a good six feet away from him. The two stared at each other for what felt like a long while.

"So," Torin said to break the silence. "You are Ruadan, I am assuming."

"Why are you not like your friends over there?" The man asked. His voice was soft, but each word sounded as though he was struggling to speak. "How does the curse not take?"

"Does it matter?" Torin asked. "I do not ask you why you have nails that long. Even though I am quite sure you use them to scratch those hard-to-reach places on your arse."

"Hm," Ruadan said. "Why are you here?"

"We are here because you attacked us on the river for no bloody good reason. We are here because you killed men of ours. We are here to..."

"No," Ruadan said. His voice sounded like a sharp whisper that could cut through anything. "Why are *you* here, Norseman?"

"I am Druid now," Torin said sternly. "Let my friends go of this curse you bestowed upon them."

Ruadan looked over at Torin's companions and nodded. One of the Druids that was with Ruadan stepped forward and snapped her fingers. She was thin and had all black hair. White paint with red lines graced her face. Obviously, a magic user of some kind.

In an instant, the curse was lifted. However, the feathered Druids then turned their weapons towards the struggling captives.

"I wish to speak with you, and *only* you," Ruadan said. "Please, come with me."

"No," Torin said. "I will not follow you into some horseshite trap. Speak to me here. I do not have time for your games."

"Hm," Ruadan said. "Fine."

The man used his left hand to pull his skull mask off and showcase his face. It was battle-hardened and older. His red hair and beard had small streaks of gray in them.

"As you have guessed, my name is Ruadan and these people that have you surrounded are my family. The Celtic Druids of the Crow. We have been searching for the leader of your people for quite some time since he betrayed us and attempted to start his own clan. I do not fault you and your friends for joining his clan. He has taken our values and bestowed them upon you. So, in that respect, I only ask for him. If you can give me Cathbad, I will spare you and your village and you can make it your own."

Torin spit at the ground before Ruadan. "Do you think I do not know what a pile of shite that is? I used to be a king. Do you know how many false promises I gave? I know that nothing is going to stop you from killing us all."

"Hm," Ruadan said. "You may have been a dishonorable leader, but I am not. I keep my word."

"I highly doubt that," Torin said.

"So, explain to me then, Norseman. Why is it you, a king, are now invading one of my camps and intervening in a matter that simply has nothing to do with you?"

"Because it has *everything* to do with me!" Torin shouted. "There is a reason I am here. There is a reason your little curse did not affect me! There is a reason you will fall by *my* hand!"

Ruadan squinted his eyes before putting his mask back on.

"Really?" Ruadan said, before tapping his iron nails together. "Because I have faced many Norsemen in my time. Many stronger than you. And none have ever seemed to even come close to ending my life. I doubt a failed king and outcast will be able to achieve any different."

Torin roared and swung his sword at Ruadan, but missed wildly as the red-haired man jumped away quickly. The feathered Druid leader then snapped his nails together which forced the surrounding Druids to grab Torin's companions and force them to their knees. Torin quickly turned around and noticed what consequences his outburst had.

"Wait, wait, wait!" Torin said, holding his hands up, his right one still holding his sword. Each one of his friends had a blade to their necks. "Do not hurt them, please."

"Hm," Ruadan said as he looked at the Norseman. "You actually *care* for these people."

"Aye," Torin said, surprising even himself. He hadn't cared about anyone in such a long time that this feeling was a bit new to him. People were just objects. Tools to use to further his own saga. But not these ones. These people that he had fought with in one battle meant more to him than anyone who spent time with him in Ragnar's army. And he had just put them in danger.

"I am sorry," he said.

Ruadan sighed and stepped forward towards his captives. He stopped at Daegal and used the nail of his pointer finger to lift his chin up. He examined the young man's every feature.

"Stop... please..." Torin pleaded again. "I will go with you."

"Torin, I had already asked for that favor earlier, to which you responded by attacking me. So, unfortunately, I have no other choice but to show you that I mean what I say. I am to be *feared*. When I speak, I will be *heard*. And when I strike, I strike to *kill*.."

Ruadan quickly jumped from Daegal to Camma and

put all five of his nails in her throat. Torin screamed with rage as Ruadan gripped and pulled, tearing Camma's throat out. Torin gripped his sword tightly and jumped to Ruadan.

The feathered Druid dodged each strike without any trouble at all. He then interrupted Torin's swing by grabbing the hilt of the sword and smiled behind his skull mask. Torin's eyes were wide and actually showed a bit of fear.

"I tried to teach you, Norseman," Ruadan said. "But I suppose I will have to kill *all* of your friends."

CAW!

*

Torin saw flashes of another land. One where he took the form of a Snake. One where a crow sat perched upon the branch of a tree.

"Torin," the Raven spoke. "Relax your mind. Heighten your senses. This man is nothing compared to what you have faced."

"How can I save my friends and get out alive?" the Snaked hissed.

"You know what you must do. You must become your former self. You must strive for your vengeance. Someone took your life from you. You must take it back and these fools stand in your way..."

The serpent hissed and flashed its fangs.

"Kill them," the Raven said. "Kill them all..."

*

Torin came back to reality. Ruadan still held his hand and weapon still. Torin's eyebrows creased and his mind filled with rage. His mouth made a soft growl. The growl morphed into a shout, which finally became a world-shattering battle-cry. He used his other hand and stepped forward, punching Ruadan in the face hard enough that it broke his skull mask and knocked him on his arse. Torin felt the leather that tied around the hilt of his sword. He felt the weight of his weapon. The power of it.

With one swift motion, he jumped onto the Druid that was holding Ari and slit his throat wide open. Ari quickly turned around and grabbed the dying man's weapon and she quickly punched the curved blade into the Druid's chest that was holding Daegal in an explosion of blood.

Golmac noticed and swung his head backwards, cracking the Druid's nose that held him. Torin finished off the kill by swiping his throat with his blade. Golmac quickly picked up a sword and the four of them stood back-to-back and awaited the other Druids.

"I guess we will not be speaking after all," Ruadan said while he stood up. His face showing a bloodied nose. He fluttered his nails together, creating a cricket like chime. His feathered Druids stepped closer and closer until Torin and his friends' backs were against the wooden logs that made the camp's walls.

Torin quickly looked behind him and noticed they were luckily in front of the spot where they entered. There was a gap that they could escape through, but if Ruadan set his men on them quickly, they would be overrun.

"There is nowhere to run, Torin!" Ruadan said happily. "It is the end of your days and the end of Cathbad's! I will..." he broke off as flames spread high into the sky, catching a few of his Druid's on fire. They screamed and attempted to pat the flames out, but to no avail. Everyone looked over at one of the campfires and noticed that Camma was laying there, holding her neck as blood gushed out. Using her other hand, she reached into a small pouch and threw some dust on the campfire again, creating another massive explosion of flames. Torin looked at her with wide eyes. She looked back at him and nodded her head as she gurgled on her own blood. Torin nodded back, and he turned to his other friends.

"We need to leave now!" Torin yelled.

Daegal went first through the gap between the logs. Ari second, Golmac third and Torin last. After they were all outside the walls of the village, Torin commanded for everyone to run and to not to turn back.

Inside the village, sparks and fire lights surrounded Ruadan. He then turned his attention to Camma. He squinted his eyes as he began walking towards her, his men burning in the background. She, however, smiled through her pain and reached behind her back. Ruadan took notice and stopped his walk. She had pulled a small sack from behind her back and readied herself.

A Teine...

Ruadan's eyes widened as he knew the weapon, and he twisted in the other direction. Camma smiled as she threw the Teine into the campfire.

As Torin and company were around a hundred yards away, they heard a massive explosion behind them. Logs and people went flying. The group paid no mind to it and kept pumping their legs harder and harder through the darkness of night. They eventually arrived at the hill where they surveyed the camp earlier that day.

They stopped and tried to catch their breath. Ari fell to her knees in exhaustion.

"Camma..." Golmac said as he panted. "She..."

"Did...did she...kill him?" Daegal asked, hunched over with his hands on his knees.

"No," Torin said. His breath catching up with him faster than everyone else's, especially Golmac. "We just pissed him off."

XXI

An Internal War

Njal could feel the bitterness of the air on his skin. His brown horse could to as it walked through the last stretch of the forest before reaching the city of Birmingham. The clouds above were dark and gray, each one threatening snowfall. Knud was on his horse beside Njal as well as two members of the Fire Clan, who were there in case any bandits wished to try their luck on the road. It had been four days since they left Eaglecrest, and each day felt colder than the last.

"This cold makes me miss Muspel," Knud said as he looked at the sky above him. "I thought we were nearing the end of the winter months."

Njal did not respond. He was in his own mind. Thinking about how they had just passed the forested area where he had fought his old friend, Ulf, for the first time. Where Frigyth was stabbed and he had to rush off into the woods and find the witch, who eventually became a close friend to him. He wondered if her shack was still there. If it was empty now. Or if maybe that's where she and Halfdan now lived. They could be right inside the trees to his right, and he would have no idea.

He wished to see them again.

He missed them...

"Njal?" Knud said, which broke the Norseman out of his trance.

"Aye?" he replied, looking forward now. "My apologies. What did you say?"

"Nothing important, really. Just speaking of the weather."

"Ah," Njal said.

Knud looked at him and felt a bit of sadness for the man. He needed to speak of his troubles, not bottle them inside. He decided to speak.

"Do you have any idea what you are going to say to her?" Knud asked.

Njal took a few moments before speaking. "No..." he finally said. "I cannot even think about it. Seeing her up there and taking up the mantle of her father... it is going to crush me, Knud."

"I know. But showing her that you still care enough to support her will leave a positive statement. Perhaps you both could work this all out. You just need to speak with her privately."

Njal noticed a few flakes of snow beginning to fall around him.

"I intend to," he said.

*

After a while, it started to become dark. A white-gray sky was becoming a darkened gray and blue. The snow was falling steadily, but not really sticking to the ground. The travelers finally neared close enough that they could see the tops of the Birmingham walls in the distance. And as they got over a small hill, Njal's eyes filled with tears.

On the lefthand side of the road, Njal could see the old remains of Alvin's farm. They still stood there, burned and broken, but they were still there. Njal closed his eyes and thought back to his life there. It was peaceful and calm.

He was forever grateful for the life he now lived. But as of late, a growing part of him wished he never met the girl with the red cloak behind the alehouse. If he hadn't, none of this would have happened.

"But then Aelred would still be the ruler in these lands," Knud said randomly, knowing exactly what Njal was thinking.

Njal turned and looked at Knud with wide and shocked eyes. He wiped a tear from his face.

"Come on, Njal," Knud said, shrugging. "I assume those ruins are the farm you were raised in. Your reaction to seeing them said it all. I know what went through your head. You are wondering if you chose the correct path. Well, I can promise you that you have. I know this one is hard, and it has left you broken, but you have made the world better because of it."

Njal said nothing as they passed the ruins of Alvin's farm.

"Think about it," Knud continued. "England is far

better now than it was. Our people are thriving on the coast, and although it hurts deeply, Birmingham is about to have a ruler that will stay our ally due to your personal relationship with the woman in charge. I mean, alliances with the Englishmen was something not a single one of us were even considering until you came along. Our people are safer. *Their* people are safer."

"I know," Njal said as they passed the ruins of Alvin's farm. "It just feels strange being back here under these circumstances, that is all."

After a short period, the group finally arrived at the city walls. The gates were wide open, allowing people to come and go as they pleased. Njal gave a little smirk to see that had not changed. Inside, the city was lit up with lanterns and torches as the snow fell steadily. There weren't many people walking around, likely due to the weather. Njal was pleased to see the city hadn't changed very much at all, inside or out. They made it to the courtyard where Ivar's old alehouse was and where Njal waited for Frigyth. However, Njal was saddened to see that The Ironside was not its name anymore. He decided not to examine the name anymore. To him, it would always be called the Ironside. So, the new name didn't even register.

"That was Ivar's old alehouse," Njal said as his horse slowly walked by.

"Ah," Knud replied. "I wish I could have met him."

"Me too."

After they passed through the marketplace, they found their way to the castle gates, where two guards stood with spears in one hand and shields in the other.

"Halt!" one guard shouted. "What is your business here?"

"I am Njal Tokeson, king of the Norse people, and we were invited to the funeral and coronation of the new lord."

"Ah," the guard said. "Right then. You and your men have rooms down at the Dragon Inn. Tell the innkeep that you are Wigberht's guests and he will get you settled. The funeral begins at sundown tomorrow, followed by the coronation. Please arrive on time."

"We do not get castle rooms?" Knud asked Njal softly so that only he could hear.

Njal shrugged his shoulders and said to the guards, "you have our thanks."

The Norsemen turned their steeds and headed towards the courtyard of the city. That was where the inns and alehouses were. Once they got there, they noticed that, in fact, Ivar's old alehouse was now called the Dragon Inn. Njal's attempt to keep the name of the inn the Ironside in his head was now all for naught.

"I wonder why they would put us here?" Njal asked as they began stepping off their horses and hitching them to the post outside.

"Sentimental, maybe?" Knud said. "Perhaps Frigyth thought it would make you happy."

"No," Njal said. "She knows that it would make me think about everything that led to this moment. That it would make me feel responsible for Ivar's death. That it would make me think of her. She would not do this. Something does not seem right."

"Of what exactly?" Knud asked.

"I do not know yet," Njal said before walking inside the inn. Inside, the fireplace crackled in the corner. The orange glow from the fire lit up an old man's face as he sat behind a desk. He had gray hair and a decently long beard that was colored the same.

"Hello," Njal greeted, trying to force a smile while ignoring the nostalgia.

"Hiya, there!" the old man said happily. "What can I do ya for?"

"We are in town for the funeral," Njal said. "We should have some rooms ready for us. I am Njal Tokeson and this is Knud, as well as two men from our home."

"Yes, of course," the old man said, looking down at his book. "I have two rooms for you all, one bed in each. You will have to double up on the beds."

Knud sighed. "No need. My men and I will take the one room and you can take the other."

"No, Knud, I can..." Njal attempted to say.

"This will not be a debate. You deserve it," Knud said, to which Njal smiled sadly.

"Alright... thank you."

Knud nodded his head.

The innkeep handed the two keys over the desk to the Norsemen and they went to their respected rooms. Njal gave his companions a nod of his own before entering his room.

Inside, he began to undress. He threw his black leather armor off to the side as well as his gauntlets, boots, and bear cloak until he was in only a black tunic and black pants. He laid down on the bed and looked up at the wood ceiling. The howling of wind could be heard outside.

The storm must be getting worse.

He then closed his eyes and tried to enter the Land of the Spirits. But...

Nothing.

He still couldn't understand why he was able to see those flashes of the realms when Edward came to visit him. He had been cut off from the other world since Odin visited him.

"I could really use your guidance right about now, Ingrid," Njal said to himself quietly.

He sighed, then decided that he should rest. He tried his best to quiet his mind. After some time, the Bear King eventually fell into a deep slumber.

XXII

Embers in the Fire

The cold showed its face as the people of Eaglecrest all curled up in their beds with their fur blankets and loved ones. Those that were still awake sat in front of their fires, attempting to stay warm. Winter was ending, but it was ending with a vengeance. Any sign of dark clouds could mean snow, so people spent their days chopping down trees for firewood or hunting for pelts to make into blankets.

The village of Muspel, however, was a bit different. The night was hot, just as it always was. The stone furnaces and iron enforced walls of the buildings and homes would keep heat inside; especially since a good half of the village was built within the side of a cliff.

The people of Muspel would sleep with as little clothing as possible that night as a shipment of minerals and volcanic rock was brought in by Icelandic traders earlier that day and the work that those were used for made the village especially hot.

Sigrid, however, sat alone in her cell with a different type of clothing.

When she was first thrown into the cell, she was wearing her Jarl's armor. The brown leather vest, brown tunic underneath, the brown pants and boots to match. However, she was given a lighter shirt and new pants so she could live out her sentence a bit more comfortably. She had set her Jarl armor to the side and used her orange and black cloak as a blanket most nights.

If she needed it, of course.

This, however, was not one of those nights. The heat outside had radiated its way indoors, and she sat in her cell with sweat dripping off her head. She was dressed in her Jarl's armor.

She was hot, yes, but her clothing was needed. She sat and waited in the lonely, dark, and moss-covered cell in the lower levels of Muspel. That is until she heard footsteps.

Her eyes glanced through the bars at the staircase where a soldier dressed in all black showed his face. He was young. Probably had around twenty winters at his back. His red hair was well groomed and his beard was spotty and not yet full. He was in pretty decent shape, a bit on the skinnier side, though.

"Hello, Jarl Sigrid. I am supposed to bring you your dinner so... here," the young man said, a bit nervous. He handed her a piece of bread through the bars. He made sure to let go as soon as her fingers touched the item of food so she couldn't grab him.

"Thanks, half-wit," Sigrid said, before taking a large bite from the bread. Sweat collecting on her brow.

"You are welcome," he said sincerely, paying no mind to the name calling. "Is there anything else I can do for you?"

"What are you, my servant?" Sigrid said sarcastically.

"Well, it is just that," the boy stuttered. "You are still a Jarl. One that... well, one that I look up to. So, if there was anything else I could get you, I would be happy to."

Sigrid stopped eating and looked up at the lad. "Well, I appreciate that," she said. "And actually, I think there *is* something you can do for me."

The guard awaited her response.

"Do you mind telling me what time it is?" she asked.

"Late evening, m'lady," the young man answered.

"Hm," she smiled. "You seem like a good age. Not a bad body. Decent hair..."

The guard titled his head at her in confusion.

"I would like to hump you," she said nonchalantly.

The man took a step back. His cheeks turned as red as his hair. "W...What?"

"Would you like to hump me?" she asked, biting her lip. "I have not humped in sometime and I could really use it. I promise I will sit in my cage like a good girl when we are done."

"I...I do not think I..."

"Why?" Sigrid said before gasping. "Gods... You are a virgin!"

"No, no," the man said, becoming flustered. His face could not have gotten more red.

"Yes, yes!" Sigrid said, throwing the bread to the side and stepping up to the iron bars of her cell and grabbing them. "Do people make fun of you?"

"I..." the guard stuttered before dropping his head. "Yes..."

"Well, I promise I will not tell a soul," Sigrid said, making a sad face, pursing her lips. "I will make you a deal. If we hump now, you will not be a virgin anymore and people cannot make fun of you and I can finally get it out of my system. Then, I will stay right back in my cage. Huh? What do you say?"

"I... I should not."

Sigrid grabbed her leather vest and opened it from the middle, showcasing her brown shirt she had underneath. She then lifted the shirt up enough to show the young man her breasts.

"Come on," she said, biting her lip. "You could be holding these right now."

The young guard contemplated everything before making the decision. There was no way it could be a trap. Sure, she was in a cell, but she was a Jarl of a very respected clan. She had to abide by some sort of honor.

Right?

The guard reached behind his back and grabbed the keys for the cell door. Sigrid began to laugh in a sensual tone. The guard then fiddled with the key ring until he found the right one before putting it in the slot of the lock and unlocking the door. He opened it and kneeled down towards Sigrid. She reached behind his head and pulled him close, kissing him instantly.

She put her hand on his groin and began to rub up and down. Repeatedly until she heard a slight commotion coming from upstairs. She then grabbed his pants by the waist and began pulling them down.

However, she felt something. Something that she needed.

Somebody screamed upstairs.

The guard's eyes widened, and he quickly pulled away from the Jarl's embrace. But before he could do anything, Sigrid grabbed the seax he had sitting at the belt on his trousers, unsheathed the weapon, then used the blade to slice the young man's neck wide open in a fountain of blood.

Her expression was stern and rageful as she threw the gurgling corpse off of her body before standing up. She tucked in her shirt again and closed her vest back up. She then reached down for her cloak and attached it to her shoulders.

Suddenly, footsteps could be heard coming down the stairs, and Sigrid readied herself. But to her excitement and relief, it was only two of her loyal clan members.

"Oh, thank Odin," she said. "What is the situation?"

"The soldiers are distracted by the furnace explosion. We must leave quickly, though, if we are to escape without any trouble."

"Alright, lead the way, boys," Sigrid said with a smirk. "Let us return to Demut so we can be armed and break Alf out of his cell. Then we can destroy that pathetic whining dog, Njal."

"Yes, Jarl Sigrid," the men replied before taking off up the stairs.

Sigrid smiled from ear to ear.

XXIII

All Things Must End

"Both of you, go on a relax. Or walk around the village and do as you please," Knud said to the two men. "Njal and I are planning to travel down to the farm he grew up on."

The two Muspel soldiers nodded their heads and expressed their appreciation. That was when Knud, all dressed in his armor again, left the room and noticed Njal standing on the outside of his own.

"Good morning, Njal," Knud said as he shut the wooden door to his room behind him.

"Hello, Knud," Njal said, trying to force a smile. "How did you rest?"

"Cannot complain. You?"

Njal swallowed hard. A frog arose in his throat.

"Let us get going, aye?" he finally asked.

Knud nodded his head.

"Shall we take the horses?" Knud asked.

"No," Njal replied as the two stepped outside of the inn. "I would rather walk."

Njal and Knud spent the morning buying and eating some breakfast before making their way to the farm around midday. The clouds were low but scattered that day. Any time a cloud would come overhead, it would release some snow or rain and sometimes both. But every time the cloud would pass, the sun would raise the temperature by what seemed like ten degrees.

"Such strange weather, is it not?" Knud asked as his feet crunched the mixture of dirt and fallen snow from the night before with each step.

"Aye," Njal replied as his eyes glancing around. His mind was filled with memories of this road. He used to walk to and from Birmingham all the time. This time, he was doing it as a much different person.

"So," Knud began. "Tell me about this, Alvin. I would very much like to hear of your life before all of this."

Njal didn't speak for a moment and before he did, he sighed.

"Well, when I first arrived here in England, my plan was nothing more than to charge head first into London's gates and kill Aelred, even if it killed me. And I was more than aware that it would. But again, if I succeeded, and he died, I did not much care. That *revenge* was all I cared about. So much so that I would rather have died with Aelred than learn what to do with my life after I succeeded." Njal cleared his throat. "But one day, I was met by a handful of soldiers. I tried to fight them off, but

I was overpowered. But instead of killing me, they decided to throw me into slavery. The only lords around here at the time that even had a slavery option for Norsemen were Birstain and Eacnung. Winchester was obviously too far, so I ended up here. In Birmingham."

"That is where you met Alvin?" Knud asked.

"Aye. I remember standing up on the wooden platform. Looking out at all the people who wanted me as their slave. Everyone looked at me like I was the devil. But they needed workers, and us Norsemen were the only option." Njal paused and held a look of amazement on his face. "Gods, they hated us... That is, except for one man who stood in the back. His eyes looked at me with what looked like sincerity. Kindness. That man bought me and raised me like his own son. I was very lucky."

"Hm," Knud said with a smile.

But then Njal stopped in his tracks. The burned farmhouse came into view a good distance down the road. After a long pause, he kept walking. Each step towards the area brought back memories. Njal did not say another word until he reached where the front door of the broken down building would've been.

"The day he died," Njal began. "I saw the flames from far away and did not stop running until I reached this point. Some words were painted on the door and I entered. I heard Alvin's coughing from the other room. That is where I saw him and watched him pass on from here to the next life."

"I am so sorry," Knud said.

"If Odin does not allow this man into Valhalla, I will travel to the Soul Road in Helheim and fetch him myself."

"What if he is in his god's Heaven?" Knud asked as he noticed a small wooden cross on the blackened floor.

"Then his god better take care of him as well as he took care of me."

The two Norsemen stayed in the farmhouse a bit longer until they decided to head back to the inn and prepare for the funeral that was set to begin at sundown.

*

Njal and Knud were dressed in their black leather armor, black pants, black gloves, and black gauntlets. They had their swords strapped to their hips and their respected cloaks to their shoulders.

The clouds eventually came together to create a snowstorm. Not a baffling blizzard or anything like that. More like a calm and relaxed storm. The wind was minimal and the snowflakes steadily fell as the sun set behind the horizon. However, due to the cloud cover, nobody could see the ball of light.

The two Norsemen stepped outside of the inn and noticed the entire city of Birmingham was walking in a crowded line towards the castle. Nobody spoke and everyone had a sad look on their faces. Some were holding lanterns and others large candles to help light the way. Njal and Knud stepped forward and molded their way into the line of people. They continued walking until they finally reached the castle, whose gates and doors were wide open, allowing everyone to enter.

For most, this would be their first time inside the castle walls. While that seemed like an exciting thought, it wasn't. The people of Birmingham knew that Birstain had his hands tied to being Aelred's puppet. However, that never stopped him from trying to be fair and look out for everyone. And betraying Aelred in the battle on the coast showed everyone that he truly did care for them, and the entirety of England, for that matter.

Inside the castle walls now, Njal noticed that everyone was coming to a stop in the throne room. There were already quite a few people formed in a crowd before the throne, which was now an altar. In fact, the throne room looked quite a bit different now. There were banners hanging high above that showcased Birmingham's sigil, there were candles that lined up to the dais, and the stained glass windows were all now just regular windows.

"I am not standing back here behind all of these people," Njal said to Knud. "Come on, let us find somewhere else."

"You have a better spot?" Knud asked as Njal was already heading off in another direction. He didn't receive an answer.

Njal continued weaving himself in the opposite direction of the rest of the townsfolk until he exited the castle gates. Knud, not far behind, grew confused but stayed silent. Njal then branched off away from the crowd and stomped over to a large tree. There, he grabbed the body and used the branches to climb up.

Knud grew even more confused; however, he still decided the silence was the best option here. Njal then balanced his way on a branch that looked like it led to a small window. He used his hand to push open the window, and he climbed through. Knud, without question, did the same, and the two men found themselves inside a tight and cramped area. A small hole in the wall before them which offered a view of the throne room.

Knud looked down and noticed a few books, all about stories

of the Norsemen. He realized that this must have been a hiding place for Frigyth when she was young. Knud smirked at that. The girl was smart.

Njal made quick work of the wall passage, which opened, showcasing the balcony of the throne room below him. It was empty. Not a single person stood there. Njal then steadied himself and jumped down. Knud followed the same.

The two Norsemen were now standing on the balcony that overlooked the throne room. Njal approached the wooden railing of the balcony and rested his forearms on it as he examined the people below him.

There were so many.

People who were weeping with sadness and pain. Njal realized how many people loved Birstain. He thought back to that day on the hill. The look on Aelred's face when he saw Birstain change sides.

Njal smirked a bit at the thought.

After a brief period of silence, and even more townsfolk entering the throne room and some even having to stay outside and listen in, a priest walked out onto the dais and stood behind the altar. He said a few things that neither Njal nor Knud could understand. The priest then made a weird hand gesture that everyone else in the throne room followed suit. Then, they all said, 'amen' after.

Knud and Njal didn't understand any of it, but they didn't need to. They knew it was a prayer for Birstain as well as an honoring to their god. Suddenly, the priest stepped back, and a man stepped up onto the dais and stood in front of the altar. Njal recognized him.

The young and handsome Wigberht.

The young leader of the royal guard looked around the room for a moment. He noticed the two Norsemen standing on the balcony. His eyes meeting Njal's. He gave a slight smirk before speaking to the people of Birmingham. Njal was unsettled by that.

"People of Birmingham! Today we honor somebody very important to all our lives. Somebody who never gave up hope, even when things seemed impossible to overcome. Somebody who *single-handedly* put king Edward back in the throne. The true king that England deserves..." his next words were muffled as Knud looked over at Njal.

"I think I understand your prior cautious feelings now," he said.

"Fuck," Njal mumbled with squinted eyes.

Single-handedly.

That word alone showed that Wigberht was not a friend. He and everyone else in the country knew that Njal and Birstain together helped find Edward and put the crown back on his head. Eventually, Wigberht said something that made Njal's heart stop.

"Let us welcome the daughter of this wonderful man. The lovely lady Frigyth."

Njal felt his throat close. His heart beat faster and faster, waiting for his eyes to finally see her again in something other than his dreams. And then, in an instant, there she was.

Wigberht stepped off the dais as Frigyth stepped on. She stopped at the altar and looked at everyone. Her brown wavy hair was just recently cut back to her shoulders and her blue eyes could be seen sparkling even from the distance Njal was at. She was wearing a black dress that was quite baggy.

Both Njal and Knud silently questioned her attire, as that was something Frigyth would never wear.

"My father was many things," she began to say. "But a coward was not one of them. For so long, everyone, admittedly even myself, thought he was weak for taking Aelred's beating for as long as he did. Especially after the death of my mother. I hated him for so long. That is... until I finally came to understand *what* he was going through. He could not try to avenge my mother by throwing everything he had at Aelred. No. He had to worry about the rest of us. He let his lust for revenge go because he knew that by attacking Aelred, he would have killed us all in the process. He took the beating so the rest of us could be free. I never thought of it that way until I had my own journey and fight against Aelred. And when I saw my father in that clearing in the woods back on the coast, I saw him finally able to release his anger and take his revenge. Without him, I would be dead. Without him, we all would be dead. He truly was our savior and could not have been a better father given the circumstances..."

Again, her words faded out as Njal's thoughts raced.

"Birstain was their savior?" Knud asked.

"What is happening?" Njal asked as his heart felt sadness. His mind tried to believe they were playing up Birstain's role because it was his funeral. But they were also lying and exaggerating.

But there was something else.

Something about Frigyth's appearance.

Knud noticed it first, and even *his* heart dropped. A bead of sweat formed on his brow as he looked at Njal, who still hadn't seemed to have noticed yet. Knud sighed and knew that the ride back home would not be a pleasant one. He stayed quiet.

"I wish I could have had more days with him as my father and not as the Lord of Birmingham, but he did not just have me to look after. He had all of you. And I hope to be just as good a lord as he ever was... I will miss you, father."

Frigyth finished off her speech before she stepped off the dais and the priest approached the altar again. He began speaking, but Njal's eyes followed Frigyth over to where she stood by Wigberht. There, Wigberht put his arm around her and kissed her cheek as she released a tear from her eye.

Njal felt the bile rise up in his throat. Anxiety gripping every part of his body. His heart pounded and his muscles constricted. The raging inferno inside of him sparked as his stomach dropped.

And then, he saw where Wigberht put his hand...

On her stomach...

Njal realized it...

Chills spread through his body. He couldn't believe it. He wanted to burn the entirety of Birmingham to the ground. He clenched his fists and felt the tears form in his eyes.

"Knud..." he choked. "We need to get the fuck out of here..."

"I understand," Knud said. "Let us go, then."

Suddenly, before they began their exit, Frigyth's piercing blue eyes met with Njal's. Her eyes widened as she saw him. She gave Wigberht a slight push off as Njal creased his eyebrows and began walking down the stairs of the balcony. Knud was close behind. They pushed through the crowd of people before they exited the castle gates.

Fat snowflakes were falling heavily now.

Njal kept trying to move quickly. Weaving his way through the hundreds of people until he finally broke free from the crowd. With Knud not far behind, he stomped his feet on the cobblestone pathway toward the inn until he heard it from behind him...

"Njal?"

He stopped in his tracks and hesitated to move or say anything. So, he didn't.

"What are you doing here?" the voice said again.

Njal clenched his fists before finally turning around and facing the woman he loved.

"We were invited..." he said coldly. "Now I can see that you were not the one that invited us."

"Who did?" Frigyth asked.

"We will be leaving now," Njal said as he tried turning the other direction.

"Njal, stop," Frigyth said. "I want to know why you are here."

"As I said before, we were invited," Njal said, his heart shattered into a million pieces.

"By whom?" Frigyth asked again.

Njal couldn't hold it in anymore. Tears formed in his eyes. "After everything we have been through... All the blood... All the death... it was just *that* easy for you, huh?"

"Njal, I..."

"No," he interrupted. "I honestly cannot hear anything that you have to say. You have broken my heart, Frigyth. I know I messed up and I know that Alf affected me horribly, but you did not even allow me to change. You just left. Gone. When I needed you most. And now, seeing you with that bastard. Pregnant with his... with his child? I cannot take any more of this heartbreak."

"What did you expect from me?" Frigyth shouted. "I was alone. You were always away, and I was in a place where I did not feel wanted by any of your people. I felt like an outcast and you were too busy for me to talk about my troubles! Wigberht is always there for me."

Njal didn't show rage. Only sadness. He spoke softly. "I felt like an outcast in Birmingham every single day of my life. But when I found you, I felt like I belonged somewhere. And my travels across England were to make a better life for us. For the family I wished to have with you. Apparently, my patience is stronger than yours. And do not blame your inability to speak your mind on me. You had every opportunity to talk to me about your troubles and you chose not to. Why? I do not know. But you decided to leave instead of talking and working things out. You decided to hump that man and have his child. You decided this life for yourself. The outcome will be nothing but your own doing."

Frigyth began to cry, but she tried to stand tall. "My father is dead, Njal. I am hurting a great deal. Speaking to me like you are on this day is pure savagery."

"Well, speak to your little Wigberht about why we are here. He is the one who invited us, after all."

Frigyth was angry at that. She immediately grew mad at Wigberht. He invited Njal there just to show him what he had lost, as if it was some sort of game. As if it was some competition.

"I am sorry, Njal," Frigyth said. "I am sorry that it did not work out. It appears as though your love for me was stronger than mine was for you. I am sorry that I hurt you. But I am going to have to ask you to leave."

"When I say, 'I love you,' I mean it. You need to find the definition of the word before you speak it back," Njal said as he turned around. He walked with Knud in silence for a moment before...

"Get the hell out of here, heathen!" a voice said from the shadows. Njal turned around quickly and saw Wigberht step out from behind a building. "Nobody wants your kind here anymore."

"Wigberht! Silence!" Frigyth scolded.

"Oh, aye," Njal said. "He sure is an honorable man, is he not, Frigyth?"

"I invited you here to show you that you no longer have a chance. Every next attempt at getting her back is futile. She belongs to me. England is ours," Wigberht said. "You idiotic man-child."

Njal scoffed. "Without me, you would still be under Aelred's rule."

"So? He was ridding the world of pathetic heathens like you. I was all for it!"

Frigyth looked at Wigberht with hurt and confusion.

Njal stopped and tilted his head. "What did you say?" he stomped towards Wigberht before he stopped an inch away from him and stared into his soul. "If you truly believe that, then why did I not see you on the battlefield that day? Are you a dog, Wigberht? One that has all the bark and yet none of the bite? Perhaps you stood there with your tail between your legs and pissed on yourself when I roared my battle-cry as I removed Aelred's head. Believe me, I am not the man you wish to piss off."

"At least my pecker can create a child," Wigberht said with a smile.

Njal grunted and grabbed Wigberht by his neck and raised him high before choke-slamming him down hard onto his back, knocking the wind out of him. Njal stepped over him and gave him a single hard punch that knocked the man out, taking two teeth with him.

Njal looked up and saw Frigyth. She didn't even try to stop it.

"I...I am so sorry, Njal. I did not know he had those beliefs. I..."

"Shut your mouth," Njal said, pointing a finger at her. "This is the man you chose over me. He is your problem now. We are done here."

Njal stepped away from the unconscious Wigberht and turned towards Knud, who was watching it all, and the two walked back towards the inn. Frigyth wished she could have told him the truth. That she still thinks about him every day. That she *did* love him. But she knew that they could not be together if she was the Lord of Birmingham and he was the king of his own people.

Wigberht's words struck her almost as much as they did Njal. She was not aware he had those feelings. And going behind her back to invite Njal as some sort of competition or game made her wish that she didn't have his child in her belly. After a couple months of confusion, she didn't know if she loved Wigberht. But after this, she knew she never would.

She bit her teeth hard as she watched the true love of her life walk away.

XXIV

Weakness is a Sickness

Torin swung open the wooden door to Cathbad's hut. The Druid leader's eyes widened as he examined the blood-stained Norseman that stood in his doorway.

"What happened to you?" Cathbad asked with worry, immediately standing up from his chair. "Where is everyone else?"

"Down by the fires fetching food and water..." Torin said coldly as he stomped in the room. His eyes stared at the wall as he spoke. "We lost Camma. She sacrificed herself for us to escape..."

"Damnit, Torin!" Cathbad shouted before Torin could say anymore. "I told you not to go! You have doomed us..."

"Shut the *fuck* up!" Torin roared with the weight of a thousand thunderous horns. His voice then returned to normal once he saw Cathbad's face of worry and freight. "This Ruadan weasel that you are so afraid of. He was there. He tried to show me fear but failed."

Cathbad creased his eyebrows. "What do you mean?"

Torin took a few steps forward, his eyes staring straight into Cathbad's. "I broke his little mask as well as his nose. I have shown him that *I* will not be stopped. I have shown him that together, we can kill them all."

Cathbad sighed and put his hand on Torin's shoulder. The Norseman clenched his jaw at that.

"My friend, you may have broken his nose, but you led Camma to her death. I do not wish that for any more of my people. Therefore, I have decided that we are going to move."

Torin's eyes filled with rage. He brushed Cathbad's hand off his shoulder with his own. "What did you just say?"

"You heard me..." Cathbad said, a bit irritated now.

"I cannot believe it," Torin began. "We *hurt* him, Cathbad! We have shown that we can kill him! He knows that we cannot be easily beaten. He is not to be feared! We must fight for our land! Our home! We cannot let some bastard try to take it all from us!"

"If we stand and fight him, he will kill us all."

"But, I..."

"No!" Cathbad scolded. "That is my decision, and that is final! We are leaving tomorrow morning, so you best pack your things."

Torin wished to ask more questions.

Where would they go? What happens if Ruadan picks them off on the road or in unfamiliar territory? What happens if they run into English soldiers on patrol? Do they start a war with England?

Every question had weight to it and needed to be answered. However, Torin couldn't stop himself from thinking of one single word...

Weak.

Weakness is a sickness.

He always told himself that. His code was if you had any bit of weakness inside of you, you must learn to master it and make it a strength in some form or another. Cathbad's weakness was his fear of Ruadan. The man at their doorstep. The man who killed Camma. The man who burned down Wolves Hollow. The man that killed the young Druid scouts. The man that would stop at nothing but to kill Cathbad.

Torin scoffed, turned towards the exit, and walked to the doorway before stopping.

Without turning around, he said, "You make us all conquer our fears before we join. Yet, our leader is more frightened than anyone. Your fear is a weakness. And weakness is a sickness."

Torin walked out and slammed the wooden door behind him before letting Cathbad reply in any capacity. He stomped his feet towards his own hut. He swung open the door and closed it behind him.

The Norseman let the rage that was boiling inside of him out. He roared and approached his small wooden table before grabbing the edge and flipping it over. Everything on top crashed to the ground. He then began kicking the table into pieces while screaming like a madman.

Once the table was nothing but slivers of wood, he

began to calm down. His breath still heavy but he began to think. He had an idea. One that brought him back to his meeting with Odin. He closed his eyes and thought hard. He thought about the Land of the Spirits. He thought about becoming the serpent.

After a few moments, his eyes opened. He felt the cool breeze brush off his scales. He looked up and saw the massive trees that sat above him and the bluish orange sky above those. He slithered around. At first, the feeling was strange. Not having legs. His tongue felt weird in his mouth. His eyes felt big and wide.

He tried to speak, but nothing but a hiss left his mouth.

Angry, he tried again. This time, his hiss released his fangs. Venom and spittle flew out. Echoes of "Odin" could be heard throughout the world. The Snake continued to try repeatedly until he heard the caw of a Raven on the branch above him.

The Snake looked up at the Raven before trying to speak again.

"Calm yourself," the Raven said. "Breath... in and out... Focus on the words you wish for me to hear. Then... speak them. I will help you a bit."

The Snake closed his eyes and did as the Raven told him. He breathed in and out. Focused on the following words and then... suddenly...

"Is Ruadan to be trusted?" the Snake asked. His voice was not fully there. The words were mostly echoes but could still be understood.

"How do you mean?" the Raven asked, confused.

"Ruadan is the man you need to kill in order to reach Njal. In order to achieve your revenge."

"I know…" the Snake echoed. "But Cathbad needs to be removed or we will all die. Can I trust Ruadan to make a deal? Does he truly *only* wish for Cathbad's head?"

"Torin, my word," the Raven said, surprised. "Are you considering asking Ruadan to kill Cathbad for you so you can keep your Druid friends alive? Then kill Ruadan and take his Druids, too?"

"I need an army to defeat Njal," the Snake echoed.

"I do not want you killing my people, though, Torin," the Raven cawed. "I wish for your successes in defeating Njal, but I do not want you killing my people just so you have your throne back."

"Who said anything about a war?" the Snake asked. "I need an army to be feared. I need an army to destroy what Njal loves most. Then, when he wishes to fight, we will fight like how we did the first time we met. Like Norsemen."

"You are going to create a war with England?" the Raven asked.

"One thing at a time, Odin," the Snake hissed.

"Hm," the Raven said. "Do what you must. I will make sure to warn you if I sense Ruadan has any ill intentions."

"Thank you, allfather," the Snake said before the world changed around him and he woke up as Torin once more.

*

He waited until the village was asleep. A full day of packing up the entire village had everyone in deep slumbers that night. So much so that nobody noticed the Norseman sneak his way down the wooden stairs and through the village.

The night was calming. The stars were out, the chill of the air wasn't as cold as usual and the nocturnal animals were all making their calls into the endless abyss of the night sky.

Torin reached the tall grass that announced the end of the village boundaries and he stopped. He turned to look back at the village one last time. He inhaled and exhaled deeply. His thoughts racing. He knew that this was a massive decision that could either greatly improve his newfound life or completely destroy it. He thought about every viable option to keep Cathbad alive in his head again. In each one, he saw the man leading his friends... his family, to death. Especially with him being so stubborn in his decision about what they should do.

He was just so afraid.

Cathbad... the man that found Torin. The man that chose to give him another chance when no one else would. The man that gave him his new life. Gave him his new love in the form of Ari.

Ari...

If Torin let Cathbad go through with his plan of moving the Druids to another location, she would never be safe. Not from Ruadan and not from anyone in England who wishes to rid the country of the Druids.

I must keep Ari alive. And by doing this, I will achieve enough power to fulfill my revenge and keep anyone and everyone I love safe. I am sorry, Cathbad, but your inability to change your mind will be your downfall... Fear is a weakness and weaknesses must be conquered.

Torin nodded to himself before turning and heading through the tall grass back to where the camp they left the night before was. Or where the remains were. He walked, each step feeling like a different thought in his head. A different way to defeat Ruadan and keep Cathbad and his village alive. A different way to survive by avoiding Ruadan entirely. But nothing came to mind. Nothing logical, anyway.

Torin then thought about Odin as he passed a small river about two miles from the Fenlands. Odin had told him that this was the only way. Odin gave him his blessing. Those words repeated in his head repeatedly.

Odin gave me his blessing. I cannot waste it. I WILL not.

Suddenly, his eyes widened as he had the sudden urge to move his head to the left. Once he did, he felt a small piece of iron whoosh past him, cutting his neck a bit. A trickle of blood forming. Torin quickly turned around and noticed three dark figures standing in front of him about ten yards away. All of them covered in black feathers and the one in the middle holding a bow.

"Wait!" Torin shouted. "I must speak with Ruadan. Please."

The three figures all tilted their heads in confusion at the Norseman's words. The one holding the bow then reached behind him and grabbed another arrow from his quiver and loaded it onto the shaft.

"I will give him Cathbad..." Torin said coldly now. The rage of vengeance flowing through his life blood like a drug. Pure adrenaline filling to the top. So much so that he felt he was going to explode. However, the rage simmered back down when he saw the Druid put the bow down and nudge his head as to say, *come with us.*

Torin did just that and followed the Druids to wherever it was they were leading him to.

*

It took a decently long while to reach where the Druids were leading Torin, but not long enough to where the sun wanted to crawl up into the sky. In fact, it seemed almost darker once Torin could see the wooden walls of the camp under the dim moonlight. The walls were dark themselves. Torin noticed that not a single torch had been lit anywhere outside or inside the walls when the gates opened up.

The Druids led him through the camp. Torin had expected everyone to be asleep with how dark it was in the camp, but they weren't. He felt a strange feeling inside of his head. One that he was quickly able to calm, but some of the effects remained.

They have a curse upon their village as well.

Torin noticed the Druids under the cover of night. Their black dressings and feathers made them look like shadows. However, one of the effects of the curse made all of their eyes glow a piercing red. Torin was very uneasy seeing that, but he thought back to his training. He remembered killing the giant in his visions and the shadows that watched him. This was nothing more than that. Torin had conquered that fear already. He gritted his teeth and snarled as he passed by the shadows and their glowing red gaze.

The Druids finally led him to a large building. One that didn't seem permanent, but more permanent than the small tents of the other camp he visited. The feathered Druids opened the door and pushed him inside before closing it behind him.

It was pitch black inside.

Not only that, but there was no noise.

Just pure silence and darkness.

That is, until after a few moments, Torin heard the flutter of iron scratching against itself. Even in the brief time he spent around Ruadan, he knew that the sound was his finger nails.

Suddenly, red glowing eyes floated in the darkness. The fluttering sound of his fingernails got louder and louder until the red eyes were a few inches away from Torin's.

"Hello, Ruadan," Torin said calmly. "No need for your theatrics. I am not frightened and you know that. I am here to speak with you about Cathbad."

"What could you possibly have to tell me about Cathbad?" Ruadan said. His words sounding like a thousand screams at once.

"I am here to make a deal," Torin said. Still looking into the red glow of Ruadan's eyes.

"After the destruction you have caused," Ruadan croaked. "I will be making no such deals and will instead be ripping your throat out and feeding it to the children."

Torin felt nothing. No fear, no pain, nothing.

"I grow tired of this," the Norseman said. "Do you wish to kill Cathbad or not?"

"You would let him die?" Ruadan asked. "Why would you do such a thing?" The flutter of his nails growing louder and faster.

"I do not wish for him to die. Not at all. But in my

discussion with him, *my* choice was to fight while his was to run, thus putting us in further danger. I have grown to love the life I now have, and I owe it to him. However, I know that by following him down this path, he would also be the one that strips that life from me by killing everyone I have grown to love. Therefore, I have come to make a deal with you. Cathbad. And only him."

"Hm..." Ruadan said. His breath carrying like a silent scream of terror. "A respectable decision on your part. So, you will give me Cathbad if I leave the rest of your village alone?"

"Aye," Torin said. "It only seems fair."

"What about the destruction you have caused already? You killed my men on the river and destroyed a camp of ours. Not to mention, I have a few nasty scars from the fire that whore created."

"Your people attacked *us* on the river. We had no choice but to fight back. They never even gave us an option for a conversation. You also killed a few young scouts of ours, as well as Camma. And she was a dear friend to us all. Therefore, I only think it is fair that we go through with this deal. You know we have some mighty fighters on our end and I know you have some on yours. Would you not rather take Cathbad without any more bloodshed?"

Ruadan began to laugh. A horrifying laugh that echoed throughout the night. His red eyes radiating a cosmic dust in the darkness.

"A Norseman trying to find a peaceful agreement? Is this the end of times?" he asked.

Torin was having none of it. "I am just a man trying

to save the people he cares about. I will sacrifice one if it means protecting everyone else."

Ruadan's laugh ceased. "I respect that. You and I are not so different, as a matter of fact."

"I am nothing like you," Torin grumbled.

"Oh, but you are," Ruadan said. "You are a man who wishes for vengeance. Who needs it. *Craves* it. I have that craving every single day. So, by you giving me that on a silver platter, you now have a friend in me, Torin."

"Good," Torin said.

"You have my word," Ruadan said. "No harm will come to your people." He snapped his fingers and the sensation in Torin's head faded. Suddenly, torches were lit and Torin could see everything inside the building he was in. Including Ruadan, whose eyes were no longer a glowing red and masked in shadows. Torin noticed his nose was bent to the side, which gave him a little satisfaction.

"Now, how do you wish to proceed?" Torin asked.

"Silently."

*

Ari woke up with crust in her eyes and a bit of phlegm in her throat. The last few days were tiring, and she needed the rest, but her body was unable to get it. Every time she closed her eyes, she would imagine herself on the battlefield fighting alongside her friends, killing every Druid of the Crow in sight. That is until her dreams would force the sound of fluttering metal into her mind, which scared her. After that, she would see Camma's face as she grabbed for her throat, which was no longer there.

The same dream... every night.

She sighed as she swung her legs around and sat up so that her legs were hanging off the bed. She rubbed her face and sighed again. She then stood up, headed over to her large wooden chest that she had sitting in the corner of her room, and she changed her clothes and secured her bones on her hand and forearm. She then walked out of her hut and felt the cool air flow through her blonde hair and tickle her face. She noticed the few other Druids that were out and about and said hello. Some were chopping wood, others were cooking small vegetables for breakfast and a few were sharpening their bone swords or bone-tipped spears. It was the day of the big move.

After Torin shed the light on Ruadan to the entire village before heading off to the camp where they lost Camma, Cathbad had no other choice but to explain everything to every-one. Once he finished his speech that day, everyone was angry with him for withholding the valuable information from them. That was when Cathbad finally spoke about how they were all a family and needed to be on the same page from there on out. But after Cathbad told everyone his plan for leaving the Fenlands, many people were angry and, like Torin, wished to stay and fight. They showed this by sitting on a dry patch of dirt where the bonfires were usually held and they would sharpen new bone weapons every day, all day, since Cathbad's speech. They made sure Cathbad saw what they were doing.

As Ari walked on the wooden pathways that con-nected each hut, she thought about her stance on things. The last thing she wished was to be fighting in a war. She found love and peace in this life with the Druids of the Fenlands. She didn't want to lose it over a debate that really only involved Cathbad.

The thought that floated around in the very depths of her mind was if Ruadan got what he wanted and killed Cathbad, would he stop and let the rest of them live without a war? But Ari kept that thought as low as it could go in her mind as she would always remember seeing Ruadan's face. Him holding Camma's throat in his hand. He would never let anyone else live if he got to Cathbad. There was no way he would... right?

But Ari was never the one for running away, either. She felt as though running from your problems showed fear and weakness, which is something that Cathbad taught everyone to try to overcome. But when your own leader is so afraid of someone that he wishes to pack everything up and go, it's hard not to look at him as weak.

Ari made it to Torin's hut, and she knocked on the door. After a few moments, there wasn't an answer. She knocked again and again. But still. Nothing.

"Torin?" she said, knocking one more time. "Are you in there? It is just I."

Nobody came to the door, so she grabbed the door handle and let herself in. However, there was nobody inside. Ari creased her eyebrows in confusion and thought about where he might be. But then she noticed something else. His table was thrown on its side and all the items that were on top were scattered around the floor or broken. She became worried.

Did someone come in and take him? Was it Ruadan?

Her heart beat faster as the thought filled her mind. She quickly shut the door and ran out of the hut, across the wooden walkway, and over to Cathbad's. She didn't even bother to knock as she swung the door open.

Inside, she was quickly taken aback by what she saw.

Cathbad was sprawled out asleep in his bed, a large cup of mead was spilled on the ground and vomit was spread out by his face. He obviously went to bed drunk.

Ari grew angry. She turned and exited the hut and went down the stairs and approached the men that were sharpening the bone swords.

"Do we have any water jugs?" Ari asked without breaking stride.

"Aye," one of the men said. The two of them then watched Ari enter a small tent and exit a few moments later with a large container of water in her two hands.

"If anyone asks, there was a small fire in Cathbad's room," she said as she passed them.

"You got it," the other Druid said as he chuckled.

Ari then walked up the stairs and across the walkway and into Cathbad's hut. She stomped up to his bedside and immediately flipped the container so all the water poured out onto Cathbad and his bed, waking him up.

"Ah!" he shouted as he jumped up and onto the floor. He looked up at Ari, who was standing there with a disappointed look on her face. "What the hell, Ari?"

"Don't you *dare* ask me that question," Ari said coldly. "There is a blood-thirsty demon out there looking for us and yet, you are up here drinking yourself into oblivion!"

"Quiet your voice, please. My head really quite hurts."

"I do not give a shite! Torin is missing from his room and all of his stuff is thrown around in his hut. There looks to have been a struggle. If we lost him, then..."

"He is probably just angry about the decision to move. He spoke to me yesterday and was *not* happy. I respect the man, but his hardened head is a weakness to him."

Ari snarled. "And your fear of Ruadan is a weakness to all of us."

Cathbad grunted as he stood up. "What did you just say to me?"

"You heard me," Ari said. "This version of you is not the one I chose to follow. Nobody would ever follow... *this*," she said, gesturing to the vomit on his bed and empty mead cup.

Cathbad moved to strike her, but due to his hangover, Ari saw it coming and she pushed him lightly. His eyes widened as his hangover caused him to lose his balance and he fell back onto his arse.

"Clean up your shite, Cathbad," Ari scoffed. "I appreciate everything you have done for us but this... I will not follow this man any further."

Cathbad's head pounded so hard that he threw up in his lap. Ari looked at him in disgust and shook her head.

"I suppose we are not leaving today after all," she said as she turned and walked out of his hut.

She looked around and made a decision. If Ruadan had actually captured Torin, then she needed to get him back. She made her way to Daegal's hut. She needed help. But before she could do anything, she noticed a large man walking on the path from the river. He was the very Norseman she was planning to rescue.

*

"Where the bloody hell have you been?" Ari asked Torin as he walked through the village.

"I had to go for a walk early this morning," Torin said. "I was quite angry with how my last conversation with Cathbad went, so I needed to calm myself."

Ari put her head down as they arrived at Torin's hut. "Yes, I saw inside. I was worried you were captured."

Torin laughed as he opened the door. "No, no. I just needed to release some anger and frustration."

"Well, I went to speak with Cathbad and he is not handling the situation very well. He was sleeping in mead and vomit..." she said as she watched Torin undress. "We will leave tomorrow morning instead."

Torin scoffed as he put a fresh shirt on. "He is going to get us all killed, Ari. You know that."

"If he keeps acting like this, then yes."

"Ari, there is no time to allow him to change. We have to act now."

"What do you suggest we do?" Ari asked him as she watched him attach his leather belt to his waist. The sword she gave him sat in its sheath.

"Now? I wish to hunt with you. I wish to get as far away from this living nightmare as possible and return to reality tonight."

Ari smiled. "I like the sound of that."

*

Ari and Torin enjoyed each other's company for the rest of the day. They traveled three miles away and hunted whatever they could gather. Mushrooms, flowers, rabbit, and even a whole deer. After they cleaned the deer, they decided to rest under a large willow tree by a small pond. They both undressed and washed themselves in the pond before they made love to one another under the tree. When they were done, Ari held onto Torin and rested her head on his chest as he looked up at the branches and leaves of the willow tree that danced in the breeze above him.

"Do you see a life with me, Torin?" Ari asked suddenly.

Torin didn't take any time answering her question.

"Of course," he said sincerely. "Being with you has given me a new purpose in life."

She smiled and nuzzled herself in his bare chest. She then lifted her head up and kissed his shoulder.

"I was worried you would not because you are a bit older than me."

"Hey!" Torin said jokingly.

"No," she said, laughing, then turning serious. "You know I do not mean it like that. I just mean... Well, you have more life experience than I do. I did not think I would be mature enough for you, I suppose."

"Ari, the experiences you have been through... they would harden and mature anyone. I love who you are. Every single part of you."

She lifted her head and kissed him on the lips. Her blonde hair tickling his bare chest.

"I have fallen in love with you, Torin. I wish to have a family with you. A quiet life built by peace. One away from war and pain."

"That is what I am trying to achieve," Torin said, looking at the sun that was threatening to set behind the horizon now. "I promise, my love. We will find peace in this lifetime."

Ari kissed him again before they decided to dress and head back to the village.

*

It had been dark for some time once Ari and Torin finally returned to the village in the Fenlands. They had noticed most of their fellow Druids were asleep in their huts while some sat up talking around the three separate campfires. One of those that were still up was Daegal, who looked at the returning lovers with wide eyes.

"Where were you two all day?" he asked before taking a gulp of mead from his wooden cup. The small fire crackled in front of him.

"Just needed to get away from everything," Ari replied.

"Mind if we sit with you?" Torin asked.

"Please," Daegal said, shrugging his shoulders and gesturing to the tree stumps that acted as seats.

"What are you doing up?" Ari asked as she and Torin took their seats.

"Just thinking, is all," he replied.

"About what?" Torin asked.

"It is nothing..."

"Please," Torin said. "We wish to know."

Daegal looked up into the night sky for a moment.

"You know," he began. "I tend to feel like everything that we do here has so much impact and meaning. Whether it be for our lives or the lives of others. But when I stay awake in the late hours of night and look up into the Heavens, I cannot help but feel so insignificant. Like every one of my problems is just... worthless."

"I understand that feeling," Torin said.

Until you have a god tell you that he needs you in order for him to stay alive, Torin thought. *Then your problems feel like they have massive weight to them.*

"It is quite extraordinary, Daegal," Ari said, looking up.

"Torin, I mean to apologize," Daegal said, looking at him from across the fire, which looked like it needed another log soon. "At first, I thought you were an arsehole. I took you for a man that used abuse to keep people in check. However, after Wolves Hollow, I realized that everything you said to me was true. I mean, you fear nothing while our *actual* leader has so much, he is attempting to run away. You ran straight towards the danger and tried to kill it. We lost Camma, but we gained trust in each other. I would follow you onto any battlefield."

He raised his cup in the air. Torin nodded back. He looked around the camp before speaking. He heard some rustling in the bushes to his right.

"I appreciate your kind words, Daegal. So, you *do* trust me?" Torin asked as he stood up.

"I trust you with my life," Daegal said. Ari looked at Torin in confusion.

"Do *you* trust me?" Torin asked her.

"Yes, of course. What..." she said before the sound of a man struggling hit their ear drums.

They all turned their attention towards the huts and walkways that sat over their heads. They noticed a man in black leather armor with feathers protruding from his shoulders and neck area holding Cathbad in his arms. He had long fingernails which were inches away from Cathbad's neck. The man was wearing a deer skull as a mask.

Looks like he fetched himself a new mask.

Suddenly, dozens of feathered Druids emerged from the shadows and stepped into the light of the campfires. All with their weapons drawn. Curved swords and back steel tip spears. Ari pulled her hand-axe from her belt as she entered a defensive stance.

"Cathbad!" she called out as she eyed her surroundings. Everywhere she looked, feathered Druids of the Crow stood. "Torin! What do we do?" She noticed he didn't move at all. He just stood there and looked at her.

"Do you trust me?" he asked again. Daegal did not move either. He just followed what Torin was doing. Ari's face turned. "Druids of the Fenlands!" Torin yelled out, attempting to wake everyone. "Please exit your huts with open arms! We have something we must discuss!"

After a few moments of silence, the Druids of the Fenlands began to exit their homes. Their eyes meeting the shadows that were crowding their village.

"Please pay no mind to them!" Torin said. "You will be fine! Your families are safe!"

"Torin?" Ari shouted as the people began making their way down the steps and onto the clearing where Torin and the others were standing. "What the bloody hell is going on here?"

"There was no other choice, my love," Torin said. "Cathbad was going to get us killed. This way, we do not waste any lives on a pointless feud between two men. It is the best course of action for both clans."

Ari's face was that of disgust. Her thoughts ran wild. "I cannot believe what I am hearing," she said. "He gave you a new life! He took you in! Took us all in! The way you repay him is by handing him to the enemy?"

Everyone was finally gathered in the clearing below. Ruadan still held Cathbad up top on a pathway, though.

"He was going to kill us all, Ari," Torin said as he tried to approach her. He tried to touch her arm, but she backed away and raised her hand-axe.

"Back up!" Ari said. "I am disgusted. Mortified! And to think I had love for you..."

"Do not do this," Torin said. "I did this for you. Can you not see that? I did this for all of you!" he shouted now. The village was quiet. "With Cathbad drinking himself into oblivion and his cowardice, he would have led us all to early deaths. We have a home here, a place where we are safe and Cathbad wished to abandon it all! Out there, we would never stop fighting! We would never stop being hunted until there was no one left *to* hunt!"

He cleared his throat.

"And so, I have decided to strike a deal with Ruadan to hand over Cathbad. In doing so, Ruadan has promised to not take any more lives. No more blood will be spilled because of this false and fearful leader of ours! He has tried to train everyone in mastering their fears and yet he was more afraid than anyone here! When those boys came back with their heads missing, what did Cathbad do? He wished to run! I decided to fight back! With me as your leader, I can promise you, we will be strong! We will have allies in Ruadan. We will grow our people and kill those who have wronged us! Together, we can create a force that England has never seen before!"

The Druids of the Fenlands nodded their heads, and some audibly agreed. Daegal being one. That's when Golmac's colossal body made his way through the small crowd and approached Torin. Everyone stood in silence to see what the large man would say. Once Golmac stood next to Torin, he looked up at Cathbad.

"Please, Golmac..." Cathbad said quietly before Ruadan used his nail to make a slight cut in Cathbad's neck. A bit of blood trickling down.

Golmac looked at Torin, then back at Cathbad.

"I love you, Cathbad. You were a father to me," Golmac began. "But when it came to fighting for us, you decided to run. You decided to drink. Torin decided to fight. As much as it hurts... I have to side with Torin."

The Druids began to cheer.

Ari seemed to be the only one who was disgusted and felt betrayed. Torin looked at her and smiled.

"You see, my love?" he said. "This is the most logical choice."

"You may have forced them to see the façade. But I will not be fooled by a snake. I now know what kind of ruler you were." Not seeing another option, Ari looked up to Cathbad and mouthed the words, *I am sorry*, before turning and running off into the darkness. The feathered Druids tried to stop her, but Torin told them to stop and let her go.

"She just needs time. She will return to me," he said, a bit saddened.

Ruadan then grabbed his mask and pulled it off, showcasing his face and all of his red hair and facial hair.

"Torin!" he shouted down. "I am very impressed by the work you have done here. You have showed these people what their so-called leader truly is. A coward. Now, because of your kindness, nobody else here must die."

The Druids of the Crow cheered. The Druids of the Fenlands, while they agreed with the situation, stayed silent as they looked at their leader. The love for him was there, but the love for their lives was more prevalent.

"And now, for the conclusion of our feud..." Ruadan said, his voice like ice.

Ruadan grabbed the top of Cathbad's head by his hair and shoved him down to his knees. He then held him there as he raised his other hand and fluttered his nails together.

"I have waited a long time for this moment, Cathbad! You stole the woman I loved from this world. You have avoided me for so long and yet, you still lose! She will finally be avenged!"

Cathbad's eyes were glued to Torin's. The Norseman could feel the anger from where he was standing. Cathbad never looked away. Not even when Ruadan swung his arm down and used his nails to grip his throat. Cathbad's eyes never looked away from Torin's. Not even when Ruadan squeezed tightly, causing a river of blood to flow from the holes in his throat. Cathbad's eyes never looked away from Torin's. Not even when Ruadan pulled his throat out, leaving a gaping hole in his neck. Finally, Cathbad's gaze was interrupted by his life fleeing his body and Ruadan kicking his corpse off the walkway and face first into the ground below.

The feathered Druids cheered as Ruadan raised his arms in glory and pride. Torin could not help but look at Cathbad's body. He didn't smile. He didn't feel pride.

He felt sadness. Pain.

That is until he thought back to Odin's words. With Cathbad out of the picture, Torin was now leading the Druids of the Fenlands. With just a little more patience, he could achieve the same with the Druids of the Crow.

The important thing was, he was one step closer to having his revenge against Njal Tokeson.

XXV

No Going Back

The gates of Eaglecrest opened as the stars above flickered in the twilight of early evening. The torches and lanterns were being lit inside the village walls by the guards.

Njal, Knud and the other two men they had with them rode their horses inside and gave a nod to everyone who was going about their business in the vicinity. The men all stopped, dismounted, and hitched their horses at the stables. Knud gave a brief nod to his men and whispered something to them before looking at Njal. The two men turned and headed off towards the marketplace, which was still quite busy.

Knud approached Njal and whispered to him, "The spies will meet us in the Great Hall."

Njal nodded his head. "Then let us not waste any more time."

Something seemed strange as they walked through

the village towards the Great Hall. Everyone had a weird look on their faces, as if they wished to say something, but decided to hold their tongues. Nobody said hello, they would just nod or say the words, "my king" as they passed by Njal.

"Something has happened here," Njal said softly to Knud.

They finally made it to the Great Hall and entered the extensive building. Inside was dark. The light of the fire pit was just beginning to grow as the flames began to take hold of the heaping amounts of wooden logs that were sitting inside. Two men were standing straight up by the throne, both dressed in all black.

"Jarl Knud. My king," they both said in unison before looking at Njal. "We thought you would like a bit of warmth, so we lit the fire for you. We hope that is alright."

"Of course," Njal said. "You have my thanks. Now what exactly has happened here? Everyone is acting like there is some big secret."

"That is because we had informed the people that we would be the ones to tell you. We would rather you get situated before we break the news."

"What news?" Knud asked, a bit impatient.

"It is Sigrid. She killed one of the guards and broke out. She returned to Demut and the Horse Clan has cut off all contact with us. They burned down three homes that they said were 'on their land' and they announced that they are no longer a part of Eaglecrest."

Njal's hate fire burned inside of him. "How did she escape?" he asked through gritted teeth.

"We do not know, sir. He was quite young."

Njal looked at Knud. "Why would you have a 'young' guard watching Sigrid?"

Knud sighed. "His father was a friend of mine. The boy wished to be a man. I gave him one chance. He failed... *I* failed, my king."

Njal grunted. "What of my brother?"

"He is still in the cell downstairs. We have personally seen to it that he be fed twice a day, just as you have asked. However, I cannot say he has eaten every meal we have brought him."

"What, he is just not eating?" Njal asked.

"We believe he has lost the will to live. All he does is face the wall. His food has begun to pile up and mold," one of the spies said.

"How long since you last saw him eat anything?" Njal asked.

"Around three days, sir."

"He must have heard the news of Sigrid."

"Aye," the other spy said. "That was our thought, too."

"But how could he have heard that?" Knud asked.

Njal sighed. "It does not matter now. I will go talk to him. But Knud, we need to speak about Sigrid as soon as possible. If she cut ties with us, that means she could attack us at any time. We need to prepare for that. As for the rest of the evening, everyone try to get some sleep but keep one eye open for anything suspicious. Do not be afraid to call for me on the horns. I do not care what time of night it is; I will be there. Let us double the men on the wall."

Knud watched his spies nod their heads and walk

towards and out the door of the Great Hall. He then looked at Njal and dropped his head. "I am sorry I failed you, Njal. I was trying to give the young lad a chance at becoming a man. He was supposed to guard that evening only."

"I understand, but I cannot say that I am not disappointed. You knew how she could charm men. A young boy would fall right into her trap. If you make another mistake like this again, there will be consequences. We must be smarter than that."

"I understand, Njal," Knud said, reaching his arm out. Njal met his forearm with his hand and they nodded at one another.

"Now, go get some sleep," Njal said. "I will think on what to do about Sigrid."

Knud nodded again before stepping towards and out the doors to the Great Hall. Leaving nothing other than Njal and the crackling of the fire pit inside. He looked up into the tall wooden ceiling and closed his eyes. He thought back to what had transpired in Birmingham. The pain he felt in his heart.

The rage.

He lost the woman he loved, his best friend left his side, and he was now about to go speak with the last remaining member of his family. Who tried to overthrow him and was sitting in a cold cell down the stairs.

Njal opened his eyes and made his way to the stairs. He walked down them slowly until he saw the cell. He quietly approached and looked inside. There, his brother laid on his side with his back facing the cell bars. Njal looked around and saw the corner where his brother used as a toilet. He then looked down in front of him and saw the plates that were piled up with moldy bread and chicken. He then looked at his brother again.

"You cannot keep starving yourself, Alf..." he sighed. "What do you need? I will fetch you whatever it is you are craving."

Alf didn't reply.

"I know you are awake," Njal said again, waiting for any sort of response. "Fine. I guess I will just sit here all night."

Njal then sat down and looked at his brother's back. He waited another few moments before speaking again.

"I want you to think of a scenario," Njal began. "I want you to imagine that it worked. Your plan, I mean. Let us say you successfully overthrew me and locked me in that very cell you find yourself laying in. Now, you know I would not be happy, but part of you would wish for me to understand and forgive you. Perhaps enough to where I would fight by your side when you released me some time later."

He cleared his throat.

"Well, that is where I am right now, except you are me in that scenario. I understand that you are mad and frustrated, but do you blame me for what I did? You were conspiring to overthrow my rule after I let you in and took care of you. I want you to realize how hard hearing that was for me. All my life, I wanted my family back. I wished to kill Aelred because he took my family from me. But then you arrived on the docks that day and I was so happy. I could finally have a piece of my family back. Now, you sit in this cell due to *your* actions. I understand that you are angry, brother, but if the tables were flipped, you would not hesitate to do as I have done."

Alf moved his body and began sitting up. He looked a bit skinnier since Njal had seen him last. He then turned around and showcased his long and untamed beard and looked at Njal.

"I do not blame you for doing what you did, brother," Alf said. "You are correct. I would have done the same. And I wish things were different, I really do. But I just think that your way of running things will get us killed in the end. We need to be strong in order to survive."

"This way is father's way. I am trying to honor him."

"Njal," Alf said, shaking his head. "Father's way got him and everyone else killed. Maybe his way of peace and expansion is not the way forward."

"Obviously, Ragnar's way of violence and conquering was not working either."

"Then maybe there is a middle ground. One where you can be strong and sturdy but focus on expansion and peace," Alf said, to which Njal widened his eyes.

"Do... do you actually mean that?" Njal asked.

"Do I strive for peace in my life? No," Alf said. "But I have seen the way these people look at you. They do see a true king in you, brother. I have to admit that if the people believe in your way and they all want peace, then who am I to stand in your way?"

Njal couldn't believe what he was hearing. He was so happy to hear these words coming out of his brother's mouth. But he knew he couldn't be stupid and trust him immediately. That had to be earned again. But it gave Njal a bit of hope.

"I appreciate that, Alf," Njal said. "I will take your advice into consideration, as I do agree. Being a powerful leader in this world is something that I must be if I wish for our people to survive. But by not solving every problem with violence, we can create alliances and expand our way of life."

Alf nodded his head. They didn't speak for a few more moments before Alf looked up at his brother.

"Can I see her?" he asked.

Njal's slight smile faded.

"Alf, I... I do not think that is such a great idea," he said. "Without her in your ear, you are speaking much more clearly. Do you understand that?"

Alf dropped his head.

"I do..." he said. "I just have fallen so madly in love with her. She is the one I wish to spend the rest of my life with, Njal. Even if you send us both away to live in isolation, I will be happy. I do not need to be king. I do not need to be here. I just want her."

Njal sat in thought for a moment. If only Sigrid was still in her cell, Njal could bring that proposition to her and... who was he kidding? He knew the reason Sigrid even wanted Alf in the first place was. She didn't actually love him, she just wished to hurt Njal through his brother.

Heartless bitch, Njal thought to himself. *If only Alf could see what the rest of us do...*

"I will speak to her," Njal said. "Perhaps we can come to some sort of..."

BOOM!

The wall behind Njal exploded, bricks and wood went flying. The force of the blast threw Njal sideways until he cracked into the other wall. Alf covered his eyes, but then looked up into the dust and smoke. He saw shadows moving in the dark, becoming clearer and clearer every moment. The dust finally settled enough to showcase Sigrid, who was dressed in brown leather armor and had her sword and orange and black wooden shield in her hands.

"Care to get out of here?" she said, smiling.

"Sigrid!" Alf shouted. The other shadows turned out to be around fifteen of the Horse Clan members.

Sigrid quickly broke the lock with her sword and opened the cell door. Alf jumped to her and they began kissing wildly.

"Sigrid!!" A voice shouted from the other side of the room. Everyone looked over to see Njal slowly getting to his feet. "What is the meaning of this?!"

"You locked me in a cell for speaking the truth. Now I have returned to take back what is mine and mine only," she said, looking at Alf and biting her lip. "Now, let us leave or I will kill you where you stand."

"I will not let you poison my brother's mind anymore. It is over for you." Njal unsheathed 'The Call of the King' with a hum and growled as he entered an offensive stance.

"Men," Sigrid said. "Clear the way upstairs for us. Five of you stay and make sure he does not make it out of here alive."

Sigrid began to make her way upstairs, following her men, and Alf stood and looked at Njal. He then looked up at Sigrid, then back at Njal.

"I love her, brother... I must follow her."

Njal dropped his head as he saw Alf run up the stairs, following Sigrid. He then looked up and noticed the five remaining members of the Horse Clan that were coming towards him.

Three of them held spears while the other two held swords. Njal waited until one of them punched their spear forward before he made his move. He dodged the spear tip and watched it go past his face before grabbing the shaft with his open hand and pulled it forward, bringing the man's body right into Njal's blade, killing him. Njal quickly pulled his sword from the man's body as he gripped the spear tightly in his other hand. He flipped the spear around and cocked his arm back quickly, then swung it forward, sending the spear straight into one of the Horse Clan member's necks.

Njal then rolled forward and sprung upwards, slicing his sword straight through another warrior's groin. He pulled his sword out and then swiped the man's head off as he focused on the remaining two.

Njal roared with a blood splattered face as he charged one of the men. He dodged a swing of a sword and chopped down hard, removing the man's arm. Blood sprayed from the wound and Njal punched the blade of his sword forward, exploding out of the man's back.

He then felt a pain in his arm that caused him to let go of his sword, which was still lodged in the man's chest. Njal turned to see the last man swung his spear forward, and the tip grazed his arm.

He was disarmed as the last enemy readied his spear again. Njal's hate flowed through his veins. His rage boiled in his heart. His grief fueled his muscles. He erupted and jumped at the man. He tackled him to the ground and began punching his face repeatedly. Each blow was filled with so much physical and emotional weight behind it that the man stood no chance. Njal stopped his punch, then lowered his head and gripped the man's neck with his teeth. He bit down hard and pulled up, pulling his jugular with him.

Njal spit the meat from his mouth. He breathed heavily as he got back to his feet, ran over to his sword and pulled it from the body of the Horse Clan member, then ran up the stairs.

When he got to the top and began making his way to the front door, that was when he felt the pain. He stopped moving and looked down to see the tip of a sword protruding out of his stomach. A bit of blood trickled down his mouth with a cough.

The blade was pulled back through, which dropped Njal to the ground. He looked up and saw Sigrid standing there with a smile on her face.

"Oh, Njal," she said as she walked around him slowly. "I have seen you fight! I knew you were going to make quick work of my men. But fight with my *mind.* I have always been smarter than you!"

"You fight... without honor..." Njal coughed. He tried to get up, but Sigrid kicked him in the gut. He coughed up more blood and grunted in pain.

"Fuck honor," Sigrid said. "Honor does not win you anything in this world. Taking what you want, *when* you want it, does."

"Where is... Alf..." Njal asked.

"Do not worry about him. If he rules as great as he humps, then our people will live on forever," she laughed.

Njal closed his eyes. He calmed his mind. He let his feelings flow through him.

There...

He felt it.

The Land of the Spirits.

Or was it the Valkyries on their descent to swoop him up and carry him to Valhalla?

It mattered little. He knew where the 'Call of the King' sat on the floor. He knew where Sigrid was. If tonight was the night he was going to Valhalla, he was taking her with him.

Quickly, he opened his eyes and gritted his teeth. He reached for his sword and used all of his energy to jump and throw his body into Sigrid's. They both flew and crashed onto the floor. Sigrid got the wind knocked out of her as she landed hard on her back. She tried to reach for her sword, but Njal's face popped into her vision. He stood over the top of her and clenched his jaw. His face was covered in blood, her men's and his own. He slowly raised his sword high above him, the blade pointed downwards.

He released a mighty battle-cry as he brought the blade down hard. It punched straight through Sigrid's chest as the rest of the blade went through the wooden floor below her.

She coughed as she spit up blood. She looked at Njal in his eyes with creased eyebrows. She did not expect this. One moment, she was standing above him, his death close, then the next, she was on her back with the sword that killed Aelred imbedded in her chest.

Njal held her gaze in her final moments. He could see the shock in her eyes. The fear. The slight fright of what came next. Would she be taken to Valhalla? Or would she be destined to walk the Soul Road for eternity?

Her eyes went lifeless as her head drooped back onto the floor.

Sigrid had died.

"NOOOOO!" Njal heard a horrifying scream from behind him that broke him away from his bloodlust trance.

He spun around and saw Alf standing in the doorway. Four members of the Horse Clan were behind him. Alf slowly walked towards the scene as his eyes filled with tears.

"What did you... What did you do?" he said.

"Brother... stop... please. She attacked me..." Njal said. "I cannot stand... I am in pain. Please."

Alf approached and began to bawl as he saw the scene fully now. "No... she said she forgot... she forgot her old sword inside. She said she wished to grab it before she joined us... She..."

"Alf, I am..."

"NO!" Alf screamed. "You killed her... You killed my only happiness."

"I would have died myself if I had not..." Njal said as he stumbled onto his backside. He used his hand to put pressure on his own wound.

"Enough! Enough, enough, ENOUGH!" Alf cried. He wiped the snot from his nose. "Njal... you have taken from me everything. My only chance at a peaceful life. You stole it. I have nothing else..." he looked down at his love once more before looking at his brother.

"You can live for family," Njal pleaded before grunting with pain. "We can start over. Help me make a better world."

Alf stared at Sigrid's lifeless body for a long moment as the firepit crackled and popped in the background.

"Because we are kin, I will let you see another day," Alf said coldly. "But when Skoll and Hati finally meet in the sky, I will be waiting for you in the forest. And there... I will kill you."

Njal watched with wide eyes as Alf leaned down and gripped 'The Call of the King' and pulled it out of his fallen love with a crunch. He threw the sword across the Great Hall and picked up the body of Sigrid. He then carried her outside the doors of the Great Hall.

Njal heard the horns blow outside and fighting commence as he lay there, still trying to put pressure on his wound, which was bleeding profusely. He grunted in pain again.

When Skoll meets Hati.

The two wolves that continuously chase and sun and moon across the sky. It was said that once they catch their prey and engulf them, Ragnarök would begin.

The end of times.

The end of the gods.

Outside the Great Hall, the guards at Eaglecrest were fighting the Horse Clan members as Alf paid no mind to anyone. He just walked straight to the main gates with a dead Sigrid in his arms. Anger and rage building up inside of him. He was a man who had lost everything. And a man who loses everything is awfully dangerous.

XXVI

A New Alliance

It was a brisk night in the Fenlands. A few days had passed since the death of Cathbad. Torin had been appointed leader, mostly by himself, but nobody disagreed. Ruadan and his Druids decided not to return to Ireland and stay in England for a while as they discuss an alliance. Alliance talks between Torin and Ruadan had only gotten them to agree that the Druids of the Crow would search nearby for a new home. Therefore, if anything happened to one or the other clans, the other clan wouldn't be very far and could help rather quickly.

However, both leaders had ulterior motives. Torin, obviously, wished to take control of the feathered Druids as well. He was constantly thinking of ways to dispatch Ruadan in silence, but couldn't find the right time.

Not yet, at least.

Ruadan's motive, however, was unknown. Torin continued to

speak with him often to try to get even a small understanding of what he was after, but he could not figure it out.

On this particular evening, Ruadan was walking along the elevated wooden pathways of the village. He was heading for Torin's hut.

Torin, on the other hand, was kneeling down and praying to Odin in the corner of his hut. His prayers began to shift into ways he could kill Ruadan again.

Could I defeat him head on? Challenge him to a duel? No... he thought. *I have not seen his full set of battle skills yet. Maybe I could...*

There was a knock at the door.

"Aye, come in," Torin shouted, to which the door opened and Ruadan entered. He wasn't wearing his wolf skull mask, only his black leather and feathered attire.

"Torin," Ruadan croaked. It was still hard for Torin to get used to his voice, which sounded like iron scraping together matched with a high-pitched whistle. "I wish to speak with you about some things."

Torin nodded and stood to his feet. He gestured to the chairs and table he had sitting in his hut. The two men walked over and sat down across from one another.

"What is it?" Torin asked.

"Firstly, how are you enjoying your new position?" Ruadan asked.

Torin took a moment to speak. "I am doing alright."

"Come on," Ruadan said. "We are allies now. We must speak truthfully to one another."

Torin nodded his head. He wasn't going to be truthful about

everything. But he remembered how good it felt when he would speak of his problems or his past with Ari. How freeing it was. Speaking of his issues to someone else made his mind empty of all the hate and rage and allowed him to think much more clearly.

"I must be honest," Torin started. "I believed Ari was going to come back. She has not yet and I am starting to worry."

Ruadan nodded his head before clearing his throat. "You know, I had my woman stolen from me once. I felt like I could have both a woman and lead my people to glory, but I have come to realize that you can have one or the other, never both. If you are a leader and you have a woman, she will either become a target for your enemies or she will not agree with your decisions and leave you. Even though those decisions were for the betterment of your people."

Torin was silent for a moment. "What did you wish to speak with me about?" he finally asked, realizing that speaking to Ruadan about his problems wasn't the same as speaking to Ari.

It was worth a shot.

"I have been thinking about our alliance a bit further," the red bearded man said. "I would like the Druids of the Fenlands to join the Druids of the Crow. Our people can coexist and thrive. We can destroy our enemies and conquer much of this country."

Torin looked unamused.

"My people do not wish for war against England, Ruadan," Torin said sternly. "We wish for peace. We wish for nobody to bother us. This is why I gave you Cathbad without a fight."

Ruadan shook his head.

"I thought you Norsemen wished to die on the battle-field so you can reach Valhalla," Ruadan said. "Not die a farmer's death with no saga to speak of."

"Cathbad gave me a new life," Torin said as he looked into Ruadan's eyes from across the table. "What I did to him hurt me deeply, but it was the best option for the people I have come to love."

"And I am gracing you with another option," Ruadan replied. "If you fight alongside me, I can grow the family that you have come to love. I can find you glory and pride. Please, consider this."

"As I said before, Cathbad gave me a new life. If I did not fight for him in his final moments, what makes you believe that I will fight for you in any form?"

That cut Ruadan. The red bearded Druid realized that Torin was going to be a lot harder to frighten or manipulate. But he didn't care. His mind was set. Torin was going to be his new toy.

"Torin," he began. "I will ask you to join me on my little adventure. There is a small village about a day's ride from us. I will show you what we can do and after that, you can decide if you truly want peace."

"Fine."

*

The snow was falling lightly around them as a late winter storm hit the country. The storm stretched from the Fenlands all the way to Birmingham as the sky was colored a dark gray. The Druids all prepared their weapons as they stood crouched within the cover of the surrounding forest. Every one of the Druids had feathers attached to their clothing. Every one of them except for Torin and Daegal, who were standing up front by Ruadan.

Their lips were closed as their eyes were peeled at the small community that stood directly in front of them, maybe a good thirty yards away, and sat in the clearing of the forest. There were four small houses, as well as an alehouse and a blacksmith. The biggest building had a pointed roof with a cross on the top.

"Christians..." Daegal said quietly.

"Ruadan," Torin whispered. "Do you allow your people to believe in another god?"

Ruadan nodded with his wolf skull mask strapped tight over his face. "Yes..." he whispered back. "As long as they fight for our survival and put our people first, I do not mind what god they put their faith in."

"Hm," Torin said. "These people seem to be Christians."

"I can see that," Ruadan said. He then made a movement with his hand and the fifteen Druids he brought with him began to move.

Quietly.

Torin looked at Daegal and whispered. "We are here to watch how he recruits for his clan, nothing more. I do not wish to be a lap dog to Ruadan's expansion."

Daegal nodded as he gripped his bone sword.

The two of them began to move. Their feet crunching in the sheet of already fallen snow. As they grew closer, Ruadan put his hand up for everyone to stop, which they did. They could hear muffled music being played in the alehouse. However, it wasn't the happy and joyous music that you would hear in a regular alehouse. It was sad and monotone. Torin didn't spend much time with Christians, but he knew their way was far different from his. He thought back to when he had raided an English village of his own when he ruled Eaglecrest.

He had brought back some prisoners and threw them in the dungeon of the Great Hall. He remembered waking up in the middle of the night to them singing a song in unison. He marched down the stairs and commanded them to stop their singing, to which they didn't. He then killed them one by one. Each one singing the song until their last breath. The Christian faith was strong.

Torin snapped out of his trance and looked at Ruadan, who just made another hand motion to tell his men to keep moving. Once they reached a spot behind one of the wooden homes, the feathered Druids all made sure nobody was watching and they scattered to different areas around the village. They waited behind the corners of the houses, under wooden carts, and even on top of the small buildings. Ruadan made a flutter with his nails as one of the feathered Druids approached him. The Druid of the Crow reached in his black leather vest and pulled out a decent sized wooden stake. It had a black wrapping around the top.

Ruadan pulled a pinch of some kind of dust from a pouch on his belt and dusted it all over the black covering on the stake. He then used a flick of his iron splinted nails to create red sparks which showered over the stake and immediately engulfed it in flames. He then took the stake and threw it in the window of the house he was crouched behind. That's when somebody inside screamed. Ruadan made his move and rushed to the front door and waited. The first person out of the house was a small and skinny man with no shirt. He had obviously been sleeping. He took one step before he was knocked out cold by Ruadan. That was when the music in the alehouse stopped. Everyone exited the buildings they were in and noticed a man in all black with a wolf skull on his face, standing at the edge of the village. He fluttered his nails together, making a horrifying sound. The people all jumped when the house next to him exploded in flames. That was when Druids from all sides began to exit their hiding places. The people began to scream in horror. A woman decided to run into the forest but before she could, she was punctured in the chest by a spear.

Torin and Daegal watched as everyone who tried to run was killed. Two men ran back into the alehouse but immediately ran back out. A feathered Druid also exited the building a few moments later, spear in hand.

Everyone was eventually pushed towards the center of the village where the Druids all forced them to their knees. Those who wouldn't stop screaming and crying were cut down without hesitation. Torin and Daegal watched with wide eyes from behind everyone.

"Torin," Daegal said, his eyes glued to the scene before him. "Why do I feel disgusted?"

"Because Cathbad at least gave people second chances. This is just... monstrous."

Ruadan then approached the circle of captives and spoke with his creaky voice.

"My name is Ruadan the Silent, and I am here to offer you a chance. One where you can forget your present life and focus on a new one. One built on family. One built on trust. If you can do for me what you do for your god, then you will be rewarded with power and glory. We will take the throne from Edward. We will dispatch any that try to oppose our will. Now, is there anyone excited about my offer?"

Nobody said anything. However, that didn't stop Torin from repeating what he had just heard in his head.

We will take the throne from Edward? He really does wish to build an army big enough to take England! This man is mad!

Torin and Daegal watched as the captives said nothing. Ruadan used his nails to puncture an old woman's neck before he ripped out her throat.

"Well?!" he screamed.

A man stood up quickly. He looked to be on the younger side. He had a patchy beard that hadn't grown in yet. His eyes were watering and sweat dripped from his brow, even though snow had been falling. Ruadan examined the man.

"Have you come to your senses, boy?" Ruadan asked as he fluttered the blood off his nails.

The boy began to sing. Loudly and proudly. It was another language, but Torin could hear the words. He remembered that song. The same one those prisoners sang before he killed them. He looked at Ruadan, who was growing angry. That was when each one of the captives stood and started to sing along. Every one of them, young or old, sang that song until their last breath, which inevitably came as the Druids began to cut them all down in a bloody mess.

Torin examined Ruadan and saw himself. His old self. He had created a new life for himself but then quickly threw it away, all for revenge. He had found love. Peace. Happiness. And now, it was all gone due to his lust for vengeance.

But as he thought about everything he had gone through, he realized that this would not be for nothing. His vengeance *is* what mattered. He had the allfather's favor. He had worked this hard and lost too much. He was not going to be stopped. He thought back to Ruadan's words about Edward. The feathered Druid was going to take the fight to all of England.

If I let him bring the fight to Edward, I will grow further from my destiny. I will lose my friends and newfound family. All the coincidences. Ari being the childhood best friend of Njal's whore, Ari wielding the hand-axe of the man I killed, and witnessing Ruadan go through the same event that occurred to me as Jarl all those years ago. It all means something. I need Ari back. I need to keep my people alive. I need to kill Njal.

"Ruadan," Torin said loudly. All the Druids looked at him as they wiped their weapons clean of blood.

"Yes, my friend," Ruadan said as he approached.

"Did you mean what you said? Are you going to take the fight to Edward?" Torin asked, his eyes still glued to the pile of dead bodies of the Christian villagers before him.

"Yes," Ruadan said. "I believe we have enough strength with you in my growing army to destroy that little bastard that sits upon the throne," he laughed. The rest of the feathered Druids did the same.

"Nothing will stand in the way of my destiny..." Torin said softly to himself.

"What was that, my friend?" Ruadan asked as he still laughed.

"Ruadan the Silent, I hereby challenge you to singular combat for the command of your throne..."

Ruadan's laugh and smile faded as all eyes were focused on the large Druid of the Fenlands.

XXVII

Skol and Hati

Night had its grip on the world. The stars fluttered above as a large Norseman sat on the edge of his bed with his chin resting upon his folded hands. The sounds of the crackling fire pit in the other room made him think back on his life. Fishing and hunting with his father. Then watching his father die not soon after. Learning the ins and outs of running a farm and laughing with the Englishman. Then holding the old man as he took his last breath while the farm burned around him. Meeting the English woman and falling in love with her. Then seeing her pregnant with another man's child. Seeing the Norse woman on the battlefield proud and unafraid. Then to her lying beneath him. Her eyes wide and afraid. He remembered the face she made when he brought his blade down hard, punching through her chest. It was a look of shock and worry. A look of pain.

He was pulled from his trance as he felt a sharp pain

in his own stomach. He quickly put his hands over the spot that hurt. His jaw clenching. Once the pain subsided, he sighed and stood up, grunting in the process.

It had been three weeks now since that fateful night. The people of Eaglecrest were preparing for spring to arrive now. They had not received snow in quite some time, which excited a lot of people. It meant better hunting conditions, better fishing, and, well, better weather. However, something was coming. Something that Njal wasn't aware of. Not until his brother had told him on that night.

The meeting of Skol and Hati.

The two wolves, Skol and Hati, were the offspring of Fenrir the Wolf, son of the god Loki. The two Jotuns would spend all of eternity chasing the gods Sól and Mani, who embodied the sun and the moon. It was said that at the dawn of Ragnarök, the wolves would finally meet the sun and the moon and devour them whole.

The only people who knew of Alf's last words before taking the body of his fallen lover and wandering off into the empty English wilderness, was Knud and some of his men. Njal didn't wish to inform his people that Skol and Hati would succeed in their chase and the dawn of Ragnarök would begin. That would cause panic and fear, and they were not even sure if Alf was speaking the truth. How could he even know of such a thing? Was he in tune with the Nine Realms? Could he speak to the gods?

Perhaps when you lose everything, you feel as though you are already dead. And then, the afterlife and reality do not seem so different.

Njal continued to watch the skies, though. He had to. His brother was a threat to him now. To his people. He thought back to Torin. He let him live and now he was who knows where, scheming and planning every way to take his own revenge. Njal knew he could not make the same mistake twice. His brother *had* to die. So, in this meeting that would, by Alf's account, occur when Skol and Hati met in the sky. It was going to result in the death of one Tokeson brother.

Njal was angry, though. He felt Alf begin to understand him when he visited his younger brother in the cell that night. But as soon as Sigrid showed up, his entire demeanor changed. And once Njal plunged the blade of his sword through Sigrid's chest, that thread of fate was set in stone. Alf would never forget that.

Njal regretted plunging his sword into her. He regretted that every single day since that night. He thought back to his choice and tried to think of any other possible outcome, but he couldn't think of one. He still regretted what he did. He realized that with her dead, it would be impossible for Alf to see her as anything other than the way he did. The only thing now were memories and stories. And if any spoke bad on Sigrid's character, Alf was too stubborn to listen.

In the following weeks since that night, Njal had made it known to the Horse Clan that they would no longer exist. They had the choice to either merge with the Eagle Clan or go through the trials of the Fire Clan and become a member there. Njal figured it was the best course of action because he did kill their leader after all.

Their Jarl.

If they still stayed in Demut and appointed a new Jarl, who's to say that the new Jarl wouldn't rise up and attack the other clans out of revenge? Disbanding the clan entirely seemed like the best way to show that the people of Demut could still enjoy their lives, even though they were in a different clan. Besides, Njal's speech about how times are changing and that everyone inside the community was a part of one massive clan surely helped people make the change. And Demut itself was to become an outpost. Strictly for the use of training and combat purposes.

Suddenly, Njal felt the pain in his stomach again, but he pushed that aside. Njal didn't wish to spend the time waiting for the confrontation with his brother by doing nothing *but* wait. He understood the community needed to keep expanding. Especially after Edward gave them the permission to do so.

The first thing on Njal's list, though, was to find a new seer for the village. There was no seer since Ingrid left with Halfdan, and nobody else had the Seiðr magic that Ingrid did. And the question of how Alf knew that Skol and Hati would succeed in their quest to devour the celestial objects they chased was something he needed answered.

That night, Njal was going to travel towards the swamps of the Fenlands where word was that there were some Druids there. Njal was told about the Druids by Alvin when he was young. They hid in the shadows and used Seiðr magic to confuse and terrify their enemies. Njal was going to journey to them and try to strike up a deal for somebody who could become a seer for their village.

He knew that it was a controversial decision due to the Druid that would be chosen probably not being of Norse blood. But he didn't care. The village needed a seer and since nobody had arrived in since Alf, well, as far as Njal could tell, the last Norseman in the world were in Eaglecrest. Or, if the story Alf told Njal was true, there were some living in Norway in the village of Sten.

Njal gritted his teeth at that. He grabbed his bear cloak and pinned it to his shoulders before securing 'The Call of the King' onto his waist. His beard was now medium length but well groomed and his blond hair was shaved at the sides, showcasing his bear tattoo. He looked in the corner of the room and saw a black and red wooden shield. It was a bit smaller than any shield he used, but that's because it wasn't made for him.

It was made for Frigyth.

The only love he ever knew. Njal was so angry at her and yet, his love for her was still there. He felt that if he should die on his journey, he would at least like her to be there with him in some form or another. He walked over to the shield, picked it up by the rim, and he put it behind his back.

He took one last look at his bedchamber. He could practically see Frigyth's naked body still laying in his bed. His heart hurt at the thought that she would never be there again.

Njal then stepped out into the throne room of the Great Hall. He passed by the large fire pit and his large knotwork carved throne before stepping outside. He felt the brisk nighttime air as he walked through the village. Each house was under the cover of darkness and dreams. The only light to be offered were the torches that were lit on every pathway of the village. Njal continued down the path to the stables and main gate, where Knud was waiting for him.

"How are you on this fine night?" Knud asked, dressed in black. "Feeling any better?"

"Aye," Njal said, approaching.

"Are you sure you do not want me to come with you?" Knud asked as he watched Njal grab the reins of his brown horse before petting its mane.

"I am sure," Njal said. "It should only be a ten-day trip at the most. I need you to stay here in case there is some sort of attack. Since that night, I have kept my eyes and ears open. Sigrid and her men were able to attack me too easily. We need to prepare in case Torin or someone else tries the same."

"Understood. I will watch the village closely while you are gone. I hope you have a pleasant trip with the people of the swamp," he joked. "Bring us back another seer. All this talk of the stars above has even *me* a bit frightened."

"You have my word," Njal said with a smile. "Be seeing you, my friend."

"Be seeing you."

Njal got himself up on his horse with a painful grunt, and he steadied himself on top. He then looked at the four warriors who were joining him and nodded his head. They did the same, and the five of them took off into the night. Knud watched his friend leave the village on his galloping horse.

*

The group journeyed from midnight till midday before deciding to stop for a break. No words were spoken other than Njal's occasional "watch for bandits" advice. They exited the tree line and noticed the seemingly endless hills of England's topography. The sun was shining, but the air was still brisk. In the distance, a bit of low hanging gray clouds could be seen.

"We will rest here," Njal said as he turned his horse to a patch of dirt within the sea of green grass. "Get the food and water you require out of the packs. We will not be staying very long."

Everyone followed their instructions. They all dismounted their horses and began digging in their saddlebags for the food and water they brought along. The leather water containers were small, but everyone began drinking them like there was an endless supply.

"Make sure you save some for the trip home," Njal said, not looking at them but hearing their gulps. "We are heading to a swamp. The water there will not be good to drink."

The men stopped drinking and secured their lids back on. They put them back in their bags and began grabbing their food. Pieces of bread and day-old cooked chicken breasts that were wrapped in cloth. One of the men began to make preparations for a small fire to warm up the chicken. That was when another of the men looked up at the sky.

"Sir," Njal heard from behind him.

"What is it?" he replied.

"Máni..."

"What?" Njal asked as he turned around. He noticed the young warrior pointing up at the sky. Njal looked up and saw it, too. The moon could be seen high in the sky but was slightly faded out by the sun's brightness. It was close to the sun.

Too close.

Njal's heart dropped.

"Are they supposed to be that close?" the warrior asked. The other warriors stopped what they were doing to spectate on the phenomenon.

"No…" Njal said coldly. "No, they are not."

The men all looked in amazement and gasped.

"Grab your things," Njal said. "Return home."

"But sir, what…" one man began to ask.

"Now…" Njal interrupted sternly, his eyes still focused on the placement of the moon.

The men didn't hesitate to move then. Packing all the things they had just unpacked before mounting their horses again. Njal nodded to them all and watched as they took off quickly in the direction from which they came. The young Norse king continued to watch the sky as he felt a strange feeling in his stomach, and it wasn't his wound. Whatever was about to happen, it was fated. He hopped back onto his brown horse and slowly made his way back toward Eaglecrest. The direction of the sun and the moon.

Memories entered his mind as he watched the moon close in on the sun. Memories of his mother and his father. He hoped that they would see he didn't have a choice now. He hoped that if he fell and entered Valhalla, that they would still love him. He hoped that if he slew his brother, then they would still accept him with loving arms. After all, it wasn't Alf's fault that he was acting the way he was. He grew up not knowing what love was and his first feeling of it was with Sigrid. She poisoned his mind and tried to steer him in the way of her agenda, and she succeeded. She may not have loved him, but he sure loved her. That was why, when Njal killed her, there was no turning back.

After an hour or so, Njal noticed something laid across the middle of the road in front of him. Something large and surrounded by a pool of dark red. The towering willow and aspen trees acted like a veil of green above him. The closer he got, the easier the object was to make out.

It was a horse.

One that Njal recognized from the Eaglecrest stables. It laid on its side and its head was removed from its body, but sat only a few inches away.

Njal grunted as he stepped off his own horse. He looked around and saw a thin dirt pathway to his left. One that led into the tall trees. He creased his eyebrows and looked at his horse one more time with a sad look. He patted its mane and looked towards the path again. He took his first step into the unknown.

Each step felt like more weight being added onto his back. He did not wish for this fight. He did not wish for anything like this. As he continued to walk deeper into the woods, he stared up at the sun. It was becoming so close to the moon now that the moon was barely visible anymore. The crisp breeze tickled his beard as he thought back to before Alf. Only a few months prior, he was living a happy life with Frigyth in his arms and Halfdan by his side. The young king would give anything up to go back to those times. But alas, his choices were his own, and now he was here.

Crack

Njal's eyes shifted quickly from the sky and down towards the sound of branches cracking. Sure, it could have been a wild animal, but he knew it wasn't. Njal reached behind him and pulled Frigyth's black and red wooden shield from his back and slid the straps onto his left arm. His blue eyes scanning the entire forest that surrounded him.

Nothing.

He continued down the pathway for a little longer until the smell of burning timber struck his nostrils. After a few more steps, the sound of crackling firewood struck his eardrums. After a few more steps, he saw the source.

There was a large pyre in the middle of a clearing. It stood about three feet high and was already wrapping itself in flames. A body laid on top surrounded by burning blankets, beads and jewelry and an orange and black wooden shield with a knotwork style horse painted on the front. The plumes of black smoke began to stretch high into the air.

Next to the pyre was a man. A large man wearing a green and black cloak, brown leather armor, and boots and gauntlets to match it. He was holding a green and black wooden shield in his left arm as well as his long steel sword in his right hand. His head peering up at the smoke.

Suddenly, his gaze shot towards Njal. The piercing green hue to his eyes made a chill go down Njal's spine. The two men stared at each other for a long moment until the man turned to look at the pyre again, which was now completely engulfed in flames.

"I thought you might want to be here as I send her off to Valhalla. So, I waited until this day to proceed. I know she does not mind," Alf said as he looked up into the smoke and closed his eyes. "I can feel her here with us."

"How did you know of this day, brother? How were you aware of Skol and Hati's success?" Njal asked.

"When you lose everything that is worth living for, you are pretty much dead already," Alf said. "Since that very moment, I have been only three steps away from Odin's Great Hall."

"Brother, please," Njal pleaded one last time. "We do not have to do this. There is more to this life for you. There is..."

"You killed her." Alf interrupted softly.

"Of course I did!" Njal shouted. "She attacked me! What was I supposed to do? Let her kill me?"

"She would not have killed you," Alf said, his voice still soft. "Only injure you enough to hand the throne over to me."

"She stabbed me!" Njal screamed, spittle flying from his mouth. "I had no other choice but to release not only me, but you, from her prison! She was evil, Alf! She turned my own brother against me when we should be fighting on the battlefield together! Please... Please see the truth in my words. I promise, if you walk away now, we can..."

"Enough!" Alf roared with thunderous bass in his voice. "Please..." he shed a tear. "I am in so much pain. I do not wish to live with this pain any longer."

"I understand your feelings..."

"How?" Alf interrupted. "How could you possibly understand what I am feeling?"

Njal paused for a moment and took a breath. "You remember Frigyth, yes?" Alf nodded. "When I returned to Birmingham for Birstain's funeral, I came to find that she is with child. But... not mine. In fact, the child is from an Englishman who used his charm to spite me. Why? I do not know. But the pain of that. I cannot bear either. And while I am truly sorry for what happened with Sigrid, you must know that her actions were hers, just as mine were mine. We must pay the price for the choices we make."

Alf breathed heavily and wiped a tear from his cheek using his forearm. "I am... I am truly sorry, brother," he said. "Seems as though we both lost our love."

Njal smiled sadly. Believing his brother might be coming around. Could they find peace in their loss? Could they lean on each other to achieve the peace they both desperately needed?

Suddenly, the world grew darker. Above them, the sun was being covered by the moon. Skol and Hati were devouring their prey. A darkened orange glow covered the world.

"But if that man killed Frigyth," Alf said. "Would you kill him to avenge her? To right his wrong?" Njal's face dropped to a serious one. "Because Frigyth is still alive. Sigrid is not. You sent her to Valhalla and so it is only right that I do the same to you. She deserves that."

Alf jumped at his brother quickly, swinging his sword downward, causing Njal to raise his shield. The blade struck Njal's shield so hard that Njal fell to the ground. He kept his shield raised as Alf continued to strike the shield repeatedly sending splinters of wood all around them. His battle-cry was full of pain and rage. Njal noticed the blade was breaking through the shield and he knew he needed to act quickly. He looked down and saw where Alf's feet were planted. One foot on each side of his body. Njal quickly threw his knee up, crunching into Alf's groin, making him yelp and fall to his back.

Njal used this to his advantage as he quickly got up off

the ground and unsheathed 'The Call of the King' and pointed it at his brother.

"Damnit, Alf!" Njal shouted. "Stop this nonsense! I do not wish to kill you!"

The sun was now completely covered by the moon. The world was in darkness. The ashes and embers of the pyre floated around the two brothers as they stared at one another.

"And you will not," Alf said as he got to his feet. He readied his weapons before charging again. The two brothers collided. Weapons swinging and shields banging. Their brows were wet with sweat and their muscles were working as hard as they could. Each one trying to gain an advantage over the other, but the brothers were equally matched.

Alf swung his sword hard as Njal dodged behind an aspen tree. Alf angrily swung twice more and Njal noticed that his brother's aggression was getting the better of him. He was getting sloppy. Njal noticed another aspen tree behind him and waited for Alf to approach and ready his blade again. Njal quickly spun around so that he was behind the tree and watched as Alf's blade struck and lodged itself into the base of the aspen tree. Njal used this to his advantage, and he punched his brother hard in the nose and watched him let go of his sword and fall to his back.

"Alf," Njal began as he watched his brother struggle to his feet. "This is your last chance. I am warning you."

"That is the difference between you and I, brother," Alf said finally on his feet. He pulled a large hand-axe from behind his back. "I punish those who wrong me. They must pay with their lives."

"Your logic will leave you with nobody to call friend. People make mistakes. You must learn to forgive them," Njal said, gripping his sword tighter. "That is what father strived for."

"Well, I respectfully disagree," Alf said.

"And that is why I am king..."

Alf growled and charged his brother once more. He swung his hand-axe downwards and Njal dodged it. He saw the blade immediately change direction as it made its way up towards his face, but he was quick to dodge that attack, too. However, Alf's attack didn't stop there. He immediately swung his hand-axe downwards. Njal was off-balance due to dodging the first two attacks, and he had no choice but to use what was left of his shield.

The blade of Alf's hand-axe struck and lodged itself in Njal's shield and the two fell to the ground again. Njal used his momentum to roll over, and he took Alf with him. The two brothers rolled further until they reached a steep hill. Their bodies broke apart as they began their descent, both picking up speed. Rolling further and further down the hill. Grass and dirt flying up into the air. Both men grunting as each hit during their descent caused immense pain. Njal's path down the hill was harder as his body struck a tree right where his wound from Sigrid's blade was. The two finally slowed down and came to a stop as the hill evened out in a forest of aspen trees.

Njal was on his back as he grunted, trying to make his way to his feet. The wound in his stomach pulsating with pain. He could feel the blood leaking from it.

Alf was on his stomach and he began to push himself up, spitting blood in the process. Alf scanned the area and noticed

Njal's shield had slid off his arm and was lying close to him, his hand-axe still lodged inside. His eyes widened as he quickly got up and ran to his weapon. Njal heard the commotion, and he looked at his brother and noticed what he was doing.

Njal grunted as he picked himself up and looked around for his weapon. He saw the silver blade of 'The Call of the King' about five yards away. He jumped to his weapon and reached his hand out, but right before he could grab it, he saw the lethal end of a hand-axe come down and cut right through his pinky and ring finger. Njal jumped, fell onto his back, and screamed in pain as blood spurted out from the now stumps on his right hand.

Alf stood over him, in between his brother and his sword. He grunted as he gripped his hand-axe.

"This is the end of your reign, brother," Alf said. "I have watched you fail over and over again. Leading our people down a path that will get them all killed. Whatever father taught you; it is not the way of survival. It is the way to annihilation."

Njal grunted as he crawled his way further away from his brother. He looked up and saw the aspen trees that surrounded them. The darkness of the sky still present.

"You must understand that this brings me no joy," Alf continued, walking towards his bleeding brother. "But it is necessary. It will bring me peace."

The struggling and crawling Njal approached the trunk of an aspen tree. One that featured a large wooden sliver that pointed upwards. Then, Njal stopped when he heard his brother raising his arm to strike true. Njal gritted his teeth and turned around quickly. He punched his right foot forward, kicking his brother's knee in. Alf toppled forward, his face crashing into the trunk of the aspen tree.

Alf screamed in pain. Njal quickly rolled and stood to his feet. He examined his brother's condition. Alf's left leg was bent at the knee in a way it should not have bent. That small sliver of the aspen tree's trunk was now lodged in Alf's right eye. He tried to hold his hand up to it, but the blood continued to pour out.

Njal looked down and quickly picked up Alf's hand-axe that was laying at his side. He then raised it high into the air and he hesitated. With his brother screaming below him, all he could think about was seeing him arrive on his ship that day. Dancing with him in the Great Hall or seeing his spear strike the boar during their first hunt. Their talk of their parents down by the water. All the wonderful memories came to Njal's mind at once.

He forced himself to break free of his trance as he shed a tear. His brother looked at him with his one good eye in anger and pain. Alf tried to reach up and grab Njal, but Njal used his foot to keep his brother down.

Njal creased his eyebrows and roared with the pain of a thousand seas and swung the hand-axe down hard, striking his brother in the head. Alf's screams of rage and pain turned into soft grunts. Njal roared again as he pulled the weapon out with a crunch and swung down again. His battle-cry became a sob. He struck again, and again, and again, blood flying high into the air until Njal exhausted himself.

He stuck one last time before dropping the weapon and

falling to his knees. He broke down and began to bawl as the blood of his brother stained his face.

Now the only sound in the forest was the sound of the whispering aspen trees. The world starting to become light again. Njal stopped his sob for a moment and looked up into the sky. The sun was beginning to show itself once more.

Although the world was not ending, Njal's world already had. He sat there alone in a of the sea of trees. Covered in blood.

His brother dead below him.

XXVIII

One Door Closes...

The early spring air was crisp as the sun was beginning to set behind the horizon. The world had returned to normal. Sounds of the trees whispering their thoughts struck the Norseman's ears. They were the only witnesses to what had occurred between Njal and his brother.

The young king was covered in blood as he limped by the funeral pyre for Sigrid, which was now nothing but blackened ash. Njal felt the nubs of his two fingers throbbing as more blood leaked from them, as well as the wound in his stomach. 'The Call of the King' was secured in the sheathe that sat upon his hip as Frigyth's broken shield was left behind with Alf's body.

He would return to them.

After his body was healed, he would return. Despite what had happened, he wanted to give his brother a proper funeral.

But his body had hurt. He had lost too much blood. He was too weak to carry Alf's body back with him now.

Njal continued down the thin dirt pathway that was covered in grass. His head began to throb and his vision blurred. Njal stumbled a bit before losing his footing and falling down the slight descent. His brown horse a good ten yards away from him.

That's when he heard it.

The cawing of a raven. Njal rolled himself around so that he was looking up at the sky. The bluish-purple of the heavens above him mixed with the fluttering branches of the blooming aspen trees filled his vision. The cawing continued as Njal closed his eyes...

And fell unconscious.

That was when the cawing had morphed into the sound of Knud. His horse galloping quickly beneath him.

"Njal!" the Fire Jarl shouted, noticing his friend. "There he is!"

There were six members of the Fire Clan riding with Knud, all on their own horses.

"Quickly!" Knud shouted as he approached and jumped off his horse. He sprinted to Njal's body and kneeled down. He held his hand by Njal's mouth and nose and felt a slight breath. Two of his men stepped off their horses and approached. "He is alive," Knud said. "But hurt. Quickly, get him on a horse and bring him to the healer!"

The Fire Clan members lifted Njal up and did as they were told. Knud hopped back on his horse and followed his men as they returned to Eaglecrest.

*

Njal slowly opened his eyes. His vision blurred for a moment. Somebody stood in front of him. They said something, but all he could hear were muffled sounds. He felt strange. He felt something he had not felt in quite some time. As his body was waking up, he felt the Bear. It sat in the middle of a clearing. Golden runes carved into its white fur. The Bear looked around and noticed the towering pine trees, the monstrous yet beautiful mountains in the distance, and the floating blue runes around him, fluttering like fireflies.

He was in Asgard, the land of the gods.

Suddenly, Njal's body awoke fully. He heard the words from the person that was standing before him. He saw their face. Their black hair and matching beard. Streaks of gray throughout both.

"H...Halfdan?" Njal stuttered.

"It is me, my friend," Halfdan said with a smile upon his face, a tear forming in his eye.

Njal smiled and shot up, hugging his dear friend. Njal broke down in tears as Halfdan hugged him back.

"I am here, Njal," Halfdan said. "I am here."

The two hugged each other for a long while.

"Where have you been?" Njal asked as he broke away, his head beginning to hurt, but he didn't care. "I never thought I would see you again."

"I know," Halfdan said. "I thought the same. After I left, Ingrid and I found a delightful piece of land by Winchester. We built a small house and bought three cows. Every single day I thought of you. Thought of Eaglecrest and the rest of our people. I felt horrible that I left when I did. You are my best friend...

my brother. And I left you when I should have been there for you. Helped you through things. There is always going to be a time for Ingrid and I to live in peace. But leaving you when you needed me most, well, that was a real shite thing to do to you and I am truly sorry."

Njal smiled sadly and nodded his head. "I thank you for your apology, but I do not need it. Everything that I have been through since you and Frigyth left has helped me become a smarter and stronger leader. This pain that I feel, well, I caused it. I was so quick to turn to my own blood that I forgot everybody else. I treated you all horribly, and I paid for that. So, *I* am sorry, Halfdan."

The berserker smiled and put his hand on Njal's shoulder. "Thank you, my friend. You are becoming very wise."

Njal chuckled a bit. "So, I am assuming Knud wrote to you?"

"Aye," Halfdan confirmed. "He explained the events. I do not wish to speak of them if you do not want."

"No, no," Njal said, before sighing. "I would love to tell you everything, brother."

The two of them spoke for hours as the fire pit crackled in the other room.

*

About a month had passed and word got around England about Sigrid and Alf. Njal had recovered from his injuries and had met in Gulgruve for a rendezvous with King Edward. The two of them discussed the repairs and expansions of the large village as part of their agreement. Both English and Norse would live there, together, in peace. The two also discussed what had occurred since the last time they spoke. Edward offered his condolences, and Njal accepted them. They shared a large bottle of wine before they both happily returned to their homes.

Halfdan and Ingrid had also moved back to Eaglecrest. It did not take long for Njal to discover that Ingrid was pregnant and Halfdan was very happy because of it. They moved back into Ingrid's hut that sat on the cliff side overlooking the village. The witch held prayers during dusk as Halfdan traveled to Demut daily to help train the young Norsemen into becoming powerful warriors. Ingrid also began training the young women of the village in the ways of Seiðr Magic in an attempt to create more of a bond with the gods.

Njal had spent time with Ingrid, attempting to contact Odin. However, he could not be found. Njal had visited the dwarves of Niðavellir, the Jotuns of Jotunheim, and even the Fire God Surtr in Muspelheim. He could not *wait* to tell Knud of that meeting, although it short. But Odin was nowhere to be found. And that was most definitely concerning.

*

After some time, summer had come in full force. The sun was bright and the weather hot. The trees and flowers were in full bloom and were beautiful to look at. Njal was returning from a hunting trip with Halfdan. The two men sat upon their horses as they looked upon the village they had helped build from afar.

"It is quite different from when we first journeyed here, is it not?" Halfdan said with a smile on his face, his horse walking steadily below him.

Njal looked from Eaglecrest's walls to the surrounding

roads and homes that led to Demut and Muspel. He remembered only seeing Eaglecrest when they first traveled the road from the valley. Now the village had expanded into surrounding homes and businesses. Multiple clans of Norse people who would never have lived together doing exactly that. It was impressive and Njal couldn't help but be proud.

"I do, my friend," he replied before the two went silent for a moment as they took in the sights, the salt of the sea striking their nostrils. "Are you excited about becoming a father?"

Halfdan laughed. "You know, Njal, that little bastard is not even here yet and I know there is nothing I would not do for him. I cannot wait to take him fishing and hunting. Watch him strike down his first boar. Or tell him stories of my days with Ragnar and how we defeated Aelred. However, I would like you to be present for that story."

"Sounds like a grand idea," Njal said, smiling.

The two were quiet for another moment as they closed in on the village.

"Hey," Halfdan said, his voice soft now and his smile fading. "I wish to say again how much I am sorry about Frigyth. I feel responsible..."

"No, no," Njal began. "She made her own choices. You had no idea she would replace me with that bastard, Wigberht. It is not your fault."

Halfdan smiled sadly as the two went on into the main gates of Eaglecrest. They proceeded to hitch their horses at the stables.

"I will meet you at my home for dinner, yes?" Halfdan asked.

"You cannot keep me away," Njal said, smiling. He then nodded his head and began walking to the Great Hall.

He opened the wooden door to the large building and walked inside. As he made his way towards his bedchamber, something caught his eye. He turned and noticed a crème piece of paper sitting on his throne. It had his name written on it and a red wax seal with a sigil that he was familiar with.

It was from Birmingham.

Njal felt a bit strange inside. Anxiety rising throughout him like raging rapids. He hurried to the letter and picked it up before walking to his bedchamber. He sat down on the edge of his bed before breaking the seal and unfolding the letter.

He began to read.

Dear Njal,

I hope this letter finds you well. I was informed of what had happened with Sigrid and Alf. I am truly sorry. I know family is important to you. Whether that be your family by blood or the family you create. Like a bear, you protect your own at all costs. I would be lying if I did not say that I miss being a part of that family.

Since I left, I have been attempting to fill the void in my life that leaving you created. I have tried hunting, painting, and even finding new love. However, nothing has worked and as you know, that love I found was false. No matter how many times I tried to tell myself it was real, I know now it was not. You will be happy to know that Wigberht is no longer in Birmingham and has been exiled to Scotland. However, I will still be a mother to his child.

I am sorry for the pain I have caused you. For leaving you when I should have stayed and helped you. When I should have been more honest with you. It was my choice and I see now that I chose

wrong and now I must live with the consequences. I hope that one day,
you can forgive me.

My love for you will never fade.

Yours always,

Frigyth

Njal finished the letter and sighed deeply. A part of him wanted to drop everything and race to Birmingham, but he knew better. She had left him. She was having someone else's child. There was no going back to her. He knew he would not be able to love that child like his own. He knew that even if he could, being so far apart and attempting to be together would never work. They were on two separate paths now. Their time was over. Njal stood up and walked out into the throne room and approached the fire pit. He looked down at Frigyth's letter one more time before throwing it into the flames.

It was time to move on.

Suddenly, the horns of arrival struck Njal's eardrums. He perked his head up and began walking to the front door. As he exited, he made his way down the pathway of the village. Before long, he noticed a crowd forming by the front gates. Njal quickly picked up the pace and approached.

"Everyone move," Njal shouted, to which the villagers did. Once the crowd was separated, Njal noticed a blonde woman standing before him. Her blue eyes looked at him. He could tell she wasn't Norse. Her clothes were light and brown, some of it still featuring fur from the animal it was made from. Njal looked down and noticed her forearm. From her elbow to the tips of her fingers, she had animal bones strapped to her in a way that looked like the meat was removed from her arm, and only bone remained.

"Hello there," the woman said in an English accent. "Are you by chance, Njal Tokeson?"

"Aye," Njal said skeptically. "And who might you be?"

"My name is Ari," she said. "Pleased to meet you."

XXIX

Until We Meet Again

The sky was a dark blue now. The horizon was lit up with a deep orange glow that faded into purple. That summer night's breeze made Njal's slicked back blond hair dance. His braid no longer present, the Bear tattoo still showing proudly. The Norseman stood upon the dock in silence as the fireflies fluttered around him and the crickets sung their evening songs.

Before him was a wooden boat. One that had runes carved across the hull and the bow. Njal slowly jumped over the hull and onto the boat. Sitting on top was a pyre. Full of flowers, weapons, gold and silver that all surrounded a body.

The body of his brother.

Njal sighed deeply before sitting down on a chest of silver next to the pyre. He looked up into the beautiful dusk sky.

"I hope you are showing the gods how to properly

drink a horn of ale, brother," Njal said softly. Tears began to fill his eyes. "I hope you are with mother and father..."

Njal broke down, crying into his hands. After a few moments, he pulled his hands away and looked at the sky once more.

"I love you all. I will be with you soon enough. But my job here is not yet finished. I will attempt to make you all proud if I have not done so. I promise," he said. "Brother, you told me of a group of Norsemen that took Sten from you. Well, I will not stand for that. Sten is *our* home. I will travel there and take it back. Peacefully or violently, Sten belongs to us. I will take it back for you, father."

Njal stood up and looked down at his brother, who had a sheet covering his body. He then stepped back onto the dock and grabbed the rope that was keeping the boat steady. The Bear King untied it and threw it onto the boat with his brother.

He then grabbed the hull and pushed it so the boat began to slowly make its way downriver. Njal then approached a finely crafted bow that was leaned against a barrel and he picked it up, his missing fingers now healed stumps. He steadied the weapon in his hands and grabbed an arrow that was lying on top of the barrel. The tip was covered in a hemp wrap. Njal then scratched the tip across his iron bracer, creating a spark that lit the tip of the arrow like a match. He then loaded the arrow into the bow and pulled back on the string.

As he breathed in and closed his eyes, he released the arrow. It flew high into the air until it finally came down and struck the pyre on the boat. Before long, Njal watched the pyre erupt in a mountain of flames. He watched the boat float down the river until it could not be seen anymore.

"To Valhalla."

About the Author

Cal Neubert is a former colligate athlete that had his career cut short because of a severe nerve injury in his shoulder. Neubert handled the life-shattering moment by writing his thoughts down in a journal. He ended up enjoying that so much, that the writing morphed into poems, then to short stories, and not after long, his first full-length novel, The Cleansing, which released in 2022.

While readers enjoyed the horror that Neubert brought to the table, he wished to hop over to the historical fiction and fantasy genres. There, he unleashed The Bear King Trilogy. Following the success of The Call of the King, and The Fate of the King, Neubert promises a heart-stopping conclusion in...

The War of the Kings.

Neubert also enjoys anything that has to do with nature, movies, and sports. He is a diehard Miami Dolphins fan and loves anything Star Wars, Marvel, and DC.